Salted Caramel SORCERY

BEWITCHED BY CHOCOLATE
MYSTERIES

BOOK SEVEN

H.Y. HANNA

CONTENTS

CHAPTER ONE

Caitlyn Le Fey bit her lip in concentration as she stared into the heavy copper pot filled with the clear, viscous liquid. As she watched, the glass-like surface of the liquid began to roil and churn, first at the edges, then drawing inwards, until the whole pot was bubbling gently. She glanced anxiously at the fire beneath the pot, wondering if she should reduce the flame. Whatever happened, she couldn't let things burn; otherwise, it would all be over. Steam rose from the pot, caressing her face with warm, damp fingers, and she blinked to clear her vision, but she didn't take her eyes off the bubbling solution.

Slowly, the pale, colourless liquid became tinged with the faintest touch of gold, which deepened gradually into a light amber colour. Caitlyn leaned closer, holding her breath. *How much longer?* Her hand hovered over the pot handle, but before she could grip it, the door behind her swung open and a young woman burst into the room.

"Holy guacamole, Caitlyn, I've been looking for you everywhere!" the young woman cried. "I thought you'd be with the Widow Mags at the Manor, supervising the set-up for the ball. I didn't realise you were still stuck here in the village."

Caitlyn glanced distractedly at her cousin before jerking her eyes back to the pot. "I thought I'd be of more use here than at the Manor. We've only got two days to go until the ball, Pomona, and you know we're catering all the desserts and sweet treats for the buffet."

The other girl came over and peered into the pot with interest. "Mmm, that smells good... What is it? Caramel sauce?"

Caitlyn nodded.

"What's it for?"

"I don't know. The Widow Mags hasn't told me yet—she just told me to make enough to fill several jugs." Caitlyn gave a self-deprecating laugh. "It's the first time I'm making it myself, without her supervising, and I didn't think it would be this stressful!"

Pomona grabbed a wooden spoon lying on the counter. "Why don't you give it a stir? It might speed things up—"

"No!" cried Caitlyn, lunging for the spoon. "No, you mustn't touch it! It might make the sugar crystallise and that'll ruin everything. You have to let the sugar dissolve and boil without disturbing it." She peered into the pot again. "It's not long now. I need to wait until it reaches just the right shade of deep amber, then I'll know it's the right temperature to add the cream—"

"Can't you just use a candy thermometer?" asked Pomona impatiently. "That's what everyone does back in America."

"I'm not making caramel candy. This is caramel sauce, and you don't need a thermometer for that. Besides, you know how the Widow Mags feels about what she calls 'newfangled gadgets'," said Caitlyn with a wry smile. "She won't ever use them, and she doesn't want me relying on them either. She says I need to hone my natural instincts."

Pomona rolled her eyes. "For Pete's sake, Caitlyn, you're just gonna listen to her? What's the point of having 'modern technology' if you're not gonna use it to make life easier? You can't, like, let these people keep you stuck in the Dark Ages!"

Caitlyn looked up, startled by the other girl's contemptuous tone. For all her feisty attitude, Pomona had always seemed to hold the Widow Mags in great respect, and although she and Caitlyn were essentially recent newcomers to the village of Tillyhenge, Pomona had seemed to warmly embrace her "new English home". She had never used words like "these people" before or suggested the local residents were somehow different.

3

"Well, the Widow Mags is right in a way," said Caitlyn gently. "If I really *am* descended from witches with a special ability to tap into the magic powers of *cacao*, then I should have an innate sense for working with chocolate, an instinct that goes beyond what common kitchen instruments can do. Learning to find that power and harness it is part of my training."

Pomona pulled a face which said: "Yeah, whatever." Then she brightened and said, "Anyway, listen, I came to ask you: what are you wearing to the ball?"

"I don't know... I haven't really thought about it, to be honest," muttered Caitlyn, turning back to the pot. The bubbling, frothing liquid was a rich amber colour now, and Caitlyn racked her brains, trying to remember if it matched the shade of amber that the Widow Mags had shown her the last time they made caramel sauce. *Is it ready? Or should I let it boil a bit longer and get a bit darker?*

"You haven't thought about it?" gasped Pomona. "Caitlyn! This is, like, the first masquerade ball you've ever been to! It's gonna be a huge deal! All these people are coming and it's in a freakin' *ballroom*, with live music and dancing and everything—I can't believe you haven't thought about what you're gonna wear! It's the day after tomorrow!"

"I know, I know, but I just... I just haven't really had much time to think about it! It's been completely crazy here, helping get things ready for the ball. It's

4

not just the desserts, you know—the whole buffet is going to be chocolate-themed. The Widow Mags has been working with the Manor kitchen staff for weeks, creating a signature menu which uses the flavours of chocolate and cocoa in savoury dishes."

"Huh? How does that work? Like chocolate-flavoured steak?" asked Pomona, pulling another face.

Caitlyn chuckled. "Don't knock it till you've tried it. And yeah, actually there *is* going to be a 'steak in Belgian chocolate-and-coffeeBelgian-chocolate-and-coffee sauce' on the menu, plus a 'cocoa-crusted beef tenderloin', which sounds absolutely delicious! It'll have a punch from warm spices like cinnamon, allspice, and peppercorns, but also a smoothness from the bittersweet cocoa." She looked at Pomona excitedly. "Oh Pomie, I think it's going to be amazing! Aside from the money that the Widow Mags is getting to cater the ball, it'll really help to showcase her talents and promote the chocolate shop. I think they're going to put little signs by the buffet, mentioning *Bewitched by Chocolate* and giving details of how to find us in the village. With so many high-society guests coming, it could be a game-changer in terms of finally raising the shop's profile."

Pomona waved a hand. "Yeah, okay, I get that the catering is important. But your costume is important too! And it's such an easy choice for you: you can go as a famous witch from mythology! You know, like Circe... or Medea... and then you could wear an awesome Greek costume with, like, a long white draping gown and gold arm cuffs—"

"I'm not going as a witch," said Caitlyn flatly.

"Why not? It would be so cool in an ironic way. I mean, you really *are* a witch!"

"Yes, well, I'm not sure I want to advertise that."

Pomona shot her an exasperated look. "Why not? Jeez, Caitlyn, I don't know why you're always trying to hide all the time. Man, if I was a witch, I'd be shouting it from the rooftops!"

Caitlyn gave her cousin an affectionate look. "Yes, but you know I'm not you, Pomie. You like getting attention and standing out from the crowd; I don't."

"Are you ashamed of what you are?" demanded Pomona. She leaned forwards, her hands clenching into fists. "Don't you realise how lucky you are, Caitlyn? If *I* was the one who found out that I was descended from a long line of witches, if *I* knew that I could develop powers, that I could use magic—" She broke off suddenly, breathing hard.

Caitlyn drew back, staring at the other girl in surprise. While Pomona had often seemed wistful, she'd never seen her cousin look so agitated and upset about her own lack of supernatural ability. She opened her mouth to answer, then gasped and whirled back to the stove as she heard an ominous hissing sound. She cried out in dismay as she saw the thick, dark brown liquid bubbling up over the edges of the pot.

"Nooo!" Caitlyn gasped. "It's burning!"

She grabbed the pot handle with one hand and yanked it off the stove, hurriedly turning off the flame with her other hand. Then she held the bubbling concoction at arm's length as she walked over to the sink. A horrible pungent smell of burning sugar filled the kitchen, making her almost gag.

"Ugh!" cried Pomona. "That really stinks!"

"It's all your fault," said Caitlyn irritably. "If you hadn't distracted me with all that stupid talk about costumes for the ball—"

"It's not stupid," said Pomona in a sulky tone. "Costumes are just as important as the food."

Caitlyn sighed as she stared down at the black sludge steaming in front of her. Carefully, she set the pot down on the edge of the sink, wondering if she should let it cool a bit before attempting to scoop out the ruined caramel mixture. But she was worried that if she waited too long, the burnt sugar would congeal and stick to the bottom of the pan in a hard lump. Hurriedly, she boiled the kettle, then poured the hot water into the pot. She was pleased to see the thick sludge begin to dissolve, and she used a wooden spatula to scrape the sides and bottom of the pot, loosening the caramel mixture further.

As she worked, Caitlyn tried to ignore Pomona, who was still grumbling about her lack of a costume, but finally, she interrupted her cousin impatiently:

"Look, can't I just wear that nice summer dress I got for the garden party a couple of months ago? You know, the one in that gorgeous sea-green chiffon. It's really pretty and I can just add a mask and pretend I'm a sea nymph or something... Anyway, does it really matter what I wear? I mean, it's not as if I'm the guest of honour or anything. No one is going to notice me or be looking at me anyway."

"What d'you mean: 'no one is going to be looking at you'? The most important person at the ball is going to be looking at you," said Pomona indignantly. "Okay, so I know James Fitzroy would probably think you look beautiful if you turned up wearing a burlap sack, but seriously, don't you wanna meet him looking drop-dead gorgeous for once, instead of the way you usually do, with no make-up and your hair a mess and chocolate all over your faded jeans?"

Caitlyn didn't answer, pretending to be engrossed in scrubbing the burnt sugar from the bottom of the pan. Pomona was right, though. A part of her did desperately want to surprise James Fitzroy with a glamorous transformation. The handsome owner of Huntingdon Manor and the surrounding estates (which included the village of Tillyhenge) was every girl's dream: a "modern-day Mr Darcy" who combined charm, intelligence, and aristocratic good looks with a calm authority and a warm empathy for others—not to mention the sexiest British accent! Caitlyn had fallen for him from their first chance meeting out in the woods, but as a shy, bookish girl who'd always struggled with embarrassment about her curvy figure, she'd never dreamt that James might return her feelings.

Not that we are *officially in a relationship or anything,* Caitlyn reminded herself hurriedly. In fact, their one attempt at a date so far had been a total disaster. She still cringed every time she thought about it. And they had both been so busy recently that they had hardly seen each other since then, never mind tried to make another arrangement. She knew that James cared about her and—even more importantly—that he wasn't repulsed by the idea that she was a "witch". It should have been enough, but Caitlyn longed for more. She longed to know for certain that James loved her, to know what it was like to be kissed by him...

Her cheeks warmed at the thought, and she ducked her head even lower, hoping that Pomona hadn't noticed. Still, her cousin was right: she was hardly likely to get her first kiss with James if she continued presenting her most unflattering side to him! Caitlyn sighed. It wasn't as if she didn't want to arrive in a gorgeous costume and turn heads at the ball. The problem was, she just didn't have Pomona's confidence. She envied the way the other girl could always wear the most outrageous outfits with fearless aplomb. Despite having a similar body type to Caitlyn, Pomona flaunted her large hips with pride and never shied away from clothes that drew attention to her fuller figure.

Caitlyn glanced at her again now: her cousin had teased her blonde hair into a bouffant mane around her head and was wearing a hot pink velour jumpsuit that clung to every curve of her body, coupled with designer sneakers with platform heels. Caitlyn smiled to herself. Pomona looked like she belonged in a Hollywood lounge bar rather than in a homely cottage kitchen in the English Cotswolds!

Then her smile faded as she caught sight of the necklace peeping out from the collar of the jumpsuit. Caitlyn felt a familiar stirring of unease as she stared at the huge glittering black diamond nestled against Pomona's throat. Ever since her cousin had been gifted that diamond choker, Caitlyn had felt uncomfortable at the sight of the glittering black gemstone. At first, she'd dismissed her misgivings but gradually, she'd become convinced that it wasn't just her imagination. There *was* something about that stone—some kind of malevolent aura—and worst of all, it seemed to be affecting Pomona in some way, spreading out like an invisible stain.

Caitlyn shivered at the sinister image in her mind and wished fervently that she had some way of convincing Pomona to give up her favourite new accessory.

CHAPTER TWO

The door to the kitchen swung open again and a lanky girl of about eighteen came rushing in. Caitlyn's face broke into an involuntary smile of affection. If Pomona was the flamboyant "American cousin" that she had grown up with, Evie was the awkwardly sweet "English cousin" she had gained when she arrived in Britain earlier that year in search of her birth family. When her "mother"—American singer Barbara Le Fey—had died unexpectedly last year, Caitlyn had been shocked to discover that the woman she had called "Mom" all her life hadn't given birth to her. In fact, she had originally been found as an abandoned baby in the Cotswolds, and many of the things she had taken for granted in her life—such as Pomona being her blood cousin—were completely thrown out the window.

Since then, Caitlyn had been desperate to find out the truth about her past, and it had been an even greater shock to learn that, not only did she have "witch blood" in her veins, but that she, too, could conjure spells and enchantments if she worked on developing her powers. As someone who had never believed in magic, Caitlyn had suddenly found herself in the middle of an identity crisis! But the dismay had quickly turned to delight when she'd found her real family here in Tillyhenge. It had been wonderful getting to know Evie, who was four years her junior and very much the younger sister she'd never had, as well as Evie's mother, her aunt Bertha—a warm, maternal figure who had instantly made Caitlyn feel welcome.

Her grandmother, the Widow Mags, however, had been a different kettle of fish. *Or should I say, cauldron of chocolate*, thought Caitlyn with a wry smile. Brusque, cantankerous, and fiercely independent, the old woman had rebuffed most of Caitlyn's efforts to get closer to her. But despite all this, Caitlyn had come to realise that beneath her grandmother's prickly exterior was a wise and compassionate heart. It was a side that she wished more in the village could see. Instead, most of the residents of Tillyhenge viewed the old woman with fear and suspicion, labelling her the "local witch" and whispering that the sweet treats in her chocolate shop must have been enchanted by black magic to taste so good...

Caitlyn came out of her reverie to realise that Evie was excitedly telling Pomona about her own costume for the ball. She walked over to join the other two girls at the wooden table in the centre of the kitchen.

"...couldn't decide between a fairy or an elf, but then I got a book from the library and there was an illustration of a woodland elf and she looked gorgeous!" said Evie breathlessly. "I thought maybe I could base my costume on that picture—"

"What about your ears?" asked Pomona. "You can't be an elf without pointy ears. Do you have any good prosthetic ones?"

"Oh, no, I've got something *much* better!" said Evie, grinning. "I'm not going to bother with trying to find a real costume. I don't think I'll ever find anything to match the picture in the book anyway. So I've decided to use a glamour spell instead."

"What's a glamour spell?" asked Caitlyn just as Pomona squealed and said: "Omigod, you mean *glamour* is real?"

Evie nodded eagerly, then she turned to Caitlyn and explained: "Glamoury is an advanced form of witchcraft where you use magic to make the world see you the way you want to be seen. It's not like Transfiguration, where you physically change yourself. With a glamour, you don't actually transform, but rather, you hide your reality and produce a... an illusion that's so real that it fools everybody."

"And you can choose what the illusion is," chimed

in Pomona. "Isn't that awesome? Like, if you wanted to go blonde, you could just use a glamour spell to change your hair colour instead of having to dye it. It's how you get all these legends and folk tales about beautiful women turning into ugly crones," she added, giggling. "It's 'cos they fooled everyone with a glamour."

"Wow..." said Caitlyn, thinking of her lifelong embarrassment with her big hips. She knew that being pear-shaped was simply the result of her genes; no matter how much she dieted or exercised, she couldn't really change. But how wonderful it would be if she didn't have to change at all but could simply alter the way people perceived her!

"I never knew you could do glamour spells," said Pomona, looking at Evie with new respect.

"Well, I can't, actually. It's very advanced magic," Evie admitted. "But you can learn anything online these days, can't you? And I found a website yesterday of a witch who specialises in Kosmetike Glamoury! She's just published *101 Shortcut Spells to Greater Allure* and also a limited-edition *Book of (Eye) Shadows*, and she's got a channel on YouTube, and she has hundreds and thousands of followers! She says she has different incantations to help you become more attractive, like a Sleek Hair glamour and an Acne Exorcism charm... If you follow her instructions, you could become so glamorous and alluring that no one would be able to resist you!"

"Maybe you should be careful, Evie," said Caitlyn

uneasily. "You just never know with online things. I mean, how do you know who's really on the other end? It's not like walking into a real shop or meeting a real person, is it?"

"Aww, c'mon, Caitlyn—what century are you living in?" complained Pomona. "Everyone shops online these days! And it would be *so* awesome to be able to use glamours!" Her eyes sparkled. "Imagine if you could really change the way you looked with just a couple of magic spells. Like, if you hate the way your nose looks, you could use a glamour spell instead of going for a nose job. Holy guacamole, half the Hollywood docs would go out of business! Caitlyn, maybe you should—"

Caitlyn made an exclamation of annoyance.

"What?" said Pomona. "I'm only trying to help—"

"No, no, it's not you," said Caitlyn, bending over the wooden table. "It's these annoying ants! I don't know where they keep coming from. I've wiped the table so many times and cleaned everything, and still, they keep coming back."

She pointed to a trail of black ants marching across the surface of the wooden table and clustering around a small puddle of sugar syrup which had been spilled on the table earlier.

"Ugh! I hate ants. Looking at them always makes me feel itchy," muttered Evie, scratching her arms as she watched the crawling black insects.

"Why don't you just zap them with some pesticide?" asked Pomona.

"I don't want to spray chemicals in here," protested Caitlyn, gesturing to the various containers of cocoa powder, cream, sugar, butter, and other food items spread across the table.

"Mum always uses herbal sachets," Evie offered. "She says they work really well to repel insects, although I always tell her I think she should just use magic—"

"Yes, of course—magic!" cried Pomona, snapping her fingers. She turned back to Caitlyn. "Why don't you use witchcraft on them?"

"What do you mean... hex them?" said Caitlyn, laughing. "Don't you think that's overkill? I mean, they're just ants—"

"Yeah, but they're being really annoying," said Pomona, turning back to look at the trail of insects with a glint in her eye.

"They're not doing it on purpose," said Caitlyn. "I mean, they're just doing what ants do. They look for sugar and take it back to the nest. You can't punish them for following their natural instincts."

"Oh no?" said Pomona with a little smile.

Caitlyn turned away to grab a kitchen cloth, saying with a sigh: "I'll wipe the spill up and hopefully they'll—"

Evie gasped and Caitlyn jerked back to see the younger girl pointing at the table surface.

"Look! Look at what they're doing!"

Caitlyn looked down: the trail of ants had broken up and reformed. Instead of marching towards the puddle of sugar syrup, the tiny black insects were now crawling up the side of a *bain marie* she had set up earlier. The Widow Mags had stressed that using a "hot water bath" was the safest way to melt chocolate without burning it, and Caitlyn had been proud of her home-made effort, using a shallow oven tray filled with boiling water. Now the *bain marie* was no longer being used, although steam was still rising from the hot water in it.

Caitlyn watched in bewilderment as the ants crawled up and along the edge of the tray. There was something strange about the way they were moving— it was almost as if they were resisting, their tiny legs braced, and yet they were being pushed forwards by some invisible force. Slowly, agonisingly, they crawled to the top of the oven tray where they clung to the edge, their antennae waving madly.

Caitlyn glanced at Pomona, who was leaning over the *bain marie* and staring down at the ants, her expression intent.

"Pomie... are you...? What are you doing?" she whispered.

Pomona grinned, not taking her eyes off the ants. "Teaching them a lesson."

CHAPTER THREE

Caitlyn drew a sharp breath. *No, it can't be true...* and yet there was no denying what it looked like: somehow, Pomona was controlling the ants, forcing them close to the edge, to the steaming water and imminent death.

"No, Pomie—stop it!" cried Caitlyn, grabbing the other girl's arm.

The sudden movement broke Pomona's concentration and her eyes snapped away from the *bain marie*. Instantly, the ants' tiny bodies relaxed, as if an invisible puppeteer had cut the strings, and they scrabbled away from the water's edge—all except one. Caitlyn watched in horror as the tiny insect clung desperately for a moment to the side of the tray, then tumbled down, falling into the hot water. Instantly, it spasmed, then curled up into a small, blackened ball.

"You've killed it!" cried Caitlyn.

Pomona peered into the water, then shrugged. "So what? Jeez, Caitlyn, what's the big deal? People kill ants all the time. I'll bet you killed a few when you were wiping up the table before."

"Yes... but... that's different," stammered Caitlyn, her eyes still riveted on the tiny, shrivelled insect now floating on the surface of the water. "This... this was like you were forcing them to suffer."

Pomona rolled her eyes. "'Forcing them to suffer'... they're just stupid ants, for crying out loud! They're *insects*! If they're gonna come into the house and climb on our table, then they deserve to die."

"How did you do it?" asked Evie, regarding Pomona with a mixture of awe and unease. "It was magic, wasn't it?"

Pomona leaned back and folded her arms, a little smile playing at the corners of her mouth. "Maybe," she said.

"You can do magic?" gasped Evie.

Pomona shrugged, although her smile widened. "Yeah. Kinda. I think." She hesitated, then added, "I've just been noticing little things in the last few weeks..."

Caitlyn looked at her warily. "What kind of things?"

"Oh, you know... like when you get really mad at someone and wish bad karma on them... and then it happens!" Pomona chuckled. "Like, there was this one guy who was driving next to me when I was coming back from Oxford yesterday and he was being a total jerk. First, he was tailgating me, and then he overtook me and pushed in front and was, like, hogging two lanes right in front of my car. And every time I tried to get around him, he would veer really close, as if he was trying to ram into me, and all this time, he was looking out his window and smirking at me, like he thought he was really cool and funny. Well, I got really mad, and I thought in my head: 'I wish you would swerve into the side of the road, you bastard'... and guess what? He did!"

Caitlyn stared at her. "What happened? Did he crash?"

"Nah... he just sorta swerved all over the place and then he got back in control of his car. But I saw his face. He looked kinda scared." Pomona smiled with satisfaction. "I was curious if I'd imagined the whole thing, so I looked at his car again and wished really hard that he would swerve... and he did it again!" She laughed in delight. "He looked *really* freaked out then. He slowed right down and pulled over and let me pass. It was awesome!"

Caitlyn looked at her cousin in horror. "It's not awesome at all, Pomona! He could have been killed!"

"Aww, gimme a break!" said Pomona. "It's not like the guy actually crashed, okay? He just got a really bad scare, and believe me, he deserved it. I'll bet he's gonna be a lot more polite and careful on the roads now, and how's that a bad thing? I just made the world a safer place."

"But what if he hadn't been able to regain control of his car? What if he had swerved and hit a tree or something? You would have been responsible for someone's death!"

Pomona jutted her bottom lip out mutinously. "It's not like I tried to kill him, okay? I was just mad and wished some bad karma on him—don't tell me you've never done that! How was I supposed to know it would come true? It wasn't like I did it on purpose."

"But you did just now," said Caitlyn accusingly. She pointed at the *bain marie*. "What you did just now—you deliberately forced those ants into harm's way."

Pomona hesitated, then she shrugged and said, "Yeah, okay, so maybe I did. So what? Like I said, they're just stupid insects."

"That's not the point! They might just be insects today, but what's next? Animals? People? You… you can't do this, Pomona, whatever you're doing," said Caitlyn urgently. "It's wrong and cruel and—"

"Aww, lay off!" said Pomona, scowling. "I'm, like, so sick and tired of your 'holier-than-thou' attitude. Ever since you discovered that you're a witch, Caitlyn, you've turned into a real killjoy, you know that? You're so freakin' uptight! You think magic should only ever be used for—" Pomona put on a high-pitched, sarcastic voice: "—'noble causes', right? Man, next you'll be telling me I can only use spells for charity and self-sacrifice!"

"That's not true!" Caitlyn protested. "I'm not saying that at all. I just think that magic gives you an unfair advantage and you shouldn't use it to do harm—"

"Maybe it was all just a coincidence," Evie spoke up, her timid voice cutting into their argument. "I mean, maybe the other car just swerved because the man was driving like an idiot; it was just a coincidence that Pomona was looking at him at the same time. And those ants... well, maybe it was just random bad luck that they happened to climb up onto the *bain marie...*"

For a moment, Pomona looked as if she would argue. Then she said with a shrug, "Yeah, maybe it was just coincidence." She shot Caitlyn a narrow-eyed look. "*I'm* not the one who overreacted."

Caitlyn started to say something, then she stopped herself. Maybe the others were right; maybe she *was* overreacting. After all, it *was* true that she would probably have killed quite a few ants herself if she had wiped them with a cloth. Still, that seemed different: a simple, practical action with the ants being killed as an unfortunate consequence. Not a deliberate manoeuvre to force them to their deaths. *Besides, it wasn't just ants being killed; it was the way Pomona—* Caitlyn thought back again to the expression on her cousin's face and shivered. *Pomona almost looked like she* enjoyed *watching the ants march to their deaths...*

Caitlyn gave herself a mental shake. What was

she thinking? Of course Pomona hadn't enjoyed killing the ants! And wasn't she being silly to get so upset over a few insects making a nuisance of themselves? She took a deep breath and released it, deliberately relaxing her shoulders.

"Yes, well… maybe I did overreact a bit. Sorry," she said, giving Pomona a half-hearted smile.

Pomona accepted the apology with bad grace. "Well, I'm gonna head back to the Manor. If you want help with your costume, you know where to find me." Turning, she flounced out of the kitchen.

There was an awkward silence after she left, then Evie said: "I … I'd better go too. I'm supposed to be looking after the herbal shop, because Mum has to take some things up to the Manor. You know she's providing all the candles and other Mabon decorations for the ball?"

"Mabon decorations?"

"Yes, didn't you know? It's Mabon in a few days' time. Mum says the marketing team at the Manor rang her up because they've decided to call it the 'Mabon Ball', and they need help decorating the Ballroom. So she's got loads of things she needs to take up to the Manor."

"Shall I come help?" Caitlyn offered. "The chocolate shop is closed for the day anyway, so I don't need to worry about customers." She gestured to the pot which had held the ruined caramel mixture and sighed. "And I think I need a break from this anyway!"

***

Twenty minutes later, Caitlyn hefted the last box of items into the boot of her aunt's hatchback, then climbed into the front passenger seat next to her Aunt Bertha, who was busily tucking the voluminous folds of her purple kaftan into the car before pulling the driver's door shut. Caitlyn had never seen Bertha wear anything other than purple kaftans—she must have had dozens of them, in all styles and fabrics!—and it seemed that, despite the autumn chill, her aunt was sticking to her wardrobe staple. But she had added a grey woollen cloak on top, as a concession to the cold weather, and a thick scarf draped over her frizzy red hair, which she wore piled on top of her head.

"All ready?" she asked, smiling at Caitlyn.

Caitlyn nodded and smiled back. It was funny how just being with Bertha made her feel better. There was something wonderfully soothing about her aunt's presence, whether it was due to her calm, practical manner, the maternal warmth that radiated from her kindly face, or even the gentle aroma of scented herbs that always seemed to surround her. Whatever it was, Caitlyn leaned back in her seat and let out a deep sigh, feeling some of the tension leave her body.

"Something the matter, dear?" Her aunt glanced at her.

Caitlyn hesitated. She was desperate to talk to someone about what had happened in the cottage kitchen and, even more, about the worrying changes in Pomona's attitude the last few weeks. It was so tempting to drop everything in Aunt Bertha's lap and just rely on her advice. But something held Caitlyn back. Perhaps because it would feel too much like a betrayal to talk about Pomona behind her back. Besides, what if Evie was right, and these issues were just strange coincidences?

"Oh... not really... um... just tired," she mumbled.

Her aunt looked at her shrewdly, then she said in a gentle voice, "You know you can talk to me in confidence, dear, about anything that's bothering you. A problem shared is a problem halved, as they say."

"Thanks... er... I'll remember that." Caitlyn forced a smile and gestured to the boxes filling the back of the car. "So... um... Evie was telling me this is all to decorate the Ballroom in honour of something called 'Mabon'? What's that?"

"It's another name for the autumn equinox," Bertha explained as she started the car and set off on the road out of the village. "In Latin, 'equinox' means 'equal night' and refers to a day in the year when there are exactly twelve hours of day and twelve hours of night. There are actually two such days: the spring equinox and the autumn one. The latter is when we celebrate Mabon—a festival which honours the summer harvest and reminds us that it is also a time to prepare for the coming darkness of winter."

"Oh, so that's why there are so many fruits and things in the boxes," said Caitlyn.

Bertha nodded. "The traditional way to celebrate Mabon is with an altar of harvest fruits and vegetables—things like apples, pears, blackberries, elderberries, even rose hips. These are made as offerings to the goddess and also shared between those in the community, so that everyone can give thanks and count their blessings."

"Are they going to set up an altar at the ball?" asked Caitlyn, surprised.

Bertha laughed. "Oh no, nothing as dramatic as that. But the marketing team did think it would be nice to decorate the Ballroom with various touches linked to Mabon, so perhaps a display of autumn fruits as a centrepiece in the middle of the buffet, or harvest decorations on the tables around the room... and I've been advising them on the colour scheme too."

"There's a specific colour scheme for Mabon?"

"Well, it's really just the colours of autumn and the harvest, I suppose. You know, green, yellow, brown, gold... and red, of course, for apples. Feasting on apples is one of the key things associated with Mabon," Bertha explained. "And of course, apples are an especially important symbol in witchcraft and magic."

"Really?" said Caitlyn, her interest piqued. She forgot about Pomona for a moment. "I never realised apples had such a special significance."

"Oh, apples are found in the legends and mythology of many cultures around the world, dear. They're connected to healing and renewal, to immortality, and also to youth and beauty and fertility. You know, in Greek mythology, a golden apple was the real cause of the Trojan War. And in Norse legends, there is an apple tree in Asgard which will give eternal youth to anyone who eats of its fruit. Here in England, the ancient Celts and Druids believed that apple trees were sacred, and in the old laws, chopping down an apple tree was punishable by death."

"Wow, that's a bit extreme, isn't it?"

Bertha smiled. "Perhaps. But you have to remember that people really did believe in the magical powers of apples back then, so it was a very valuable fruit to them, over and above its place as food. For example, they used to believe that if you cut an apple into three sections and rubbed the pieces onto a sick person, then buried the pieces in the ground, the apple would draw out the illness and deposit it into the soil instead." She shook her head ruefully. "Shame it isn't so easy in real life to cure sickness with an apple."

"You mean the famous saying—'an apple a day keeps the doctor away'—isn't true?" asked Caitlyn with a grin.

"Oh, apples *are* very good for you; there's no doubt about that," Bertha replied. "They're high in fibre and vitamins, and they're a rich source of polyphenols, which are antioxidants believed to help with all sorts of things like lowering cholesterol, controlling diabetes, and preventing cancer and heart disease. Polyphenols might even protect your brain as you age, so you're less likely to succumb to conditions like Alzheimer's... and all without resorting to magic!"

Caitlyn looked at her aunt curiously. She'd always thought it interesting that although Bertha was a fully practising witch, her aunt didn't seem to use magic spells very often—much to Evie's frustration.

"So do you ever use apples in magic spells to cure things?" she asked.

"I have done occasionally, but mostly I prefer using my traditional herbalist knowledge when I recommend remedies. Plants and herbs have many wonderful powers, you know, which can simply be unlocked with a mortar and pestle, without having to resort to charms and incantations," said Bertha with some asperity. "Besides, because of their association with fertility and beauty, apples are more often used in love magic than in healing, particularly for divination."

Caitlyn looked puzzled. "Divination?"

"Oh, you know, trying to find out if somebody loves you or the name of your true love—that sort of thing," said Bertha with a dismissive sniff. "But most of the practices are not 'proper' magic, dear. They're really just silly superstitions."

"Like what sorts of things?" asked Caitlyn.

Bertha threw her an impatient look. "Now, don't you start messing about too! I'm always telling Evie not to waste time on such nonsense, but the girl just won't listen. She will believe the most ridiculous things. For example, one of the most common Mabon traditions is using an apple to find your soulmate. They say that if you peel an apple—keeping the skin whole as one long piece—then when the peel drops off the apple and lands on the floor, it will form the first letter of the name of your true love." She shook her head in exasperation. "I came home last week to find that Evie had ruined a whole batch of apples trying to peel them correctly!"

Caitlyn hid a smile and hastened to assure her aunt, "Oh, I'm just asking out of curiosity. Old folklore and superstitions are always fascinating."

"Hmm... yes, well, from what I've seen, I hardly think you'll need to resort to an apple peel to find your answer," said Bertha with a teasing look.

Caitlyn blushed and turned quickly to look out the window, relieved to see that they were turning into the main gates of the Huntingdon Manor estate.

CHAPTER FOUR

The chat about Mabon traditions had helped to distract Caitlyn from her troubled thoughts, but as they pulled up in front of the manor house, Aunt Bertha said:

"Mabon should be of particular interest to Pomona, actually—after all, she's named after one of the goddesses associated with the festival."

"Oh? Pomona always says she was named after the Roman goddess of fruits," said Caitlyn.

"Well, yes, and the goddess Pomona is a keeper of orchards; she's responsible for the flourishing of fruit trees. So she is always portrayed bearing a cornucopia or a tray of ripening fruit... and the cornucopia, or Horn of Plenty, is a traditional symbol for Mabon," Aunt Bertha explained. "In fact, I've suggested to the Manor marketing team that they should try to get hold of some decorative cornucopias—you know, the kind filled with fake fruit—to decorate the buffet. There is no more distinct symbol of Mabon than the cornucopia."

The mention of Pomona brought all of Caitlyn's worries flooding back as she got out of the car and began helping her aunt take boxes out of the boot. When she carried the first box up the front steps of Huntingdon Manor, however, she was momentarily distracted to find the front door open and unattended.

That's odd... where's Mosley? she wondered as she stepped into the empty front hall.

The next minute, she heard footsteps, and she turned to see a middle-aged man hurrying down the hallway towards her. It was Giles Mosley, the Manor's butler, although he looked so uncharacteristically flushed and dishevelled that Caitlyn eyed him in surprise. Despite proudly describing himself as a "modern butler", Mosley had rigid ideas about the importance of etiquette and traditions. In fact, Caitlyn often wondered, with some amusement, whether the butler had secretly been teleported from England's Victorian era! He insisted on addressing everyone in the most ridiculously formal way and was constantly scandalised by the new master's attempts to modernise the estate, including James's preference for a casual, friendly relationship with the Manor staff. Furthermore, he always maintained an impeccable appearance in a discreet dark suit and immaculately pressed shirt, with his hair carefully combed into a neat side-parting.

Today, however, his hair was in wild disarray, with strands sticking up in all directions. His tie was crooked, his collar bent, one of his trouser legs was upturned, and several buttons were missing from his jacket. As he got closer, Caitlyn noticed he had what looked suspiciously like dried dog slobber hanging from one ear, and when she saw the black kitten in his arms, she smiled to herself. She could make a good guess as to what had caused the butler's dishevelment.

"Miss Le Fey!" he cried, hurriedly trying to straighten his clothing with one hand while holding the squirming kitten in the other. "Please accept my apologies for not receiving you. I was obliged to leave my post due to... er... a disturbance that required my supervision."

"I don't suppose the disturbance had anything to do with this little scrap of mischief?" asked Caitlyn, laughing and pointing to the kitten, who was now attempting to climb up onto the butler's shoulder.

Mosley winced as the kitten's tiny claws dug through the fabric of his jacket, but he maintained a stoic expression as he said: "It appears that the preparations for the ball are particularly fascinating to felines. Nibs has been following members of the staff around as they transport items from the Portrait Gallery to the Ballroom, which has resulted in an incident of leg entanglement."

Caitlyn tried not to giggle at Mosley's language. "'Incident of leg entanglement'... are you saying someone tripped over Nibs?"

"Not exactly. As you may know, his lordship's dog, Bran, is the kitten's devoted companion. Unfortunately, he is not quite as adept at squeezing between moving legs..." The butler grimaced delicately.

"You mean Bran smacked into someone while trying to follow Nibs?" said Caitlyn, wincing in her turn as she imagined the scene. A collision with a huge English mastiff was not to be recommended. "Oh no! Was anyone hurt?"

"Fortunately not, madam," said the butler gravely. "The maid involved managed to regain her balance without dropping the priceless divining crystal she was carrying, although she did require the aid of a... er... strong alcoholic restorative afterwards to sustain her nerves. However, I am pleased to report that there were no casualties in the incident, human or otherwise. Nevertheless, I felt that it was prudent to remove the kitten from the vicinity." He made a surreptitious attempt to smooth down his hair. "I... er... slightly misjudged the effort required to catch him."

Caitlyn stifled a laugh. "Well, I'm glad you managed to catch the little monkey! How come you're taking things from the Portrait Gallery to the Ballroom?" she added curiously.

"It was a directive from the Manor's new marketing team," Mosley explained. "As you know, there is healthy competition between the various villages in the Cotswolds to attract tourists and local visitors. Tillyhenge has always stood out for its paranormal history, no doubt because of the proximity of the circle of standing stones on the hill behind the village, as well as the associated local legends. The marketing team are keen to maximise this. Therefore, they decided to change the name of the event this year to a 'Mabon ball' instead of the more common 'hunt ball' that normally occurs every autumn."

"Oh, right... but I still don't see why that means you have to move things from the Portrait Gallery to the Ballroom," said Caitlyn, puzzled. "What things are you moving, anyway? Surely not the oil paintings?"

"No, no, we are moving select artefacts from Lord Fitzroy's father's occult collection," Mosley hastened to explain. "The marketing team wanted to showcase some of the iconic items in the collection as part of a campaign to highlight Olde English legends and folkloric traditions in the local area, and his lordship agreed. The items will be placed in specially commissioned display cases situated around the Ballroom, and it is hoped that they will provide interesting viewing and talking points for the guests—" He broke off and winced again as Nibs, who had been sniffing the butler's earlobe with interest, suddenly began nibbling it with his tiny but sharp teeth.

"Here, I'll take him," Caitlyn offered, hastily putting her box down on the floor, then reaching up to grab the kitten.

"Thank you," said Mosley, straightening his jacket and looking relieved. He glanced at the box that Caitlyn had set down on the floor. "Can I be of assistance, Miss Le Fey?"

"Well, I'm sure Aunt Bertha would be delighted with another pair of hands," said Caitlyn with a smile. "She's brought lots of things to decorate the Ballroom. I think your marketing team are going to be delighted." She turned to lead the way back out to the car.

"Er... has your aunt met with any resistance in the village?" Mosley enquired as he followed her.

Caitlyn paused to look back at him. "What do you mean?"

"In terms of helping to create a 'Mabon ball'," the butler explained. "It is my understanding that several of the villagers are unhappy about the change in direction. They see it as an invitation to court pagan devilry and allow witchcraft to flourish in the village."

"But that's ridiculous!" said Caitlyn impatiently. "Surely they understand that the whole thing is a PR stunt? It's just a way to get media coverage and publicity for the ball—and hopefully for the Manor and the village too. That would ultimately benefit them, if it means more visitors and business in the area."

"I'm afraid that many of them do not view it that way," said Mosley, looking worried. "There is much fear and prejudice in the village. I hope it will not boil over on the night of the ball."

With Mosley summoning several other members of staff to help Bertha unload the car, Caitlyn soon found that her participation wasn't needed. So instead, she focused on trying to keep hold of a squirming Nibs, who was desperate to join in the action.

"*Meew!*" cried the kitten, trying to wriggle free.

"Oh no, you don't," said Caitlyn, holding the little body firmly against her. "You've been causing enough trouble already."

The kitten gave another protesting cry and squirmed again, rolling in Caitlyn's arms and scrabbling with his back feet. His tiny claws raked against the bare skin of her inner wrist and she gasped, jerking her hand back reflexively and releasing her grasp on the little cat. Instantly, Nibs took advantage, leaping out of her arms and landing nimbly on the ground.

"Nibs!" cried Caitlyn, lunging to grab him.

The kitten gave her a cheeky look as he evaded her easily, then scampered back towards the manor house.

"Nibs! Come back!" shouted Caitlyn, exasperated, as she chased after him.

The kitten dodged around a maid carrying one of

Bertha's boxes, darted through the open front door, and disappeared. Huffing with annoyance, Caitlyn hurried after him. She reached the front door herself just in time to see the little bottlebrush tail disappearing around a corner further down the main hallway.

"Nibs!" she called, dashing after him.

By the time she reached the corner, though, there was no sign of the kitten. Caitlyn wandered slowly down the hallway, glancing left and right at the rooms opening off on either side. This was one of the private wings of the Manor, which was not open to the public tours, and most of the doors to the rooms were shut. As she reached the end of the hallway, however, she found one which was slightly ajar. Caitlyn had stayed at the Manor often enough now that even the private areas were fairly familiar to her, and she recognised it as the door to James's study. Had Nibs gone inside?

Hesitantly, she stepped up to the door and knocked. There was a rustle of papers, then she heard a deep male voice call: "Come in!"

Stepping inside, Caitlyn found James Fitzroy sitting behind the mahogany desk dominating one side of the room. He looked deep in thought and there was a slight frown on his handsome face as he stared down at the desk, but his expression brightened as soon as he saw her. Caitlyn's heart skipped a beat as she saw the warmth in his grey eyes.

"Caitlyn! This is a nice surprise."

He rose quickly and came around the desk towards her, his hands outstretched. For a wild moment, Caitlyn thought he was going to pull her into his arms, but then he stopped and dropped his arms to his sides. There was an awkward silence. Finally, James cleared his throat and asked in a formal tone:

"How are you?"

"I'm fine, thank you," said Caitlyn stiffly, whilst inside she wanted to scream with frustration. Why was it that she and James always seemed to end up doing this ridiculous polite tiptoeing around each other every time they met again? She looked at him hesitantly and asked: "Am I disturbing you?"

"No, no. I'd just finished a call." He paused, his frown returning. "It was with Inspector Walsh, actually."

Caitlyn looked up in surprise at the mention of the CID detective. She had met Inspector Walsh several times, during his investigations into various murders that had occurred in Tillyhenge and at the Manor in the past few months, but she hadn't heard of any particular crime recently.

"Is something wrong?" she asked.

James's frown deepened. "I'm not sure," he said slowly. He hesitated, then said, "Gerald Hopkins is dead."

"Dead? But... I thought the doctors said he was improving, and they were hopeful that he could wake up soon?"

James nodded grimly. "They were. They only put him in a medically induced coma because of his head injury, to allow his brain time to heal, but when I last spoke to them, they seemed very pleased with his progress. They were talking about bringing him out of the coma soon, and I was looking forward to speaking to him after the ball. But I've just been informed that he died unexpectedly last night."

"Oh." Caitlyn wasn't quite sure how to respond to the news.

She had mixed feelings about Gerald Hopkins, an academic with expert knowledge in witchcraft and the occult, who had made a name for himself as a modern-day "witch hunter". He had been an old colleague of James's father and his arrival in Tillyhenge several weeks before had coincided with the murder of a woman who had proclaimed herself to be a witch, but who had turned out to be a fraud using fake promises to con people into paying her for custom spells and supernatural protection. Although Hopkins himself had not turned out to be the murderer, that hadn't lessened his evil in Caitlyn's eyes. She could still vividly remember the night she had been trapped in an icy pool of water in an icehouse on the estate: Gerald Hopkins had stood at the water's edge and looked down at her with cold, contemptuous eyes, refusing to help her simply because he believed her to be a witch...

He had also tried to turn James against her, accusing her of bewitching him and calling her the most dreadful names, and Caitlyn still couldn't think of Hopkins's words without a surge of anger. So she had found it hard to muster up much sympathy for him when he had injured his head during a struggle with James and had ended up in a coma. Even now, she found it hard to feel sorrow for the man's death. The only regret she felt was that she would no longer be able to ask him all the questions she'd wanted to. There had been so much Gerald Hopkins had hinted at, so much left unsaid, and Caitlyn was sure that the truth about the Fitzroy family's history would provide answers to her questions about her own family and past too. Now, though, it looked like the old witch-hunter was taking his answers with him to the grave.

"Did he have a heart attack or something?" she asked James.

"They're not sure. That's why Inspector Walsh is involved."

Caitlyn raised her eyebrows. "Are you saying they suspect foul play?"

"Possibly. To all appearances, Hopkins looked as if he had died of a heart attack, but there were some strange features in his reports which couldn't be explained by the hospital procedures he'd had."

"What do you mean, strange features?"

James looked up, his eyes meeting hers. "He looked like he'd been tortured."

CHAPTER FIVE

Caitlyn caught her breath sharply. "*Tortured?* But how...? Do they know what happened?"

James shook his head. "The hospital was particularly chaotic last night—someone had hacked into the internal system and caused an outage in their electronic medical records, which resulted in complete havoc, as you can imagine. Operations were put on hold, medical procedures cut short, emergency triaging compromised... So it's hardly surprising that no one checked on Hopkins for a long time. When a nurse finally did, she found him dead in his bed."

"Didn't they see anyone go into or come out of his room?"

"No, there was too much confusion. However, they did notice something in his records. The outage had affected the machines recording his vitals, so there was significant data missing, but from what little information was available, it looked like there were several large spikes in his respiration, blood pressure, and heart rate—the kind indicative of great stress or pain. It looks like Hopkins did die of a heart attack, but not the normal type. Something—or someone—had used pain to deliberately stress Hopkins's heart to the point where it simply gave out."

Caitlyn recoiled. "You mean... someone tortured him to death? But why would anyone do that?" she asked in a horrified voice. "I mean, torture is usually used when someone wants information—"

"Exactly," said James.

Caitlyn stared at him, her mind whirling. So she wasn't the only one who had wanted answers from Gerald Hopkins. There were others who were prepared to go to far greater lengths. She shivered. The thought of the old man, alone in the hospital, being tortured for his secrets, made her feel queasy. However much she disliked Hopkins, she wouldn't have wished such a fate on him.

After the last murder had been solved, she had thought that things were finally settling down in Tillyhenge. The spate of unusual deaths and strange occurrences had seemed to be over, and life seemed to be returning to some kind of normal. But now she realised that she'd been living in a fool's paradise. The trouble hadn't disappeared at all—it had simply been simmering beneath the surface.

Caitlyn's thoughts returned to Pomona. There, too, things had been bubbling away out of sight. She had been trying to convince herself that everything was fine and that she was simply imagining things, but Pomona's odd behaviour had only increased in the last few weeks. And after what had happened with the ants, she could no longer ignore it or explain it as simple paranoia.

"James," she said suddenly. "Have you... have you noticed anything different about Pomona?"

"Pomona? In what way?"

Caitlyn shrugged helplessly. "Just... in general. She's been staying here the last few weeks, so you've seen quite a bit of her, haven't you?"

James inclined his head. "You know she's welcome to stay at the Manor for as long as she likes. In fact, Pomona has stayed so often in the past few months that I don't think the staff even regard her as a guest anymore."

"And you haven't noticed anything she's said or done recently which seems a bit odd?"

"What do you mean by 'odd'?" James grinned at her. "A lot of people would think that everything Pomona does is a bit odd. She's not exactly the picture of conventional decorum, is she? I think she scandalises Mosley at least once a day with something she says or does. I keep expecting him to resign in horrified disapproval, leaving me to find a new butler!"

43

Caitlyn laughed reluctantly. "No, you're right. Pomona is an expert at breaking the rules and defying social conventions. But I don't mean outlandish behaviour, I mean..." She trailed off, trying to find the right words, then burst out: "Have you noticed her doing anything that seems mean or cruel?"

James raised his eyebrows. "Not that I can think of, off the top of my head... why?"

Caitlyn shrugged again. "Maybe I'm just imagining things, but... I feel like Pomona has changed. She... she seems to really enjoy it when someone or... um... something... is punished. You know, like karma."

"Ah. Well, Pomona has always been much more outspoken than the rest of us, and she's not afraid to show her glee when people get their comeuppance. I'm sure we all have similar thoughts; she's just more honest about voicing them!" James gave a self-deprecating laugh. "To be honest, as a repressed Englishman, I admire her ability to speak up and not always be worried about being polite or offending others."

"No, that's not what I meant. It's more than that. It's almost like..." Caitlyn paused, reluctant to voice it. "Well, like she seems to enjoy watching them suffer."

"Are you talking about a specific incident?" asked James. "Perhaps if you told me what happened, then I could understand you better."

Taking a deep breath, Caitlyn recounted Pomona's account of the man with the swerving car, as well as the incident with the ants in the Widow Mags's kitchen.

"What really bothers me is the feeling that she seemed to get a kick out of watching those ants squirm," she said as she concluded. "It was almost as if Pomona was enjoying their terror as they were forced near the edge of the hot water."

James laughed. "That's a bit melodramatic, don't you think? After all, they were just ants. Could you really feel their fear?"

"I know they're really small and you can't see their faces or expressions or anything, but you can feel something from them," Caitlyn insisted. "All living creatures have an... 'energy'... and I could feel theirs shrinking back in fear."

"But perhaps you misunderstood Pomona's reaction. I mean, if someone suddenly thought that they have magical powers, they would probably be thrilled, and this would be reflected in their face. So maybe what you saw wasn't Pomona enjoying what she was doing to the ants—if she *was* doing anything, which I would seriously question—but what you saw was her delight with what she *thought* was her newfound 'ability'," James reasoned. "After all, Pomona has always been fascinated by magic and the paranormal, hasn't she? In fact, I've always wondered if she wasn't secretly a bit envious of you finding your true identity. If anyone has wanted to be a witch all her life, it's Pomona!"

Caitlyn was silent as she digested James's words. It was true. Ever since they were little girls, when they used to spend school holidays together, she could remember Pomona eagerly trying a variety of occult practices—from tarot cards and Ouija boards to astrological charts and crystal divination. Her cousin had even joined a Hollywood "coven" at one point. But despite her fervent attempts, Pomona had never been able to find any supernatural powers in herself. Caitlyn had always thought it a terrible irony that she—someone who had never believed in witchcraft—had been the one to discover her magical ancestry, when Pomona would have done anything to be in her place.

"It's highly unlikely that Pomona has suddenly gained the ability to do magic, no matter how much she'd like to think so, and much more likely that it was just a series of strange coincidences," continued James. "I know it seems incredible, but it *is* possible. The same way it seems unlikely you could flip a coin and get ten heads in a row—but that doesn't mean that it can't happen."

"It's not about whether Pomona really used magic or not," Caitlyn argued. "It's more the way she seemed to be pleased—"

"But it *is* the possibility that she used magic that's really bothering you, isn't it?" said James. "If you had seen Pomona smack a mosquito or swat a fly, would you have felt so upset that she showed satisfaction at killing it?"

"N-o-o," Caitlyn admitted. "But that seems different, somehow." She paused, struggling to find the words to explain. "I mean, if I swat a fly, then it's no different to a predator going after prey. The fly has a chance. It can get away from me if it's fast enough and I'm not skilled enough to swat it. But what Pomona did to those ants—it was like forcing another creature's will to bend to yours using magic. That seems unfair and... and cruel, in a way..."

"I think perhaps you are ascribing motives that weren't there," said James gently.

Caitlyn sighed. Could she have been completely wrong?

"Look, I wouldn't worry too much," said James, giving her a reassuring smile. "I'll definitely keep an eye out for anything unusual in Pomona's behaviour, but I think—"

They were interrupted by the sound of heavy padding footsteps approaching in the hallway outside, and an enormous beast lumbered into the study. It had massive jaws beneath drooping jowls, paws the size of proverbial dinner plates, and an adorably bewildered expression on its huge, wrinkled face.

"Bran!" said James, smiling at the English mastiff. "Look—one of your favourite people has come for a visit."

Caitlyn braced herself, expecting the dog to bound over with his usual enthusiastic, slobbery greeting.

But the mastiff hesitated just inside the door, whining anxiously.

"What's the matter, boy?" asked James, going over to lay a hand on the huge head.

The mastiff whined again and turned back towards the hallway. He looked back over his shoulder at them, his dark eyes imploring silently.

"I think he wants us to follow him," said Caitlyn, going over to join James.

James took a step towards the dog. "What is it, Bran? What are you trying to tell us?"

The mastiff wagged his tail, then whined again. When James didn't move, he came back and clamped his huge jaws gently around his master's arm, giving it a tug. Then he whined again, sounding more urgent this time, and shuffled his paws.

"I wonder if it's something to do with Nibs," said Caitlyn suddenly. "The only other time I've seen him behave like this was when he came to tell me that Nibs was stuck on a dangerously high window ledge—do you remember?"

"Hmm... well, Bran *is* very protective of the little scamp," James agreed. He followed the dog out into the hallway and said, "All right, boy. Show us what's bothering you."

The mastiff's wrinkled face brightened, and his tail wagged harder. Turning, he began a slow, lumbering trot down the hallway. But instead of heading for the front part of the manor, as Caitlyn had expected, he went in the opposite direction, leading them to the old servants' staircase at the rear of the house. There, he bounded slowly up the steps, moving with surprising agility for such a giant dog. At the top, he led them unerringly down the corridor until he reached a thick oak door. Heavily studded with metal and sporting a brass ring-pull for a doorknob, it looked like it belonged in a medieval dungeon more than in the upper storey of an elegant Georgian manor.

Caitlyn recognised it as the door to the Fitzroy Portrait Gallery, which housed the oil portraits of James's ancestors, in addition to his late father's prized occult collection.

"Oh! I wonder if Nibs is trapped inside the Gallery," she guessed. "Mosley was telling me that the staff were moving some items from your father's collection to the Ballroom. Maybe they left the door unlocked and Nibs slipped inside. I was actually looking for him just now when I came to your study. He was getting under people's legs—literally!—and I was trying to keep him out of mischief, but he gave me the slip."

James shook his head in reluctant admiration. "For an undersized kitten who nearly drowned, that little monkey can certainly keep you on your toes!" He reached for the brass ring and shoved hard against the heavy wooden door.

As Caitlyn had expected, it was unlocked and swung open noiselessly on well-oiled hinges to reveal a long room that ran the length of the manor house.

She wrinkled her nose in anticipation but was surprised to find that the atmosphere in the room was better than normal. The air, normally heavy with dust and the cloying smell of mould, was slightly fresher—probably due to the recent comings and goings of the staff and the door being kept open longer than usual. The place still had an oppressive air, though, with a row of oil paintings along the wall facing the windows and a series of shrouded shapes filling the rest of the room. These looked ghostly and ominous, although Caitlyn knew that they were nothing more sinister than furniture covered with white sheets, and display cases containing the items from the old Lord Fitzroy's occult collection. Still, she disliked the room, and she followed James reluctantly as he stepped inside.

CHAPTER SIX

Caitlyn was just about to call for Nibs when she realised that they were not alone. A man was standing at the far end of the Portrait Gallery. At the sound of their entrance, he whirled around and Caitlyn saw a look of irritation flash across his face— so brief that she thought she might have imagined it—before it was instantly smoothed over by a bland smile. He looked to be in his forties, with a tall, wiry figure and a suavely handsome face. He was dressed in a pinstriped, three-piece suit—the kind normally worn by bankers or British politicians, although somehow he managed to make it look fashionable rather than stuffy and conservative. In fact, from the top of his artfully tousled hair to the tips of his polished Italian shoes, he was the epitome of perfect male grooming.

And yet, despite his impeccable looks and dress, Caitlyn found the man almost too urbane and handsome for her taste. She glanced at James next to her and couldn't help comparing the two men: the master of Huntingdon Manor might not have been as perfectly oiled and groomed, but there was something much more dashing in the way that James wore his navy zip-neck sweater and dark jeans with casual elegance, the simple look seeming to highlight his broad shoulders and tall, athletic frame.

"Daniel," said James with mild surprise. "What are you doing here?"

The other man gave a self-deprecating laugh. "You've caught me red-handed, I'm afraid! I was satisfying my insatiable curiosity. I'd heard so much about your late father's famed collection of occult objects, I was dying to see it for myself. I was fortunate to find some of your staff in here, removing some of the items." He gave a conspiratorial grin. "I hope you don't mind, old chap—I told a slight fib, said you'd given me permission to look through the rest of the collection and so they could leave the keys to the door with me."

"No, of course... you're welcome to look around," James said as he and Caitlyn went over to join the other man.

"I do hope you're going to introduce me to your charming companion, James?" The man flashed Caitlyn a brilliant smile and held out a well-manicured hand, his eyes widening with calculated admiration. Caitlyn flushed slightly as she took it. Next to her, James cleared his throat and said:

"Caitlyn, this is Daniel Tremaine, who arrived at the Manor last night. He'll be staying with us for a few days." He turned back to the other man. "This is Miss Le Fey, who lives in the village."

"In Tillyhenge?" said Tremaine, regarding her with interest.

"Yes, I live with my grandmother," Caitlyn replied.

"But surely you're not a local resident? Your accent... it sounds a bit unusual—"

"I was born in England, but have grown up mostly overseas," Caitlyn explained. "My... um... adopted mother was American."

"And yet you don't sound very American either?"

"Well, I was home-schooled, and my tutor was British." Caitlyn could see what his next question was going to be and forestalled him. "My adoptive mother was a singer, and she was a bit of a nomad. She liked moving around, even when she wasn't 'on the road' touring, so I never stayed anywhere long enough to attend a normal school. We also didn't live in the United States very much."

"Ah, that explains the unusual accent," said Tremaine, smiling. "Not that it isn't charming, I hasten to add. What we might call 'transatlantic', perhaps? So what brought you to Tillyhenge?"

Caitlyn hesitated, trying to think of a way to shorten a long, complicated story. "I came to the

Cotswolds searching for my birth family, and I was lucky to find my aunt and grandmother both living in the village. My grandmother owns a chocolate shop in Tillyhenge and I'm living with her."

"A chocolate shop! How delightful. I must take myself down to the village to sample your sweet delights sometime," said Tremaine, leaning closer and putting a slight stress on the words "your sweet delights".

Caitlyn shifted uncomfortably. She knew that this was probably typical of the kind of sexual banter that was common in the sophisticated circles Tremaine moved in, but she felt unsure how to deal with it. She glanced at James and saw him frowning slightly.

Hastily, she asked, "What about you? What do you do, Mr Tremaine?"

"Oh please—call me Daniel," he drawled, smirking. "And what do I do? Well, you could say that I provide a civil service at Her Majesty's pleasure."

"I'm sorry?" said Caitlyn, puzzled.

"Daniel means that he works for the British government," said James shortly.

"How dull you make that sound," said Tremaine, giving James a reproachful look. "And here I was hoping to impress Miss Le Fey with the importance of a high-flying diplomatic mission." He turned back to Caitlyn and said, with exaggerated regret, "Alas, I have to admit that my job is far more mundane: I am simply an accountant in the obscure bureaucracies of the British government. Although I must mention that analysing budgets and balancing figures for Her Majesty's Service can be more exciting than you think," he added with a wink.

He glanced at James. "In fact, I believe your father was a servant to the Crown in his own way, was he not? And other members of your family in previous generations, going all the way back to the time of King James I?"

"I'm afraid I have little interest in my family's past allegiances to the Crown," James replied. His tone was polite, but it was obvious from the coolness in his grey eyes that he wasn't prepared to discuss the topic further.

A muscle tightened in Tremaine's jaw, but his voice was light and teasing as he said: "Really? That's lackadaisical of you, James. I have to confess, if it were me, I would have been consumed with curiosity and desperate to find out more." He turned and gestured around the gallery. "Take your father's obsession with the occult, for instance. I would have been fascinated to know why and how he amassed such an unusual collection of objects..." He walked over to the nearest shrouded shape and lifted the white sheet, peering underneath. "There is a veritable treasure trove in here! Look at these... black moon crystals, bone daggers, spell jars ..." He leaned down to peer closer at something in the glass case. "Aha! And that looks like a Vlach magic talisman from Serbia..."

Caitlyn watched him, startled. The few times she

had peeked underneath the covers, she'd had trouble naming half the things in the display cases, and yet Daniel Tremaine seemed to be very familiar with the objects.

The accountant dropped the sheet and moved on to another covered piece. This time, when he pulled the sheet back, it revealed a Victorian umbrella stand in the shape of an elephant's foot.

Caitlyn drew back in disgust. "Ugh! Is that real?"

"Yes, I'm afraid so," said James, grimacing. "A cruel and vile practice that's thankfully obsolete now. I would get rid of it, except that it's an antique with historical value."

Tremaine seemed less interested in the gruesome umbrella stand than in what it contained: a collection of rods and staffs of various shapes and sizes, including a gnarled birchwood broom which looked like it had come straight out of a children's storybook on witches. He rifled through the collection, then pulled something out and looked at it keenly. It was a long wooden staff with a forked top, capped in metal, that resembled the horns of a goat or a deer.

"A stang," he murmured. "And a perfect specimen too, made exactly as it should be—of ash, and shod in iron."

"What is it for?" asked Caitlyn, curious in spite of herself.

"It's a ritual staff. In some traditions, it's believed to symbolise the Horned God. And in witchcraft, it's used to direct energy or aid in spirit flight, or simply as a mobile altar."

"You seem to know an awful lot about witchcraft traditions for an accountant," James commented.

Tremaine gave an easy laugh. "It's just a little hobby of mine. Some men like to spot planes, other men like to home-brew beer... I'm fascinated by the occult."

"You should meet my cousin Pomona," Caitlyn blurted. "She's just like you. Ever since we were little girls, she's been obsessed with witchcraft and magic, and anything to do with the paranormal."

"Ahh... sounds like a girl after my own heart," Tremaine said smoothly.

He turned back towards the umbrella stand, stepping around another piece of shrouded furniture. Something shot out from underneath the folds of the white sheet and caught his ankle, causing him to trip and stumble.

"What the—!" Tremaine regained his balance and looked down in bemusement.

Caitlyn followed his gaze and bit back a laugh as she saw the little black paw appear from underneath the white sheet again and wave around, swiping at empty air. Daniel Tremaine had obviously been the victim of a feline ambush!

"Nibs, there you are..." She swooped down and extricated the kitten from the folds of the sheet.

"*Mew!*" cried Nibs, struggling in her hands.

There was an answering bark and, a minute later,

Bran came bounding over from the other side of the gallery, where he had been disconsolately sniffing and searching for his little friend. The English mastiff barged past Daniel Tremaine, nearly knocking the man off his feet, and making him drop the stang in surprise.

"Careful!" shouted James, grabbing the forked staff just in time before it fell on Caitlyn.

"I'm okay," Caitlyn assured him, although she looked askance at the sharp points on the forked end. She was grateful that James had caught the stang before it fell on her.

"Good God, Fitzroy, that dog of yours is a menace!" said Tremaine irritably, annoyed at losing his aplomb. "He ought to be locked up!"

"Bran is a gentle giant," James said. "He's normally very calm and he would never hurt anyone intentionally. But I agree he can be clumsy at times," he conceded in an apologetic tone. "I'm sorry he startled you."

Caitlyn braced herself as Bran came up to eagerly lick Nibs's face.

"*Mew!*" cried Nibs, even more indignantly this time as he found himself coated in dog drool.

Caitlyn tucked the kitten securely under one arm, then reached down to loop her other hand through Bran's collar.

"Maybe I'd better take these two out of here," she said ruefully.

"Yes, good idea," said Tremaine quickly. As James

tried to follow, Tremaine put a hand on the younger man's arm. "Actually, James, if you don't mind hanging around for a bit, I'd... er... love the chance to pick your brains about your father's collection."

"Well, I don't really know much—" James demurred.

"Oh, I'm sure you know more than you think."

James acquiesced, although he didn't look particularly enthusiastic. He glanced at Caitlyn. "Will I see you before the ball?"

"Probably not," she said with a regretful look. "We're up to our ears—literally!—in chocolate. We've got so many things still to prepare for the buffet. I don't think I'm going to have an hour to spare between now and the start of the ball."

"Well, then... I'll look forward to seeing you then." He gave her a smile that made her insides melt a little.

Caitlyn hustled the animals over to the door, but as she was about to leave the gallery, she glanced back over her shoulder. The two men had turned away, but she could see that Tremaine was watching her from the corner of his eye, obviously waiting for her to leave. As she went out and shut the door firmly behind her, she couldn't help wondering why the accountant seemed so keen to speak to James privately.

CHAPTER SEVEN

Aargh! Why did I think I could simply wear this?
Caitlyn looked despairingly at her reflection in the
mirror. She had really thought that she could reuse
the beautiful dress she'd bought for the Fitzroy
Summer Garden Party a few months ago and wear it
to the Mabon Ball. Now, though, as she smoothed the
simple chiffon sheath over her hips, she realised how
naïve she had been. Everyone else would probably be
in full masquerade, with glittering, glamorous
costumes, and her dress—pretty as it was—seemed
suddenly woefully inadequate. *It might even look rude
and disrespectful to James*, she thought with dismay.
*As if I can't be bothered to make any effort for the
biggest event in the Huntingdon Manor calendar.*

Caitlyn sighed, wishing that she had paid more
heed to Pomona's remonstrations to organise a

proper costume. But there was nothing she could do now. The ball would begin in a few hours and there was no time to find something else to wear. The best she could do was put a mask over her eyes and hope that no one paid her much attention. *Maybe if I put my hair up and add some accessories to it, I'll look more like I'm in costume?* she thought, lifting her thick red tresses and piling them atop her head, then tilting her head to one side to examine the effect.

A muffled thump interrupted her thoughts and Caitlyn glanced across at the en suite bathroom door. Pomona had insisted that she and Evie come over to the Manor before the ball, to get ready in one of the guest bedrooms there, rather than try to dress in Caitlyn's room above the Widow Mags's chocolate shop. Caitlyn had demurred at first, wanting to remain with her grandmother to help with any last-minute preparations for the catering, but now she was glad that Pomona had insisted. It would be nice simply being able to walk downstairs to the Ballroom, rather than having to worry about travelling from the village in their ball outfits. And the spacious guest suite, with its full-length mirror and luxurious en suite bathroom, was heaven compared to her cramped attic bedroom.

Evie had rapturously agreed when they'd first been shown to the room and had immediately disappeared into the en suite with her things. Caitlyn frowned slightly as she realised that nearly forty minutes had elapsed since the younger girl had shut herself in the bathroom. Another thump made her glance at the closed en suite door again. *What's Evie doing in there?* She would have expected the other girl to have come out by now, proudly displaying her transformation. She walked over and knocked gently on the bathroom door.

"Evie? Are you okay?" she called.

"Uh… yeah… I'm fine!" came Evie's muffled voice.

"Do you need help?" asked Caitlyn, starting to turn the door handle.

"No, no!" There was another thump. "No… I'm fine… honestly… I'm just… er… getting ready."

Caitlyn looked doubtfully at the closed door, then shrugged and turned back to the mirror. She was just about to gather her hair atop her head again when there was a knock on the room door. The next moment, without waiting to be answered, Pomona barrelled into the room, her arms full of sparkling gossamer fabric.

"Pomie! I thought you were getting ready in your own room," said Caitlyn in surprise.

Pomona waved a dismissive hand. "I've still got, like, ages. Anyway, I knew you'd need more help than me." She put a hand on her hip and gave Caitlyn's dress a scathing look. "You really think that's good enough for the ball?"

Caitlyn hung her head. "No, you were right. It's not appropriate at all. But I haven't got anything else remotely suitable, and it's too late now to try and find another outfit. There aren't any costume shops nearby—I think the nearest place that might have anything decent is Oxford, and there's no time to go there now."

"Ah...!" Pomona smiled smugly. "Well, I kinda guessed that you'd end up in this situation, so I made contingency plans... TA-DA!"

She held up her arms and shook out the folds of gossamer fabric, revealing a shimmering ballgown in the most beautiful shade of aquamarine. It was strapless, with a sequinned bodice that moulded to the body and hips, then flared out into a full fishtail skirt. There were more sequins stitched onto the gossamer fabric which covered the fishtail skirt, and they were cleverly placed so that the overall effect looked like a scatter of rainbow-hued scales.

"Oh my God... it's gorgeous," Caitlyn breathed, staring at the dress in delight. "But how—?"

Pomona smirked. "I used a bit of magic."

"Magic?" said Caitlyn quickly.

"Online shopping magic," said Pomona, chuckling. "I did an internet search after I left the chocolate shop the other day and I picked out the perfect outfit from this great online designer emporium." She sneezed, then continued. "Express delivery too! It arrived yesterday, just in time." She thrust the dress at Caitlyn. "Go on! Put it on!"

A few minutes later, Caitlyn stood in front of the mirror once again, but this time she was eyeing herself with surprised delight. Not for the first time, she felt incredibly grateful for Pomona's sense of fashion. Her cousin seemed to have an unerring eye for clothes which highlighted her pear-shaped figure in the most flattering way. Caitlyn twisted and turned, admiring herself in the mirror. Somehow, despite the emphasis on the curve of her hips with the fishtail style, the overall effect was graceful and elegant. The vivid aquamarine colour seemed to make her red hair glow against her bare shoulders, and the dress was so cleverly designed that it really did look as if her legs had been replaced by a shimmering mermaid's tail.

"You gotta wear your hair down," declared Pomona. "That's what all sea sirens do. But I got you these clips that you can use, to dress things up a bit. Oh, and this matching mask." She handed Caitlyn several diamanté hairclips made in the shape of sea stars, together with a beautiful Venetian-style mask encrusted with tiny pearls and sparkling seashells.

Caitlyn took the items gratefully. "Oh, Pomie... They're beautiful. You've really thought of everything." She threw her arms around the other girl in an impulsive hug. "Thank you! I really don't know what I'd do without you. You're the best!"

"Yeah, yeah, tell me something I don't know," said Pomona, grinning as she squeezed back.

Caitlyn felt a stab of guilt as she thought of her recent suspicions. Seeing Pomona now, and how generous and thoughtful she was, it seemed ludicrous to imagine that she could ever be intentionally cruel. *I must have been wrong*, thought

Caitlyn. *It was all just a bunch of silly coincidences, and I blew it up into something bigger with my paranoid imagination.*

"Are you gonna wear that with the costume?" Pomona asked, wrinkling her nose as she pointed at Caitlyn's neck. She sneezed again.

Caitlyn's hand crept up to the rectangular stone pendant that she wore on a simple ribbon around her neck. Her runestone necklace. The one that had been around her neck when she had been found as an abandoned baby. The only thing she had linking her to her past—and one of the things that had remained a mystery despite all the other revelations she had uncovered since arriving in Tillyhenge.

Well, not a complete *mystery,* Caitlyn reminded herself. After years of trying, she had finally made some progress deciphering the runes engraved on the surface of her pendant. Using a hag stone—a rare stone with a natural hole in the middle, believed to enable you to see things concealed by spells and enchantments—she had been delighted to discover that the strange symbols could change shape, reforming into letters... words she could read. Unfortunately, the words themselves hadn't made much sense, and the hag stone had been inadvertently lost soon afterwards. Caitlyn felt the familiar sense of frustration as she ran her fingers over the etched surface of her runestone. She had been so close to getting some answers at last!

"Caitlyn? Did you hear me?"

She blinked and looked up to see Pomona blowing her nose. Her cousin's voice was muffled by the tissue as she repeated her question about the runestone.

"I always wear it, Pomie. You know that. I never take it off."

"Yeah, but it'll totally ruin the look of the costume," Pomona complained. "Can't you, like, put it in a purse or something, just for tonight? Or you could leave it here in the room. It'll be perfectly safe."

"No." Caitlyn's fingers closed protectively around the hard edges of the runestone. "I'm not taking it off."

"Well, then... why don't you wear it around your wrist as a bracelet, then?" suggested Pomona. "At least that way it won't be so obvious."

"I suppose..." said Caitlyn. She watched doubtfully through the mirror as Pomona reached behind her to untie the ribbon from around her neck and then looped it twice around her left wrist, before tying a neat knot to secure it in place.

"There. Now it kinda looks like a cool charm bracelet," said Pomona, smiling with satisfaction.

Caitlyn held her arm up and wriggled it, eyeing the runestone which was now dangling from her wrist. Then she glanced at her reflection in the mirror again. Pomona was right: her costume did look a lot better without the runestone around her neck. *It's just for one night*, she reminded herself. Then her eyes strayed to her cousin's reflected figure in the mirror—and to the sparkling black gem strung around *her* neck.

"What about your necklace?" she asked in a casual voice. "Why don't you take it off for the night as well?"

"Are you kidding?" said Pomona, stroking the black diamond pendant and admiring her reflection as the jewel flashed and glittered. "This is gonna go perfectly with my costume and—" She broke off to sneeze again and grab more tissues from the box on the bedside table. When she emerged from the wads of tissue at last, she peered into the mirror and groaned. Her nose was red and starting to swell.

"Are you okay?" asked Caitlyn.

"Yeah, my nose has been itching ever since I unzipped the garment bag containing your costume. I don't know... something's making me sneeze... and my eyes water too," Pomona grumbled, grabbing another tissue to dab at her eyes. She let out a wail as she looked at her reflection again. "I can't go to the ball looking like this!"

"Maybe you have an allergy to something that was in the garment bag?" Caitlyn suggested. She lifted the folds of her skirt and brought it to her face. It smelled faintly musty. "I'll bet they haven't rented out this costume in ages, and it was probably stored with loads of other costumes in a tight space or something, with dust mites and mould spores everywhere."

"What? Mould spores? *Eeuww!*" Pomona looked

disgusted. Then she sneezed again.

Caitlyn hurried over to the bedroom windows and threw them wide open to allow the fresh air in.

"Thanks," said Pomona, sniffing as a cold breeze wafted into the room. "I think that's a bit better."

"You should probably ask Mosley for an antihistamine too," suggested Caitlyn as she hurriedly took her costume off.

"Those things always make me drowsy," grumbled Pomona.

Caitlyn slipped her gown back onto its hanger, then hung it up on the other side of the room, away from Pomona. "I'll put it back on after you've left," she said.

"How come you're not affected?" said Pomona peevishly.

"I suppose everyone has different allergies. Just as well, since I have to actually wear the costume!" said Caitlyn with a wry laugh. "I hope Evie won't be affected too, otherwise I'll have to keep away from both of you for the rest of the evening."

"Speaking of Evie, where is she?" asked Pomona, looking around in surprise. "I thought she was getting changed with you."

"She's in the bathroom." Caitlyn glanced at the en suite door, then lowered her voice. "She's been in there for ages. I don't know what she's doing in there."

Pomona marched over to the en suite and rapped sharply on the closed door. "Hey, Evie? What's going on in there, honey? You fall down the toilet or something?"

"Er... no... I'm fine," came Evie's voice.

"Well, how come you're taking so long?" complained Pomona. "If you don't open the door, I'm gonna come in—"

The next moment, the door swung open to reveal a stunningly beautiful young woman standing on the threshold. She had long red hair which hung like a silky-smooth waterfall down her back, and a delicate, heart-shaped face with a pert nose, rosebud mouth, and big brown eyes thickly fringed by dark lashes. She was dressed in a medieval-style green tunic with a matching leather lace-up bodice and soft suede boots, and a small circlet of gold encircled her head, just above the dainty, pointed ears peeping out of her hair.

Caitlyn and Pomona stared at her, open-mouthed. Finally, Pomona said:

"Who... who are you? What have you done with Evie?"

The beautiful woman stepped forwards, smiling widely. "It's me! *I'm* Evie!"

The other two girls blinked incredulously.

"Honestly, it's me!" the young woman insisted, coming out of the bathroom.

Caitlyn and Pomona backed instinctively away, even though they couldn't take their eyes off the woman. Her every move was as lithe and graceful as a dancer, and she seemed to exude a mesmerising aura, which made it impossible to tear your eyes away from her.

"Holy guacamole..." Pomona breathed. "Evie... is that really you?"

"Yes, it's me!" The beautiful woman laughed. "Do you mean it's worked? You don't recognise me?"

"Man, I thought you were Aphrodite come to life or something," said Pomona, staring at her in wonder. "You're, like, the most beautiful woman I've ever seen!"

Caitlyn shook her head in disbelief. "What did you do, Evie?"

"It's a glamour spell!" Evie beamed. "It's made me beautiful!"

"You were always beautiful, Evie," said Caitlyn gently. "Just maybe not in the conventional way."

Evie scowled. "No, I wasn't! I hated the way I looked, with my frizzy hair and my freckles and my flat chest..." She hurried over to the mirror and admired her voluptuous new bust. "Oh my Goddess! Look at my cleavage! The girls at school will never make fun of me now—"

"The girls at school won't even *recognise* you now," said Pomona, chuckling. "How the heck did you do it? I mean, no offence, Evie, but you said glamours are advanced magic and you're not like some super-experienced, powerful witch."

"It's that online witch I told you about!" Evie explained eagerly. "I ordered her spellbook and I've been watching the post like a hawk 'cos I was so afraid Mum might see it before I could grab it." Evie flashed the other two girls a guilty look. "She'd be really annoyed if she found out what I was spending money on. She thinks online witches are all frauds and their spellbooks are just scams."

Secretly, Caitlyn thought that her aunt was probably right, but Evie looked so happy and excited that she felt bad bursting the younger girl's bubble.

"Anyway, it arrived yesterday, and I stayed up all night practising," continued Evie. "You know, glamour is a very advanced form of witchcraft—it's a kind of mind control, really—and normally you have to be a really powerful witch to be skilled enough to do it. But this spellbook gives you all the hacks and shortcuts, so you don't have to spend all the years training that you'd normally do!"

Caitlyn started to make a sarcastic comment about shortcuts, then bit her tongue. Instead, she said: "Are you sure it's safe?"

"Of course, it's safe! You're not really changing anything about yourself, see? It's just an illusion."

"But... you don't look like yourself at all," Caitlyn said, frowning. "I mean, don't get me wrong, Evie—you look beautiful. But... but you look like someone else entirely!"

"That's the whole point!" said Evie with delight. "I don't *want* to look like me. I've drawn a veil over my real appearance and projected an illusion of what I want to look like instead."

"But—"

"That is so awesome!" Pomona cried, obviously not sharing Caitlyn's concerns. "Does the spell, like, break at midnight or something?"

Evie shook her head, grinning. "No, that's the best part! A glamour can last for several hours or even days."

"You mean, you're stuck looking like that?" asked Caitlyn in dismay.

"What's so bad about that?" asked Pomona. "She looks gorgeous!"

"Yes, but are you saying you can't reverse a glamour spell?" Caitlyn persisted, looking at Evie worriedly.

The younger girl shrugged. "Well, you *can* 'switch' a glamour spell on and off if you're a really powerful witch and you know all the proper advanced techniques to manipulate magic. But the spellbook I ordered uses 'instant' shortcut spells, and for those, you don't get so much control. So you just have to wait for the illusion to wear off by itself." She glanced at her reflection in the mirror again. "Anyway, like Pomona said, what does it matter? It would be great to keep looking like this! In fact, I think I'm going to top it up again before it fades entirely, so I can remain looking beautiful and—"

"What about your mother?" Caitlyn demanded. "Isn't she going to notice that her daughter has completely disappeared?"

Evie looked slightly chastened. "Oh. Yeah. I hadn't thought that through yet..."

"Aww, don't be such a party pooper!" said Pomona, rolling her eyes at Caitlyn. "Bertha will be busy in the kitchen all evening, helping the Widow Mags. She's not gonna see Evie until after the ball— let the girl enjoy her evening! We can worry about what to tell her mom afterwards."

"But—"

"Ooh, quick, let's get a selfie!" exclaimed Pomona, grabbing her phone and leaning close to Evie. Then she frowned at her phone screen. "Wait... you look just like your old self in here."

Evie leaned over to look. "Oh. I suppose glamours don't work through a camera lens," she said in disappointment. "Maybe the glass acts as a filter, blocking out the illusory magic?"

"What a bummer." Pomona started to lower her phone, then she glanced at the phone screen again and gave a shriek. "Yikes, is that the time? I gotta go change! See you guys later!"

A minute later, she was gone. The room felt strangely silent and empty without Pomona's effervescent presence. Caitlyn glanced at Evie, then said hesitantly:

"Evie, do you really think this glamour thing is a good idea?"

Evie raised her chin. "Yeah, I think it's the best thing that's ever happened to me!" Then, as if to forestall any further awkward questions, she added hurriedly: "I'm... I'm going downstairs first. See you at the ball!"

Left on her own, Caitlyn wandered into the bathroom to stare at her reflection in the mirror. Then she rummaged in the make-up bag on the vanity counter and pulled out a mascara wand. Turning back to her reflection, she sighed and said: "Well, I guess it's my turn for some glamour... the old-fashioned way!"

CHAPTER EIGHT

Caitlyn hesitated just outside the doorway to the Ballroom. She knew that she was terribly late—it looked like most of the guests had already arrived and the ball was well under way. She had purposefully dawdled in her room, fiddling with her costume and hair and make-up, telling herself that she needed to get the details "just right". But if she were being honest, she had to admit that she'd just been finding an excuse to delay coming down. Although she—like Pomona—had grown up with a celebrity mother and was no stranger to Hollywood parties, she had never been comfortable with the glitz and glamour of that lifestyle. While her cousin had basked in the limelight, Caitlyn had always preferred to stay in the wings, shyly watching everyone else around her and enjoying things in her own quiet way.

So the thought of stepping into a huge room full of strangers at such a high-profile occasion was incredibly daunting.

She wished that Pomona was there with her. She wouldn't have felt so intimidated if her vivacious cousin had been by her side. But although Caitlyn had stopped by Pomona's room before coming downstairs, she had found it empty, with no sign of the American girl anywhere. Sighing, Caitlyn smoothed down the shimmering fabric of her fishtail skirt again. Then she took a deep breath and straightened her shoulders. She wasn't a shy little girl anymore or a tongue-tied teenager, always hiding in the shadow of her more confident cousin, she reminded herself. She shouldn't be needing to rely on Pomona—she was an adult now, and she had to learn to face things on her own. *Besides, I'm in costume; with this mask covering half my face, I'm probably totally unrecognisable*, she told herself.

Feeling braver, Caitlyn took a deep breath and stepped through the double doors to join the throng. Instantly, she felt herself caught up in the exuberant atmosphere as she looked around the spectacular Ballroom. Sparkling crystal chandeliers graced the high, vaulted ceilings, and a series of gold embellishments and mirrored panels decorated the walls around the huge room. A small chamber orchestra was ensconced at one end of the Ballroom, its members enthusiastically playing a Viennese waltz. On the other side of the room, which opened out into a small alcove, there was a sumptuous buffet laid out next to an impressive five-tiered fountain. Crowds of people milled about, talking, laughing, and drinking, as white-gloved waiters glided past, refilling champagne glasses and offering canapés from silver trays.

It would have looked like any other high-society ball, except for the arrangements of autumn nuts, harvest fruits, dried branches, and flowers decorating the side tables, and the dozens of white candles lining various ledges around the Ballroom, their flickering flames reflected eerily in the mirrored panels. An enormous cornucopia had been placed in the centre of the buffet table, with all manner of fruits and vegetables spilling from its open cavity, and piles of red apples were scattered on surfaces everywhere. And most arresting of all were the glass cases placed strategically in the corners of the room, displaying intriguing treasures from the old Lord Fitzroy's occult collection, such as elf-shot amulets, ritual chalices, pentacle altars, and even what looked like a creepy, mummified Hand of Glory.

Wow, thought Caitlyn, looking around. *The marketing team have really gone to town on the Mabon theme!*

It looked like the guests loved the dark fairy-tale atmosphere, though. Caitlyn could see several people pointing to the decorations and talking excitedly, whilst others posed dramatically next to the displays, showing off their outfits as friends took photos. There was a mind-boggling array of costume types, and it looked like everyone had made a huge effort to take part in the masquerade—from sinister demons to ethereal fairies, wild monsters of myth to mysterious beauties of legend. Caitlyn felt a rush of gratitude to Pomona once again for her thoughtfulness in organising a suitable costume—she would have felt terribly underdressed and horribly embarrassed if she'd come downstairs in her simple summer dress.

Thoughts of Pomona made Caitlyn wonder again where her cousin was. She stood on tiptoe, straining to see through the crowds. It was frustrating because she didn't know what costume Pomona would be wearing, so she had no idea what she should be looking for. Switching tack, she searched for a glimpse of Evie, but, again, she drew a blank. In fact, with the masks covering faces, and the outlandish hairstyles and costumes changing people's appearances, it was difficult to recognise anyone. Caitlyn knew that James had invited all the local residents to the ball, but despite his own down-to-earth and inclusive attitude towards his staff and tenants, some in the village and surrounding farms would still not feel comfortable alongside the Manor's high-society guests, and she doubted that many would attend. Suddenly, she felt very alone, despite the crush of people around her.

Then she caught sight of a stunningly beautiful woman dressed in an elf costume on the other side of the room. *Evie!* Belatedly, Caitlyn realised that she had been looking for her young cousin's "true form" when she had scanned the room earlier. She had temporarily forgotten about Evie's glamour, but now she saw that it was certainly working well! Evie was surrounded by a cluster of young men, all vying for her attention. Some were solicitously offering her food and drink; others were whispering flirtatiously in her ear; one handsome young man was even down on one knee, staring up at her adoringly. Caitlyn smiled to herself. In spite of her earlier worries, it was nice to see Evie receiving so much admiration for once—although from the expression on her younger cousin's face, she looked more bemused than anything else!

Caitlyn turned away and drifted to the edge of the dance floor. She watched wistfully as couples whirled past in perfect time to the dreamy music being played by the orchestra. *What about James—where is* he? *Why hasn't he come looking for me?* Then she felt ashamed of her self-pitying thoughts. After all, she was the one who had deliberately delayed coming down—she could hardly expect James to have remained by the door, waiting for her! As host of the party, as well as owner of the estate, he would have had to circulate and look after his guests, particularly the important sponsors for the local charities who were hoping to benefit from this ball.

Even as she had the thought, Caitlyn spotted James on the other side of the dance floor. He looked breathtakingly handsome in his Phantom of the

Opera costume, with the stark elegance of his black-and-gold brocade jacket and silk cape highlighting his tall, muscular figure, and the silver half-mask lending an almost sinister edge to his aristocratic features. He was dancing with a slender blonde woman, whirling her expertly between the other couples, and they looked stunning together. Caitlyn saw several eyebrows waggling and meaningful looks exchanged as other guests watched them, and she was reminded uncomfortably of the fact that James Fitzroy was considered one of the most eligible bachelors in England. All her old insecurities came flooding back, and Caitlyn wondered if she had been crazy to think that the master of Huntingdon Manor would choose her above all the other beautiful, sophisticated women surrounding him.

She was pulled out of her forlorn thoughts by the sound of a familiar crotchety voice enquiring:

"Have you seen my teeth?"

Caitlyn whirled to see a stooped old man dressed in a black suit and tails that looked like it had been unearthed from the wardrobe department of a historical drama production unit. In fact, he himself looked like something that had been dug out from an ancient attic, with his rheumy eyes, sunken mouth, and few wispy hairs carefully combed across his balding head. He carried himself with a certain dignity, though, and would have looked perfectly respectable—were it not for the fact that he was leaning over the shoulder of a startled woman, peering hopefully into her champagne glass.

"Porcelain amalgamate, pointed ends, more alabaster than ivory, I think... about yea long," the old man told her, demonstrating with a bony thumb and forefinger. "Not a bad replica of my original fangs, actually, although you don't get the same overbite, of course."

"I... I beg your pardon?" stammered the woman, staring at him.

"Are you saying that you've dropped your dentures in my wife's drink?" demanded the woman's companion.

"Not very likely, but you never know where teeth can turn up, do you? It's the confounded dentist. Told him vampire fangs need extra finesse in attachment, but he dismissed my concerns," grumbled the old man. "I thought he would be better than the last chap, but he turned out just as useless!" He sniffed. "Still, what do you expect from someone who did most of their training on ogre teeth?"

"Oh... that's a good one, mate," said the husband, laughing suddenly and raising his glass in a toast to the old man. "You're really getting into character, aren't you? Word of advice, though..." He cast a disparaging look at the old man's suit. "I'd get a better costume next time, if I were you. You don't look anything like a vampire."

"What? How dare you!" spluttered the old man. "I do not need a costume to look like a vampire—I *am* a vampire!"

The husband burst out laughing. Before he could respond, Caitlyn grabbed the old man's arm and hastily hauled him away from the couple.

"Viktor! What are you doing here?" she demanded.

The old man gave her a grumpy look. "Looking for my fangs, of course. What else?"

"No, no, I mean, what are you doing here at the ball? How did you sneak in?"

Viktor looked affronted. "Sneak in? I do not sneak! I am an Ancient Guardian Protector. We are the most respected warriors in the Underworld. There are none to match us in duty or honour... Anyway, as it happens, I had an invitation—from the lord of the manor himself," he added huffily.

"James? James invited you to the ball?" said Caitlyn disbelievingly.

"Yes, he happened to come upon me when I was hanging upside down, having a nap in my favourite corner of the Manor Library ceiling. Good cobwebs there, you know—keeps the draughts out. Anyway, he looked a bit startled to find me, but very decent chap. Impeccable manners. Asked me how I was, and we discussed the weather, of course, like any two civilised Englishmen... and when he heard of my predilection for toffee apples, he invited me to come and sample them at the ball, seeing as they were to be one of the special treats offered in the buffet." Viktor smacked his lips. "I must say, that old witch Mags knows what she's doing with caramel sauce, I'll give her that. Best toffee apples I've tasted in a century!"

The old man brightened suddenly as the exuberant notes of a new piece of music filled the Ballroom.

"Ah! The polka-mazurka! This was my favourite dance back in the 1850s. Dum...dum-dum...dum!" He gave a little sideways skip and a hop, then grabbed Caitlyn's hand enthusiastically. "Come, I will show you, my dear—"

"Oh no, Viktor, I don't think that's a good idea..." Caitlyn started to protest, but Viktor was already dragging her into the centre of the room.

The next moment, Caitlyn found herself clutched in Viktor's bony arms and whirled around the dance floor. *For a six-hundred-year-old vampire, he sure is nimble on his feet,* thought Caitlyn, struggling to keep up with Viktor's fancy footwork.

"Dum...dum-dum...dum," sang Viktor happily, swinging Caitlyn around with gusto.

She had to clutch at her skirts to stop herself tripping, and gave a yelp of surprise as Viktor suddenly twirled her outwards to the end of his arm.

"*Oomph!*" Caitlyn gasped as she collided with another couple. She turned in dismay and saw that she was facing an elderly matriarch in a sequined black gown, with enormous ostrich plumes in her hair and a scandalised expression on her face. "I'm terribly sorry—"

Before she could finish, she felt Viktor's bony

hand groping for her arm again. But unfortunately, he seemed to have trouble seeing clearly and he grabbed the arm of the matriarch instead. The woman gave a shriek of shock and outrage as the old vampire yanked her into his arms and twirled away with her.

"Wait! Viktor—" Caitlyn cried, trying to follow them, but her route was cut off by the swaying bodies of other dancing couples.

"It looks like you'll have to accept me as a poor substitute," came a smooth voice beside her.

Caitlyn turned to see that the old matriarch's dance partner was sweeping her a mocking bow and offering his hand. He lifted his mask slightly to give her a wink and she realised with a sinking heart that it was Daniel Tremaine. He was the last person she wanted to dance with, but it seemed too rude to snub him, so Caitlyn reluctantly put her hand in his. She stiffened slightly as she felt his arms go around her, pulling her close, then she forced herself to relax as they whirled back into the throng of dancers.

CHAPTER NINE

"So, Miss Le Fey, how are you enjoying the ball?"

Caitlyn jerked back in surprise. "How... how did you know who I am?" she asked.

Tremaine laughed. "In my line of work, you learn to recognise people's true identities, no matter how good their disguises."

"In your 'line of work'? As an *accountant*?" said Caitlyn dubiously.

He smiled, unperturbed. "Naturally. It's important to be able to see past fake façades when you're dealing with financial matters." He looked at her pretty decorated mask with amused disdain. "And masquerade costumes are child's play. In any case..." His gaze swept upwards, over the fiery tresses which curled around her face and spilled over her shoulders. "Your hair... it's hard to disguise a colour so distinct. Red like that does not come out of a bottle. If you'd really wanted to remain incognito, you should have worn a wig, perhaps, or kept the hood that you had on earlier."

Caitlyn looked at him, confused. "What hood?"

"The one you were wearing before the ball commenced. I came down early and decided to look in the Ballroom to see how the preparations were going. There were no staff about, but I saw you by the fountain next to the buffet."

Caitlyn frowned. "You couldn't have. When I arrived at the Manor with Evie—with my younger cousin—we went straight up to the guest room to change, and I didn't come down until a short while ago."

"I definitely saw you. As I said, it is hard to disguise hair as vivid as yours."

"I'm not the only red-haired girl in the world," protested Caitlyn.

"I have yet to see anyone else at the ball with hair like yours," said Tremaine, glancing around the room. "So if we discount the guests, are you saying there is another young woman in the village with hair the same shade?"

"No, not really," Caitlyn admitted. The only other redheads in Tillyhenge were Aunt Bertha and Evie, but their hair was a paler, carroty shade of red, whereas Caitlyn knew that hers was a deep crimson, with golden highlights that caught the sun. It was the one feature of her appearance that she felt unabashedly proud of, the one thing that gave her a bit of confidence when she was feeling insecure about her figure and her lack of style and sophistication. Still, that didn't explain how Daniel Tremaine could have seen her hair when she had been nowhere near the Ballroom earlier that day...

"You must have been mistaken," she insisted. "That couldn't have been me. Did you see her face?"

"No, not directly."

"Then how can you be sure it was me just based on a glimpse of her hair?" demanded Caitlyn.

"There is more to a woman than simply her face," said Tremaine. "There is the way she holds herself, the lines of her body, the aura around her..." He gave her a wolfish grin. "I enjoy women—enjoy looking at them, observing them, admiring them, and I never forget a woman I've seen. Besides..." He paused as he twirled her slowly in a circle. "You're a special case. Anyone *really* looking would have noticed a special quality about you. They would have seen that there's more to you than meets the eye."

Caitlyn drew back from him. "I... I don't know what you mean."

"Oh, I think you do. That shy wallflower act may fool others, but it won't work with me. I think you're very aware of the power you have, especially the power to lead men astray."

"What—?" Caitlyn gasped an incredulous laugh. She didn't know whether to be insulted by his heavy-handed innuendos or to laugh at his ridiculously melodramatic words.

Before she could reply, Tremaine leaned suddenly closer, so that his lips were next to her ear.

"You're a beautiful woman, Caitlyn Le Fey, and beautiful women have to be careful. You know, in another age, you would have been branded a witch and burned at the stake just for enticing men with that glorious hair and those enchanting hazel eyes."

Caitlyn flinched and would have pulled away from him, except that he tightened his hold on her, his arm like a band of steel around her.

Tremaine laughed. "Relax—I'm teasing. No one's going to harm you. After all, you're not *really* a witch... are you?"

She stared at him, but Tremaine's face was hard to read, being partially covered by his mask. She could see his lips pulled back in the semblance of an easy smile, but it was a smile that didn't reach his eyes, she noted. And despite his words, a part of her couldn't help feeling that he had been deadly serious...

Tremaine lifted his arm to twirl her again, and, as he did so, he glanced at her raised wrist. Caitlyn saw his eyes narrow as he caught sight of her runestone necklace, looped around her bare wrist.

"That's an unusual charm bracelet," he said. "Those engravings... they're witch's runes, aren't they?"

"Y-yes, that's right," said Caitlyn, startled.

"Do you know what they mean?"

Caitlyn shook her head.

"Where did you get it from? Was it a gift?"

Caitlyn eyed him warily. The questions were asked in an idle tone, but she couldn't help feeling that Tremaine was intensely interested. "No," she said, not bothering to explain and hoping that he wouldn't ask further.

"I wondered if it might have been something from the late Lord Fitzroy's collection of occult artefacts," he mused. "A trinket, perhaps, that you'd admired and decided to keep for yourself?"

"No, of course not!" said Caitlyn, indignant. "I would never remove anything from the Manor without James's permission."

"I beg your pardon," said Tremaine smoothly. "I wasn't implying that you stole it—simply that you may have been given *carte blanche*, as it were, to help yourself to anything that you liked." He smiled thinly. "James wouldn't be the first man to show weakness where a woman was concerned."

"No, this is mine," said Caitlyn curtly. "It's... um... a sort of family heirloom."

"Ah...I see."

They were at the edge of the dance floor now, and as she was spun around, Caitlyn glanced sideways and met the eyes of a woman watching them from the crowd. She was exotically beautiful, of Chinese or other East Asian descent, and aside from her striking looks, she stood out because she was not in any obvious disguise—although the green silk *cheongsam* she was wearing was more than a match for any costume. What startled Caitlyn, though, was the intensity of the woman's gaze, and even as they danced away again, she could feel the woman's eyes still following them, like the red laser sight from a sniper's rifle. She was immensely relieved to hear the music ending, and she could barely pull her hand out of Daniel Tremaine's fast enough as he gave her a final twirl, then swept her a mocking bow.

"I... I need to pop to the Ladies'," she mumbled, to forestall any further conversation from him, and turning, she dived into the crowd.

It wasn't until she had put a good distance between them that Caitlyn slowed down. *Ugh...* She looked down at the hand Daniel Tremaine had been holding. She felt unclean after their little interlude, and she almost decided to go to the Ladies' for real, so that she could give her hands a good scrub. Then she gave herself a mental shake. *Don't let him get to you. Tremaine is just a creep who loves himself and thinks he's so clever with all that heavy flirting and those stupid sexual innuendos.*

Caitlyn looked up again and caught sight of the buffet nearby. Her spirits lifted. She'd get something to eat instead, she decided. *Mm, yes, something rich and chocolatey. Nothing like a peanut butter and mocha truffle or a salted caramel fudge to take your mind off everything for a few decadent moments!*

As she arrived at the buffet and surveyed the smorgasbord of dishes, Caitlyn recalled that there weren't just sweet treats on offer—as she had told Pomona, the whole buffet was chocolate-themed. Even though she had helped the Widow Mags plan and prepare the menu, it wasn't until she saw the sumptuous variety displayed in front of her that she really appreciated the old witch's genius in incorporating the flavours of chocolate and cocoa into so many savoury dishes.

Aside from the Belgian chocolate steak and cocoa-encrusted tenderloin that she had told Pomona about, there was also a dark chocolate and wild mushroom millefeuille, a beautifully roasted joint of venison served with chocolate, fig, and turnip, a duck-breast salad with burnt coconut, pineapple, cashews, and smoky cocoa powder, and—taking pride of place next to the cornucopia in the centre of the buffet—a large dish of roast grouse with sweet caramelised figs, beautifully glazed heritage carrots, and a velvety chocolate-porter sauce.

On the opposite side of the buffet was a display of treats from the Widow Mags's chocolate shop: rich fudge brownies and decadent chocolate puddings, cocoa-dusted chocolate beans and succulent chocolate-dipped apricots and strawberries, creamy chocolate-and-hazelnut torte, and white chocolate parfait...

Caitlyn smiled to herself, Daniel Tremaine temporarily forgotten, as she began heaping food onto her plate. And when she reached the end of the buffet, she was delighted to discover that the fountain was no ordinary water feature—instead, a rich, buttery, salted caramel sauce spurted from the top and drizzled down the five tiers in a smooth amber flow.

So this is what all those jugs of caramel sauce that the Widow Mags wanted were for! she thought, standing back to eye the fountain in admiration. There was a large tray on a pedestal next to the fountain, displaying an array of marshmallows, cookie chunks, fresh strawberries and apple wedges, pretzels, doughnuts, and pieces of chocolate cake. Caitlyn eagerly helped herself to one of the fondue sticks in a nearby jar and speared a large piece of apple, then held it out under the flow of caramel. She watched with mouth-watering anticipation as the rich, creamy sauce drizzled over the piece of apple, coating it with glossy treacle sweetness. She'd just pulled the fondue stick out of the fountain and was raising the caramel-coated apple to her lips when a voice said:

"I'd be careful if I were you."

Caitlyn looked up to see a woman standing on the other side of the fountain and her eyes widened as she recognised the mysterious Asian beauty who had been watching so intently when she had been dancing with Daniel Tremaine. Caitlyn eyed her curiously as the woman came closer. She looked to be somewhere in her thirties, perhaps, with flawless skin and luminous, almond-shaped eyes. Her black hair was teased and swept back in a rock-chick style that was at odds with the very traditional *cheongsam* she wore, and yet the overall effect was fashionable and elegant. Diamonds sparkled at her ears and dripped off her wrists and fingers, and she spoke with the kind of refined enunciation usually associated with British high society.

"I'm sorry?" said Caitlyn politely.

The woman came forwards to join her next to the fountain. "You wouldn't want to get burned, would you?" she said.

"Oh, the caramel sauce isn't hot," Caitlyn said, waving the fondue stick she was holding.

The woman laughed contemptuously. "I'm not talking about the caramel, you fool. I'm talking about Daniel Tremaine."

Caitlyn blinked. "I don't understand—"

"You think you can handle him, don't you? You think you can manipulate him, flirt with him—"

"I wasn't flirting with him!" said Caitlyn indignantly. "I think you've completely misunderstood the situation. Mr Tremaine asked me to dance, that's all."

A cynical smile curled the corners of the woman's mouth. "And I suppose, while you were in his arms, he impressed you with tales of daring foreign exploits and clever subterfuge. After all, there's nothing as sexy as the thought of hidden danger in a glamorous setting, is there?"

"Danger? I think you've got Mr Tremaine mixed up with someone else," said Caitlyn with a laugh. "He's just an accountant who works for the British government—"

"Is that what he told you? If you believe that, then you're even more of a fool than I thought." She gave Caitlyn a pitying look. "You have no idea what you're dealing with. Let me give you a friendly word of advice: don't fall for Daniel Tremaine's charms. He always wants something—the question is whether you're prepared to pay the price to give it to him."

Caitlyn shook her head, baffled by the woman's cryptic words. "I'm sorry, I really think you've got the wrong end of the stick. I'm not romantically interested in Daniel Tremaine—or in any other way, really! I only met him for the first time the day before yesterday and he's just a passing acquaintance."

Before the woman could reply, there was a commotion on the other side of the Ballroom. Caitlyn turned swiftly to see a flurry of movement near the main entrance. Curious, she left the buffet and jostled her way through the crowd, rising on tiptoe every so often to try and see above the heads of people. All around her, she could hear excited murmurings and whispers:

"Who are they?"

"Oh my God, look at her costume!"

"Do you think those are real...?"

"Do you know who they are?"

Finally, Caitlyn pushed her way to the front of the throng and stepped out to see a couple standing at the entrance to the Ballroom. They had obviously just arrived, and the man was escorting his female companion into the party. Caitlyn caught her breath. Despite the elaborate costume and mask, she knew instantly who the girl was: Pomona.

CHAPTER TEN

Caitlyn stared at her cousin: Pomona looked like someone straight out of myth or legend. She was wearing a gown made of a silky green fabric, which left her shoulders bare and was moulded to her curvaceous figure, parting on one side to reveal one tanned and shapely leg. She had eschewed the more common face mask tied around the head, instead opting for an ornately decorated mask on a stick, which she brandished with dramatic flair. Her black diamond choker hugged her throat with a cold metal embrace, the dark jewel seeming to sparkle more brilliantly than ever under the light from the Ballroom chandeliers.

But it was Pomona's head that everyone's eyes were riveted on: where her mane of sun-kissed blonde hair used to be, there was now a writhing mass of snakes. For a heart-stopping moment, Caitlyn thought that they were real snakes. Then, as she looked closer, she realised that they were cleverly fashioned from some kind of rubber and flexible fabric, so that they wriggled and coiled with every small movement that Pomona made. Even her breathing caused them to writhe and slither across each other, giving the impression that they were alive.

She's come as Medusa, Caitlyn realised, thinking of the infamous Greek she-monster who could turn men to stone with a simple glance. It was a spectacular transformation and Pomona was milking every moment of it. She stood with her head tossed back, a hand on one hip, and a delighted smile on her lips as she surveyed the room. Pomona had always liked causing a stir, and she couldn't have made a grander entrance.

Still, glancing at the crowds around her, Caitlyn realised that it wasn't just Pomona's costume that was capturing everyone's interest. It was also the man standing next to her. Dressed all in black, with a simple black domino cape, he should have been dull and inconsequential compared with the other male guests in more elaborate costumes, and yet there was an aura around the man which made him stand out, a sense of mystery and power which drew all eyes to him. He was wearing a mask—a sinister black bauta-style Venetian mask, which covered all of his face and obscured his features behind the artificially prominent nose and beak-like chin. Only his eyes were revealed, blazing out from the gilded eye holes.

Caitlyn felt her heart give an uncomfortable jolt. She would have known those piercing blue eyes anywhere. It was Thane Blackmort, the "Black Tycoon"—an enigmatic billionaire who had appeared, seemingly out of nowhere, and conquered the business world with grace and ruthlessness. He had confounded the media with his ability to both grab the headlines and yet remain a complete mystery at the same time. For despite all the titillating stories about his wild parties and his eccentric habits, like dressing only in black, drinking only black vodka, and flying only in his black private jet, no one could really dig up very much information about him.

Caitlyn knew, though, that Blackmort was not a popular person in the local community. Many were furious and disgusted with his recent attempts to buy up large tracts of private land for modern development, regardless of how much it would damage the wild, unspoilt beauty of the Cotswolds countryside. In fact, Tillyhenge itself, as well as large parts of the Fitzroy estate, had been in Blackmort's sights, and Caitlyn, together with the village residents, had been hugely relieved when James had flatly turned down all of the billionaire's offers.

Now, she wondered how he had ended up on the guest list for the ball. She had always got the impression that Thane Blackmort was *persona non grata* at Huntingdon Manor. Then she saw the defiant tilt of Pomona's chin and the challenging light in her eyes, and she realised that it was her cousin who had engineered for the billionaire to come tonight, under the guise of being her "escort". Caitlyn felt a flash of surprise. Pomona must have known the controversy she'd cause, bringing Blackmort to the ball. It was almost a direct insult to James's hospitality. Why had she done it? Pomona might have been exuberant and outspoken, but she was never normally malicious or even just plain rude.

Caitlyn started forwards, but Pomona was already turning away, with Blackmort at her side, his black domino cape swirling behind him. They made an arresting sight, and the crowd parted before them like the proverbial Red Sea. Caitlyn quickened her steps, trying to intercept them, but found her way blocked by another guest—a large, jovial-looking man dressed in a short Roman toga, with a wreath made of fake vine leaves and clusters of plastic grapes on his head.

He stepped in front of the couple and said in a slurred voice: "Hello-hello... that's shome costume you've got there, luv—*hic!* Medusha, eh?" He leaned forwards and gave Pomona a wink. "The shnakes kind of gave it away..."

She giggled and replied, "And I'll bet you're Bacchus, the god of wine?"

The man hiccupped and clapped with glee. "Right first time, luv! Own a brewery in real life, actually, so

I thought it wash the perfect costume. And you, Shir..." He turned towards Blackmort and squinted at him. "Who are you shupposed to be?" He eyed the dark, sombre costume, then gave a drunken chuckle and said: "Don't tell me, don't tell me... you're the god of death, right?"

Caitlyn saw a gleam come into those piercing blue eyes, and she heard a note of secret amusement in Blackmort's voice as he inclined his head and said:

"I am whatever you wish me to be."

"Ooh... very good, very good," said the man, grinning and swaying on his feet. "I like your shtyle, man. *Hic!* Bet you're a hit with the ladies. You must give me shome tips—"

He lurched towards Blackmort, and two men instantly materialised out of the crowd. They were dressed all in black as well, their bulging biceps clearly defined through their tight black shirts, and for a moment, Caitlyn thought they were bouncers hired by the Manor to provide security. Then she realised that they were Blackmort's men. They grabbed the drunken man before he could come too close to the billionaire and hauled him back.

The people watching began to murmur in alarm, then everyone's attention was diverted as the crowd parted and James Fitzroy stepped out. A slight hush fell over the Ballroom as everyone waited to see how he would react to his new guests. Caitlyn could tell from the hard line of James's mouth that he was not best pleased to see Blackmort, but she also knew that the last thing he wanted to do was to cause a scene. He held out a hand and said with perfunctory courtesy:

"Good evening, Mr Blackmort. What an unexpected pleasure."

Slowly, Blackmort removed his mask and shook James's hand, his eyes still showing that gleam of sly amusement. "I hope that it is, Lord Fitzroy. I would hate to think that I was trespassing on your hospitality."

"James always told me that any friend of mine is welcome at Huntingdon Manor," said Pomona, adding with a challenging look to James: "I was surprised that Thane wasn't on the guest list already."

James had removed his Phantom of the Opera mask, but his face was still a mask of politeness. "Due to the cap on guest numbers, we aren't always able to invite everyone—I'm sure you understand," he said.

"Naturally," said Blackmort with urbane coolness. "But now that I am here, I hope you can spare me a moment of your time, Lord Fitzroy. My secretary has been attempting to contact you to arrange a second meeting to discuss my offer, but so far, she hasn't had any success. You are a difficult man to get hold of."

"I apologise. My schedule has been particularly full lately. But in any case, I did not see much point in a second meeting. I thought I'd made my feelings very clear: there is no part of the Fitzroy estate that is available for sale, and especially not the section which contains the hill with the stone circle."

Blackmort smiled slightly. "Everything is for sale at the right price."

James's mouth tightened. "I beg to differ."

"I'm not talking merely of money," said Blackmort. He glanced around, conscious of the crowd around them and the people avidly trying to listen to their conversation. Turning back to James, he said, "Perhaps we should continue this conversation in a quieter place."

James hesitated. It was obvious that he had no wish to speak to Blackmort, but at the same time, he didn't want to fuel the village gossips either. Finally, he inclined his head and said: "I will have my PA contact your secretary to arrange a suitable time."

Blackmort gave a slow, triumphant smile. "I shall look forward to our next meeting, Lord Fitzroy. And now..." He turned and held a hand out to Pomona, who had been hovering next to them. "I think it is time for a dance. Shall we?"

The crowd rippled and moved back as Blackmort led Pomona out onto the dance floor, just as the music from the chamber orchestra swelled once more. Caitlyn watched uneasily as the billionaire pulled her cousin into his arms. Pomona tossed her head back and laughed with delight as Blackmort began moving swiftly to the music, spinning her around with breathtaking speed. Caitlyn had never seen her cousin look like that, with her face alight and her eyes sparkling almost as much as the black diamond that glittered at the base of her throat.

She glanced around the crowd, seeing many others also watching the dancing couple. Then she caught sight of a familiar figure standing at the edge of the dance floor. It was Daniel Tremaine, and his eyes were trained on Blackmort and Pomona with a disturbing intensity.

CHAPTER ELEVEN

"Caitlyn! At last—I've been looking for you everywhere!"

Caitlyn jerked her gaze from the dance floor and turned to see James striding towards her. She felt a mixture of shyness and elation as she saw the warmth in his grey eyes.

He caught both her hands in his. "Where have you been? I was about to send a search party out for you."

"I... I delayed coming down for a bit," Caitlyn confessed. "Just so... you know... I could slip in after everyone had arrived..."

"Why on earth would you want to do that?" James looked astonished.

"Well, it's just... arriving at a big party where you don't really know anyone... I mean, I'm not very good at chatting to strangers, you know, and..." Caitlyn ducked her head in embarrassment. "I thought it would be easier once everyone was busy dancing and drinking and stuff... you know, people would be less likely to notice me."

James shook his head in exasperated affection. "You're a nutter," he said. "You wouldn't have been alone, you know. I was waiting by the entrance for you for ages. So you would have been with me and I would have introduced you to everyone as they arrived."

That would probably have been even worse! thought Caitlyn, imagining all the curious stares and probing questions she would have had to endure. She was well aware that there was constant speculation and gossip among the Manor staff and village residents—not to mention members of the wider community—about her relationship with James Fitzroy. Many just couldn't seem to understand how the handsome owner of Huntingdon Manor could be interested in her when he was surrounded by so many society beauties. In fact, Caitlyn squirmed inside every time she thought of the vicious rumours and accusations that had been thrown at her:

"Lord Fitzroy's got his pick of beautiful, sophisticated girls from all over England. Why would he fall for a fat little frump like her? With a bum like that?"

"She must have bewitched him, cast some kind of evil spell on him..."

"No man could be enthralled like that by natural means. She used black magic to possess his mind and bind him to her..."

Caitlyn gave her head a sharp shake, banishing the memory of those hateful voices, and looked back at James.

"It's okay. I actually preferred doing it this way," she said, smiling up at him. "And... and please don't feel that you have to look after me. Honestly. I'm perfectly happy just people-watching from the sides and—'

"Oh no, you're not getting rid of me that easily, Miss Le Fey," said James, giving her his charming lopsided grin. "Now that I've found you, I'm going to thoroughly neglect my duties to all my other guests—"

"No, you can't do that!" cried Caitlyn. "You're the host of the ball. You have to—"

James laughed. "I'm teasing. Don't worry. I've more than done my duty," he said with a slight grimace. "I've wined and dined and danced and hobnobbed with all the people I'm expected to. Now, I intend to enjoy the party... with the one girl I've been waiting to dance with all night."

Caitlyn blushed and felt a rush of happiness as James squeezed her hands, then turned and led her onto the dance floor. The orchestra was playing a soft, lilting melody and she felt as if she was stepping into a fairy tale as James slipped his arms around her and they glided effortlessly into the throng of dancing couples. A thrill went through her as she savoured the moment: the sparkling chandeliers above, the glittering Ballroom around them, the romantic swirl of her skirts as they spun around the dance floor, and the tall, handsome man looking tenderly down at her—it was every girlish Cinderella fantasy come true.

And it was so different from dancing with Daniel Tremaine earlier! James had none of the other man's arrogant manner and showy turns. Instead, he moved with a quiet, commanding grace as he guided her expertly around the dance floor, his arms protectively around her as he shielded her from the other whirling couples. Even with James's care, though, Caitlyn found herself swinging perilously close to several other dancers. The Ballroom seemed to have got much more crowded, and soon she began to feel uncomfortably warm in the crush of bodies surrounding them.

"Are you all right?" asked James as she stumbled slightly.

"Yes, fine. It's just... it's a bit warm, isn't it?" Caitlyn said, catching her breath.

James gazed across the Ballroom, frowning slightly. "Yes, it is rather. I'm afraid Mosley might have been a bit too enthusiastic with the thermostat adjustments earlier; he was very worried that the guests—particularly the female ones—would be cold, you see." He gestured to the far end of the Ballroom where French windows looked out onto a wide stone terrace. Despite the chilly autumn evening, one of the glass doors was open. "Would you like some fresh air?"

"Yes, thank you," said Caitlyn, and a few minutes later she stepped gratefully out onto the terrace, feeling the warmth from the Ballroom spill out with her.

She pulled off her mask and took a gulp of the crisp night air, almost relishing the sting of the cold on her overheated cheeks. Looking around, she noticed that there were others who'd had the same idea of escaping the muggy atmosphere of the Ballroom. A few figures were huddled by the stone urns next to the terrace steps, and she could hear the soft murmur of flirting couples, as well as make out the lazy swirls of cigarette smoke from those who'd nipped out for their nicotine hit.

James put a solicitous hand under her elbow and guided her gently to the far edge of the terrace, where a stone balustrade formed a sort of balcony to lean on. From here, the music of the orchestra was faint and distant, and the clamour of talk and laughter faded to a muffled hum. A large tree growing nearby spread its canopy over them, casting deep shadows around them. Despite the presence of the couples on the other side of the terrace, it felt almost as if they were completely alone. Caitlyn was suddenly very aware of how close James was standing next to her.

She licked her lips, feeling her heart begin to pound. Was James going to kiss her? She found that she couldn't look at him, and she cursed the wave of shyness that seized her. Why couldn't she handle the moment with confidence and aplomb? Suddenly she wished that she had been more like Pomona growing up. Her bubbly cousin had practically made dating an Olympic sport in her teens and had collected "types" of boys like others collected hair accessories. But Caitlyn had always been a shy, bookish dreamer who had little experience of boys and even less of sex. And now, here she was with the man who had stolen her heart, and she was too embarrassed to let him see that at the age of twenty-two, she still hadn't ever been kissed "properly".

"It's... it's a lovely evening, isn't it?" she said breathlessly. "It's lucky that it's not raining or... or... um..." She faltered, groping for another subject at random. "So... er... do you know Daniel Tremaine very well?"

James had slipped an arm around her waist and had been drawing her closer, but at the mention of Tremaine's name, he stiffened and pulled back.

"No, not really. He contacted me out of the blue a few days ago and mentioned that he was in the area. Apparently, he was an acquaintance of my father's. He sounded very keen to visit the Manor and I felt obliged to offer him my hospitality."

"Oh." Caitlyn digested this for a moment. "Did your father ever speak to you about him?"

James shook his head. "Not that I recall. But to be fair, my father and I were never close. We didn't have the kind of relationship where we talked much about our personal lives. I certainly never told him much about my friends and acquaintances, and vice versa."

"Tremaine seems a bit young to have been in your father's social circle," Caitlyn commented. "I mean, he's only in his mid-forties at most. Whereas your father would have been almost thirty years older than him."

"I think it was more of a work acquaintance than a personal friendship."

"Oh... I thought he might have met your father through their mutual interest in the occult," said Caitlyn. "He seems to know a surprising amount about witchcraft and magic."

James gave a casual shrug. "People have their side interests and hobbies." He shifted restlessly, then said with mock reproach, "I'm beginning to feel a bit jealous that I brought you out here to this romantic spot and all you want to do is talk about Daniel Tremaine."

Caitlyn gave an apologetic laugh. "Sorry."

James smiled. "Don't be. Just getting a moment alone with you is treat enough."

He reached up, his fingers gentle as he brushed a strand of hair from her temple. The featherlight touch made her shiver—with surprise or anticipation, she wasn't sure which—and she felt goosebumps tingle down her spine. Her heart pounding, Caitlyn raised her eyes slowly and gazed up at James. It was too dark to see his eyes clearly, but she could feel the intensity of his gaze. Then her breath caught in her throat as he began lowering his head to hers.

Slowly... oh so slowly...

Caitlyn gasped softly as she felt his lips brush hers, the merest whisper of a touch—and then her gasp turned into a scream as a dark figure popped up suddenly next to them. An old man stuck out his scrawny neck, thrusting his wrinkled face next to theirs.

"Have you seen my teeth?"

James gave a startled cry and stumbled backwards, releasing Caitlyn, who had to clutch the balustrade beside her for support.

"*Viktor!*" Caitlyn couldn't believe that he'd just ruined what could have been the most wonderful moment of her life. She wanted to throttle the old vampire. "What are you doing here?"

The old man glowered at her. "Looking for my fangs, of course. I've been searching for them all evening and I still can't find them. It was those dratted chewy salted caramels." He felt his jaw petulantly with long, bony fingers. "One bite and my gums practically stuck together! Must have yanked my fangs out of their sockets, and they probably dropped out of my mouth—"

"Well, we haven't seen them," said Caitlyn irritably, wishing the old vampire would hurry up and leave, so she and James could be alone again.

"Look, why don't you go and ask Mosley to help you?"

"Eh? Who's Mosley?"

"He's the Manor butler," James spoke up, looking slightly bemused by the whole situation. "I'm sure he'll be able to assist you."

Viktor looked sceptical. "Got experience looking for lost teeth, has he?"

"Yes, just go... *go!*" Caitlyn gave Viktor a gentle nudge.

The old vampire started to turn away, then he swung back all of a sudden and looked at her and James. "What are the two of you doing out here?"

"Er..." Caitlyn couldn't help blushing and hoped that the dark would hide the colour in her cheeks. "Lord Fitzroy and I are... um... talking."

Viktor eyed James up and down suspiciously. "I have observed you hovering around Caitlyn, young man. What are your intentions towards her?"

"My... my intentions?" James looked dumbfounded.

"Viktor!" Caitlyn hissed. "It's none of your business."

"Of course it is my business," said Viktor huffily. "I am your guardian uncle. I need to protect your maidenly virtue."

"*Viktor!*" groaned Caitlyn, her face really flaming now. "This is the twenty-first century. You can't—"

"Lord Fitzroy? *Lord Fitzroy!*"

They were interrupted by a commotion at the French windows and, the next moment, Mosley rushed out onto the terrace. It was so unlike the butler's normally dignified carriage that Caitlyn broke off to stare. Mosley spied the three of them at the edge of the terrace and hurried over, his usually impassive face tight with anxiety.

"Sir!" He stopped next to James and mopped his brow with a pristine white handkerchief. "Your lordship, there's some trouble at the front of the Manor. I think you need to come immediately."

CHAPTER TWELVE

Caitlyn blinked in surprise as she followed James out of the front door of the Manor. Assembled on the large circular driveway was a group of people, mostly women, who were huddled together, chanting and waving home-made placards. She identified many as residents of Tillyhenge, and she recognised the middle-aged woman at the front of the crowd as Vera Bottom, the sister of a local dairy farmer.

Vera was a thin, sour-faced spinster who lived with her widowed brother and seemed to spend most of her free time preaching against the evils of witchcraft and magic to anyone who would listen. And unlike her brother, Jeremy, who had always treated the Widow Mags with warmth and courtesy, Vera went out of her way to be hostile to the old witch and anyone connected with her. Now, she raised a fist above her head and joined the others in shouting:

"Save Tillyhenge from witchery!"

"Don't corrupt our village with filthy black magic!"

"We don't want pagan evil here!"

The group was advancing towards the front door and Mosley hurried to intercept them.

"I'm afraid I cannot let you pass, madam," he said to Vera, spreading his arms out. "There are guests inside and—"

"We have a right to go in too. Lord Fitzroy invited everyone in the village; he said we're all welcome. Ask him!" Vera jabbed a finger in James's direction.

"Yeah! You can't stop us! We have a right to free speech!" cried a woman next to Vera. Her voice was shrill and piercing. "That means we can protest where we like!"

"Not on private land, you can't," snapped Mosley, losing his composure. "The right to protest only applies in public spaces. Assembling on private grounds without the owner's permission is trespassing."

"Oh yeah? And what you goin' to do? Shoot us?" asked a man, thrusting his face aggressively into Mosley's.

The butler bristled. "If you will not leave of your own accord, I will not hesitate to call the authorities and have you arrested, sir!"

"It's all right, Mosley," said James, going down the front steps to join the butler. He leaned towards Mosley and said something low in the latter's ear, which sent the butler hurrying back into the Manor. Then James turned towards the crowd and said in a pleasant voice:

"Good evening, ladies and gentlemen. I understand you have some concerns and I'd be very happy to address them. But perhaps we could discuss them at another time, in more appropriate surroundings?"

Vera stepped up to James, her arms akimbo. "You told us we'd be welcome at the Manor tonight. Are you going back on your word, Lord Fitzroy?"

"Of course not," said James with perfect courtesy. He gave her a steely-eyed look. "However, the invitation was for you to come and enjoy yourselves at the ball, not to stage a protest outside the Manor."

"How can we enjoy ourselves when you're encouragin' all sorts of heathen practices an' demon worship?" demanded the woman next to Vera.

"Yeah!" another chimed in. "It's bad enough that we've 'ad to put up with the likes o' that ol' witch in the chocolate shop and 'er daughter peddling 'er 'erbal poisons in the village, but now you want us to support some kind o' voodoo fest, with ritual sacrifices and shameless orgies—"

James burst out laughing. "I'm sorry, but I do think your imaginations have run away with you. This is simply a fancy-dress party. People have been holding masquerade balls since the eighteenth-century, and there's nothing wrong with the innocent pleasure of dressing up in masks and costumes."

"Not so innocent when everyone's dressing up as demons and monsters and other vile creatures!" cried Vera.

"Not everyone is dressed as demons and things like that, although I agree that monsters of myth and legend are very popular," said James in a quiet voice. "But there are also plenty of guests dressed as Little Bo Peep, Aladdin, Paddington Bear, Sherlock Holmes..." He smiled. "And I can assure you, there are definitely no sacrifices or orgies."

Faced with James's quiet authority and calm, amused manner, several people began looking a bit shamefaced and started shuffling their feet. A few started drifting towards the back of the group, as if they wanted to leave.

But Vera was not so easily mollified. "We heard that you had altars!" she hissed. "Why do you need altars if you're not performing sacrifices? Don't think you can hide it from us. Jessica told us what she saw."

She pointed to a blonde woman who had been standing to one side, a bit removed from the rest of the group. Caitlyn noticed that the woman had been busily scribbling in a notepad, in between snapping photos with her phone, and now she looked annoyed as her name was mentioned. She hunched her shoulders slightly, as if in an unconscious attempt to deflect attention away from herself.

"Go on, Jessica—tell Lord Fitzroy what you told us," urged Vera.

Grudgingly, the woman said: "I was outside *Herbal Enchantments* and saw the owner loading her car with various items. I recognised them as things used to decorate Mabon altars. I'd seen them used before in 'hearth and home' rites performed by covens of self-proclaimed witches."

"Well, it's true that Bertha brought several traditional items used to mark the Mabon festival, but I hardly think apples and corncobs and baskets of dried fruits are that sinister, do you?" asked James reasonably.

Caitlyn saw several villagers give reluctant grins as Jessica looked discomfited. She dropped back, allowing others to move in front of her, so that she melted into the rear of the group.

Vera flushed, still unwilling to give up. "Why do you have altars then?" she demanded.

"I'm not sure where you got that idea from, but there aren't any 'altars' as such," said James. "My marketing team simply thought that it would be nice to decorate the Ballroom with various things associated with autumn. It's no different to hanging holly and mistletoe around the place at Christmas."

"That's different. Mabon is a pagan festival!" spat Vera. "It's an evil occasion celebrated by witches and others practising black magic."

"I'm afraid you're mistaken. Mabon *is* a festival celebrated since ancient times, but it is simply a harvest festival, a time for giving thanks for the successful crops of summer and the fruits of the orchard," James explained patiently. "In a way, it is no different to the North American tradition of Thanksgiving—"

"Eh? We ain't stupid! Thanksgiving's in November," scoffed the woman with the shrill voice.

"Yeah," said the belligerent man. "An' we know that Mabon's tied to the autumn equinox. That's on the twenty-first of September, a couple o' days from now. So it can't be linked to Thanksgivin' at all, 'cos that's much later in the year."

"Well, in actual fact, the original Thanksgiving celebration was in early October, which is not that far from now," a new voice said coolly.

Caitlyn turned in surprise to see Daniel Tremaine step out of the front door. He was followed by Mosley and a couple of waiters, all bearing large silver trays. They remained standing at the top of the steps, but Tremaine sauntered down to join James in front of the villagers. He gave the assembled group a patronising smile and continued in a lofty voice:

"The beginning of October is a much more logical time to give thanks, when you consider the agricultural calendar. After all, that's when you would learn how well your crops had done, how fat your animals had got, and how your family was going to eat during the coming winter. It's only because various American presidents, like Abraham Lincoln, tried to change the date that Thanksgiving was moved to the end of November—"

"*Daniel Tremaine!* You bastard, are you following

me?"

Everyone stared as the woman called Jessica suddenly pushed to the front of the group and launched herself at Tremaine, eyes flashing and hands clenched into fists.

The accountant caught the woman's wrists as she lashed out at him. He glared at her. "Jessica Hyde! What are you doing here?"

"What am *I*—? How dare you ask me that, you sadist!" spluttered the woman, looking furious. "*You're* the one who followed me to my house and tried to intimidate me, to shut me up, just because your bosses didn't like what I was writing. *You're* the one who threatened to hurt my daughter if I ever revealed that the British government—*aaahh!*"

Jessica gave a cry of pain as Tremaine moved suddenly, yanking her sideways and twisting her arms, so that her wrists were contorted against her body. She writhed and struggled, screaming and cursing, but she couldn't pull her arms out of his cruel grip.

"Daniel! That's enough," said James sharply, moving towards them.

Tremaine let Jessica go, but not before he'd leaned close and hissed something into her ear. She staggered back as she was released, a mixture of fear and fury on her face. Caitlyn expected the woman to start shouting again, but she remained silent, her eyes smouldering as she glared at Tremaine and rubbed her bruised wrists.

There was a shocked silence. There had been a disturbing element of raw violence in the brief struggle, and even the villagers who had been protesting the loudest looked uneasy. Several of them began casting longing looks at the driveway behind them, as if wishing that they'd never left Tillyhenge.

Daniel Tremaine gave James an ironic smile and said, "My apologies. I let my temper get the better of me." He jerked his head towards the assembled group, as if to say: "all yours"—and then he turned and sauntered back to join Caitlyn by the front door of the Manor.

James frowned slightly as he watched the other man for a moment, then he turned back to the villagers. Clearing his throat, he smiled and said:

"Look, it's cold out here and I'm sure many of you would appreciate a hot drink. I've asked Mosley to bring some hot chocolate…"

He glanced over his shoulder, and Mosley immediately hurried forwards, followed by the two waiters. The silver trays they were bearing were loaded with mugs of hot chocolate. Even from a distance, Caitlyn could smell the wonderful rich aroma of sweet cocoa and see the fragrant steam curling upwards in the chilly night air. Placards were dropped and protests forgotten as the group surged around Mosley and the waiters, everyone reaching out eagerly for a steaming mug. There was silence for a few moments as people slurped their creamy, chocolatey drinks, and Caitlyn could almost hear a collective sigh of contentment rise from the group.

"Cor... this is fantastic," said the man who had been aggressive to Mosley earlier. He was standing next to the butler now, regarding him with jovial goodwill as he drank his hot chocolate.

"Mmm, yes... never tasted hot cocoa so rich an' creamy," agreed the woman next to him. She took another greedy gulp from her mug, then looked in surprise at Vera, who hadn't helped herself. "Here, Vera—you not havin' any?"

"I'm not touching that filth!" hissed Vera, recoiling slightly. "And you shouldn't be either! Don't you know that the Widow Mags is catering for the ball? That chocolate is straight from her kitchen, and that means you're drinking something from the cauldron of a witch!"

The other villagers looked at each other doubtfully. Caitlyn could tell from their expressions that despite their recent outcry, they were now struggling to link the innocent mugs of delicious hot chocolate in their hands with evil witchery. The fear and distrust that surrounded the Widow Mags in Tillyhenge meant that many villagers had never tasted her treats themselves and had condemned her based only on rumour and hearsay. But now, with the delicious chocolate warming their bellies, it was a lot harder to believe in its supposed menace.

"But Vera—have you tasted it?" asked the woman, offering her a mug. "It's bloody good! It's not like a potion or anythin'."

"That's the whole point! That shows it's full of black magic," insisted Vera. "There's no way normal chocolate could taste so good naturally. It has to have been bewitched!"

"Well, if this is what bein' bewitched tastes like, then hex me all you want," said the man next to Mosley, smacking his lips and laughing.

The others in the group joined in, and several clapped each other on the back and cheered as they drained their mugs. Vera made an infuriated noise, then she whirled and stormed off down the driveway leading out of the estate. A few villagers drifted after her, but most of them remained clustered around Mosley and the waiters. They were now joking and laughing with James, and regarding him with newfound respect.

"Very clever," said an amused voice next to Caitlyn. "Defuse the conflict, calm the situation, and seduce with sweet indulgences..."

Caitlyn turned quickly. She'd forgotten that Daniel Tremaine was standing next to her. He was watching the scene with approval, a speculative gleam in his eyes.

"James Fitzroy has all the makings of a great leader and politician, if only he realised it," he murmured. "All he needs is guidance to use those talents for the right cause..."

CHAPTER THIRTEEN

"Who was that woman?" Caitlyn asked Tremaine. "The one who attacked you."

The accountant shrugged carelessly. "She's a journalist—one of those New Age hippy-dippy nutcases. You know the type: always preaching crystal healing and aura therapy and all that mumbo jumbo."

"She seemed very angry and upset," said Caitlyn. "What she said, about being intimidated and silenced—"

Tremaine rolled his eyes and gave an exaggerated sigh. "You're not swallowing that rubbish? These people always bang on about the same old thing: government conspiracy theories and claiming they're being spied on or persecuted. It's really just to make themselves feel important, you know," he said contemptuously. "It gives meaning to their pathetic, empty lives." He turned towards the front door. "I'm heading back to the Ballroom. I haven't sampled the delights of the buffet yet, and those mugs of hot chocolate have just reminded me of what I'm missing." He offered her his arm, his suave smile back in place. "Coming?"

Caitlyn shook her head. "No, thank you. I'll wait for James."

She watched thoughtfully as Tremaine disappeared back into the house. It occurred to her that the accountant had skilfully deflected her questions and not really provided any explanation of his history with Jessica Hyde. She turned back to the group on the driveway, searching the assembled faces, but she couldn't see the journalist. Had Jessica left with Vera?

The villagers were moving towards the front door now, shepherded by Mosley and the two waiters, but it was a very different group from earlier. Gone were the hostile attitudes and belligerent chanting. Instead, everyone was talking and laughing good-naturedly, their faces flushed and smiling.

"...are you sure you wouldn't like to come and join the ball?" James was asking. "You know you'd be very welcome."

"Naw... not really our scene," said one of the men, looking sheepish. "Wouldn't feel comfortable with all your poncy friends—er, I mean, all your guests, your lordship."

Several others in the group nodded and chimed in with their agreement.

"Please, none of this 'your lordship' business. My name is James, remember?" said James with a crooked smile. "Well, all right, if you won't join us... how about if I get the caterers to make up some hampers for you to take home to your families? We have lots of food and it'll be a shame if you don't get to sample all the delicious items on the menu."

Everyone's faces brightened and there were several murmurs of surprise and thanks. The group followed Mosley and trooped eagerly into the Manor, all talking animatedly.

James paused beside Caitlyn and gave her an apologetic look. "I'm sorry, but I think it would be better if I went with them, rather than just leave things to Mosley—"

"Oh, of course," said Caitlyn quickly. "You don't have to worry about me. Honestly. I can look after myself. I'll just head back to the Ballroom."

"I'll come and find you as soon as I can," James promised.

Caitlyn made her own way back to the Ballroom and arrived to find most of the guests clustered around the French windows, peering out at the view of the grounds beyond the terrace. Curious, she joined them and was just in time to see a sleek black helicopter land in the middle of the lawn, its rotating blades whipping up a wind force that flattened the branches of the trees nearby. Murmurs of awe and appreciation rippled through the watching crowd. The lights from the house showed a tall figure striding towards the helicopter, accompanied by two burly men, and Caitlyn realised that it was Thane Blackmort. Was he leaving the ball already? Apparently so, for—as she watched—he boarded the helicopter, followed by his bodyguards, and then the sleek black machine rose once more and disappeared into the night sky.

Caitlyn turned away from the windows, frowning in puzzlement. Why had Blackmort left the party so early? And where was Pomona? Her cousin hadn't been accompanying the billionaire just now, so she had to still be at the Manor. Caitlyn scanned the Ballroom, searching for Pomona's distinctive Medusa costume, but she couldn't see it anywhere.

Restlessly, she drifted across the room, peering through the crowds for any sign of the American girl. She turned at last towards the alcove where the buffet was. She'd half expected to see Daniel Tremaine there, but there was no sign of the accountant. Caitlyn paused in front of the display of dishes, recalling absently that she'd left a plate of food by the salted caramel fountain earlier. She looked around for her abandoned plate, but, not surprisingly, it was gone, no doubt cleared away by one of the waiters. She wondered for a moment if she should try again with a fresh plate, but her appetite seemed to have deserted her. Instead, Caitlyn found her thoughts returning to Pomona.

She turned and looked across the Ballroom again, scanning the guests with increasing urgency. *Where is she?* Caitlyn felt silly, but she couldn't shake off a sense of worry around her cousin. She made one last search around the Ballroom, then went back out into the adjoining ante-hall. Here, the music and general hubbub from the party were fainter, and it was obvious that several guests had escaped out here for a break. There was a pair of women huddled near the Ballroom entrance, their heads together as they gossiped and giggled; three men stood facing each other, talking in low voices, their manner suggesting an earnest business negotiation; a young couple was tucked behind a marble bust in the far corner, kissing passionately; and two older ladies sat on a *chaise longue* beside the wall, their faces showing relief as they slipped their feet out of their shoes and stretched their cramped toes.

Leading off the ante-hall was another room—a small sitting room, with a comfortable arrangement of plump sofas gathered around a fireplace. Caitlyn walked over and peered in the doorway. It looked empty, but just to be certain, she stepped inside and walked over to the sofas. She was startled as she rounded the back of a two-seater to find a beautiful young woman crouched behind it.

"Oh my Goddess! Oh... it's you, Caitlyn." The young woman breathed a sigh of relief.

"Evie?" Caitlyn blinked, still trying to get used to the other girl's new look. "What are you doing here?"

"Shh! Keep your voice down!" hissed Evie. She grabbed Caitlyn's hand and yanked her down into a crouching position as well, so that they were both hidden by the back of the sofa. Then she rose slightly to peer over the top, back through the doorway into the ante-hall and the Ballroom beyond. "Is he out there?"

"Who?"

"Viscount Astley."

Caitlyn shrugged helplessly. "I have no idea who that is, so I wouldn't know even if I *did* see him." She gave Evie a curious look. "I didn't realise that you were friends with a Viscount."

"I wasn't—until an hour ago!" said Evie with a sigh. "I met him in the Ballroom, and he just won't leave me alone! He keeps hovering around me and telling me how beautiful I am—"

"Well, isn't that nice?" asked Caitlyn with a laugh. "That was what you wanted, wasn't it? Your glamour is making you irresistible."

Evie gave her a haunted look. "I... I don't know... I didn't think it would be like this! I mean, it's lovely to feel beautiful for a change, but all these young men keep following me everywhere and bringing me food and drink, or chairs for me to sit on, and asking me to dance and worrying that I'm hot or cold, and telling me I look gorgeous... I just can't get a moment to myself! And Archie—Viscount Astley—is the worst! He keeps quoting Shakespeare and awful poetry to me; he's even proposed twice already and said his heart will crack with despair if I don't love him!"

Caitlyn burst out laughing. "I'm sorry," she said, trying to stop as Evie gave her a disgruntled look. "But you have to admit it's pretty funny. The image of you spending the whole evening running away from lovelorn young men..." She dissolved into fresh giggles.

"It's not funny at all!" Evie fumed. "Archie even kissed me! I thought I'd given him the slip when I sneaked out of one of the French doors in the Ballroom, but he followed me onto the terrace and started saying he wanted to marry me. I told him he must be joking but he said no, he would show me how much he loved me by kissing me—"

"Did he hurt you?" asked Caitlyn, aghast.

"No, no... it was a nice kiss, actually," said Evie, flushing and looking down. She twisted her hands. "I mean, he didn't really force himself on me or anything. It was just that... well, I didn't expect him to swoop down like that and it was... it was my first 'proper' kiss, you know, on the lips, and... and now he's ruined it! It was supposed to be Chris—" She broke off suddenly and flushed an even deeper red. "Anyway, I... I just couldn't make Archie believe that I didn't want to marry him. He said—"

She broke off suddenly and tensed as they both heard a young male voice with an incredibly posh British accent calling:

"*E-van-geline!* Oh, Evangeline, darling... where are you?"

"That's him!" gulped Evie, hunching her shoulders. "What am I going to do?"

Before Caitlyn could reply, a young man in a harlequin jester costume hurried into the small sitting room. He was very good-looking, with perfectly tousled blond hair, gleaming white teeth, and soulful brown eyes that swept the room eagerly.

"Evangeline! Here you are!" he cried, rushing towards Evie. "Darling, how could you have left me bereft like that? Did you think that you could shake me off and I'd forget you? No! Put that idea from your mind! For as Hamlet once said: *'Doubt that the stars are fire, Doubt that the sun doth move his aides, Doubt truth to be a liar, But never doubt I love'*!"

"Oh Goddess..." groaned Evie, putting her face in her hand.

Caitlyn felt her lips twitch, but she fought the urge to laugh. The young man turned towards her with his megawatt smile.

"Oh, I do beg your pardon—allow me to introduce myself: Archibald Cummings, Viscount Astley—at your service!"

"Er... hello... I'm Caitlyn Le Fey," said Caitlyn, still trying not to laugh. "Maybe I should leave you two alone," she added, backing away.

"No!" hissed Evie, clutching her arm. "No, don't leave me, Caitlyn!"

"Oh, darling, I'm so happy to have found you at last," cried Viscount Astley. "You've inspired me so much that I've even written a love poem myself. Yes, it just popped into my head! It's not Shakespeare, of course, but I fancy that it's not bad..." He gave a modest cough, then cleared his throat. "*Ahem-ahem...*" Puffing out his chest, he began to recite:

"Men are from Mars, women are from Venus,
You are my vajayjay, and I am your penis—"

"*AAAGGGHHH...!*" Evie stared at him in horrified disbelief. Then, with a wail, she hitched up her skirts and ran out of the room.

Viscount Astley blinked stupidly for a moment, then hurried after her, shouting: "Wait! Evangeline, darling, you haven't heard the rest of the poem yet—"

Caitlyn followed them out of the room, but by the time she was out in the ante-hall, there was no sign of either of them. She chuckled to herself, wondering where Evie was going to hide now. Then she sobered as she recalled her original search for Pomona. Turning, she left the ante-hall and wandered down the hallway which led away from the Ballroom. She tried to consider all the places that Pomona could have gone. The Library was not far from here, but her cousin wasn't a bookworm at the best of times. Somehow, Caitlyn couldn't imagine Pomona deciding to go to the Library when a party was in full flow. In fact, Pomona had always been the life and soul of any event, so even if she'd lost her escort for the evening, surely she wouldn't be retiring from the heart of the action already?

Caitlyn turned a corner and found herself in the disused wing at the rear of the Manor. She recognised the same old servants' staircase that Bran had led them up a few days ago, when they were searching for Nibs. There was a door next to the staircase with a little wooden sign erected next to it, displaying the letters "W.C.". It must have been a rarely used toilet that had been opened to provide an overflow option to any guests who couldn't find free facilities closer to the Ballroom. In fact, as she approached, the door to the toilet opened, and a man in a Roman toga stepped out, adjusting the wreath of vine leaves and plastic grapes on his head. Caitlyn remembered him as the man who had accosted Blackmort and Pomona in the Ballroom earlier. On an impulse, she called out:

"Excuse me... have you seen the girl in the Medusa costume?"

The man stopped and peered at her. His face had the slack, blurred look of someone in an alcoholic haze, and, for a moment, Caitlyn wondered if he was too drunk to remember.

Then he said: "Oh... yeah, I shaw her a few minutes ago, actually... on my way to the toilet." He swayed slightly as he pointed up the staircase. "She wash—*hic!*—going upstairsh."

"Thanks," said Caitlyn, wondering if she should offer him help getting back to the Ballroom or whether that would insult his masculine pride.

She watched until he had tottered back up the corridor and disappeared around the corner—still upright—then, satisfied, she turned towards the staircase. Hitching her long fishtail skirt up so as not to trip on the gossamer folds, she took the steps two at a time and arrived, slightly breathless, at the top of the staircase to find herself in the same familiar corridor that she had been with James and Bran a few days ago. A short distance down the corridor was the thick, metal-studded door of the Portrait Gallery.

Caitlyn frowned. Had Pomona gone in there? She noticed that the door was slightly ajar and, as she put a hand on the brass handle, she paused for a moment to listen. There was no sound from inside. A feeling of apprehension and unease crept over her skin, like the tiny feet of a dozen insects, and she felt her pulse beating unsteadily. Suddenly, she didn't want to go inside. But she forced herself to reach out and push the heavy door. It swung open with a soft whisper, rather than the dramatically creaking hinges of horror movie clichés, and Caitlyn gave a self-deprecating laugh, chiding herself for her silly paranoia.

She stepped inside the Portrait Gallery, the familiar musty smell enveloping her as she looked around. The lights were off, but the curtains had been left open, and the moonlight coming in through the tall windows played over the eerie shapes of the furniture draped in white sheets. The place looked empty, and she was about to turn and leave, when something made her hesitate. Caitlyn frowned, peering down the long room.

"He-hello?" she called. "Anybody here? Pomona?"

There was no reply. Caitlyn hesitated again. All she wanted to do was leave and shut the door behind her, but instead, something—some sort of premonition—made her step inside and start walking across the Gallery. Her long fishtail skirt swished across the dusty floor, muffling her footsteps, as she weaved between the white-draped furniture to reach the other side. She had only gone a few feet when she stumbled, tripping over something. She glanced down, then bent to pick up a thin serpentine object on the floor. Her fingers slid across a cool, scaly surface and the object moved suddenly in her hands.

Caitlyn stifled a scream, almost dropping it again, before she realised that it wasn't alive. She held the object up to the light and recognised it at once: it was one of the incredibly lifelike rubber snakes that formed part of Pomona's wig in her Medusa costume. It had been so cleverly designed that it seemed to wriggle even as she held it in her hands. It had obviously come loose and fallen off the wig. *What is it doing here though?* wondered Caitlyn.

She hesitated, then tucked the rubber snake into the top of her bodice for safekeeping. She would give it to Pomona later, in case her cousin wanted to try and reattach it to her wig. Then, after a moment's hesitation, she started once more across the Gallery.

Why am I doing this? It's obvious there's no one in

here, Caitlyn thought. But she continued doggedly until she reached the other end of the long room. As she had expected, she saw nobody, but recalling the scene with Evie downstairs, she walked around a large baroque sofa just to be sure. As she stepped behind it, she stumbled again. This time when she looked down, she froze.

There was a human hand lying limply next to her feet. Her gaze travelled up the connecting arm and she caught her breath as she realised that there was a man sitting slumped forwards on the floor behind the sofa. She dropped to her knees beside him and pushed him upright, then gasped and jerked backwards, her eyes widening in horror.

A two-pronged metal rod was protruding from the man's torso, the sharp ends of the "horns" piercing the man's chest. Blood had seeped out from the wounds, and it was obvious, even before she registered the ghostly white skin and blank stare, that he was dead. Caitlyn felt nausea rise in her throat as she focused on the face and recognised the suavely handsome features.

It was Daniel Tremaine, and he had been impaled by the witch's stang.

CHAPTER FOURTEEN

Caitlyn strained her ears, trying to listen through the door. She could hear the murmur of men's voices on the other side, but not clearly enough to make out what they were saying. She turned away from the door and bit her lip, undecided about what to do. The officer who had brought her to James's study had instructed her to remain there and wait for Detective Inspector Walsh to join her, but it had been nearly ten minutes now and there was still no sign of the CID detective.

She sighed and began pacing the room, then paused as she felt the cool, sinuous shape tucked into the top of her bodice rub against her skin. Slowly, she drew it out and stared down at the thin rubber snake which coiled across her palm. The long, slinky body ended abruptly, for instead of a tail, there was a flap where it had originally been attached to a Medusa wig.

Pomona's wig.

Caitlyn shrank away from the thought. But she knew that it was the logical conclusion and the only one that the police would jump to if she showed them what she had found in the Portrait Gallery, not that far from Daniel Tremaine's body...

On a sudden impulse, she turned towards the corner of the room dominated by an enormous dog bed. It was where Bran normally lay when his master was in the study, and it was a luxurious affair, with a sofa-style base surrounded on three sides by a bolster to keep draughts out, and an additional memory-foam topper mattress in the centre, to support the mastiff's huge bulk. There was a large dent in the middle of the mattress, a sign of Bran's recent presence, and it was liberally covered in dog hairs and dried drool.

Caitlyn looked at it thoughtfully for a moment, then she bent down and lifted one corner of the topper mattress to peer underneath. Sandwiched between the sturdy foam base of the sofa bed and the topper mattress were more canine hairs, dog biscuit crumbs, a slightly squashed and very chewed tennis ball, and a soft toy missing half its stuffing.

Caitlyn hesitated for a fraction of a second, then she bent and placed the rubber snake down amongst the dog hairs, pushing it towards the back of the bed as much as possible. She'd just dropped the topper mattress back into place and turned away when the door to the study opened and Inspector Walsh walked in, followed by James himself.

"Ah… Miss Le Fey—won't you take a seat?" the inspector asked, indicating a chair facing James's desk.

He himself remained standing, whilst James— instead of taking the executive chair behind the desk—leaned against the wall near the door, with his arms crossed. He gave Caitlyn an encouraging smile, however, which made her feel better as she turned back to face the inspector. With her involvement in so many murders recently, she had been in this situation so many times now that she should have known what to expect and shouldn't have been nervous. And yet she found herself waiting tensely as Inspector Walsh began to question her.

The questions were fairly standard, though, and she found herself answering relatively easily, until the detective leaned forwards and asked:

"And why were you searching for Miss Sinclair?"

Caitlyn licked her lips, trying to keep her expression neutral. It was a seemingly innocuous question, but she knew enough about Inspector Walsh now to know that he was a shrewd investigator. He might have looked like a middle-aged country plod, but those old eyes missed very little. *Not that I'm trying to hide anything*, she told herself quickly. *At least, nothing that really matters…*

She gave a deliberately casual shrug and said: "No

reason in particular. I mean, I hadn't seen Pomona around the Ballroom so I was wondering where she was. You know, just to have a chat. Girls' stuff. I... um... I thought she might have gone to the Ladies' to fix her make-up or something, so I that's why I left the Ballroom to look for her."

"And you thought there might be a Ladies' in the Portrait Gallery?" asked Inspector Walsh dryly.

Caitlyn flushed. "Well, I..."

"As far as I understand, all the toilets for guest use were on the ground floor, so what made you think you might find Miss Sinclair upstairs?"

Caitlyn hesitated. If she mentioned the man who had seen Pomona, it would put her cousin irrevocably at the scene of the crime. He had been so drunk—would he remember anything? Inspector Walsh hadn't mentioned him, so she assumed that the police hadn't found the man or questioned him yet—and if they did, she could always deny that he'd told her anything...

She took a deep breath and said, in as nonchalant a voice as she could manage, "Pomona wasn't the reason I went upstairs. I just happened to... er... hear a noise at the top of the staircase and I was curious, so I went up. Then I saw that the door of the Portrait Gallery was slightly open so I went in. It was nothing specifically to do with Pomona," she said firmly. Then, throwing the ball back into his court, she said, "Anyway, haven't you asked her yourself?"

The inspector sat back in his chair. "Yes. Miss

Sinclair tells us that she was in the Library. Apparently, she felt drowsy and left the Ballroom to find somewhere to rest. She says she sat down in the Library and dozed off, and was woken up by the commotion when you discovered the body. However…" He paused significantly. "There was no one else in the Library at the time, so there are no witnesses to corroborate that."

"You're talking as if she's a suspect in the murder," Caitlyn burst out. "Why on earth would Pomona want to kill Daniel Tremaine? She barely knew him! He only arrived at Huntingdon Manor a few days ago."

"Sometimes the reasons aren't obvious until later. We have to follow all leads," Walsh said ponderously. "And your cousin is someone who does not have another witness confirming her alibi." He leaned forwards suddenly. "Doesn't it seem odd to you that she should leave in the middle of the party and go to have a nap in the Library?"

"People do get tired," said Caitlyn. "It's not unheard of. Maybe she'd had a bit too much to drink…"

"So you did not see your cousin when you went up to the Portrait Gallery?"

"No," said Caitlyn. That, at least, was the truth.

"Nothing at all—nothing you saw or heard—to suggest that she might have been there?"

Caitlyn swallowed, resisting the urge to glance at Bran's bed in the corner. In her mind's eye, she saw, once again, the rubber snake that she had found—the snake which could only be from Pomona's Medusa wig. She knew that she should have immediately turned it over to the police when they'd arrived and told them where she had found it, as well as whose costume it had come from. But something had stopped her—the same crazy urge that had led her to hide the fake snake under the mattress in Bran's bed. Now, it would look worse if she belatedly owned up.

There's no need for the police to know anyway, she told herself silently. *It doesn't really matter what I found—it's not as if it's relevant to the investigation, because there's no way Pomona could be involved in Daniel Tremaine's murder.*

Her eyes flickered involuntarily to James. Normally, she would have been glad of his presence during a police interview, but for the first time, she found herself wishing that he wasn't there. James knew her too well and she could see him eyeing her now, a slightly puzzled frown in his grey eyes as he sensed her hesitation.

Caitlyn took a deep breath. "No, there was nothing."

Inspector Walsh regarded her silently for a moment and Caitlyn braced herself for further questions, but to her surprise, the detective simply said:

"Very well. That will be all for now. I may have further questions for you, Miss Le Fey, but in the meantime..." He leaned forwards and looked Caitlyn in the eye. "I would urge you to speak to your cousin and persuade her that if there's anything she's holding back, she must come clean to the police."

Caitlyn started to murmur her assent, but she was interrupted as the door to James's study was suddenly flung open. A young constable marched in, grinning triumphantly as he escorted a blonde woman. She was cursing and struggling, trying to pull her arm out of his grasp, and Caitlyn saw with surprise that it was the journalist, Jessica Hyde.

CHAPTER FIFTEEN

"...let go of me, you pig! Let go!"

The young officer ignored Jessica, instead thrusting her towards Inspector Walsh like a puppy proudly showing off a stick it had fetched. "Look who I found skulking around the back of the Manor, guv! She took off and tried to run, but I caught her... and look, sir... blood!" He grabbed one of Jessica's hands and held it up.

Caitlyn caught her breath as she saw the bloody palms. Inspector Walsh sprang up, but, before he could speak, Jessica wrenched herself free and whirled around to face the young constable:

"I'm going to report you to the IOPC! I'm going to have you suspended for police brutality!" she snarled. "I've got contacts in the media—don't think you're going to be able to cover this up!"

"I don't need to cover up anything. I was just doing my duty!" said the young constable indignantly. "You're a murder suspect and you were seen running away from the scene of the crime!"

"Stewart—"

"The butler identified her, sir!" said the constable, turning towards Inspector Walsh. "He said he saw her trying to attack Daniel Tremaine earlier in the evening."

"Bollocks!" cried the woman. "I didn't attack him! Tremaine was the one who assaulted *me!*" She spotted James on the other side of the room and jabbed a finger at him. "Ask him! He was there. He saw what happened."

Inspector Walsh swung around to look at James.

"There was hostility on both sides, I believe," said James carefully. "Ms Hyde did launch herself at Daniel Tremaine, but he also retaliated with excessive physical force."

"He was a beast!" cried Jessica Hyde. "He did that on purpose just to cause me pain, because he loved that. He got off on it, didn't you know? He was a sadist and—" She broke off as she saw the expression on Inspector Walsh's face and realised that her belligerent words weren't helping her case. "But I didn't kill him," she added quickly. "I had nothing to do with his murder!"

"Can you explain why you have blood on your hands, Ms Hyde?" asked Inspector Walsh.

Jessica glanced at her palms, then made a motion

as if to wipe them on her trousers. The constable caught her hands just in time.

"It's my own blood," she said, starting to sound nervous for the first time now. "I tripped and fell when I was walking around the outbuildings behind the manor house, and I scraped my hands on some splintered wood."

"And what were you doing skulking around the property?" asked the inspector.

"I wasn't skulking!" protested Jessica. Then she hunched her shoulders and mumbled, "Well, okay, maybe a bit. Look, I was just being nosy, okay? I'm a journalist; it's second nature for us to poke around a bit. I hadn't ever been on the estate before, and I was curious."

"So why did you run?"

"It… it was just a reflex reaction. I mean, I knew I was sort of trespassing, and when I saw this bloke in a police uniform, I just panicked, all right?"

"Why would you panic unless you'd done something wrong?" demanded the young constable. "Why would you run unless you're guilty?"

Jessica bristled and started to snap a reply, but Inspector Walsh held a hand up, silencing them both. Turning to the constable, he said: "Stewart, go and find one of the SOCO officers and ask them to come with a kit immediately." Then, as the constable left the room, he glanced at James and said: "I'd like to ask Ms Hyde some more questions."

"Yes, of course," said James quickly, going over to

Caitlyn and putting a hand under her elbow. "We'll leave you now, Inspector. You're welcome to use my study for as long as you need."

They stepped outside and walked silently back through the house together. The festive atmosphere which had filled the Manor grounds earlier was completely gone now. The Ballroom was empty, the music and dancing halted, and most of the guests—after giving their statements—had left. A few members of staff were moving unobtrusively about, collecting used glassware, blowing out the candles, cleaning up the debris. In the front foyer, they found a few of the last remaining guests still lingering, some waiting for their transport and others speaking to a couple of police officers.

"I told Bertha not to worry about you—that you could stay the night here," said James. "So she's left already and taken the Widow Mags and Evie back to Tillyhenge with her."

"Oh. Thanks." She gave him a tired smile. "Well, in that case... do you mind if I say goodnight?" she asked. She felt completely drained after the excitement of the ball, followed by the shock of the murder and the strain of Inspector Walsh's probing questions.

"Of course not. Sleep well."

She turned towards the sweeping staircase leading to the upper floor, disappointed that James had made no attempt to give her a goodnight kiss. Still, she reminded herself that the events of the evening had completely destroyed any romantic mood, and besides, as host, he was probably still preoccupied with managing the aftermath of the ruined evening. As she put her foot on the first step, however, James caught her arm.

"Caitlyn—wait." He gave her a crooked smile. "This evening didn't quite turn out like I'd imagined."

"That's a master understatement, even for an Englishman," said Caitlyn.

James laughed. "Yes, well... I was wondering... would you like to go out for a morning ride with me?"

Caitlyn stared at him. Was the invitation a date? After their first "romantic dinner" together had turned into a fiasco, James hadn't made any further attempts to arrange another date and Caitlyn had been too bashful and embarrassed to make any moves herself—especially since it was mainly her fault that their first date had been a disaster. Now, her heart leapt at the thought of a second chance.

"I... I'd love to," she said, giving him a shy smile.

"Great! You do ride, don't you? I remember you mentioning once that you'd ridden ponies before."

Caitlyn blushed slightly as she recalled the incident: it had been shortly after they'd first met and she'd needed James's help in a rescue situation, which meant an unexpected ride with him on his stallion. She could still vividly remember the feel of his arms around her as he sat astride behind her, holding her safe on the cantering horse.

Yanking her thoughts back to the present, she

said: "It was just a few pony rides. I'm not an experienced rider," she added nervously as she thought of James's horse—a huge Percheron stallion named Arion, who looked like he'd be more at home on a battlefield than trotting across the rolling Cotswolds hills.

As if reading her mind, James chuckled and said, "Don't worry—I wasn't suggesting you ride anything like Arion. I have a Welsh cob mare in the stables who's very gentle. You'd have no problems with her."

"Oh. That sounds lovely," said Caitlyn, smiling at the prospect. "When were you thinking of going?"

"Well, I imagine you'd want a bit of a lie-in tomorrow morning, and in any case, the police will probably still be here, going over the crime scene, and I may need to remain on-site... But perhaps the day after? I can come and pick you up from the chocolate shop—"

"Oh no, it's silly for you to go to Tillyhenge and then come back. I can just drive over myself," Caitlyn offered.

"All right. I'll meet you in the stables at nine o'clock, then."

Caitlyn smiled. "It's a date." She stifled a yawn with an embarrassed laugh and turned towards the stairs again. "Sorry. I think I'd better head to bed—"

James cleared his throat. "Wait, Caitlyn—actually, there's something else I wanted to ask you."

"Yes?"

James's expression had turned serious, and he

hesitated a long moment before saying: "Were you telling the truth just now?"

She stiffened. "What do you mean?"

"When Inspector Walsh was questioning you about Pomona. You seemed..." He trailed off uncertainly.

"Seemed what?"

"Like you were holding something back."

Caitlyn was wide awake now, her heart thudding uncomfortably in her chest. "I don't know what you're talking about," she said, trying not to sound defensive.

"Why did you really go up those stairs? If you didn't think that Pomona was up there, why did you bother?"

"I told you... I mean, Inspector Walsh... I thought I heard a noise," said Caitlyn weakly.

James looked her in the eye. "Did you really have no reason to suspect that Pomona was up in the Portrait Gallery?"

"Are you suggesting that I lied to the police?" she asked, taking refuge in self-righteous indignation.

James seemed to be choosing his words carefully. "I know how much Pomona means to you, more like a sister than a cousin. She's your very best friend. It would be understandable, perhaps, if you felt tempted to lie for her—"

"Why would I need to do that?" asked Caitlyn quickly. "That implies that she's guilty. Surely *you* don't believe that Pomona has anything to do with this murder?"

James was silent for a moment, then he said gently: "I just want you to know that you can always talk to me, even if you don't feel that you can speak to the police. I hope you'll remember that."

Caitlyn nodded, unable to meet his eyes, and was immensely relieved when Mosley approached at that moment with a matter that needed James's attention. She took the opportunity to murmur a hasty "goodnight" and escape up the stairs. Their exchange echoed in her head, though, as she undressed; and when she climbed into bed at last, her mind was in turmoil. She felt terrible for having lied to James, on top of lying to the police. How had she ever got herself into this position? She wished now that she'd never kept quiet about the rubber snake she'd found.

But what choice did I have? she thought despairingly. *The police would have jumped on Pomona if I'd told them about it. They're suspicious enough of her already—they'd go nuts if they thought a piece of her wig was found so near the crime scene. And it's stupid because Pomie could* never *be the murderer,* thought Caitlyn fiercely. *So I'm saving them from wasting their time chasing red herrings.*

Sighing, she turned over and stared into the darkness. She hadn't seen Pomona since finding Daniel Tremaine's body. The police had kept them separated, and then her cousin had taken herself straight to bed after she was released from questioning. Caitlyn had passed by Pomona's bedroom door on her way to her own, but it had been shut and, not wanting to disturb her in case she was asleep, Caitlyn had refrained from knocking.

But I'll speak to her first thing in the morning, she promised herself. *I'll ask her why a piece of her wig was in the Gallery. I want to hear her side of the story first. Then I can decide whether to tell James and the police...*

CHAPTER SIXTEEN

Caitlyn drifted off at last into a troubled sleep and awoke, pale and bleary-eyed, and not feeling remotely refreshed. Still, she hauled herself out of bed and into the shower, and emerged from the bathroom twenty minutes later with her hair washed, her face scrubbed, and her mind slightly clearer. On her way downstairs, she stopped by Pomona's bedroom once more and this time she knocked firmly. But she got no response and, when she tried the handle, she found the door unlocked and the room empty. The bed had obviously been slept in and she could see the usual mess of clothes, make-up, and accessories that Pomona left in her wake, but there was no sign of the American girl.

Maybe she's gone down to breakfast, thought Caitlyn hopefully, and she hurried to the sweeping staircase leading down to the ground floor. From past stays at the Manor, she knew that breakfast was normally served in the Morning Room, and she made her way there eagerly. But when she arrived, she was disappointed to find her cousin nowhere in sight. Instead, there was a woman she didn't recognise sitting at the table on the other side of the bright and airy room.

No, wait, I do know her, thought Caitlyn as she hovered in the doorway, peeking into the room. It was the woman who had warned her about Daniel Tremaine.

"Good morning, Miss Le Fey. I trust you slept well."

Caitlyn jumped and turned to see Mosley standing behind her, impeccable as ever in his dark suit. "Oh, hi, Mosley. I should be asking you that question," she said, giving him a sympathetic smile. "You must have been up half the night dealing with the police and the forensics team and stuff..."

"It was certainly a late night, but I managed to accrue a few hours' rest, which I have found sufficiently restorative," said the butler.

"Oh. Well, I hope you get some time off today, then, to catch up on some sleep," said Caitlyn, trying not to smile at the butler's ridiculously formal language. She often wondered if Mosley had somehow been teleported from the Victorian era. She knew that James was constantly trying to get him to relax his manner and attitude, with little success.

She herself had long given up trying to get Mosley to call her by her first name, although she winced slightly every time he addressed her as "madam"—it made her feel a hundred years old!

"His lordship was kind enough to offer me the day off today, but I declined. I certainly cannot leave the running of the Manor to the general staff when there is so much chaos in the aftermath of the murder and the abrupt ending of the ball," Mosley said indignantly. Then his normally impassive face relaxed into the ghost of a smile. "However, I appreciate your concern for my welfare, madam." He gestured into the Morning Room. "Can I show you to the breakfast table?"

"Who's that, Mosley? Sitting at the table?" asked Caitlyn in a whisper.

The butler lowered his voice. "That's Mrs Vivien Kwok, who was one of the guests at the ball last night."

"Oh, I didn't realise that any of the guests were staying overnight at the Manor."

"There had not been any plans as such, but it seems that the shock of the news of the murder upset Mrs Kwok greatly. She collapsed in hysterics and was only calmed by sedation," Mosley explained.

Caitlyn raised her eyebrows. "Wow, that sounds a bit dramatic. I'm surprised they didn't think she needed to be taken to hospital or something."

"Mrs Kwok was in no position to travel last night, and one of the cellists in the chamber orchestra came forward and volunteered to stay overnight to look after her. Apparently, she has some nursing experience, and the police doctor was satisfied with that. So Lord Fitzroy was grateful to accept the offer, and he told Mrs Kwok that she could stay at the Manor for as long as she needed to recover."

"Oh, well, I don't think I'll bother her then..." said Caitlyn, starting to back away from the doorway.

"I believe it would be beneficial for Mrs Kwok to have some company this morning," said Mosley quickly. "It has been rather dispiriting for her to sit in there alone. Miss Marković—the cellist—had her breakfast earlier and has gone out for a walk about the grounds."

Caitlyn sighed. She didn't really fancy another conversation with Vivien Kwok, but after the butler's words, it would seem churlish to refuse. So she allowed herself to be led into the room and seated at the table. The other woman looked up, her face hardening in recognition as she saw Caitlyn. Seen now in the harsher light of day, Caitlyn realised that Vivien was much older than she'd first looked— somewhere in her late forties, perhaps even her fifties—although, like many of East Asian descent, her skin still retained the youthful glow and unlined appearance of a woman half her age. But there were lines of tension around her mouth and temples, and a weary cynicism in her eyes, which did more to age her than any wrinkles or sagging might have done.

"Hi... I don't think we were properly introduced at

the ball last night. I'm Caitlyn Le Fey," said Caitlyn, wondering if she should be offering a hand to shake. It seemed ridiculously formal to do that across a breakfast table, so instead she gave the woman a guarded smile. "I'm sorry to hear about your... um... I mean, it must have been a terrible shock for you, since you knew Mr Tremaine personally?"

Vivien stiffened and her gaze slid to Mosley, who was busying himself pouring Caitlyn's coffee. She waited to answer until the butler had finished and left the room.

"Were you expecting me to be prostrate with grief?" she said sarcastically. "I'm sorry to shatter your illusions, but I'm not going to be joining the legions of female admirers crying over Daniel Tremaine today."

Caitlyn was taken aback by the woman's hostile manner. "You seemed to be upset enough last night," she retorted.

Vivien shrugged an elegant shoulder. "Anyone would be upset if they found out that a murder had been committed in the same house they were in."

"Have the police spoken to you?" asked Caitlyn casually as she helped herself to some toast and jam.

"Why?" the other woman said, her voice sharp.

"Well, they were questioning everyone who was at the ball. I thought they'd be especially keen to speak to you, given your... um... personal relationship with the murder victim."

Vivien gave a cynical laugh. "Why don't you just

come out and say it? You think that Daniel and I were lovers, don't you?"

"Well, were you?" asked Caitlyn, deciding that the only way to deal with this woman was to be as blunt as she was.

"Yes," said Vivien after a moment. "But it ended a few years ago."

There was something in the way she said that which made Caitlyn wonder who had ended the affair. Somehow, she didn't think that it had been Vivien.

"Um... so how did you meet Daniel?" she asked. "Was it through—" She broke off. She had been about to say "through work", but as she looked across the table again, she realised that Vivien didn't look like the type who would be hunched over a computer in an office or even presiding over a boardroom meeting. No, Vivien looked more like the type of woman who would be sauntering out of London's most expensive department stores, laden with designer shopping bags, or sipping champagne at charity lunches in exclusive hotels. She was proven right a moment later when Vivien said:

"I met Daniel at a charity event organised by my husband's company."

Caitlyn glanced at the diamond solitaire on the woman's ring finger. "Did your husband not come to the ball?" she asked politely.

"My husband is dead."

"Oh!" Caitlyn faltered. "Um... I'm sorry to hear

that."

Vivien gave a humourless laugh. "Don't be. It was hardly a tragedy. I married him for his money; he married me to gain the ultimate trophy wife. There wasn't much love lost on either side." She gave a little smile. "And now I'm a rich widow."

Something in the woman's cool, supercilious manner irritated Caitlyn and prompted her to ask more prying questions than she would normally have felt comfortable doing. "Did your husband know about your affair with Daniel?"

Vivien shrugged. "Possibly. Jerry was just as good at turning a blind eye to my affairs as I was to his. As long as it didn't affect the status quo, it didn't matter." She smiled at Caitlyn's expression. "Are you scandalised? Darling, welcome to the reality of many society marriages. As long as we maintain public appearances and remain discreet, we can amuse ourselves with whomever we like."

"And Daniel Tremaine was happy to be your 'amusement'?" said Caitlyn disbelievingly.

Vivien arched an eyebrow. "Are you doubting my charms?" Then, as Caitlyn started to protest, she laughed again and said, "No, you're right. Daniel had his pick of beautiful women *and* he was ten years my junior. I don't flatter myself that he became my lover just because of my seductive appeal... No, I think he wanted an unobtrusive way to gain inside access to my husband's business dealings. After all, pillow talk is a time-honoured tool used for extracting information."

"That seems a bit of an extreme way to investigate a business, doesn't it?" said Caitlyn sceptically. "Most accountants these days would just use legal means to gain access to financial statements and such."

Vivien looked even more amused. "My goodness, you really did fall for Daniel's little charade, didn't you?"

Caitlyn remembered the woman's cryptic comments at the ball. "Are you telling me that he didn't work for the British government?"

"Oh, it's true that Daniel worked for the British government, but in an entirely different capacity."

"What do you mean?"

Vivien gave an exaggerated sigh. "Do I have to spell it out for you, darling? He was an agent. A spy. A special operative. Whatever you want to call it."

"How do you know that?"

The other woman gave a bitter smile. "Because I knew Daniel... in both the literal *and* the Biblical sense. And pillow talk works both ways."

"So as an agent, Daniel Tremaine could have had many enemies," mused Caitlyn.

Vivien Kwok smiled again, her eyes cold. "Well, let's just say I wouldn't be surprised if there were many who would have wanted him dead."

CHAPTER SEVENTEEN

After breakfast, Caitlyn renewed her search for Pomona and found the American girl at last in the Conservatory, a beautiful Victorian structure furnished in the traditional manner with floral cushions and wicker furniture, and overflowing with potted ferns and other hothouse plants. Her cousin was curled up on one of the wicker sofas next to the tall glass windows, staring moodily out at the Manor grounds. She was dressed in a simple sweater and jeans—a big difference from her exotic costume the night before—although Caitlyn saw uneasily that the black diamond choker still glittered menacingly just above the collar of Pomona's sweater. Her fingers curled convulsively as she fought the urge to reach out and yank it from her cousin's throat.

"Pomona, here you are! I've been looking for you

everywhere." Caitlyn went over to join the other girl. "Have you had breakfast?"

"No," muttered Pomona, not taking her eyes off the landscape. "Not really hungry."

Caitlyn looked at her cousin in concern. "Pomie, is something wrong?"

Pomona turned around, her eyes flashing. "Yeah, something *is* wrong! The police won't let me leave. They said I have to remain at the Manor. I'm, like, under house arrest or something!"

"Aww, come on, Pomie, you know how these things work. They like to keep everyone where they can find them easily as they go through the preliminary questioning."

Pomona shook her head. "That old dude Walsh—the way he was talking to me last night and all these questions he kept asking... like, what I was doing, and whether anyone could confirm my alibi—*alibi?* Why the hell do I need a friggin' alibi?"

"You have to see it from the police's point of view," said Caitlyn in a placating voice. "It's just part of the investigation. They have to verify everyone's movements at the time of the murder. It doesn't mean they have anything against you personally."

"Yeah, it does!" snapped Pomona. "They are treating me like some damned suspect! I kept repeating over and over that I was, like, having a nap in the Library, and all I could remember was waking up and hearing all this screaming and shouting. And then I came out and saw everyone rushing around, and I heard that someone had been murdered. That was it. But I could tell that Walsh didn't believe me. He kept cross-examining me and acting like he thought I was lying about being asleep."

"Well, you have to admit, it *was* unlike you," said Caitlyn, looking at her cousin uncertainly. "I mean, I've never seen you leave in the middle of a party to take a nap."

"It's not my fault if I felt drowsy! It was probably that antihistamine I had."

"What antihistamine?"

"You're the one who told me to take one, remember? For my allergy."

"Oh... yes, that's right," said Caitlyn, recalling Pomona's constant sneezing and watering eyes when they were getting ready for the ball.

"Well, Mosley got me some pills after I left your room. I saw on the box that one of the side effects is drowsiness, but I figured it couldn't be that bad. Maybe I shouldn't have drunk so much—probably alcohol and antihistamines don't mix. Anyway, I didn't know that it would, like, knock me out." She glared at Caitlyn. "What's the matter? Don't you believe me either?"

Caitlyn hesitated. "Pomie, did you go up to the Portrait Gallery last night?"

Pomona drew a sharp breath, her face darkening. "What the hell, Caitlyn? Are you suggesting that I—"

"No, no... I mean..." Caitlyn faltered, not sure what she meant. "Just tell me, please, Pomie—did you?"

"I wasn't in the Portrait Gallery with Daniel Tremaine," said Pomona coldly.

"Okay, well... what about earlier?" asked Caitlyn, grasping at straws. "I mean, like, maybe after you got dressed in your costume, before everyone arrived?"

"No, why would I wanna go in there?" asked Pomona impatiently. "I told you, I didn't go into that damned Gallery at all last night!"

"Well, in that case..." Caitlyn looked her cousin straight in the eye. "Why did I find one of the rubber snakes from your wig in the Gallery?"

Pomona paled. "What?" She leaned forwards urgently. "Did you tell the police?"

"No," Caitlyn admitted. "I picked it up and—"

"Omigod, you've still got it?" said Pomona, looking relieved. She sprang up. "That's great! C'mon, let's go upstairs and you can give it back to me."

Caitlyn resisted the tug on her arm. "I should really be handing it in to the police."

"You can't do that!"

"Pomie, I have to. It's evidence from the crime scene."

"So why did you keep quiet about it last night?"

"Well, I—"

"Because you knew it would make me look guilty, that's why," said Pomona, looking smug.

"Well, yes... but... that's not... I didn't..." Caitlyn stammered, trying to sort out her confused thoughts. "Look, I just wanted a chance to speak to you first. I thought maybe you'd have an explanation for why a piece of your wig was in the Portrait Gallery—"

"Well, I don't, okay? And if you hand that in to the police now, you know what will happen. They're suspicious of me already, and this will be the last nail in the coffin." Pomona shot her a malevolent look. "It'll almost be like you framing me for the murder."

"Pomie!" gasped Caitlyn in dismay. "How could you say that?"

The other girl looked slightly abashed. "Okay, I know you wouldn't really do that, Caitlyn... but it's kinda the same result. Look, if you just give it to me, then the police never need to know about it. You know what they say: what you don't know can't hurt you, right? And we're actually *helping* the police! We're saving them time, so they don't waste energy investigating something that has nothing to do with the murder."

They were the same arguments and justifications that Caitlyn had told herself the night before, and yet hearing Pomona voice them only made her more uneasy. *Does it really have nothing to do with the murder?* a voice inside her asked.

"C'mon, Caitlyn. You gotta give it to me," pleaded Pomona. "I'm leaving as soon as they let me and—"

"Leaving? Where are you going?"

Pomona looked back out the window again and said in a casual voice: "I'm going back to London."

Caitlyn's heart sank. "You mean, you're going back to Blackmort."

She tried to keep her voice neutral, but Pomona obviously heard something in her tone because she bristled suddenly.

"Yeah, so what if I am? You got a problem with that?" She eyed Caitlyn angrily. "You're just like everyone else! You've got this thing against Thane."

"That's not true," said Caitlyn weakly. "But you can't really blame people for feeling hostile towards him. I mean, he hasn't exactly made himself popular with what he's been doing locally—the way he's been aggressively buying up land for property development."

Pomona scowled. "People are so dumb. Thane is trying to make things better for them, don't they realise that?"

"By erecting big, ugly buildings all over the countryside?" said Caitlyn sarcastically.

"How d'you know they'd be ugly?" snapped Pomona. "Thane's got, like, one of the fastest-growing property development companies in the world. He knows what he's doing. Man, I can't believe people don't like him just because he wants to help bring the country into the twenty-first century! He could really improve things, like—"

"The Cotswolds is one of the most unique, unspoilt parts of England. I don't see how building modern developments all over it is going to improve it," said Caitlyn acidly. "And what about sites of special significance? Like the stone circle? Is he going to build over those?"

"No, of course not," said Pomona, waving a hand scornfully. "They'd just, like, put a fence around it or something. For example, the standing stones could be a really nice feature at the front of the development! A lot more people would get to see it. They could put a sign next to it explaining all the legends associated with it, and have a spot where people can get selfies—"

"What?" Caitlyn stared at her cousin. The thought of the stone circle being hemmed in by artificial fencing and presented like some sort of Santa's grotto in a shopping mall appalled her. "Pomie, I can't believe you just said that! You of all people... You're the one who told me how sacred the stone circle is as a site of ancient magic, and how it sits where ley lines intersect. They've stood there on the hill for thousands of years..."

"Well, that doesn't mean that they have to remain like that a thousand more. So much of England is just stuck in the past, bogged down by stupid traditions and stuff," said Pomona. "Jeez, Caitlyn, just because something's always been done one way in the past doesn't mean you can't change and find a better way!"

"Well, okay, that's true sometimes," Caitlyn conceded. "But I just can't see how this would be a 'better way'."

"That's because you don't have 'vision', like Thane does," said Pomona loftily. "He's an awesome businessman. Anyway, I don't care what you think, and I'm not gonna stop seeing Thane just because you're all too dumb to appreciate him!" She made an irritable noise and sprang up from the wicker sofa. "I'm gonna get some breakfast."

With that, she flounced out of the Conservatory, leaving Caitlyn staring after her worriedly.

CHAPTER EIGHTEEN

Caitlyn knew Pomona well enough to know that there was no point speaking to her cousin further when she was in that kind of mood. It would be better to let the other girl cool off and try to reason with her again later. In any case, she also didn't want Pomona pressuring her while she was still trying to decide what to do with the rubber snake she'd found, so a part of her was glad that Pomona had abruptly ended their conversation.

Now, she gathered her things from her room, then made her way back downstairs. She had hoped to see James before she left Huntingdon Manor. Despite everything that had happened with the murder, she couldn't help also remembering with a thrill that James had almost kissed her the night before. They hadn't really had a chance to be alone together since being interrupted, and now Caitlyn wondered, with a mixture of nervousness and excitement, what it would be like when they saw each other again.

But when she asked Mosley, she was disappointed to learn that James had been called out to one of the tenant farms on the estate early that morning and probably wouldn't return until late afternoon.

"His lordship did want to know if madam would like to take Nibs back to Tillyhenge with her?" asked Mosley, trying not to look too hopeful.

Caitlyn grinned. "Oh, sure, I'll take the little monkey back with me. It's probably about time for my turn, anyway, isn't it?" she said, referring to the "kitten-share" arrangement that she and James had worked out after they'd rescued Nibs together from a flooded quarry in the woods. Since then, the little black kitten had lived part of the time at the Manor and part of the time at the Widow Mags's cottage. *And causes havoc in both his homes*, thought Caitlyn with a smile. But she knew that the inhabitants of both places—herself included!—doted on the kitten and missed him when he was away.

"I think you will find Nibs in his lordship's study, together with Bran," said Mosley.

"Great! Do you mind getting the cat carrier while I go and grab him?" Caitlyn replied, dropping the rest of her things at the side of the foyer.

She made her way to the wing where James's study was located. As she approached, she was surprised to see a young woman lurking nearby. The woman had her back to her, but from her posture, she seemed to be listening at the door. The next moment, she reached for the handle and began slowly turning it.

Caitlyn frowned. She knew that the normal public tours of Huntingdon Manor had been suspended in the short term, given the ongoing murder investigation, so there shouldn't have been any members of the public wandering through the house. And in any case, this was a private wing, so no tourists or visitors should have had access here. She started running down the hallway, shouting:

"Hey! What are you doing?"

The young woman whirled to face her and, as Caitlyn got closer, she realised with a start how tall the other girl was—she was not petite herself, but this young woman towered at least a head taller. She was very striking, with copper-coloured hair—the kind usually associated with freckles and milky white skin—but her complexion was the olive tone more commonly seen in Mediterranean countries. Her eyes were also unusual: a vivid shade of blue-green which seemed to dominate her face as she stared at Caitlyn in surprise.

"Oh!" she cried, clutching her chest. "You scared me."

"What are you doing?" demanded Caitlyn. "This is a private part of the house."

"Yes, I know. I came to fetch my cello," said the

girl. "Mr Mosley told me that it had been moved to Lord Fitzroy's study for safekeeping. He said he'd fetch it for me this morning, but he seemed so busy when I went to find him just now that I thought I might as well come and get it myself. I was interviewed in here last night, so I knew my way."

Belatedly, Caitlyn realised who the girl must be: the member of the chamber orchestra who had volunteered to look after Vivien Kwok. Feeling terribly embarrassed, she gave a sheepish smile.

"I'm sorry, I didn't mean to be so aggressive. It's just with everything that's happened…"

"It's okay. I know. With the murder," said the girl, nodding understandingly. She offered Caitlyn a friendly smile. She spoke English fluently, but with a faint accent that Caitlyn couldn't quite place. "I'm Milena Marković. I was playing in the chamber orchestra last night. I stayed overnight to help look after one of the guests."

"Yes, I'd heard about that. It was really good of you," said Caitlyn, feeling even more ashamed of her earlier hostility now.

Milena shrugged. "It was nothing, really. I'm used to dealing with situations like that, so I offered to help."

"I'd heard that you had some nursing experience?" said Caitlyn, looking at the other girl curiously.

"Oh, not professionally. I mean, I don't work as a nurse or anything. But I'd done some part-time training as a nursing assistant, and I have experience dealing with... uh... extremely agitated patients, so that helped with Mrs Kwok."

"Yeah, I heard that she was very upset by the news of the murder?"

Milena made a sympathetic face. "She was absolutely hysterical. She kept screaming 'Daniel!' and we had to physically restrain her from running into the Portrait Gallery to see his body."

Wow, that's a bit different from the cool, indifferent image that Vivien Kwok tried to portray at breakfast, thought Caitlyn.

"Even after she was sedated, she was still restless all night—she kept waking up, sobbing, and calling his name." Milena shook her head. "I actually thought the victim was her husband, from the way she was acting, but they told me that he was just another guest?"

"I think they might have known each other in the past," said Caitlyn delicately.

Understanding dawned on the other girl's face. "Ah."

"So you're not staying with her any longer?"

Milena shook her head. "Mrs Kwok seems much better this morning. She might remain a bit longer, but she doesn't need me to watch over her anymore. It's just as well, since I need to leave soon anyway— I'm supposed to be visiting my mother; she lives in a special community not far from here and she gets quite distressed if I don't turn up." She gave Caitlyn a diffident smile. "Actually, my mother's the reason I have nursing experience. She used to suffer from extreme anxiety and panic attacks, so I'm used to dealing with that, and I know how to calm people down so that they don't hurt themselves."

"Oh, I'm sorry," said Caitlyn with compassion. "That must be difficult for you."

Milena gave that offhand shrug again. "It's been like this for many years now, so I'm used to it. I'm an only child, you see, so there's no one else to be with her. But I have to travel with the orchestra and I'm away from home a lot of the time, so it was great when she found this community. It means she can have people around her all the time." She glanced at her watch. "But she still really cares about my visits."

"Oh, well, I'll help you get your cello then," said Caitlyn quickly, feeling embarrassed again for jumping to conclusions earlier and keen to make amends.

She pushed the study door open, then stood back to let Milena enter before her. The other girl walked into the darkened room, then yelped in shock and fear, and jumped sideways, hopping on one foot.

"What? What is it?" cried Caitlyn, hurrying in after her.

She snapped on the lights, then made a noise of exasperation as she saw the culprit: a little black kitten who had pounced from behind one of the chairs and ambushed Milena's foot. He was now attacking the girl's shoe, his paws clutched around the pointed toe and his hind legs kicking excitedly against the sole, raking it with his tiny claws as if disembowelling make-believe prey.

"Nibs!" scolded Caitlyn, bending to grab the kitten.

Milena looked down and relaxed slightly. "Ohhh... it's a baby cat!" Then she gave another scream and staggered backwards as a huge shape rose suddenly from behind James's desk and lumbered forwards.

"It's all right! That's just Bran—he's very friendly," said Caitlyn quickly, feeling sorry for the startled girl. Milena was already struggling to balance on one leg, with Nibs clamped to her raised foot, and now she was faced with a slobbery English mastiff thrusting his wrinkly face into hers, his tail wagging as he tried to say hello.

"Oh my God—I've never seen such a huge dog!" gasped Milena, leaning as far back as possible.

"He's very gentle and sweet," Caitlyn assured her. She had detached Nibs at last and now held up the squirming kitten. "It's this little monster that you need to worry about," she added, chuckling.

Milena put her foot down and stood upright again, taking a steadying breath. She reached out a tentative hand and patted Bran's massive head, a slow smile spreading across her face. "He's gorgeous, actually," she said. Then she looked at the kitten in Caitlyn's arms. "And the little one too. It was just that he scared me, jumping suddenly on my foot like that."

"I think it's a new trick he's learnt—hiding under

furniture and ambushing people walking past," said Caitlyn wryly. "He tried it on someone else the other day."

Milena laughed, putting a hand to her chest again. "Well, as long as there are no more scares today... I don't think my heart could take it!"

She crossed slowly to the other side of the study, where a large cello case was propped against the wall. When she bent to lift it, though, she gave a grunt of surprise.

"Why is it so heavy...?" she muttered, shifting her position to get a better grip on the case.

"Do you need help?" Caitlyn offered, going over to join her.

Milena waved a hand. "No, no, I'm used to carrying my cello by myself. It's just..." She frowned in puzzlement. "It's not normally this heavy..."

She took a deep breath and heaved again, this time managing to lift the large black case and heft it upright. But it tilted over and fell against her, its weight causing her to stagger back in surprise. Caitlyn sprang forwards to help, but it was too late. With a cry of dismay, Milena lost her grip on the cello case. It teetered sideways, then fell over with a crash, which caused Nibs to dive under a chair and Bran to back away, barking loudly.

"My cello!" cried Milena, rushing forwards.

The impact had caused the lid of the case to flip open and Milena froze as she saw what was inside. Then she let out a terrified scream.

CHAPTER NINETEEN

Caitlyn rushed forwards to peer into the velvet-lined interior of the cello case. Her heart leapt into her mouth as she saw that instead of a large stringed instrument, the body of an old man was crammed into the case. Then her shock turned to exasperated disbelief as she realised who the old man was.

"*Viktor!*"

"Eh?" The old vampire opened his eyes and sat up slowly, unbending his lanky frame. He was wearing the same ancient black suit that he had been wearing at the ball—Caitlyn could even see a smear of dried caramel sauce on the ruffled collar of his white shirt—and he yawned, showing a pair of shrivelled yellow fangs, as he looked irritably around the room.

"What a dreadful din! Screaming and barking and whatnot... how is a vampire supposed to get any sleep around here?" he said peevishly.

"Viktor, what are you doing in there?" hissed Caitlyn.

"Having a nap—what does it look like?" said the old man huffily. He stretched and looked down at the cello case with disapproval. "I must say, it is a lot more cramped than I expected. And I thought the velvet lining would be softer."

"Viktor, why on earth are you sleeping in a cello case?" demanded Caitlyn, struggling for patience.

"Saw it in that ante-chamber outside the Ballroom. Reminded me of a coffin I once had, and I thought I would climb in to see how it compared. Must have dozed off..." Viktor smiled in fond reminiscence. "Ah... it's a great shame that coffins are not in vogue among vampires anymore. There is nothing quite like a comfy coffin. Even the simple pine ones smell so fresh and lovely."

Milena made a strangled sound in her throat, her eyes bulging as she stared at the old man. "*Upir*?" she said hoarsely. "Y... you are a vampire?"

Viktor stood up stiffly and attempted to sweep the girl a bow, nearly falling over in the process. "Count Viktor Dracul, at your service! I am one of the last vampires and one of the Ancient Guardian Pro—"

"Uh... that's great, Viktor," Caitlyn interrupted hastily, glancing at Milena's pale face. The girl looked like she was going to faint any minute. "I'm sure Milena doesn't need your whole potted history right this minute. More important is: where did you put her cello?"

"Eh? Oh, I removed it to make room, of course," said Viktor. "All the other instrument cases were full, and there was nowhere to prop it up in the room, so I put it out the window—"

"What?" cried Caitlyn. "Viktor, you can't just take someone's cello out of its case and chuck it out of the window!"

"I did not 'chuck it'," said the old vampire, glowering at her. "I placed it carefully next to some bushes growing outside the window. It is well sheltered from the elements by the eaves and the surrounding bushes. You will find it there, quite undamaged." He adjusted his jacket, straightening the hems with a jerk. "Now, if you will excuse me, I am going to find my morning glass of prune juice."

Turning, he stalked out of the room. There was a stunned silence after he left, then Milena turned to Caitlyn and said:

"Who... who was that?"

For a moment, Caitlyn was tempted to tell the other girl the truth: that Viktor was a six-hundred-and-thirty-four-year-old vampire who was also her "guardian uncle", and that he could shape-shift into his other form: a fuzzy brown fruit bat... Then she gave herself a mental shake. Was she crazy? Milena would probably think that she had lost her mind! Besides, Bertha and the Widow Mags had always warned her to keep a low profile and not to share too much about the truth of magic and beings from the

Other Realms...

Giving the other girl a wan smile, Caitlyn replied: "Um... Viktor is my uncle. He's very old and... and a bit confused. And... er... he's got quite a vivid imagination."

"Perhaps you should think about a care home or somewhere where people can keep an eye on him," Milena advised. "I mean, he could hurt himself if he starts climbing into the wrong places or falling off something."

"Thanks. I'll... er... definitely think about it," said Caitlyn, thankful that Viktor couldn't hear this conversation. The old vampire would have been incandescent with indignation! Keen to change the subject, she said, "We'd better go and find your cello. I just hope that it's still there outside the ante-chamber window."

She cast a longing look behind her as they left James's study. She'd been thinking of checking on the rubber snake hidden under the mattress in Bran's bed, maybe even removing it and taking it with her back to Tillyhenge, but now, with Milena here, there was no opportunity.

Anyway, it's probably safer leaving it where it is, she thought. Especially with Bran occupying the bed, she doubted that anyone was going to find the snake any time soon. And with Pomona pestering her for the snake, not actually keeping it with her might be a good thing. She could always return any time to retrieve it if she needed to.

They made their way to the ante-hall outside the Ballroom and, luckily, found the instrument exactly where Viktor had described. Several minutes later, they stepped out of the front door together, with Milena lugging her cello case and Caitlyn grappling with Nibs in the cat carrier, as well as her overnight bag and the garment bag containing her costume.

"Have you got a car here?" Caitlyn asked.

Milena shook her head regretfully. "No, I came on the orchestra coach. But Mr Mosley told me that there are bus services running from the nearest village—I think it's called Tillyhenge?"

"Yes, I'm headed there. Why don't I give you a lift?" Caitlyn offered.

"Oh, you live in the village?"

Caitlyn nodded. "Yes, with my grandmother, who owns a chocolate shop. It's called *Bewitched by Chocolate*."

"Ah! Yes, I remember now—I saw a little sign next to the buffet last night with that name," said Milena. "Did your grandmother cater for the ball?"

Caitlyn nodded proudly. "All the chocolate treats and desserts for the ball came from her shop, and she was also responsible for designing the chocolate-themed savoury dishes on the menu."

"Oooh, the sweet treats were *delicious*!" said Milena, half closing her eyes in remembered ecstasy. "I don't think I've ever tasted such wonderful chocolates... so rich and creamy... and—oh my God—that caramel fountain! You know, salted caramel is my favourite flavour." She giggled. "Every time the orchestra had a break, I would sneak over to try some more of the caramel fondue. If the ball had gone on all night, I would probably have made myself sick!"

Caitlyn chuckled. "I know what you mean. I didn't actually get a chance to taste anything from the caramel fountain in the end, but I'm hoping there'll be some of the sauce left at the shop. In fact, I think the Widow Mags—that's my grandmother—was planning to make some special treats with the leftover sauce." She smacked her lips. "If you haven't tasted her salted caramel chocolate fudge cake or her chocolate pots with salted caramel toffee, then you haven't lived!"

"They sound amazing," said Milena with a dreamy sigh. "I don't have the time today, but I'm definitely going to return to Tillyhenge so I can come and check out your grandmother's shop!"

***

When they got to Tillyhenge, Caitlyn parked her car, as usual, by the side of the village green and, after pointing Milena to the nearest bus stop, she shouldered her overnight bag, picked up the cat carrier, and started to make her way through the winding cobbled streets. As she walked past the familiar shops of the "village high street", she smiled as a sense of belonging hit her. It was strange to think that a little over six months earlier, she hadn't even known that this tiny English village existed, and now she felt completely at home here.

Then, as she rounded a corner and walked past *Herbal Enchantments*—Aunt Bertha's herbal shop— she was rudely reminded that while she might have embraced local life and quickly settled into her new identity as part of a "witch" family, there were those in the village who did not return the sentiments. A sharp-faced woman was standing outside the herbal shop, talking earnestly to a couple of tourists who had been about to enter. Caitlyn felt a surge of indignation as she overheard what Vera was saying to them:

"...would do well to stay well away from this shop! The owner is a witch, and you have no idea what she puts in her dangerous concoctions. Don't fall for her scams and tricks. You'll regret it!"

The tourists exchanged uneasy looks, then turned reluctantly away from the shop and hurried back towards the village green, whilst Vera watched with a smile of satisfaction.

"What are you doing?" Caitlyn burst out. "You have no right to—"

"I have every right!" retorted Vera. "I'm an honest, upstanding resident of Tillyhenge, and I have a right to protect the reputation of this village, which means preventing our visitors from suffering the evil influences of witchcraft and black magic."

"Aww, come on," groaned Caitlyn in exasperation. "Bertha is a certified herbalist! And herbal remedies have been around for centuries. I'm sure your own mother and grandmother used them. Don't tell me you think that every time you make a cup of peppermint tea, you're dabbling in witchcraft?"

"That's different," said Vera haughtily.

"What's the difference?" demanded Caitlyn. "Peppermint is a herb and you're using it for its powers to aid digestion. That's no different to using other herbs to achieve other effects."

"The difference is that I don't use things like that!" hissed Vera, pointing to something in the shop window.

Caitlyn turned to follow the woman's finger and her eyes widened as she saw what was in the display. Tucked amongst the arrangement of natural goat's milk soap, soy candles, herbal tea sachets, and loofah sponges were several little figures. They looked like home-made dolls, created from various scraps of fabric stitched together, with simple button eyes and embroidered thread for mouths, and basic "stick-man" body shapes. There was something charming and yet at the same time slightly disturbing about their primitive forms.

"If Bertha isn't meddling in witchcraft, then tell me why she has voodoo dolls in her window!" snapped Vera.

"I... they're not..." Caitlyn faltered. She had to

admit that the dolls did resemble the "voodoo dolls" that she had seen in movies. She didn't know how to reply, and she found herself backing away from Vera's accusing gaze. Trying to keep her head high, she turned and hurried into the shop.

Inside, she found her aunt behind the counter, calmly measuring out some dried herbs on some scales. She looked up as Caitlyn rushed in, red-faced and flustered, and said:

"Oh, hello, dear. I hope you didn't mind me leaving you at the Manor last night, but James assured me that you'd be comfortable staying there. Have you just returned?" She gestured to the pile of dried leaves on the scales. "I received a new batch of comfrey leaves this morning, and I'm just about to try a test infusion—"

"Aunt Bertha, have you seen what Vera is doing outside?" Caitlyn interrupted as she deposited her bags and the cat carrier on the floor by the counter.

Her aunt glanced out of the shop window, unconcerned. "Oh... is she still there? I was hoping she'd be gone by now."

"Shouldn't you call the police or something?"

Bertha shook her head. "She'll probably go away much quicker if I just don't react."

"But have you heard the terrible things she's saying about you? I just saw her scare a couple of tourists away! Surely you can't just stand by and let her give you a bad name?"

Bertha looked unperturbed. "Those with open

minds won't be swayed by her prejudice; they'll find a way to return."

"But... but what if Vera remains out there all day, every day?"

Bertha smiled placidly. "I doubt that will happen. She'll tire of it soon enough, especially if I don't react. The fastest way to put out a fire is by starving it, rather than fanning the flames."

Caitlyn looked at her aunt disbelievingly. For the first time, she sympathised with Evie's frustration at her mother's decision to always "turn the other cheek", to never rise to any provocation. Surely, sometimes, you had to stand up to bigots and bullies?

"Well... if you're not going to defend yourself, then maybe you shouldn't give her more fuel to 'fan the flames', as you put it," she said irritably.

"What do you mean?"

Caitlyn pointed to the shop window display. "Those doll-things in the window. They're giving Vera even more ammunition for her hate campaign."

Bertha raised her eyebrows. "The poppets?"

"Is that what they're called? I thought they were voodoo dolls?"

"'Voodoo dolls' are a type of poppet," said Bertha briskly. "There's a lot of misunderstanding about poppet magic. It's true that they can be used in harmful magic, but they're often used to heal as well."

"They look kind of creepy," said Caitlyn

doubtfully.

Bertha chuckled. "That's just because you've been conditioned to think of them that way—probably because of all the 'evil voodoo dolls' you've seen in films and on TV. If you had simply been given one to play with, as a little girl, you wouldn't see it as anything other than a cherished toy. They're not that different, really, from the corn dolls you often see at harvest festivals." Her expression hardened. "And I'm not going to remove them from my window display simply because of some ignorant, narrow-minded villagers. That would be showing them that I would bow to their demands. I know the poppets are not evil and I have nothing to be ashamed of."

"But—"

They were interrupted by the bell chiming at the shop door as someone else entered. Caitlyn turned quickly, hoping to see that the two recent tourists had come back, but, to her surprise, it was Inspector Walsh who stepped into the shop.

"Good morning, Inspector," Bertha greeted him cheerfully. "How can I help you today? Would you like a sage tincture to provide more clarity in your investigation? *Salvia officinalis* has been used for centuries, you know, to boost brain function and cognitive powers. I can also provide it as a herbal tea, if you prefer."

"Thank you, but no. However, you can help my investigation by explaining something to me," Walsh said gravely, coming to join them at the counter.

"When my men searched Daniel Tremaine's room at the Manor, they found *this*..."

He reached into his coat pocket and drew out something in a clear plastic evidence bag. Caitlyn caught her breath as he set it down on the counter for them to see. It contained a poppet doll with pins stuck into its body.

Inspector Walsh fixed Bertha with an intent look. "Can you tell me why this doll was found in the belongings of the murdered man?"

CHAPTER TWENTY

Caitlyn shivered as she stared at the poppet. It was similar to the dolls in Bertha's shop window, except that this one had a shrunken apple for its head. Eyes had been gouged in the surface of the brown, shrivelled fruit, and a mouth slashed beneath them in such a way as to give the disturbing impression that the doll was grimacing in terrible pain. And even more horrible were the long, gleaming pins stuck into the doll's torso with such force that some of them were bent askew.

"Oh my Goddess, that's an apple poppet," said Bertha, leaning forwards eagerly to take a closer look. "Poppets made with dried apples are very rare. Mabon would be one of the few festivals where they're seen, actually. An apple poppet like this would be highly sought after by a museum."

"Apple poppet?" said Inspector Walsh quizzically.

"Well, a poppet is a doll used in sympathetic magic, where a person can be affected by magical actions performed on something that represents them," Bertha explained. "Poppet magic can be very powerful, with the ability to target a person's health, attitudes, behaviour, and actions from a great distance away."

"Hmm," said Inspector Walsh, looking unimpressed.

Caitlyn smiled to herself. She knew that the CID detective was highly sceptical of anything to do with witchcraft and the occult. As far as Walsh was concerned, there was no such thing as magic, and he regarded any talk about paranormal causes of evil as "superstitious nonsense".

He cleared his throat and said: "So this... 'poppet', you call it... it's used to represent a person?"

Bertha nodded. "The word comes from Old English and simply means 'girl' or 'doll'. They can be made of all sorts of things, usually fabric, but also wood, clay, paper, or even wax—the important thing is how they are 'personalised' with something taken from the person they are representing, so that a magical bond can be established." She smiled at Walsh, warming to her subject. "You know, poppet magic has been used since the beginning of time. Archaeologists have found records from ancient Egypt and Mesopotamia showing the use of clay effigies to enhance spells, and when the Romans came to Britain, they brought their *kolossoi*—which are small dolls used for curses—and passed on their beliefs in folk magic."

Inspector Walsh had perked up at the mention of "curses" and now he said: "One of my constables told me this is a 'voodoo doll'. Half the Manor staff were terrified when they saw it."

Bertha compressed her lips. "As I was explaining to Caitlyn just now, Inspector, there are few practices more misunderstood and maligned than the use of poppet magic—probably due to all the bad stereotypes in the popular media. First of all, 'voodoo'—or 'Vodou', rather—is a specific set of spiritual beliefs and practices stemming from Afro-Caribbean culture. It's not necessarily linked to evil and black magic. And yes, while voodoo dolls are a type of poppet, that does not mean that anything shaped like a person *must* be used for malice." She wagged a finger at him. "Magical practice is all about intent! A poppet can be used for good or bad, healing or harm."

"Healing?" said Inspector Walsh sceptically.

"Yes, poppets were very popular, especially in England in olden times, because they were believed to stand in for a distant loved one who might need to be healed. One would stuff the doll with healing herbs, anoint it with a healing oil, and perform healing spells on it, which would then transfer to its human equivalent."

"Hmm... but this poppet, now..." Inspector Walsh

pointed to the evidence bag. "Can you tell if it's good or bad?"

Bertha looked down at the doll, her expression sober. "I'm afraid I can't tell you for certain, Inspector. You really need to ask the person who created it."

"I'm asking *your* opinion," said the detective evenly. "When I questioned the Manor staff about this poppet, they all mentioned you as someone known to be associated with such 'tools of black magic', as one of them said."

Bertha laughed. "Oh, that's probably because I've started stocking some here in the shop and displaying them in my windows, and some local residents aren't happy about that."

"Hmm... yes, so I gathered," murmured Inspector Walsh, flicking his eyes towards the shop window, through which they could still see Vera's figure hovering outside. "Tensions have been running high in the village recently. Do you think stocking poppets is wise?"

"I'm not scared of the other villagers," said Bertha, raising her chin. "And I've decided to stock these poppets because I want to try and educate people and counter all the misinformation out there."

"Well, as part of that education, you can tell me what you think of this one," said Inspector Walsh testily, pushing the evidence bag closer to Bertha.

She hesitated, eyeing the doll's anguished expression and the multitude of pins sticking into its body, then said reluctantly, "It does look as if it was created for harm."

"Do you think that has a bearing on the murder investigation, Inspector?" Caitlyn spoke up.

The detective looked thoughtful. "It might—it could give us a motive, which could lead us to a possible suspect. For example, if someone who believed all this magical mumbo jumbo thought that Tremaine had been trying to... er... hex them, he or she might have decided to 'get in first', so to speak."

"But wait... I thought you already had a suspect in custody," said Caitlyn, frowning. "That journalist Jessica Hyde? Wasn't she found with Tremaine's blood on her hands?"

"It turns out that it wasn't his blood—it was her own," said the inspector. "So it seems that she *was* telling the truth, after all, about hurting herself when she slipped and fell."

"But that doesn't mean that she couldn't have killed him as well," Caitlyn pointed out. "That could have been the reason she was running in the first place: to get away from the scene of the crime."

"It's possible, but not very likely. I've done a re-enactment with my lads and we've timed how long it takes to get from the Portrait Gallery out into the grounds behind the Manor, where Hyde was seen. There just isn't enough time. Which means that, effectively, she has an alibi." He sighed. "We had to release her this morning, as we haven't got enough evidence to keep her in custody. So I'm now turning my attention to the other guests who were at the ball."

"But do you really think someone could have killed Tremaine in a form of 'pre-emptive self-defence'?" asked Caitlyn. "That's an odd motive for murder, don't you think?"

"No more odd than the other things about this case," grumbled Inspector Walsh.

"What do you mean?"

The detective was silent for a moment, as if deciding whether to say more, then he gave an irritable sigh and said, "Well, this isn't supposed to be public knowledge, but with the Manor staff nosing around me and my men all the time, and the local grapevine being what it is, it'll probably be leaked to the village soon anyway. The murder weapon—that forked rod—"

"The stang," Caitlyn supplied.

"Another tool used in magical practice that's often misunderstood," added Bertha with a disapproving sniff.

"Yes, well, in this case, I don't think you can argue that it *wasn't* used for harm," said Inspector Walsh, glowering at her. "Now, normally, having a clear murder weapon is a cause for celebration, especially because, in this case, we even know where it came from. I understand that this stang was already in the Portrait Gallery—isn't that right?" He glanced at Caitlyn.

She nodded. "I definitely saw it there a couple of

days before the ball. It's part of James's father's occult collection."

"So the logical assumption would be that the murderer came upon Tremaine in the Gallery, grabbed whatever was to hand—in this case, the stang—and stabbed him with it," said Inspector Walsh.

"That sounds like a pretty straightforward killing, compared to some of the other murders that have occurred in Tillyhenge recently," said Caitlyn, looking at the inspector in puzzlement. "What's 'odd' about it?"

"What's 'odd' is that according to the forensics team, the angle of the wound and the damage in the surrounding tissues suggest that the stang was driven into Tremaine's body with a force that could only have come from flying at great speed through the air. Someone standing next to him and stabbing him with it could not have produced the same effect."

"Well... couldn't the murderer have thrown it from across the room? Like a spear?" asked Caitlyn.

Inspector Walsh shook his head. "Not according to my forensics experts. They say that it would have required a superhuman effort to throw the stang at such speed and with such accuracy as to impale Tremaine in that way."

"But then... if a person couldn't have thrown it by hand, how else could the stang have killed Tremaine?" asked Caitlyn.

"By magic," said Bertha suddenly. "A powerful

spell could animate an object and cause it to fly across the room, to stab or strike an enemy."

Inspector Walsh made a noise of irritation. "Just because there's some mystery attached to the method of murder doesn't automatically mean that it has to involve witchcraft and magic," he growled. "I'm sure there's a perfectly logical explanation. It will just take time to find it."

"What about CCTV?" asked Caitlyn suddenly. "I remember seeing security cameras mounted in some rooms of the Manor. Don't you have any footage of the Portrait Gallery on the night of the ball?"

The inspector shook his head regretfully. "As you'd expect, most of the security cameras are in the formal rooms—the ones that are open to the public tours. There are very few cameras in the private wings of the Manor. There *is* one in the corridor outside the Portrait Gallery, but it's not trained directly on the door of the Gallery."

"So you mean someone could slip into the Gallery without being caught on camera?"

"Yes. Nevertheless, I do have one of my officers going through all the footage. It's a slow, tedious process though, and so far, there are no obvious leads." Inspector Walsh lifted the evidence bag with the poppet doll and looked at it grimly. "This is the best we've got."

CHAPTER TWENTY-ONE

As Caitlyn left *Herbal Enchantments*, she was pleased to see that Vera seemed to have tired of her vigilantism at last and had disappeared. Caitlyn glanced warily around as she started down the winding cobbled lane leading away from her aunt's herbal shop, but she didn't see the older woman. As she rounded a corner, however, she was surprised to bump into another familiar figure: Jessica Hyde. The journalist had just finished chatting with a couple of villagers and was busily scribbling on a notepad, which was one reason she had walked straight into Caitlyn.

"Oh! Excuse me—" Jessica broke off and narrowed her eyes. "Hey, haven't we met? You're the girl who came out with Lord Fitzroy to see the protesting villagers at the Mabon Ball, aren't you?"

"Yes, that's right," said Caitlyn, surprised that the woman remembered or had even noticed her the night before. It had been a riotous scene and she had played no active part in the encounter.

As if reading her mind, Jessica grinned and said: "It's my sharp journalist eyes—I'm always on the lookout for a story."

"Is that why you're here in the village?" asked Caitlyn. "I heard that you were only released by the police this morning. I'd have thought that you'd want to go straight home to rest and recover from such an ordeal."

Jessica waved a dismissive hand. "Oh, I've been arrested by the police loads of times. That's not going to stop me missing the chance of a great scoop." Her eyes gleamed. "When the news gets out about what happened last night, there's going to be a media frenzy, and every news channel and tabloid paper is going to descend on Tillyhenge. Well, I'm not going to lose my advantage of being on the ground first! And this is just the kind of story that will grip everyone in the country..." She held up her fingers, ticking each one off as she continued: "A glamorous masquerade ball given by a rich, handsome aristocrat; a pagan festival celebrating light and darkness; a man killed by a mysterious flying weapon which people are saying was cursed; angry residents terrified of a local witch; rumours of black magic and witchcraft running rife in the village—"

"That's rubbish! There's no black magic in the

village," said Caitlyn hotly.

"Ahh... why don't you tell me your side of the story then?" said Jessica, whipping out a voice recorder from her handbag. She smirked at Caitlyn. "By the way, I heard that you're the young Lord Fitzroy's girlfriend? Is that true?"

Caitlyn stiffened. From her past life with her celebrity adoptive mother, she knew what the media could be like, and how persistent and nosy they could be. Suddenly, she wished that she hadn't stopped to talk to Jessica Hyde.

"I... I don't really have anything to say," she said, trying to turn away.

"Really? Don't you want the chance to set the record straight? I heard that this poor old woman they're accusing of being a witch—and maybe even being involved in the murder—is your grandmother." Jessica looked at her slyly. "If that were me, I'd want the chance to defend her."

Caitlyn felt a rush of irritation. She knew that the journalist was just provoking her and she shouldn't rise to the bait, but she had to bite back the indignant words that sprang to her lips. Then she had an idea.

"All right," she said. "I'll give you my account—but first I want to hear what you know about Daniel Tremaine."

Jessica's expression became guarded. "What do you mean?"

"Well, you obviously have a history with him. In

fact, based on the way you attacked him when you saw him last night, you *should* be the prime suspect."

"The police have already cleared me. I have an alibi," spat Jessica.

"Yes, but that doesn't change the fact that you had a lot of motive. I just want to know why you hated Tremaine so much." Caitlyn eyed the other woman thoughtfully. "You accused him of following you; you said he threatened your daughter... what was that all about?"

For a moment, she thought Jessica wasn't going to answer, then the woman said: "I was working on a special story—an exposé about the inner workings of the British government. Well, somehow Daniel Tremaine got wind of my investigation and he began to harass me. It was obvious that he—or his bosses, rather—were afraid of what I might dig up and wanted to shut me up."

"What do you mean 'his bosses'?"

Jessica shot Caitlyn a sideways look. "Tremaine worked for a secret branch of the British government which deals in threats of a paranormal nature. You know, witches and vampires and the forces of Dark Magic." She paused, looking defiantly at Caitlyn, as if expecting her to laugh. When she got no reaction, she relaxed and continued, "It was the scoop of a lifetime. It had taken me months of digging, wading through conspiracy theories and underground rumours to get the little information I managed to find, so the last thing I wanted was to give it all up.

In fact, I wouldn't normally be intimidated but... well, Tremaine found out that I have a daughter." She swallowed. "I'm a single mum and Mandy is all I have in the world. The way Tremaine was talking... well, he scared me." Her eyes smouldered with resentment. "So I had to agree to drop the investigation, but in return, I told him I never wanted to see him following me or coming near Mandy again."

"That's why you flipped when you saw him at the ball last night," Caitlyn realised.

"Yeah. I thought that he was up to his old tricks again, so I totally lost it. I'd warned him, you know. I'd told him that if he kept on threatening me, I'd make sure that the whole world knew about his secret organisation and the filthy work he does for them."

"What filthy work? What did he do for them?"

Jessica gave a grim smile. "Well, let's just say that Tremaine enjoyed inflicting pain on others. In fact, he probably got off on it."

Caitlyn frowned. "You mean he was a sadist?"

"Hah! Yeah, I suppose you could call him that. A professional sadist. He was skilled at the methods used to produce the most intense agony and suffering, and this was highly valued in his job." Jessica leaned forwards and said with meaning: "Pain is one of the greatest motivators when people are reluctant to give up information."

Caitlyn drew a sharp breath. "You're talking about

torture, aren't you? Are you saying that Tremaine tortured people for the government?"

"Well, somebody has to do it." Jessica gave a disdainful laugh. "Don't look so shocked. It's well known that governments have covert operatives who deal in this sort of thing. Oh, they wrap it up in euphemisms, of course—'enhanced interrogation techniques' and 'severe tactics' and all that—but it all amounts to the same thing in the end. Torture to extract information, or as a form of intimidation to influence behaviour."

"I don't believe it. The British government would never—"

Jessica snorted. "Do you really think our government is more saintly than others? The British Empire has a long history of blood on its hands; the violence and cruelty that people have suffered, especially in the colonies, is well documented."

"Yes, but that's history," protested Caitlyn. "You're talking about hundreds of years ago. In today's world—"

"You think things have changed? No, they've just got better at hiding it or smoothing things over when it's discovered. Even as recently as a decade ago, there was a well-known case of MI5 colluding in the questioning and torture of a convicted British terrorist in Pakistan. And that's not the first time that's happened." She held up her hands as Caitlyn started to protest again. "Okay, I'm not saying that it's officially sanctioned or anything. In fact, the top authorities probably have no knowledge of what goes on. Most of the official departments in the government probably aren't even aware of the existence of this 'secret society' that Daniel Tremaine belonged to. After all, the US has 'black ops divisions'... so why not the same in Britain?"

"Do you think Tremaine's murder is linked to his work for this secret branch of the government?" asked Caitlyn.

Jessica shrugged. "Why not? I'm sure there are many who have suffered at his hands, who would have been very happy to see him dead."

CHAPTER TWENTY-TWO

Caitlyn arrived back at *Bewitched by Chocolate* to find the Widow Mags standing impatiently behind the glass counter displaying her chocolate truffles, waiting for a young couple to make their selections.

"...mm... the espresso truffle cup with mocha ganache looks good... I think we'll get that—oh no, wait! What's that one?" The young woman leaned over, peering through the glass. "Dark chocolate with Madagascar vanilla... ooh, that sounds delicious... and this one here, with the chocolate ganache and chopped roasted hazelnuts, sounds good too—"

"I think we should get the crunchy English toffee dipped in milk chocolate instead," argued her partner. "Or that one with the peanut butter centre—"

"No, no, dark chocolate is much nicer—"

"What about white chocolate, babe? Look, there's one with zesty lemon ganache—"

"Oh, for goodness' sake... are you going to choose something or not?" snapped the Widow Mags, glowering at them. "I haven't got all day."

Caitlyn groaned inwardly. Her grandmother really needed to work on her customer service skills! It was hard enough getting tourists to find the chocolate shop, tucked away at the back of the village, and ignore any negative gossip put about by hostile villagers like Vera Bottom—the last thing she needed was to scare customers off once they finally came into the shop!

And it didn't help that with her fierce dark eyes and large hooked nose, not to mention her fine grey hair escaping in wild tendrils around her face, the Widow Mags looked exactly like the "old witch" often seen in children's stories and popular media. Her hunched form (due to osteoporosis) and her gnarled hands (due to bad arthritis) only added to the stereotype, and her grumpy, uncompromising manner didn't help to reassure strangers either. Now, Caitlyn could see the young couple eyeing her grandmother warily as they began to back away from the counter. Hastily, she hurried over to join them.

"Would you like me to help, Grandma, and then you can get on with whatever you were making?" she suggested gently.

For a moment, she thought that the Widow Mags was going to refuse. The old witch was notoriously proud and independent, and more likely to bristle at an offer of help than accept it graciously. But to her relief, her grandmother handed her the tongs and—with a loud "Humph!"—disappeared through the door behind the counter, which led to the back of the cottage.

Caitlyn turned back to the couple and gave them a bright smile. "Hello there! Can I help you with any of your choices?"

"Well... there are so many flavours, we weren't really sure which to choose," said the girl, coming timidly towards the counter again.

"I'll tell you what," said Caitlyn impulsively. "Would you like to have a taste of some of the truffles? That might make it easier for you to choose."

The girl's eyes lit up and her partner came forwards eagerly as well. "Ooh, can we?"

Ten minutes later, the couple left the shop carrying boxes of chocolate truffles and bonbons, as well as bags filled with chocolate-coated nougat, cocoa-dusted chocolate beans, and jars of rich chocolate sauce. Caitlyn stood at the door and watched them walk away, a sense of achievement in her chest and a smile of satisfaction on her lips. It had been one of the biggest sales they'd had in days and would bring in some much-needed income for her grandmother.

The rest of the day passed uneventfully, although, in between serving customers, Caitlyn found her mind constantly returning to the mystery of Daniel

Tremaine's murder. She also found herself worrying about Pomona and her recent strange behaviour. She wondered if she should confide in the Widow Mags but, again, something—some sense of loyalty to her cousin—held her back.

Pomona had a perfectly good explanation for why she was sleeping in the Library, she reminded herself. *I even remember her complaining that antihistamines make her drowsy when we were getting ready for the ball, and I suggested that she take some for her allergy. There's no real reason to suspect that she's involved in the murder—other than that rubber snake I found. But there* must *be a logical explanation for that…*

Caitlyn cheered up slightly when she received a text message from her cousin late that afternoon. It seemed that while Pomona couldn't leave the local area just yet, the police *had* said that she was allowed to wander as far as Tillyhenge.

Am bored. What r u doing?

Looking after the choc shop. Want to come over? Caitlyn texted back.

OK. C u later.

Caitlyn smiled to herself. It would be nice to spend some time alone with Pomona. They hadn't had much chance to do that recently, and a "girlie evening" might encourage her cousin to open up, maybe even acknowledge the change in her attitude and—

Her phone beeped again. There was another

message from Pomona:

U got that snake from my wig?

Caitlyn frowned and texted back. *It's somewhere safe.*

Cool. Must get it from u later.

Caitlyn stared down at her phone, no longer smiling. Was that the real reason for Pomona wanting to come and see her? Not because she really wanted to spend quality time together, but because she wanted to retrieve something that could be incriminating evidence in a murder investigation?

Caitlyn's troubled thoughts plagued her for the rest of the afternoon, and she was relieved when she could finally close the chocolate shop and retire to the rear of the cottage. She expected to spend a quiet evening with the Widow Mags, waiting for Pomona to join them, but, to her surprise, it was Bertha who arrived not long afterwards.

"Mother, I've managed to get you an appointment at that new immersion therapy clinic in town," she said jubilantly. "They've had a last-minute cancellation for one of their late sessions tonight. If we leave straight away, we can easily make it."

"Immersion therapy? I'm not doing that nonsense," declared the Widow Mags, jutting her bottom lip out.

"Oh, come on, Mother—it could be really good for you," cajoled Bertha. "This clinic specialises in novel treatments for arthritis. I've heard that they've had very good success with Dead Sea salts and warm water immersion."

"I don't understand—if you're a witch, why do you still get things like arthritis?" Caitlyn spoke up. "I mean, can't you just make it go away with a spell or something?"

The Widow Mags gave her an impatient look. "I cannot just 'magic' my arthritis away. Ageing is one of the most powerful forces in the world and not easily combated."

"But... but surely there are ways to use magic to stay youthful or live longer?" asked Caitlyn in surprise. "Or is that just a myth?"

"No, it is true. You *can* use magic to arrest ageing, to even turn back time... but you would have to resort to Dark Magic to do so. For me, that is too high a price to pay," said the Widow Mags heavily. She looked down at her knotted and twisted fingers, then gave an irritable sigh and said to Bertha, "Fine. I'll try this immersion nonsense. But just the once."

"Great! I'll get your handbag, Mother," said Bertha briskly, starting to bustle around. "Is there anything in particular you need? Make sure you put on an extra cardigan—it's chilly tonight—and Caitlyn, can you fetch her big coat—"

"Don't fuss! I'm perfectly capable of getting ready myself," growled the Widow Mags. She turned to Caitlyn. "Don't forget to wrap up the unused chocolate bars, then place them back in those airtight boxes, and into a dark corner of the pantry—not in the fridge, mind! The cocoa butter can stay outside as well. Just make sure you seal the jar really well... You can put the salted caramel sauce in a jar in the fridge, though," she added over her shoulder as Bertha wrapped a thick scarf around her neck, then hustled her out of the cottage.

Left alone, Caitlyn began to follow her grandmother's instructions, but she found it hard to do anything with Nibs scampering about her ankles. The little kitten had been sleeping for most of the afternoon, curled up in his basket next to the ancient Aga in the kitchen, and now he was full of beans and keen to play. He chased and pounced on Caitlyn's feet, nearly causing her to trip several times, and clambered all over the kitchen furniture, peering into bowls and containers, and playfully batting anything he could reach with his paws.

"Nibs! Stop that!" said Caitlyn, huffing in exasperation as she removed the kitten once more from a shelf in the pantry, where he was busily trying to roll a couple of onions off the ledge.

As she carried him back out, she spied the large kitchen scales on the counter and was struck by an idea. Nibs's lack of growth had been puzzling her lately. The kitten was still the same size as when she and James had rescued him several months earlier— it was almost as if he was frozen in time, stuck as an eight-week-old baby cat. The local vet had examined him and done several tests, but had been unable to come up with any explanation. Given that Nibs was bright and healthy, he had advised her to stop worrying and just accept that perhaps the kitten was naturally stunted.

But Caitlyn wasn't ready to give up on the mystery. In fact, she had wondered if there might be a "magical cause" for Nibs's condition, and she had been intending to find a "witch vet"—although she had been too busy as yet to do much searching.

It would probably help if I start keeping a record of Nibs's weight and show how it doesn't change at all, she thought, eyeing the scales. Carrying the squirming kitten, she went over to the scales and placed Nibs carefully in the centre of the metal tray.

"*Mew!*" he cried, immediately trying to climb off.

"No, no... you have to stay there... just for a second," Caitlyn pleaded, pushing the kitten gently back onto the tray while, at the same time, trying to read the wildly swinging hands on the dial.

"*Meeew!*" said Nibs defiantly, wriggling out of her grasp and launching himself off the scales. He tumbled over the side of the counter and landed on the floor, where he shook himself and promptly scampered away.

"Nibs!" cried Caitlyn in an infuriated voice.

She was just about to chase the kitten when a loud crash, followed by the sound of shattering glass, made her freeze in surprise. It had come from the front of the cottage. Caitlyn hurried out and, when she stepped into the shop area, she looked quickly around the darkened interior.

Her heart lurched as her gaze swept across the

front of the shop. Something had been thrown through the display window, shattering the glass and puncturing a jagged hole in the middle of the pane. Caitlyn went over and bent to retrieve the object on the floor next to the broken window. It was a large stone.

Teenage boys playing a prank?

Annoyed, Caitlyn heaved the front door open and marched outside. Then her steps faltered and the angry scolding she'd been about to give died on her lips as she found herself facing an angry mob of villagers. The hairs on the back of her neck prickled as she saw the ugly looks on the faces around her. Several seemed to be the same members of the group who had been protesting at the ball the night before. They were not holding placards now, but Caitlyn felt her stomach turn over when she saw what they were holding instead: crowbars, stones, hammers, and wooden sticks... *Weapons.*

She could feel the tension in the air, the sense of anticipation. They were waiting, watching to see how she would react. Any slight provocation could set them off. *I have to keep things calm*, she told herself frantically. *I mustn't show fear.* She swallowed and tried to stand taller, but before she could speak, a man stepped out of the group and spat at her.

"Witch! Demon hussy!"

Caitlyn flinched and took an involuntary step back. Her stomach felt queasy, but she was pleased that her voice sounded calm and strong when she spoke:

"What do you want?"

"We want you to get out of this village!" hissed a familiar voice. Vera Bottom stepped out from the crowd. "There's no place for black magic in Tillyhenge!"

"Yeah, we're not goin' to just sit around waitin' while we're murdered in our beds!" said the man.

"*What?*" Caitlyn looked at them in bewilderment. "What on earth are you talking about?"

"We're talking 'bout that man up at the Manor," said another woman, stepping forwards. "He was murdered by witchcraft... and we don't want to be next."

CHAPTER TWENTY-THREE

Caitlyn frowned at the villagers in front of her. "Daniel Tremaine wasn't murdered by witchcra—"

"Oh yes, he was," said Vera. "Don't you try to cover it up! I met Dot Gaskin in the post office shop, who heard it from Hannah Lowes, who got it from Susan Gorman, whose nephew works at the police station, and she said that the murder weapon was an evil witch's tool; a kind of pitchfork with the devil's horns—"

"It's not the devil's horns!" said Caitlyn in exasperation. "It's called a 'stang' and it's just a kind of rod or staff, with two prongs at the top—which are actually supposed to represent deer antlers, I think. Anyway, it's just a symbolic thing, used for rituals, like... like candles, for example."

"Oh yeah? If it's only symbolic, then why is that

man up at the Manor dead?" demanded a woman in the crowd.

"Yeah!" said another one, nodding vehemently. "I heard he was impaled by this... this stang thing!"

"Well, you can get impaled by anything, can't you?" Caitlyn pointed out.

"Not like this," said Vera, her expression both scared and jubilant. "I know what the police report said—you can't hide it from us. It said that the weapon went into him with such force that it couldn't have been done by any man." She lowered her voice dramatically. "Only the supernatural energy summoned by an evil spell could have thrown the weapon that way."

Caitlyn shook her head impatiently. "The police report never said that! It just said that there was some mystery connected with how the stang could have been used to kill Tremaine, but Inspector Walsh himself said that they would probably have a clearer picture once they got more information—"

"We don't need more information!" snarled the first man. "Only an idiot wouldn't see the answer starin' them in the face. That bloke was at a *Mabon* ball—a ball celebratin' a bloody *witches'* festival! And then he gets killed by this weapon flyin' out o' nowhere, when there's no one else around... What's that, if it's not black magic and witchcraft?"

"We don't *know* if there was no one else around," said Caitlyn, trying to remain calm. "That's what the police investigation is for—so they can find the murderer. Someone probably followed Daniel Tremaine up there and attacked him when he was unprepared."

Vera narrowed her eyes. "Yes, and that someone was probably the Widow Mags—"

"The Widow Mags was in the Manor kitchen the whole time, working with the caterers. There are countless people who can swear she was never alone the entire evening," said Caitlyn sharply.

"So what? She's a witch, ain't she?" said one of the other women nastily. "That means she could've easily put a spell or somethin' over the others and made 'em think that she was there—only she was actually off flyin' on her broom or wha'ever—"

"Oh, for heaven's sake—!" Caitlyn hung on to her temper with an effort. She took a deep breath and let it out again. *Keep calm*, she reminded herself. *Don't let them get to you.* Forcing her voice to remain neutral, she said: "Look, if you have any concerns about the investigation or information about potential suspects, then you need to speak to the police, not me. I'm sure Inspector Walsh would be very happy to listen to you."

"No, our beef is with you!" said the first man, stepping forwards and jabbing a finger at Caitlyn's chest. "You and the Widow Mags."

"We had nothing to do with the murder up at the Manor," said Caitlyn firmly.

"Doesn't matter—it's not just about this murder," snapped Vera. "The Widow Mags needs to get out!

She has no place in this village."

"The Widow Mags has as much right to live here as any of you," Caitlyn shot back.

"No, she doesn't!" cried another woman. "No one has the right to peddle witchcraft."

"Oh, for the love of..." Caitlyn gritted her teeth, resisting the urge to roll her eyes. "She's not peddling witchcraft—she's just selling chocolates!" She could never understand why the villagers were so scared of her grandmother for doing something as innocuous as selling delicious treats.

"But what's in those chocolates? How does she make them?" demanded a man in the crowd.

"Yeah!" said another woman aggressively. "How do you explain how they taste so good?"

"Because she's a skilled chocolatier!" said Caitlyn in exasperation. "Some of you are great at woodwork, right? And others are great at weaving baskets or cheese-making or knitting or whatever... Well, the Widow Mags is fantastic at making chocolates. It's no different to any other skill."

"It *is* different," a woman insisted. "I've never tasted any other chocolates like hers. It's... it's not natural, how good they taste."

"An' the way they make you feel," chimed in another woman, her face screwing up in a mixture of pleasure and disgust at the memory. "I 'ad one of 'er chocolate truffles once; it melted on my tongue an' the taste... it made me feel so... so..."

"They're bewitched," stated Vera. "That's the only

explanation. Nothing 'normal' should taste that good."

"Honestly, that's the dumbest thing I've ever heard!" cried Caitlyn, her frustration starting to get the better of her. "You're accusing someone of witchcraft just because they make the most delicious chocolates you've ever tasted? I mean... *come on*! Have you heard yourselves? Do you realise how ridiculous you sound?" she demanded, looking at the hostile faces surrounding her.

"You're just tryin' to cover up for her," said one of the men, and several others muttered and nodded their heads. "There's prob'ly all sorts o' potions an' hexes that go in them chocolates an' other stuff the old witch makes in her shop."

Caitlyn groaned with impatience. "Oh, rubbish! There's no evil potion or hexing spells or whatever! All the Widow Mags uses are the highest quality cacao beans combined with the freshest cream, the richest cocoa butter, the purest sugar... You can come in and see for yourself, if you like!" she added recklessly. "We have nothing to hide."

"Fine, we will!" the man replied.

He shoved Caitlyn aside, causing her to stumble and nearly fall, as he marched past her and into the shop. Before she could recover, the rest of the crowd had followed him in, brandishing their weapons, their voices raised in excitement.

Caitlyn felt a sudden panic. What had she done? She should have been locking the shop door firmly against them, not inviting them in! She hurried into the shop and tried to push through the crowd. She managed to wriggle through to the glass counter displaying all the chocolate bonbons and truffles, and stood in front of it, her arms flung out defensively as she turned to face the villagers.

"Look! There's a cauldron!" someone yelled, pointing to the small black cast-iron pot sitting in the alcove behind the counter.

Caitlyn glanced quickly behind her and breathed a silent sigh of relief that the ladle in the cauldron was lying immobile. The long-handled spoon was one of the few things in the shop which *was* sometimes bewitched—although it did nothing more sinister than continuously stir the hot chocolate that normally simmered in the cauldron. It was just a magical version of the mod cons found in many kitchens, but she knew that the villagers wouldn't see it like that.

"It's just got hot chocolate in it," said Caitlyn quickly. She reached behind her and ladled a generous spoonful of the rich chocolate drink into a mug, then offered it to the man nearest to her. "Here, you can see for yourself."

The man reeled back from her. "Don't you dare try to poison me, you witch!" he shouted, taking a swing at her hand.

Caitlyn gasped as the mug was knocked out of her grip and smashed on the floor, spilling hot chocolate everywhere. The villagers who had been standing nearby screamed and jerked away, hopping on one foot, as if trying to avoid stepping on acid. The fright seemed to trigger a wave of hysteria in the rest of the mob, who began kicking and smashing anything they could reach.

"No! Wait—" cried Caitlyn, watching them in horror. "What are you doing?"

She lunged at a couple of men who had picked up a beautiful chocolate sculpture the Widow Mags had created the week before. She tried to wrestle it out of their hands, but she was no match for them. Instead, she could only watch helplessly as they flung the sculpture on the floor and stomped on it, smashing the intricately created chocolate statue into several pieces. Then they turned their attention to the shelves filled with jars of chocolate sauce and hazelnut butters, nestled next to little bags filled with chocolate-covered pretzels, espresso beans, marzipans, and dipped caramels. For a heart-stopping moment, Caitlyn thought they were going to pull down the whole wall of shelves, then they were distracted by a shout across the room.

"Look! This goes to the kitchen!" a man shouted gleefully, standing by the door behind the counter and holding it open.

"That's where she cooks up her spells!" cried Vera shrilly.

"It's where she hides all her poisons!" another woman shouted.

"We've got to destroy it!"

"Aye! Destroy it all!"

There was a cheer, and then the crowd surged through the doorway, into the back of the cottage.

"No! Stop!" Caitlyn gasped, rushing after them.

She arrived in the kitchen just in time to see several villagers peering nervously into the pantry while others rummaged through the items piled on the big wooden table in the centre of the room. Caitlyn felt a flash of satisfaction. *Well, if they've been hoping to find 'eyes of newt' or 'wings of bat' or whatever other stupid cliché, they're going to be disappointed*, she thought smugly, eyeing the table. There was nothing there other than the chocolate-making ingredients that she hadn't had time to tidy up yet: slabs of dark couverture chocolate, bags of sugar and cocoa powder, a large jug of fresh cream, a tin of unrefined cocoa butter, and a handful of chocolate buttons scattered across the wooden surface.

Then her moment of glee turned into dismay as she saw a couple of men reach for the triple-tiered chocolate cake sitting on a stand at the end of the table. The Widow Mags had just completed it that afternoon, and it was an amazing creation of rich Belgian-chocolate sponge layers, frosted with dark-chocolate ganache and Swiss-meringue buttercream.

"Don't touch that!" she cried. "That's a—"

CRASH!

Caitlyn let out a wail of horror as the men shoved the cake viciously off the table. "What have you done?" she cried furiously, staring at the mess of chocolate sponge and buttercream on the floor. "That was a special client order, and it took *hours* to make!" She looked around for her phone. "This has gone too far. I'm calling the police. I'm—"

She broke off with a gasp of outrage as one of the men suddenly grabbed her and pinned her arms behind her back. "Let me go! *Let me go!*"

She squirmed and struggled to get free, but her captor was much stronger. He jeered and laughed, and she cringed back as his friend leaned over her, raising a threatening hand. Then a new voice broke into the din—a voice with a distinctly American accent.

"What the hell—? Hey! Let her go! GET YOUR HANDS OFF HER!"

Caitlyn gasped with relief as she craned her neck and saw the blonde girl standing in the kitchen doorway. *Pomona!* She had completely forgotten that her cousin had said she'd be coming over. The men relaxed their hold slightly—whether in surprise or acquiescence—and she took the chance to wriggle out of their grasp and stumble across the room towards Pomona. Her cousin stood with her hands on her hips, surveying the damage in the room, a terrible scowl on her face.

A couple of villagers shifted uncertainly, but Vera waved a disdainful hand. "It's just that American bimbo who runs around with the witch girl," she sneered.

"What did you call me?" said Pomona.

"I said you're a bimbo. A floozy," said Vera, squaring up to the American girl. "I'm not scared of you."

Pomona narrowed her eyes. "I'm gonna give you one chance to get out of here while you still can."

"Or you'll what?" jeered one of the villagers, thrusting his face at her. It was the man who had grabbed Caitlyn earlier. "You think we're scared o' the likes of you? You're not in Hollywood now, darlin'. You can't throw your money 'round here and think you're goin' to get us all suckin' up to you."

Pomona said nothing, but Caitlyn shivered suddenly at the look on her cousin's face. Pomona's normally cornflower-blue eyes had darkened until they were almost like midnight, and her mouth was set and hard. One hand went to the choker around her neck and her fingers caressed the glittering black diamond nestled against her throat as she began to slowly scan the room, pinning each villager with her cold gaze.

Caitlyn licked her lips nervously and reached out to catch Pomona's sleeve. "Pomie? Just ignore them," she said in an undertone. "They're just looking for a fight. It's not worth it. You can't win in a situation like this."

"Oh no?" Pomona smiled coldly. "Just watch me."

CHAPTER TWENTY-FOUR

Pomona swung back to face the man. "So you think you can just, like, come in here and trash the place, huh? You think just because you're a big guy, you can pick on women and assault them? Well, it's time someone taught *you* a lesson."

He gave a sneering laugh. "Yeah, and you goin' to be the one to do it, darlin'?"

Pomona didn't answer. Her eyes roved over the room and lit on the smashed remains of the chocolate cake that had been thrown off the table. She smirked. "Oh yeah... I'm gonna make sure you clean this place up and I know the perfect way to do it."

Then she turned and fixed him with an intent stare. For a moment, nothing happened, then suddenly the man twitched and began moving jerkily, like a puppet on a string.

"Eddie? Eddie, what's goin' on, mate?" cried the man next to him.

Eddie's teeth were clenched, as if his jaw had locked in place, and beads of sweat appeared on his forehead as he began staggering towards the wooden table. He moved with jerks and spasms, as if he was resisting some kind of force while he made one painful step after the other. Caitlyn caught her breath as she was reminded suddenly of the ants that had been forced up the side of the *bain marie*...

She glanced at Pomona. "Pomie, what are you doing...?" she whispered.

Then her attention was yanked back to Eddie, who'd let out an anguished cry as he suddenly found himself kneeling next to the remains of the chocolate cake. As everyone watched dumbfounded, he bent down and put his face into the mess of chocolate sponge and buttercream, eating it off the floor like an animal.

"Eddie? What're you doin'?" cried his friend, staring in bewilderment.

"He's... he's been bewitched!" cried Vera, her eyes round with horror.

The next moment, she gave a shriek as she suddenly found herself being propelled towards the chocolate cake mess as well.

"No! No! I'm not touching that!" she gasped, even as she found herself being forced to reach down and grab a chunk of chocolate sponge from the floor. Her eyes bulged and she reeled back in disgust, but she couldn't escape her own hands as the piece of cake was suddenly crammed into her mouth. "Aaagghh! Nooo! I can't... I can't... it's vile... it's witch's food!" she blubbered while she continued to scoop cake up from the floor and shovel it into her mouth.

Pomona burst out laughing, pointing at Vera's face, which was liberally smeared with chocolate ganache now. Then she turned and swept her gaze over the other villagers. One by one, they, too, started moving spasmodically towards the mess on the floor and, despite their protests, began force-feeding themselves the chocolate cake. The more horrified and repulsed they were, the more hungrily they seemed to grab the very thing they feared.

Pomona was laughing and whooping with delight as she hovered around them. Caitlyn bit her lip as she stared at the villagers. For a brief moment, she had to admit that she felt a guilty pleasure at seeing Eddie, Vera, and the others get their just desserts— literally!—but the feeling had quickly turned to shame and horror as she continued watching them.

"Pomie... no, stop... this is wrong..." she said, turning urgently towards her cousin. "You have to stop—"

"Why?" demanded Pomona. "Don't you think they deserve to be punished?"

"Well, yes... but not like this!" Caitlyn threw an agonised look at the villagers again. "This is cruel... it's torture—"

"Torture? I'm just making them binge-eat chocolate! What kind of torture is that?" scoffed Pomona.

Caitlyn turned back to the group huddled on the ground. Some of them were being forced to lick buttercream off the bare floor now, sobbing and gagging as they were doing it, and her heart clenched in pity. She had to do something—she couldn't let this continue!

Pomona isn't the only one who can use magic, she reminded herself. *I'm a witch, aren't I? I have powers far greater than hers, if only I can tap into them!* But even as she had the thought, she felt a flash of doubt. So far, all her training had focused mostly on manipulating chocolate and other small spells. She had never attempted a larger feat of magic or tried to match her powers against another. Could she do it?

Besides, what do I actually do? she wondered frantically. *What spell do I use? What incantations?* She felt a wave of panic and despair. How could she stop Pomona when she had no idea which spell she needed to direct the magical ability she had?

Then a memory of the Widow Mags's voice echoed in her mind: "...*magic is simply the ability to cause change by force of will... Spells are useful, yes— especially for novice witches who need a verbal guide to help them focus—but the power lies not in the words themselves, but in the force of the will behind them...*"

Caitlyn took a deep breath, then fixed her eyes on the villagers again, and this time she focused her mind and reached out towards the group. Almost instantly, she encountered a resistance—an invisible force that nevertheless stung like barbed wire and lashed at the villagers whenever they tried to break free. Caitlyn tried to push against it, but gasped and reeled back herself as she felt the sting of pain in her mind.

Pomona jerked around to glare at her. "What are you doing?" she demanded. "Don't mess with me! You're spoiling all the fun!"

"This isn't just 'fun' anymore, Pomona," Caitlyn shot back. "You've got to stop."

Then, before her cousin could reply, she gathered her will and projected it towards the group of villagers. She had never done this before, but something—some instinct—told her what to do. In her mind's eye, she recalled the many times she had helped the Widow Mags create her chocolate truffles, the way she had used magic to manipulate the smooth, creamy chocolate so that it poured over and enrobed the ganache centres, covering them completely. Now, she gritted her teeth and gathered all the empathy and compassion she had in her; then she imagined it pouring over the villagers—just like the thick, creamy chocolate—covering them and protecting them from the cruel stings of the invisible force that was flaying them.

Almost instantly, the group stopped eating and sagged to the floor. It was as if a puppeteer's strings had been cut. They slumped down, panting and exhausted, their faces still smeared with chocolate, but their eyes filled with relief.

Pomona cursed under her breath and turned furiously towards Caitlyn, but before she could say anything, there came a snarl from across the room. Both girls looked up to see Eddie scrambling off the floor, his face ugly with hatred. He looked wildly around for a moment, then grabbed the large kitchen knife on the counter next to him and came towards them. He raised his arm and lunged at Pomona, as if to stab her, and she dodged out of the way just in time.

"What the hell—? Fine! You wanna play dirty? I'll show you what I'm really capable of!" she snapped.

She flicked a finger, and suddenly the knife was yanked out of Eddie's hands. It rose up in the air and hovered in front of his astonished face, then spun around so that the sharp end was now directed at him.

"N-no... no..." he stammered, stumbling backwards, his eyes widening with fear.

Pomona laughed with glee. "Ohhh... yeah!"

Caitlyn's heart jumped into her throat. "NO! Pomona, you can't—"

She felt as if time had slowed down as she watched the knife quiver in the air, its blade gleaming with malevolent force. Then—at a nod from Pomona—it shot with supernatural speed towards Eddie's chest.

CHAPTER TWENTY-FIVE

"*Pomona, nooooo!*" screamed Caitlyn.

Blindly, she reached out with all her powers. There was no time to think, no time to consciously decide what to do, how to save Eddie—all she could do was react with pure instinct.

Everyone in the room gave a collective gasp of surprise as the knife suddenly transformed in mid-air, the gleaming blade becoming dull as it changed from tip to handle and became a chocolate replica of itself. It struck Eddie's chest and shattered, falling to the ground as harmless chunks of milk chocolate—like the broken pieces of a smashed chocolate Easter egg.

For a long moment, there was a stunned silence in the kitchen. Then they heard steps outside, at the front of the cottage. A minute later, the Widow Mags appeared in the kitchen doorway. She paused and surveyed the scene: the group of terrified and bewildered villagers, the mess of chocolate everywhere, the two girls defiantly facing each other, and the still-cowering figure of Eddie on the floor between them.

"What has happened here?" she asked harshly, stepping into the room.

Instantly, there were panicked whispers and murmurs of fear from the villagers.

"It's her!"

"The old witch!"

"Oh my God, what's *she* going to do to us?"

The Widow Mags glanced at Pomona, who was standing with her arms crossed, her chin up, and her eyes burning with defiance. Then she went over to Eddie and bent to help him, but he let out a cry of disgust and scooted backwards, crawling away from her.

"Don't... don't touch me!" he cried, the whites of his eyes showing.

Scrambling to his feet, he limped across the kitchen and disappeared out the door leading to the shop area at the front. One by one, the other villagers began to follow suit, picking themselves up and hobbling out—giving the Widow Mags as wide a berth as possible. Vera was one of the last to leave and, as she got to the door, she turned around and sent the Widow Mags a baleful look.

"I was right all along," she spat. "I knew you were

dabbling in black magic! And now you've trained these girls to use it too."

Caitlyn started to protest: "No, it wasn't—"

"You hexed us!" said Vera shrilly. "Don't try to deny it! And then that knife... we all saw what happened: it was bewitched—it was flying towards Eddie to kill him!"

The Widow Mags looked sharply at Caitlyn and Pomona, but before either of them could respond, Vera hissed:

"I won't forget this! Just you wait... I'm going to make sure that everyone knows what happened. I'm going to make sure that you get kicked out of this village!"

Whirling, she stormed out of the kitchen. Caitlyn started to follow, but the Widow Mags caught her arm.

"Let it be, child," she said.

"But she's got it all wrong!" cried Caitlyn passionately.

"Nothing you say at the moment will change her mind. She is too prejudiced and too scared to listen."

"But—"

"You have to choose your battles, Caitlyn, and this is not one that you will win today." The old witch turned to survey the kitchen again, noting the remaining smears of chocolate cake left on the floor, then said grimly: "Now, I'd like to know what happened here."

Caitlyn glanced at Pomona, then said hurriedly,

"The villagers came barging into the shop and started making a mess everywhere and destroying things… and then… well, we were trying to stop them…"

The Widow Mags gave her a hard look, then she turned to Pomona and said: "And what about Eddie?"

Pomona scowled. "He tried to attack us! He came at me with a knife so I—"

"*I* changed the knife into chocolate," Caitlyn cut in quickly, indicating the pieces of milk chocolate scattered around their feet. "It broke and fell on the floor. Eddie got a fright, but he wasn't hurt." She swallowed, not meeting the Widow Mags's eyes, and added in a wavering voice, "Vera was wrong. No one… no one tried to kill Eddie. It was all… um… a big misunderstanding."

Pomona opened her mouth, as if to argue, then she paused, throwing a wary look at the Widow Mags. Finally, she shrugged and mumbled: "Yeah… what Caitlyn said."

The Widow Mags was silent for a moment, her eyes moving from one girl's face to the other. Caitlyn squirmed under the old witch's gaze. She knew that she shouldn't have lied about what had happened with Eddie, but somehow, she couldn't bear to admit that Pomona could have been planning to use magic to seriously harm anyone.

Finally, the Widow Mags said in a measured voice: "There is more to this affair than you are telling me, but I see that I will get no further answers for now." She glanced at the state of the kitchen. "And there is work to do—"

"Yes, why don't Pomona and I go and clean up the shop outside?" said Caitlyn brightly.

She grabbed Pomona's hand and hustled her out to the shop area at the front before the Widow Mags could say any more. But as they began to pick up the debris, she eyed her cousin sideways, her thoughts uneasy.

"Stop looking at me like that," growled Pomona. "I can't believe how you're acting like *I'm* the bad guy here. Jeez, Caitlyn, those men were assaulting you! Who knows what they would have done to you if I hadn't arrived."

Caitlyn shifted uncomfortably, aware that Pomona was right in a way. "I *am* thankful that you came, Pomie. It's just..." She shook her head, looking at the other girl helplessly. "Did you really have to do that to them? Don't you think you went overboard?"

"Aww, come on! Those villagers were, like, vandalising the whole place. Don't tell me you weren't glad to see them get a taste of their own medicine?"

"I wanted to see them get their comeuppance, yes, but not like that," Caitlyn protested. "We could have reported them to the police or something. Why did you have to torture them?"

"For crying out loud... I made them eat *chocolate*!" said Pomona. "Man, the way you're acting, you'd think I'd burned them with hot irons or something!"

"They were forced against their will. It didn't matter if they weren't in physical pain; they were still suffering and terrified—"

"Well, *excuse me*," said Pomona, her voice dripping with sarcasm. "I didn't realise it was Touchy-Feely-Let's-Not-Scare-The-Villagers Day."

"What about Eddie?" said Caitlyn. "That wasn't just harmless fun. Vera was right—you could have killed him!"

"He came at me first," said Pomona defensively. "He was the one who grabbed the knife, not me. If I hadn't turned it on him, he could have stabbed me. Is that what you wanted?" She gave a careless shrug. "Besides, who said the knife would have gone into a vital organ? Anyway, Eddie was a jerk. He deserved whatever he got."

Caitlyn stared at her cousin. "You've changed, Pomona," she whispered.

"Well, of course I've changed—I can do magic now!" said Pomona gleefully.

"No, that's not what I mean," said Caitlyn. "In the past, you'd never have said what you just did, and you would never have enjoyed watching people suffer like that."

"Aww, get off your high horse!" groaned Pomona. "You know what your problem is? You're just jealous."

Caitlyn gaped at her. "Jealous? Me?"

"Yeah. You don't like not being the only special one anymore."

"What?" Caitlyn spluttered. "That's the most stupid, ridiculous—"

"No, it's not! You used to be the only one who was the—" Pomona put on a mocking voice. "—'special witch girl', but now I've got magical abilities too. So you're jealous."

"That's not true!"

"Yeah, it is. You're jealous 'cos I can use magic and I'm a heck of a lot better at it than you are. I mean, you've got all this witchy power and what do you use it for? To make chocolates and cookies!" Pomona said contemptuously. "That's just, like, pathetic! You could have punished those villagers yourself if you'd really wanted to—"

"I'd rather be 'pathetic' than use magic to hurt people," Caitlyn retorted. "You know very well that it's not right to use Dark Magic—or any magic, really—to cause harm."

"That's just bull!" snapped Pomona. "Who says what's right and what's not right? It's just a bunch of random rules. I mean, they used to think that it was okay to marry your brother in Cleopatra's time, right? And now, incest is, like, the biggest taboo."

"That's different. It doesn't matter what century or country it is; it's never okay to hurt others just because you enjoy watching them suffer—"

"You need to show people what you're capable of sometimes," said Pomona grimly. "Look at the Widow Mags! Man, if she could just show the villagers what kind of power she has, they'd be so freaked out, they'd never dare mess around with her again."

Caitlyn sighed. "And what would that achieve? It's

their irrational fear that's causing all the problems in the first place. Making them even more scared isn't going to solve anything. We need to help them understand and accept witches, not fear us."

"They're never gonna do that," said Pomona impatiently. "Honestly, Caitlyn, were you born yesterday? You know people never accept those who are different—and especially if the difference is the ability to do magic. People will always hate us, because we have powers that they don't. So the only way to win is to dominate them."

"You don't really mean that," said Caitlyn, aghast.

"I do and you'd better believe it." Pomona tossed a packet of chocolate toffees carelessly onto the glass counter, then scowled at Caitlyn. "You know what? This sucks. I'm sick of being chewed out by everyone when *I* was the one who saved the day! I'm outta here." Turning, she flounced out of the shop and disappeared down the lane.

Caitlyn started after her, but as she passed an overturned chair on the way to the door, something shot out and swiped at her ankle. She gasped and yelped, hopping around on one foot, until she looked down and saw the little furry black face peeking out at her from the side of the chair.

"Oh... Nibs, it's you." Caitlyn heaved a sigh of mingled exasperation and relief as she regained her balance and set both feet on the ground.

"*Mew!*" said the kitten, cheekily reaching out with a tiny paw to swipe at her foot again.

Caitlyn glanced towards the door of the chocolate shop, wondering if she could still catch up with Pomona if she hurried. Then she checked herself. Maybe it was just as well to let her go. They both needed to cool down. Chasing after her cousin now would simply result in more shouting and insults, and probably end up with her saying something that she'd later regret.

"*Mew!*" came the insistent little voice again, and Caitlyn looked down to see that Nibs was now sitting by her feet, looking up at her expectantly. He tilted his head to one side, his yellow eyes enormous, and raised one paw off the ground.

"*Mew?*" he said hopefully.

In spite of herself, Caitlyn broke into a smile and bent to scoop the kitten up. She was glad to see that he seemed unharmed. He must have found somewhere to hide when the villagers stormed into the kitchen. Even if he was only a baby cat, it looked like Nibs had already developed the famous feline instinct of self-preservation.

She cuddled him against her chest, finding comfort in his soft fur and warm purring body. After the tension and terrors of the villagers' attack, and the horrible scene with Pomona, it was wonderfully soothing just to stroke the kitten and hear the rumbling emanating from his little chest as he purred with pleasure.

Caitlyn's gaze drifted around the chocolate shop as she continued absentmindedly stroking the kitten, and she felt a surge of anger and resentment as she took in all the damage that had been done. Painstakingly created chocolate sculptures had been smashed, handmade cookies ground underfoot, packets of sweets and chocolate bars tossed around and broken, entire shelves of items pushed to the floor... not to mention the huge gaping hole in the cracked glass of the shop window. It was all going to cost a fortune to replace, and it was also the most dreadful waste of food.

Pomona was right—the villagers deserved to be punished! she thought furiously. *They* were the ones who had come looking for trouble, *they* were the ones who had vandalised the place, and—she shuddered at the memory of the two men holding her—*they* were the ones who had first engaged in physical assault.

Maybe I'm being too hard on Pomona, she thought grudgingly. Okay, her cousin had probably gone a bit too far, but then she *had* been provoked. And it was certainly true that Eddie had grabbed the knife first... what would have happened if Pomona hadn't stopped him?

Caitlyn sighed, feeling a mixture of guilt and unease. She was still disturbed by Pomona's actions, and she still felt as if there had been some undefinable change in her cousin, but at the same time, she couldn't help wondering if the other girl was right. *Maybe I* am *taking too much of a sanctimonious attitude towards everything...*

She decided to find Pomona and talk to her again

the next day. By then, they would have both calmed down and things should be easier. Feeling much better, she gave Nibs one last pat, then set him back down on the floor and turned once more to tackle the mess in the shop around her.

CHAPTER TWENTY-SIX

By the time Caitlyn had finished helping the Widow Mags clean up the mess, it was very late, and she was exhausted when she finally mounted the spiral steps to her attic bedroom. She slept fitfully and awoke late, gazing drowsily at the ceiling for several minutes before she rolled over and glanced at the clock on her bedside table. Then she sat bolt upright as she suddenly remembered her riding date with James Fitzroy. *Yikes!* She was supposed to meet him at the Manor stables in half an hour!

Springing out of bed, she rushed through a shower and got dressed as quickly as she could. She had wanted to make sure that she was looking her best for James, but there was no time to linger over hair and make-up. All she had time for was a quick sweep of mascara on her lashes and a swipe of gloss on her lips, then she hastily pulled her red tresses into a ponytail and stood back to look critically at her reflection in the mirror. The late night and disturbed sleep had put shadows under her hazel eyes, making them look enormous, and she was paler than normal. She wondered if she should attempt to apply blush to add some colour to her cheeks, then decided against it. She wasn't that adept with make-up at the best of times, and her previous attempts with blusher had often left her looking like a clown!

Maybe the fresh air and exercise will give me a natural glow, she thought hopefully as she grabbed a fleece-lined jacket to ward off the morning chill and hurried out of her room.

Fifteen minutes later, she arrived breathlessly in the stable courtyard at the rear of Huntingdon Manor to find James already there. He was talking to one of the grooms, and next to them stood two horses, saddled and waiting. One was a magnificent grey stallion—James's Percheron, Arion—and the other was a much smaller horse: a sturdy-looking mare with a rich chestnut coat and beautiful flaxen mane and tail. Caitlyn was across the courtyard before she realised it, drawn to the gentle-looking mare with her neat ears and big, dark eyes. The horse blew softly into Caitlyn's outstretched hands, the velvety muzzle nosing across her palms.

"She's looking for a sugar lump" said James, grinning as he came over to join her.

"Oh, I'm afraid I didn't bring—"

He chuckled. "Don't worry. Sugar isn't really healthy for horses, although an occasional treat won't do them harm. This one has a terribly sweet tooth though, and she's always scrounging for more." He gave the mare's neck an affectionate pat. "It's why she's called Melys. It means 'sweet' in Welsh."

Caitlyn looked up with surprise as the groom approached, offering her a pair of riding boots and a hard hat. "Oh, thanks! I was just worrying that I didn't have proper riding boots."

"You *can* ride in your own shoes, but it'll be easier to keep your feet in the stirrups if you have boots. These belong to my sister," James explained. "I'm hoping you and Vanessa have roughly the same size feet..."

They did. Caitlyn wriggled her toes in delight a few minutes later. The boots were slightly snug but not uncomfortably so, and she felt so much more "professional" now as she approached the side of the mare.

"Shall I bring the mounting step, sir?" asked the groom.

James waved a hand. "No, don't worry. I'll help Miss Le Fey up into the saddle."

He came to stand behind Caitlyn, who felt her heart rate speed up. Would James put his hands around her waist and lift her up, as he once had during that fateful night when they'd ridden Arion together? She was almost disappointed when he bent instead and cupped his hands around her knee and ankle. The next minute, she forgot all about romance as she was boosted up into the saddle. She grabbed the reins frantically, gripping the sides of the mare with her knees.

"Whoa..." said James as Melys fidgeted and tried to take off. He calmed the mare, then glanced at Caitlyn, who was still perched tensely on the front edge of the saddle. "Try to sit back and relax," he said gently. "And don't grip so tightly with your knees, otherwise she thinks you're telling her to go faster. It also unbalances you and makes it more likely that you'll come off the saddle if she makes any sudden moves."

"Oh." Caitlyn tried to comply. To her surprise, as she sat back into the saddle, eased her hold on the reins, and loosened her knees, she felt the horse relax beneath her as well.

"There. That's better." James smiled encouragingly at her. "Got the reins?"

Caitlyn nodded, adjusting the leather straps in her hands. James checked her saddle, adjusted her feet in the stirrups, then went over to his own horse. Caitlyn watched enviously as he swung up onto Arion with ease, then she gave the mare a nudge with her heels, and they followed James and Arion out of the stable courtyard.

"I thought we'd go for a hack through the woods," James said over his shoulder. He grinned at her. "Unless you'd prefer a canter over the open fields?"

"Oh no, hacking sounds perfect," said Caitlyn

hastily.

For a while, all she could do was concentrate on her horse and try to remember the instructions from her previous riding lessons on how to hold the reins and balance in the saddle. But gradually, as she got used to the rhythmic movement of the mare's body and gained confidence in her own ability, she began to relax and enjoy herself. She even laughed with delight when Melys broke into a gentle trot, and she found that she could remember how to rise and lower in her seat in time to the horse's gait.

"You ride well for an 'inexperienced rider'," said James, his grey eyes twinkling.

Caitlyn felt her cheeks flush—both from his praise and the exercise—and was glad now that she hadn't applied blusher, after all; she'd probably look like a red beacon otherwise!

"Thanks. It's funny how it all comes back to you. Like riding a bicycle, I suppose," she said.

She took a deep breath of the crisp air. It was a beautiful morning, and the woods were peaceful, with only the muffled sound of the horses' hooves and the occasional birdsong to break the silence. Many of the trees had shed their leaves so that sunlight streamed down through the gaps in the canopy in shafts of muted gold and amber. It might not have been as exciting as riding pillion with James on his stallion, but there was still something very romantic about riding side by side together through the glorious autumn foliage of the woods.

In fact, Caitlyn realised with a smile that she had almost forgotten about the events of the night before. She could feel the tension melting from her neck and shoulders with each *clop* of the horses' hooves, and she let out her breath in a great sigh.

"Is something wrong?" James said, giving her a quizzical look.

"Oh no, not at all," said Caitlyn quickly. She could see that James was still looking at her curiously, but she was reluctant to spoil the lovely mood of the morning by bringing up the events of the night before. *I'll tell him everything later*, she thought. *When we get back to the Manor.*

Soon they came to a clearing on a grassy knoll, with a view beyond the treetops to the rolling Cotswolds hills in the distance. They dismounted and left the horses browsing in the long grass, whilst they walked to the summit of the knoll and took in the vista. Caitlyn gave another sigh—a long, happy one this time—as she gazed at the landscape, with its high wolds, enclosed limestone valleys, and wooded vales.

"It's so gorgeous," she said. "You must love riding on the estate."

"I do." James glanced at her, his mouth curving in that lopsided smile which always set Caitlyn's pulse racing. "But today the company makes it extra-special," he added softly.

She felt her cheeks warm even more. For a moment, she thought that James was going to move and take her into his arms, and she was disappointed when he turned back to look at the view again, adding in a prosaic voice:

"Actually, I almost thought I would have to cancel our date. Inspector Walsh arrived first thing this morning, wanting to go over several aspects of the case, but thankfully we managed to get through most of the things fairly quickly, and I was able to leave him with Mosley to check the crime scene again."

"Have there been any developments?" asked Caitlyn.

"Well, unfortunately, the police have had to release their most likely suspect," said James. "Jessica Hyde, the journalist who was with the villagers protesting at the ball—she seemed to have a history with Daniel Tremaine and obviously still harboured a lot of bitterness towards him. But unfortunately—or fortunately, perhaps, for her—she had a strong alibi."

"Yes, I know," said Caitlyn. "Inspector Walsh came to question Bertha at her herbal shop yesterday, and he mentioned having to release Jessica from custody. Actually, I met her myself in the village a short while later."

She paused, recalling the allegations that the journalist had made about Daniel Tremaine, but before she could mention them, James said:

"Inspector Walsh told me this morning that they may have another lead. It seems that one of his officers has spotted something in the CCTV footage—

a person going into the Portrait Gallery—and the time stamp shows that it was shortly before Daniel's body was discovered."

"But wait—I thought the camera isn't trained on the Gallery door, so you can't really see who's entering or leaving it."

"Not directly, but his officer noticed that there is a console table on the wall opposite the Gallery door, which *is* in the camera frame."

Caitlyn frowned. "I don't understand how that helps. Is there a mirror above the table which shows the Gallery door in its reflection?"

"Unfortunately not, but there *is* a large antique bronze vase on the table, and the officer is sure that he can see what looks like a moving figure reflected on the surface of the vase."

"But they can't tell who it is?" asked Caitlyn, disappointed.

"Not at the moment. It's a very small, blurred image."

"Can't they just zoom in?"

"It's not as simple as that. The image is distorted by the curved bronze surface, and, of course, the dim lighting in the corridor doesn't help. But Inspector Walsh tells me that they've enlisted some digital video specialists who will work on isolating and enhancing the image. That will take time, though, so we won't have an answer for a few days."

"If they can get a clear enough picture, it might give them the identity of the murderer on a plate," said Caitlyn excitedly.

James gave a rueful laugh. "Somehow, I doubt it will be that easy. Even with enhancement, they might not be able to get a clear enough picture of the person's face to identify him or her. Probably a 'her'," he added.

"Why do you say that?"

"Well, according to Inspector Walsh, the image seems to show a figure in a long green gown. That's more likely to be a woman than a man, don't you think?"

Unbidden, an image of Pomona standing proudly in her Medusa costume came to Caitlyn's mind: the long gown made of silky green fabric that moulded itself to her cousin's body...

"Caitlyn?"

She blinked. "Sorry. Um... yes, I suppose so, although in a masquerade ball, you could have a man in a long green costume."

"I don't remember any male guest wearing such a thing," said James, furrowing his brow. "Anyway, I think the police are operating on the assumption that the suspect is likely to be a woman. Given Daniel's Casanova tendencies, it's probably not so surprising."

"Do you know a lot about his background?"

"No, not really, but I don't need to in that respect. It was obvious that he had a roving eye and could turn on the charm with the opposite sex," said James dryly.

"It's not really what you expect when you think of an accountant, is it?" Caitlyn said, turning to look James straight in the eye. "But that wasn't Daniel Tremaine's real occupation, was it?"

He didn't answer directly. "What makes you say that?"

"Well, two different women have told me that. One of them I met at the ball. In fact, she was the woman who had to stay overnight at the Manor—"

"Ah yes, Mrs Vivien Kwok," said James.

"Did you know that she had been Tremaine's lover?"

"Yes, Inspector Walsh *had* mentioned that to me. He questioned her yesterday evening, after she'd recovered from the shock of the murder, but he seems to feel that she isn't a strong suspect— literally. He doesn't think she would have had the strength to use the murder weapon in the way needed to impale the victim." James looked at Caitlyn curiously. "How did you know about her and Daniel?"

"I met her at breakfast yesterday morning, before I went back to Tillyhenge, and we... er... got chatting," said Caitlyn, thinking that "chat" was the most unlikely way she would have described her conversation with the coldly beautiful Mrs Kwok. "She admitted that she'd had a romantic relationship with Tremaine in the past, and she also told me that the whole accountant thing was just a front, a cover for Tremaine's *real* job, which was a spy for the

British government. And not only that, but a very specific branch within the government. Then when I met Jessica Hyde later in the village, she said the same thing."

She repeated what Jessica Hyde had told her about Tremaine's work for a secret society and noted that James didn't look particularly surprised. "You knew all this already, didn't you?" she said accusingly.

James was quiet for a moment, then he sighed and said: "Yes, I knew."

Caitlyn drew back, feeling hurt that he'd never mentioned anything to her. James must have sensed it, because he put out a hand and said: "I'd been meaning to tell you, Caitlyn—"

"When did you find out?"

"That day we met Daniel in the Portrait Gallery," James admitted. "After you left, he started asking me lots of probing questions about my father's occult collection. Then he revealed that he worked for a covert branch of the British government—a modern-day version of a secret society that was founded several centuries ago."

"You mean a secret society of witch hunters," said Caitlyn. "The one that your father was a member of."

James's jaw tightened. "Yes. The same one."

CHAPTER TWENTY-SEVEN

"Why didn't you tell me?" Caitlyn asked.

James's face was stony. "I just... I didn't really want to talk about it."

Caitlyn looked at him in frustration. Ever since that shocking night when Gerald Hopkins had revealed that the Fitzroy family had a long connection to a secret society, James had been distant and difficult whenever she tried to broach the subject.

To be fair, as someone who had long believed that science held all the answers, it probably wasn't surprising that James found it difficult to cope with the idea of a secret society dedicated to destroying witchcraft and magic. Moreover, it had been hard for him to believe that a secret society formed in the seventeenth century, made up of men who shared

King James's obsession with the occult, could have continued to the present day—and that its members could still believe that the forces of Dark Magic threatened Britain as much as any invading army.

But Caitlyn knew that what James really struggled with was the knowledge that he was descended from a long line of witch hunters—a practice that he abhorred—and that his own father could have been an active member of the society. She had tried to speak to him about it, but he had assiduously avoided the topic. It yawned like an open wound between them, and Caitlyn found his attitude puzzling and infuriating.

"Have you told the police?" she asked him.

"No."

"James!" Caitlyn looked at him incredulously. "Hasn't it occurred to you that Tremaine's murder could be tied to his work? To his membership of this society?"

James ran a distracted hand through his hair. "It could just as likely be linked to his sordid personal life."

Caitlyn wrinkled her nose. "A 'crime of passion'? Not that old cliché!"

"Clichés exist for a reason."

"The police obviously don't think so, otherwise they would already have gone after one of the many women that Tremaine had been involved with," argued Caitlyn. "Like Vivien Kwok, for instance. She sounds exactly like the stereotype of the bitter, jealous ex-lover. She even warned me off Tremaine at the ball! Why haven't the police gone after her then?"

"She's still on their list," said James doggedly. "I mean, Inspector Walsh said she's not a strong suspect, but that doesn't mean that she's been completely discounted. For one thing, she doesn't have an alibi for the entire evening, so she could have slipped away unnoticed to the Portrait Gallery."

Caitlyn blew out a breath. "Well, fine, but that doesn't mean that the police can't investigate the other angle too. I mean, I just can't believe that there isn't some connection between Tremaine's work for the secret society and his death." She gave a little gasp as she remembered something. "Gerald Hopkins! He was a member too, wasn't he? And he was also murdered recently. In fact, didn't the police say there was evidence of torture?"

"Possible evidence," James reminded her. "Nothing is conclusive. There were no obvious injuries found on Gerald Hopkins, remember, which was part of the mystery. If he had been tortured, wouldn't they have found some wounds or something on him?"

Caitlyn thought suddenly of the creepy poppet doll that Inspector Walsh had brought to show Bertha. "Not if the torture had been inflicted by sympathetic magic," she said suddenly.

"By what?"

"Sympathetic magic. It's a form of magical practice where you use an object—usually a doll—to represent a person, and then whatever you do to the doll is transferred to the person, even if they're far away. Inspector Walsh found an apple poppet amongst Tremaine's things. A 'poppet' is a doll that's used in sympathetic magic," Caitlyn explained.

"Hmm... the inspector mentioned finding a doll, but I didn't get the impression that he thought much of it."

"Well, he thought enough to bring it to Bertha's shop yesterday and ask her about it." Caitlyn paused as she remembered the way the poppet had looked, and gave a shiver. "It's a horrible, creepy thing, and it had pins stuck all over it. Well, what if... what if it had been used to represent Gerald Hopkins, and that was how he had been tortured? That would explain why he had no marks on him and why no one had been seen in his room—it could all have been done at a distance!"

"Voodoo dolls are just a tourist gimmick," said James scornfully. "They're a complete misinterpretation of practices from the original 'Vodou' religion that originated in Haiti and other places in the Caribbean. The dolls made by the original Vodou practitioners weren't used to inflict harm at all—they were simply a ritualistic device believed to help with healing or communicating with the dead. It was Hollywood that turned them into evil effigies used to unleash magical forces to get revenge. The whole thing is a myth."

"Sympathetic magic, itself, isn't a myth," said

Caitlyn. "Perhaps it wasn't the original intention for these dolls—these 'poppets'—but the Widow Mags and Bertha have taught me that all magic can be used for both good and harm." She added eagerly, warming to her subject: "This apple poppet was found in Daniel Tremaine's things... what if Tremaine was the one who murdered Gerald Hopkins?"

James looked at her askance. "Are you suggesting now that Daniel could do magic? That he used this... 'poppet' to torture and kill Gerald without touching him?"

Caitlyn hesitated. "I don't know... Maybe it's something he learned in the course of his work. I mean, if he really *was* a member of this secret society that deals with the paranormal, then he might have had contact with the world of witchcraft and magic, and... well, picked up some skills—"

"I thought it was only those born as witches who could work magic."

Caitlyn thought uncomfortably of Pomona and the frightening ability her cousin had shown the night before. "I... I don't think it's quite so clear-cut." She took a breath and said briskly, "Anyway, the point is—don't you think it's too much of a coincidence that Gerald Hopkins's mysterious death should have happened just as Tremaine arrived in the area? He was recovering well; the doctors were planning to bring him out of his medically induced coma... and then suddenly, he just ups and dies? That can't be a coincidence!"

"But why would Daniel have wanted to kill Gerald?" asked James. "Especially if they really were members of the same government agency? One would have thought that they would have been colleagues, maybe even friends."

"Maybe not. Gerald Hopkins was much older—he was of your father's generation. Tremaine was a younger recruit. Maybe there was some conflict between them or maybe... maybe Tremaine had been *sent* to kill Hopkins!" said Caitlyn excitedly. "Yes! Think about it: maybe Hopkins had 'gone rogue', and they were worried that he might reveal too much and they wanted to silence him, so they sent one of their younger agents—"

"Now *this* is really beginning to sound like a Hollywood movie," said James disdainfully.

Caitlyn drew back, stung. "Well, fine. What's your theory then?"

"I don't have one," said James shortly. "But if I did, it wouldn't be some ludicrous, convoluted story involving covert assassins and voodoo dolls and black magic! Why can't you just accept that Daniel's murder could have a mundane, carnal cause?"

"And why can't *you* accept that it might have something to do with a secret society of witch hunters?" Caitlyn shot back. "Tremaine came to Huntingdon Manor—he came to see *you*—for a reason. I'm sure of it. He was very interested in your father's occult collection; he was asking questions— don't you want to know why? And he left in the middle of the ball to sneak off to the Portrait Gallery—why? Don't you want to know how you and your family fit into the whole thing?"

James stared off into the distance, his jaw set. "No."

Caitlyn fumed at his handsome profile. "I never thought you'd be a coward."

He jerked around, a frown between his eyes. "A coward?"

"Yes." Caitlyn looked at him defiantly. "You're scared—scared to dig up the past, scared to seek the truth."

"Rubbish." James's grey eyes were cold.

Caitlyn felt a slight chill. He had never looked at her that way before. But she stood her ground. "It's not rubbish and you know it."

Turning, she headed back to where they'd left the horses. After a moment, James followed. He helped her mount, then they rode back in a stiff silence. Caitlyn felt a mixture of emotions churning inside her. A part of her was simply furious and exasperated at James's stubborn, unreasonable attitude. But another part of her was struggling with something more complex. She had looked forward to their romantic morning ride as the embodiment of all her girlish fantasies, and she was bitterly disappointed at how their second date had degenerated into a "fight" once again. But more than that, she was coming to the uncomfortable realisation that "Prince Charming" could have seriously clay feet. *Is this what*

*they mean when they talk about really falling in love—
warts and all?*

When she had first met James Fitzroy, all she
could think about was how amazing he was—the
perfect Mr Darcy fantasy come to life, with his
aristocratic good looks, that sexy-as-hell British
accent, and a gallant manner worthy of any romance
novel's hero. She had never dared hope that he might
return her feelings: she had always been a shy,
bookish girl, with huge insecurities about her big
hips and lack of sophisticated style, so she had never
expected someone like James Fitzroy to even notice
her, much less find her attractive. Meeting him
always seemed to reduce her to a blushing,
stammering schoolgirl, and most of her early
thoughts were consumed with the significance of his
attentions towards her. It seemed crazy to even dare
imagine that there could be a chance for them to be
together.

Then, when she discovered that, somehow, she
had managed to capture James's heart, it had
seemed like a dream come true, the culmination of
everything she could have possibly wanted, the
"happily ever after" at the end of her own personal
romance novel. Except that now she was realising
that after the "oh my God—yes, he does want me!"
moment, life goes on and things weren't that simple.
James wasn't the perfect romantic hero fantasy, after
all. He didn't always agree with her or support her
views; he wasn't always reasonable and

understanding. He was just a man, with faults and flaws, prejudices and peculiarities... and yet she still loved him.

Caitlyn was so immersed in her brooding that they were almost through the entrance to the stable courtyard before she realised that they were back at the Manor. As their horses slowed, James turned suddenly to her, his grey eyes filled with regret. "Caitlyn... listen, this isn't how I wanted the morning to—"

"Ah, Lord Fitzroy—you're back!"

They looked up in surprise to see Inspector Walsh striding across the courtyard towards them. They stopped their horses and James dismounted.

"Were you wanting to see me, Inspector?" he asked politely.

"Actually, it was Miss Le Fey I wanted to speak to," said the detective.

"Me?" said Caitlyn in surprise, as James came over and helped her off her horse.

"Yes, we had a formal complaint made at the station this morning," said the inspector gravely. "Vera Bottom has reported the Widow Mags for assault and intent to cause grievous bodily harm."

CHAPTER TWENTY-EIGHT

Caitlyn stared at the detective in disbelief. "She's *what?* That's... that's the most outrageous thing I've ever heard!" she spluttered. "If anything, *Vera* is the one who should be reported! She was the one who came to the chocolate shop with a bunch of her cronies and encouraged them to vandalise the place—"

"What?" James cried. "When did this happen?"

"Last night," said Caitlyn, guiltily recalling that she hadn't told James about the incident yet. "Vera and a group of villagers turned up at *Bewitched by Chocolate* yesterday evening, when I was alone, and threw a stone through the shop window. When I went out to confront them, they started shouting abuse and harassing me, and then they barged into the shop and started wrecking everything—"

"Ms Bottom says *you* invited them in," said Inspector Walsh. "Did you?"

Caitlyn swallowed as she remembered her rash words to the hostile villagers. "Well, sort of," she admitted. "Although not in the way she's implying! They were claiming that the chocolates had been deliberately tainted with... with evil spells and poisons and all sorts of other nonsense, and I got angry and told them that there was nothing in the treats except things like top-quality cocoa powder and fresh cream, and they could come in and see for themselves." She looked earnestly at Inspector Walsh. "But I didn't really think they would take me up on it. It was sort of like a rhetorical question, you know? Besides, even if I *had* invited them in, it didn't give them the right to start trashing the place!"

"Why didn't you tell me?" James asked.

"I was going to," said Caitlyn. "But it was such a lovely morning, I... I didn't want to ruin the mood by bringing it up, so I thought I'd just wait until we got back." She didn't add that their ride had been ruined anyway by their subsequent argument, but from the look in James's eyes, he was aware of her thoughts.

Inspector Walsh cleared his throat. "Yes, well, I've had a very different story from Ms Bottom. According to her, she and a group of villagers went to the chocolate shop in good faith to voice some concerns they had about the quality of the Widow Mags's products—"

"'Voice some concerns'? Hah, that's rich!" said

Caitlyn. "They practically accused the Widow Mags of trying to poison everyone in the village, and even suggested that she might have had a hand in Daniel Tremaine's murder. They were completely unreasonable and started smashing things in the shop, and then they pushed their way into the kitchen and, when I tried to stop them, two men grabbed me and held me down—"

James made an exclamation and reached out, as if wanting to pull her close, then he seemed to recall his surroundings and dropped his arm. "Did they hurt you?" he demanded.

Caitlyn shook her head. "No, although I don't know what they would have done if Pomona hadn't arrived and—" She broke off.

Inspector Walsh looked at her sharply. "Yes?"

Caitlyn licked her lips, uncertain what to say. She couldn't tell the truth and, in any case, Inspector Walsh, with his intense scepticism of anything to do with magic, would never believe her.

"Well, she... she surprised them, and the men let me go."

Inspector Walsh raised his eyebrows. "According to Ms Bottom, your cousin Miss Sinclair used black magic on them. She even claims that one of the villagers—Eddie Paver—was nearly killed by a kitchen knife that was bewitched to fly towards him."

"That's... that's not... I mean, *Eddie* was the one who grabbed the knife first, and if Pomona hadn't—" Caitlyn broke off again and swallowed hard. She saw

James watching her, a frown between his eyes. Taking a deep breath, she let it out again slowly, then said in a calmer voice:

"Look, I think there's been a big misunderstanding. The villagers had worked themselves up into an almost hysterical state last night and things were so chaotic... well, I think Vera might have got... um... confused and started imagining things. You know how prejudiced she is against the Widow Mags," she reminded the inspector. "And Vera is completely paranoid about anything which she thinks might be linked to witchcraft, so surely you're not going to believe her ramblings? I mean, I thought you didn't believe in magic," she challenged him.

"I don't," he said testily. "But in this case, I cannot ignore the fact that several people are making the same accusations. I've spoken to several other villagers who were with Vera Bottom last night. While there was some confusion over who the culprit was—some of them seemed to believe that it was the Widow Mags who was responsible—overall, they all echo Ms Bottom's story of being oppressed by some kind of sinister force. Now, whether or not I believe in 'black magic' is irrelevant when I have so many testimonies all claiming to have suffered severe distress at the same event." He paused deliberately, then added: "What's more, when I spoke to your grandmother this morning, she did not deny the accusations."

"You went to see the Widow Mags?" Caitlyn looked

at him in surprise.

"No, unfortunately I was required to be here at the Manor this morning, but I spoke to her on the phone. She tells me that your cousin had no involvement in what happened last night and that any complaints from the villagers could be directed at her."

She's covering up for Pomona, Caitlyn realised. She felt a rush of love and gratitude towards her grandmother. The Widow Mags might have been stubborn and cantankerous, but here she was, sacrificing what little goodwill and trust she had in the village, to take the blame for Pomona's actions.

"This is why I am here now, Miss Le Fey," said the inspector. "You are the only other witness who was present last night. So I want your account of what happened: did you see the villagers being abused? Did you see Eddie being injured by a flying knife?"

Caitlyn shifted her weight. "I... I can't believe you're even asking me that," she prevaricated. "I mean, if you don't believe in magic, then why would you take any of their accusations seriously?"

"Because there are other explanations for what happened—for instance, the villagers could simply have been *led* to believe that they were being tortured by an invisible magical force. The Widow Mags could have used hallucinogenic herbs or other substances to alter their perception of events. In that case, she could be liable for prosecution for forcing a psychoactive substance onto someone without their consent."

Caitlyn shook her head in exasperation. "This is crazy! The person who should be pressing charges is the Widow Mags herself, for damages done to her shop! There's no evidence of any... er... magical attack, whereas if you go down to the shop, you'll see that there's *plenty* of evidence of the villagers' handiwork. *They* broke in and vandalised the place! Shouldn't you be questioning *them* and charging *them* for crimes?"

"I can't when the Widow Mags refuses to press charges and has asked me to drop the whole case," said Inspector Walsh. "Now why do you think that is?"

Caitlyn hesitated. Once again, she could hardly tell the truth: *because my grandmother really* is *a witch and wants to keep a low profile*. She shrugged. "I don't know. She doesn't like to make a big deal of things."

"What exactly are the villagers accusing her of?" James asked the inspector, frowning. "You said they were 'abused'—that's a strong allegation. What are they claiming happened to them?"

For the first time, Inspector Walsh looked uncomfortable. He cleared his throat, his cheeks reddening slightly. "Ah... Ms Bottom claims that they were... *ahem*... forced to eat chocolate cake."

"They were *what*?" James said with an incredulous laugh. "I'm sorry, Inspector, but are you joking?"

"No."

"Well, I—surely you're not giving serious credence to such ludicrous claims?" exclaimed James.

The inspector looked irritable. "I am obliged to take any reports of physical abuse seriously—"

"Yes, but being 'forced' to eat *chocolate*?" James said derisively. His face hardened. "Well, regardless of whether the police will be pressing charges, I shall be having a word with the villagers myself. There's no place for vigilante behaviour in Tillyhenge, and I will make that clear to anyone who wants to remain a tenant on the estate."

He started to say more but was interrupted by Mosley appearing in the stable courtyard, summoning him to an important call. James excused himself and returned to the house. Caitlyn expected Inspector Walsh to follow but, to her surprise, he turned back to her and said:

"By the way, Miss Le Fey, have you had a chance to speak to your cousin?"

"I... yes... I mean... what about?" stammered Caitlyn, taken aback.

"I wondered if she might have revealed anything further about her actions and whereabouts on the night of the ball."

"There's nothing more to 'reveal'," said Caitlyn, trying to ignore the uneasy feeling in the pit of her stomach. "She told me exactly the same thing that she probably told you: she'd taken an antihistamine for her allergies, and it had made her feel very drowsy, so she went into the Library to have a nap.

She was woken by the commotion of people running around and shouting, after the discovery of Tremaine's body, and came out to see what had happened. That's all."

"Hmm." Inspector Walsh eyed her thoughtfully. "Well, that's interesting, because I reinterviewed one of the ball guests last night: a Mr Ken Bates, who is the owner of a local brewery and who recalled meeting your cousin earlier in the evening, when she first arrived at the ball."

Caitlyn's heart sank as she suddenly remembered the very drunk man in the Roman toga and grapevine crown who had waylaid Blackmort and Pomona when they first arrived; the very same man she'd met when she was searching for Pomona.

As if following her thoughts, Inspector Walsh said, "Apparently, Mr Bates also met you, a bit later that same evening. He had been quite intoxicated on the night of the ball and hadn't been able to answer questions very thoroughly, but yesterday, having sobered up, he came back to amend his statement. Mr Bates distinctly remembers passing your cousin on his way to one of the guest toilets and says he saw her heading up a staircase at the back of the Manor— the staircase which leads to the Portrait Gallery. He also says that he met you a short while later, and when you asked him about Miss Sinclair, he directed you up the stairs."

The detective fixed Caitlyn with a steely look. "Miss Le Fey, are you covering up for your cousin?"

CHAPTER TWENTY-NINE

Caitlyn gulped as she stared into the inspector's hard eyes. "I... I don't know what you mean."

"You said in your statement that you had no reason to think Miss Sinclair had gone up the stairs, and yet Mr Bates informs me that he specifically told you he'd seen her take the staircase—so either he's lying, or you are. Now, as far as I can see, there's no reason for him to lie, whereas there's a very strong incentive for you to want to cover up for your cousin."

Caitlyn tried to fight the sense of panic. She almost denied that she had spoken to Ken Bates at all, then she stopped herself. Instead, she said defensively, "Mr Bates didn't tell me that he saw Pomona specifically. He just said he saw a woman who looked like her going up the stairs. But he could have been wrong! He was very drunk—he said so himself—and he might not have seen things very clearly."

"I think, no matter how drunk he was, he would have been pretty clear about seeing—quote: 'a woman with hair made of snakes'," said Inspector Walsh dryly. "That matches Miss Sinclair's Medusa costume. There was no other guest at the ball in a similar disguise, was there?"

"But did he see her face?" insisted Caitlyn.

"No," conceded the inspector. "All he saw was her back."

"Well then, he could have been wrong! Come on, Inspector, you must have experience of how unreliable witnesses can be when they're drunk. And Mr Bates was really hammered—he was slurring his words and he could barely walk straight—so how can you be sure of anything he says he saw?"

"In actual fact, drunk witnesses are more reliable than you think," growled Inspector Walsh. "Recent research has shown that intoxicated eyewitnesses are actually no different from sober eyewitnesses in their account accuracy or vulnerability to distortions. But I take your point," he added, his voice softening slightly. "The lack of clear facial identification is a weakness in Mr Bates's testimony."

"Anyway, James was telling me that you might have a new lead," said Caitlyn brightly, trying to change the subject. "Something that one of your officers saw in the CCTV footage?"

"Yes. We're still working on enhancing the image,

but it seems that a vase on the table opposite the Portrait Gallery door might be showing the reflection of a person entering the Gallery, a short while before you found Daniel Tremaine. From what we can see so far, it looks to be a female—wearing a long green gown." Inspector Walsh paused significantly, then added, "Your cousin, Miss Sinclair, was wearing a costume with a long green gown on the night of the ball, wasn't she?"

"So were a lot of other people," said Caitlyn quickly. "Like... like Vivien Kwok, for instance! She was wearing a long green cheongsam on the night of the ball. I remember because I spoke to her, and I was admiring it."

"I have already questioned Mrs Kwok," said Inspector Walsh evenly. "However, I do not consider her a strong suspect."

"Does she have an alibi?" persisted Caitlyn.

"Not for the entire night," Inspector Walsh admitted. "She was seen in the Ballroom for most of the evening, but there was a brief spell when she was absent, but it was just a short visit to the Ladies'."

"Did anyone see her there? Are there witnesses to corroborate that?" asked Caitlyn quickly.

"No. However, that doesn't mean that she is lying," the inspector pointed out. "Your cousin also has no one corroborating her statement of being in the Library."

Caitlyn ignored the reference to Pomona. "Did you know that Vivien Kwok had been Tremaine's lover?

Did she tell you that?"

"She mentioned that they'd had an affair at one point, several years ago."

"Well, doesn't that automatically put her high on the suspect list?" asked Caitlyn. She reflected ironically that she was voicing support for James's theory that the murder had been a clichéd "crime of passion". But right now, all she wanted to do was shift the focus away from Pomona. "Daniel Tremaine was known as a womaniser, and Vivien Kwok was very bitter about their break-up. It was the classic 'older woman, younger man' set-up, and I don't think she ever really got over him. In fact, she came up to me after I'd been dancing with Tremaine at the ball, and from the way she was talking, it was obvious that she still feels—felt—very possessive about him. Couldn't she have killed him in a fit of jealous rage or something?"

"But why now?" asked the inspector. "From what I understand, their affair ended a few years ago. If she had wanted revenge, wouldn't she have done something earlier?"

Caitlyn shrugged. "I don't know... maybe it took a while for things to bubble up. You know how people brood over stuff. Maybe she kept hoping that they would get back together, and when she finally confronted him at the ball and he told her outright that he wasn't interested in her, she just lost it."

Inspector Walsh looked dubious. "That may be so, Miss Le Fey, but the fact remains that Mrs Kwok doesn't seem like the kind of woman who could have used that weapon to kill Tremaine. For one thing, she lacks the upper-body strength required to throw the stang through the air with enough force to impale someone."

Silently, Caitlyn had to admit that he was right. Vivien Kwok looked like she had never lifted anything heavier than a Tiffany silver hairbrush in her life.

The inspector's phone buzzed suddenly, and he frowned as he took it out. "Excuse me, I'm going to have to take this—"

"Oh, of course. I've got to go anyway... um... I'll catch you later, Inspector!" said Caitlyn, grabbing the opportunity to escape further questioning.

Before he could respond, she hurried from the stable courtyard and back into the house. Instead of heading to her car parked at the front of the Manor, however, Caitlyn made her way to the private wing where James's study was situated. Inspector Walsh's probing had reminded her forcibly that the rubber snake she'd found was still hidden underneath Bran's bed. She'd been planning to try and retrieve it this morning anyway, and now it seemed even more urgent that she get it away from the Manor and off the police's radar.

When she arrived at the study, Caitlyn was relieved to see that James wasn't there. It would have been impossible to search the dog bed if he had been. As it was, the only thing in her way was an enormous English mastiff sprawled across the mattress, snoring loudly. Caitlyn approached the dog slowly, wondering if it would be possible to slip a hand underneath the mattress without waking him up. She was just crouching down next to the bed when Bran stirred and woke up.

The mastiff's droopy eyes lit up as he saw her, and he thumped his tail on the floor in greeting. He yawned widely, showing a cavernous mouth beneath sagging jowls, then leaned forwards and began trying to lick Caitlyn's face.

"Uh... hi, Bran... *ugh*... yes... I love you too... *eeuugh*!" Caitlyn choked, turning her face away to try and avoid the huge, slobbery tongue.

She ducked her head and tried to slide her hand into the space between the mattress and the base of the dog bed. It was like trying to force your hand into a rock crevice. Bran's huge weight pressing down on the mattress meant that it was almost impossible to get even a finger underneath.

Caitlyn pulled her hand out again and regarded the dog with a sigh. "Okay, I think I need you to move, Bran. Come on... good boy... can you get off the bed for a minute?"

The mastiff wagged his tail and looked at her blankly.

"Come on, Bran," said Caitlyn, backing away and patting her thighs, trying to cajole him to follow her. "Come on, get up! Good boy!"

The mastiff looked at her, his mouth open in an amiable doggie grin, but he didn't budge. Like all giant dogs, now that he was lying down and comfortable, it was going to take a lot to convince him to get back on his feet.

Caitlyn returned to the bed and laid a hand on Bran's collar, giving it a gentle tug. "Come on... *hup!* Come on, Bran... good boy... get up!"

Again, the mastiff lay immobile, only leaning forwards to give her face another loving slurp.

"*Eeuuw!*" Caitlyn wiped the trail of dog drool off her chin.

She went around to the other side of the bed, where she put her hands on the mastiff's sizable rump and gave him a little shove.

"Come on, Bran..." she pleaded. "I just need you to get up for a moment! You can get straight back on the bed, I promise—you just need to stand up for a minute..."

She pushed and shoved his giant furry bottom until she was panting and sweating, while the mastiff lay as if enjoying a massage, a contented, vacuous expression on his wrinkled face. Finally, Caitlyn gave up and came back round to the front of the bed again. She looked down at Bran in frustration. How could she get him to stand up? Maybe she could try tickling him? Were dogs even ticklish? Or what about a treat to motivate him? She glanced around the study but there was no packet of dog biscuits or anything else to be seen that could be used as a food lure.

Caitlyn bent and tried to slide her hand

underneath the mattress once more, grunting with effort as she attempted to shift Bran's weight over to one side of the bed.

"Come on... just... move... a little bit... please, Bran..." she panted.

Suddenly, without warning, the mastiff heaved himself to his feet.

"Yes!" cried Caitlyn, delighted. Quickly, she yanked a corner of the topper mattress up with one hand and groped underneath with the other. Her fingers closed around a familiar slinky-shaped object. Jubilant, she pulled out the rubber snake and stood up again. Then she became aware that Bran was looking behind her, wagging his tail and whining excitedly. She whirled and realised instantly why the mastiff had got off his bed at last: his master had returned.

She stifled a gasp, jerking her hands behind her back, before belatedly realising how guilty that reflex action made her look. Swallowing nervously, she faced James, trying to appear nonchalant.

"Caitlyn... what are you doing?" He frowned.

"N-nothing," she said breathlessly.

He raised his eyebrows. "You're hiding something behind your back."

For a wild moment, Caitlyn considered denying it, but as she looked into James's puzzled grey eyes, she found that she couldn't bear telling him any more lies. Slowly, she pulled her hands from behind her back and held out the rubber snake to show him.

"What's this?" James came forwards to take it from her.

"I found it on the floor of the Portrait Gallery... near Daniel Tremaine's body."

She heard James's sharp intake of breath as he realised the implication of what she was saying.

"This is from Pomona's Medusa wig, isn't it?" he asked. "And you didn't hand it in to the police?"

"It wasn't... I mean, that night, when I was waiting in here to be questioned, I just..." she stammered, "I... I just sort of acted on impulse... I hid it under Bran's bed."

"You *what*?" James burst out. "Caitlyn, how could you have done that? Do you realise what this means? You've hidden key evidence in a murder investigation, just because it could incriminate your cousin—"

"But that's the whole point! It would have made Pomona look guilty and got her in trouble, when she had nothing to do with the murder."

"How do you know she's not involved?"

There was silence in the study. Caitlyn stared at James incredulously. "Don't tell me you seriously believe that Pomona—"

"Look, I don't *want* to believe it," said James, running a hand through his hair in an agitated fashion. "But we can't ignore cold hard facts—"

"I don't care about facts!" cried Caitlyn. "I *know* Pomona isn't a murderer."

"But do you really know her anymore?" challenged

James. "You said yourself that she's been acting strangely lately. You were very worried the other day when you came to speak to me; you said Pomona seemed to enjoy inflicting pain on those ants and watching them suffer—"

"That was different," said Caitlyn quickly. "You can't compare a... a prank on insects with a murder."

She tried not to think of the night before, when Pomona had stood in the Widow Mags's kitchen, watching the villagers suffer with a look of glee—or of the way Pomona had bewitched that kitchen knife to fly through the air towards Eddie. *Just like the way the stang had flown through the air towards Daniel Tremaine.*

Shoving the image away, Caitlyn took a deep breath and looked up to meet James's eyes. "Pomona isn't a murderer."

James sighed. "I know you love Pomona and she's 'family'... but you can't keep protecting her, Caitlyn. Let the police investigate. If she's really as innocent as you say, then there's nothing to worry about." He hesitated, then his expression hardened. "I don't want to have to do this, but... if you don't hand this evidence over to the police and tell them everything, then I will."

CHAPTER THIRTY

Caitlyn was fuming as she drove away from Huntingdon Manor. She didn't know who she was more angry with: James or herself. She resented the high-handed way he was forcing her to own up to the police. But she also knew, in her heart of hearts, that James was in the right: there was no excuse for tampering with evidence at a crime scene, no matter how much she wanted to protect Pomona.

Still, he could have been more understanding! she thought angrily. In spite of her protests, James had insisted that she speak to Inspector Walsh and hand over the rubber snake by the end of the day. He had even compelled her to leave the rubber snake with him for safekeeping until then, as if he didn't trust her! Now, Caitlyn felt a panicky sense of urgency as she wondered what to do.

I need to find the real murderer, she thought suddenly. She was sure that Pomona hadn't killed Daniel Tremaine—which meant that the real murderer was still out there. *If I can only find out who it is and present them to the police, then everything will be okay!* She might still get told off for withholding evidence, of course, and for trying to cover up for her cousin, but hopefully it would just be a "slap on the wrist", since it wouldn't have had a real bearing on the case anyway.

And as for Pomona... Caitlyn shifted uneasily in the driver's seat. She could no longer ignore her worries about her cousin. Even if Pomona wasn't involved in Tremaine's murder, there was still something very wrong with her. But Caitlyn didn't know where to turn. She didn't feel that she could talk to James about it anymore, and for some reason, she still felt too uncomfortable approaching Bertha or the Widow Mags. Then she thought of Evie. Yes, her younger cousin was someone she could confide in! After all, Evie had been there during that strange episode with the ants, and Caitlyn knew that she would be much more understanding than anyone else.

When she arrived back in Tillyhenge, Caitlyn made her way to *Herbal Enchantments* and was pleased to see that the shop was fairly busy. A coach full of tourists had just arrived in the village, and a large group had found their way to the herbal shop. Some customers were hovering around Bertha as she weighed out dried herbs on some scales, and others were happily browsing amongst the scented soy candles and natural medicinal teas.

Caitlyn gave her aunt a cheery wave, then ducked to the private living area at the back of the cottage, where she found Evie painstakingly grinding something with an ancient stone mortar and pestle. At least, she assumed it was Evie, for the girl in the room still looked nothing like her young cousin. Her figure was marginally less voluptuous and her hair slightly less smooth and glossy than on the night of the ball, but otherwise, she still looked very much like the stunning young woman who had captivated everyone's attention.

"Evie?" said Caitlyn hesitantly.

The other girl raised her head and her eyes lit up. "Oh my Goddess, Caitlyn—I'm so glad you came! It's been so boring; I've been here grinding willow bark since first thing this morning."

Caitlyn looked at the mortar and pestle in surprise. "Are you doing that by hand? I thought you usually bewitched the pestle to do the pounding for you, so it's a lot quicker and easier."

Evie made a face. "Yes, but I've been magic-docked."

"Magic-docked?"

"It's like being grounded, except that instead of not being allowed to go out, I'm not allowed to use magic," Evie explained. She looked forlorn. "Mum was furious when she saw my new look, and I had to tell her about using the glamour spell from that YouTube witch." She sighed. "So now I'm not allowed to use magic at all—I have to do everything the hard way."

"Wow. I'm sorry, Evie," said Caitlyn sympathetically. "How long are you grounded—I mean, magic-docked?"

"Mum said at least until the glamour is completely gone." Evie made a despairing sound. "But it seems to be taking *forever* to fade! It's been nearly two days now since the ball and I still look the same." She dropped her eyes and added in a sheepish tone, "Mum says that's why you can't trust spells from random witches on the internet—you don't know the quality of the witchcraft used to create them or whether the incantations have been tested properly."

"Maybe you just need a bit more time. I mean, you do look a lot more like yourself already," Caitlyn said with an encouraging smile, thinking that a little white lie was sometimes necessary.

Evie gave her a worried look. "But Mum said that dubious-quality spells can leave permanent bad effects. What if... what if I remain looking like this forever? What if I can never return to the 'old' me?"

"But I thought you were delighted with the change! I mean, this is exactly how you've always wanted to look, isn't it?"

"I... I don't know," said Evie miserably. "I thought it would be wonderful to be glamorous and beautiful at last, but... nothing's turned out the way I expected! I had a terrible time at the ball, and then yesterday, when I walked past Chris in the village, he... he wouldn't even talk to me."

"What do you mean, he wouldn't talk to you?" asked Caitlyn, surprised.

Chris Bottom was the local teenage heart-throb who had all the village girls sighing wistfully. Evie had long worshipped him from afar, too shy and insecure to imagine that Chris could ever like her—especially when his aunt Vera was constantly warning him to stay away from her family. But thankfully, Chris seemed to share his father Jeremy's much more open-minded and tolerant attitude. At any rate, he seemed to turn a deaf ear to Vera's poisonous words and had often gone out of his way to be kind to Evie. So Caitlyn was startled to hear that he might have snubbed her young cousin.

"I thought Chris was always nice to you," she commented. "It's not like him to be rude and unfriendly."

"Well, he wasn't rude, exactly. It was just... I tried to say hello and he just stood there with his mouth open, staring at me. It was like... like he was too scared to speak to me!"

Caitlyn eyed Evie's face and figure with amusement. "You know, Evie, you might be a bit intimidating to a teenage boy at the moment."

Evie sighed. "But I—"

She broke off suddenly and hunched her shoulders as they heard the faint sound of a male voice with a very posh British accent outside the windows.

"Hullo! Hullooo! Evangeline, darling, are you there?"

"Oh my Goddess! It's him!" cried Evie, crouching down quickly so that she wouldn't be visible from the window.

"Who?" asked Caitlyn in puzzlement.

"Archie—Viscount Astley!" hissed Evie as she crawled underneath a table. "Get down, Caitlyn! He'll see you!"

Caitlyn obediently dropped to her knees. "The guy from the ball? What's he doing here? I thought he would have left already."

"He was supposed to leave straight after the ball, but he's decided to stay on. He's taken a room at the village pub, and he keeps coming around here and standing outside the window, reciting poetry to me," groaned Evie.

As if on cue, they heard the voice outside clear its throat theatrically, and then start booming:

"Hear my soul speak:
The very instant that I saw you, did
My heart fly to your service; there resides,
To make me slave to it..."

Caitlyn guffawed. "My God, which century is Archie from? He looks like he's only in his twenties, but he speaks like someone from Shakespeare's time."

"That *is* Shakespeare," said Evie, making a face. "It's from *The Tempest*; I remember 'cos we did it at school. And last night, he was throwing pebbles at my bedroom window and reciting lines from *Romeo and Juliet*."

Outside, the quivering, melodramatic voice continued:

"... And the sunlight clasps the earth
And the moonbeams kiss the sea:
What is all this sweet work worth
If thou kiss not me?"

"How long does he go on for?" whispered Caitlyn. "You can't keep hiding like this, Evie. You've just got to go out and tell him politely that you're... well, that you're not into him. Say it in iambic pentameter if that will help him understand," she added, grinning.

"I've already tried!" Evie said, heaving a frustrated breath. "Not in iambic pentameter, I mean, but I did try to explain that I don't like him *that* way. But he won't listen! He just keeps asking me to marry him again."

"What about Aunt Bertha? Can't she talk to him?"

"Mum says I got myself into this mess, so I need to learn to deal with it myself," said Evie morosely. Then she brightened. "Oh wait—has he gone?"

They both listened. It was true: all was silent again outside. Cautiously, Caitlyn stood up again and tiptoed over to the window, which looked out onto the lane behind Bertha's cottage. It was empty.

"All clear!" she said over her shoulder.

Evie crawled out from under the table and gave a loud sigh of relief. "Thank Goddess! Maybe Archie has finally got tired of things and given up."

Somehow, Caitlyn doubted it, but she decided not to be a wet blanket. Instead, she changed the subject: "Listen, Evie, I actually wanted to talk to you about Pomona."

"Pomona?"

"Yeah, you know what happened with the ants the other day—weren't you bothered by that?"

"But I thought we all agreed that it was just a coincidence."

Caitlyn sighed. "It's not coincidence, Evie." She told the younger girl what had happened in *Bewitched by Chocolate* the night before.

"Oh my Goddess!" Evie's eyes were round. "I'd heard some talk in the village, but it was mostly about Grandma, and you know how they're always spreading nasty rumours about her, so I didn't believe most of it... So you mean it was *Pomona* and not Grandma who hexed Vera and her friends?"

Caitlyn nodded soberly. "Yeah. It was almost as if Pomona was a different person."

"Do you think it's that black diamond necklace?" asked Evie. "I mean, it's supposed to be cursed, isn't it? I remember Pomona telling us that the main jewel is one of the missing pieces of the Black Orlov diamond, and wasn't that diamond, like, famous for cursing anyone who owned it? There was a New York jeweller who jumped off a skyscraper and a Russian princess who committed suicide... Maybe Pomona's fallen victim to the diamond's curse?"

"I think it's more than the necklace—I think it's the man who gave it to her: Thane Blackmort," said Caitlyn grimly. "People talk about someone being a 'bad influence'—well, Blackmort is the living embodiment of that! He's an *evil* influence. Ever since Pomona met him and started spending time with him, she's been different. It's like she's slowly changing into someone else, and now I feel like I don't even know her anymore."

"If Blackmort has bound Pomona to him with some kind of Dark Magic, that's going to be much harder to break than a curse," said Evie, looking worried. "You'd need a banishing spell."

"A banishing spell?"

"Yeah, it's a form of manipulative magic. But witches usually use it for small things—you know, like to get rid of unwanted or negative energies. You'd need a really powerful banishing spell to free Pomona. And..." She bit her lip. "You need her to take part in the ritual."

"I'll talk to her," said Caitlyn. "I'll persuade her to take part."

Evie looked doubtful. "She'll lose all her new magic powers, you know. She might not be happy to do that."

"She would if she knew what she's becoming," insisted Caitlyn. "I'm sure the old Pomona—the *real* Pomona—is still in there, somewhere! I just need to reach her." She looked earnestly at the younger girl. "In the meantime, Evie, can you work on finding a banishing spell we can use?"

"Me?" Evie looked dismayed.

"Yes, I wouldn't know where to start, whereas you know so much more about magic in general because you've been brought up as a practising witch, and you've got access to your mother's spell books."

"I'm not supposed to be doing *anything* with magic at the moment," said Evie anxiously. "Not even to read or research spell books for fun. If Mum catches me..." She gulped, then she took a deep breath and raised her head, meeting Caitlyn's eyes. "But I'll do it for Pomona."

Caitlyn reached out to squeeze the other girl's hand. "Thank you!"

"There's just one thing," said Evie hesitantly.

"What?"

"Tomorrow is Mabon—you know, the autumn equinox, when there'll be exactly twelve hours of day and twelve hours of night."

"Yes, your mother explained all that to me," said Caitlyn. "So?"

"Well, Mabon is known as the cusp; it's the day when darkness begins to defeat the light. If Blackmort is using Dark Magic to impel Pomona, the power of that bond will grow even stronger once

Mabon passes and we enter the final season of the year."

"So what are you saying?" asked Caitlyn, trying to ignore the ominous feeling in her chest.

"If we don't manage to do the banishing ritual successfully by sunrise on Mabon morning—by sunrise tomorrow—then even a powerful spell might not be strong enough to free Pomona."

"You mean... the change could become permanent?" asked Caitlyn in horror.

Evie nodded, her eyes wide. "The real Pomona could be lost forever."

CHAPTER THIRTY-ONE

"Hello, girls. How are we getting on in here? Evie, have you finished grinding the willow bark yet?"

Caitlyn and Evie jumped and whirled to see Bertha bustling in through the doorway. She came over to join them and peered into the mortar.

"That's looking good," she said with an approving nod.

"What are you going to use it for?" asked Caitlyn.

"I'm making up a new batch of natural pain-relief capsules," Bertha explained. "Dried feverfew and white willow bark—both crushed into a powder and then mixed and combined. The feverfew is great for relieving migraines, and willow bark is nature's pain killer. It contains salicin, you see, which is a chemical similar to the salicylic acid used in commercial aspirins."

She glanced at her watch, then turned to Caitlyn and said with a smile: "Now, can I ask you for a favour, dear? I have a friend who lives in a small commune nearby, who often provides me with supplies. I had a nice surprise this morning, as Stella sent me a message saying that she'd had a bumper crop of feverfew this summer, so she has loads of dried flowers to spare—which will be perfect for this batch of capsules I'm making. She also has bags of comfrey and burdock roots, hawthorn berries, and even some rose hips." Bertha beamed with anticipation. "So I'm going to pop over and I need Evie to come with me, to help me carry a few things. I was wondering if you wouldn't mind looking after the shop for a bit—"

"Um... actually, Mum, why doesn't Caitlyn go with you, and *I'll* stay?" interrupted Evie. "I've still got a few things to finish up here."

Caitlyn glanced up and saw the meaningful way that Evie was waggling her brows. She realised that this was a chance to get Bertha out of the house, so that the younger girl could access her mother's spell books.

"Um... yes!" said Caitlyn quickly. "I'd love to come and help you, Aunt Bertha."

Bertha looked surprised. "Oh... well, of course."

Twenty minutes later, Caitlyn got out of her aunt's car in a small clearing in front of an old, rambling country mansion. She looked around with some surprise. "Wow, this isn't what I imagined," she commented.

Bertha regarded her with amusement. "Were you expecting long-haired hippies walking around, smoking questionable herbs, and doing yoga in the nude?"

Caitlyn laughed awkwardly. "Sort of, I suppose..." She looked around again. The place looked like a respectable small country estate. It was set on several acres of land, with most of it being open meadow land, bordered by a strip of woodland, and established plots for vegetables, fruits, and herbs closer to the house. She could see sheep and pigs in the distance, as well as a flock of chickens running about, followed by peeping chicks, and people busily working in the gardens and outbuildings.

"There are a lot of misconceptions about communes and intentional communities," said Bertha tartly. "Most people think they're some kind of cult, or full of rabid tree-huggers who grow everything they eat and wear, and refuse to touch technology. It's all nonsense, of course! Lots of communes are filled with 'normal' people who still do all the conventional things like have a job, bring up families, enjoy hobbies, et cetera, and they live in their own private spaces within the commune, and they don't have to share meals or income if they don't want to. It's really all down to an individual community's values and philosophies. At the end of the day, communes are just groups of people who choose to live in an alternative way to what's common in modern society!"

Caitlyn looked at her aunt, surprised by her impassioned speech. "I didn't realise you knew so much about communes, Aunt Bertha."

Bertha flushed, looking slightly sheepish. "Sorry. I used to live in a commune for many years, you see, and it's a way of life that's still very close to my heart."

Caitlyn stared. "You lived in a commune?"

Bertha nodded, turning her head to gaze out over the landscape, her expression nostalgic. "Yes, many years ago, when I was a young woman. Not here. It was a commune up in Scotland." She paused, then added, "It was where I met Evie's father."

Caitlyn's eyes widened even more. She'd always wondered about Evie's father, but had never dared ask too much about him. It had always seemed too much like rude prying, especially when both Evie and Bertha never mentioned him.

"Is he still in a commune now?" she ventured.

Bertha laughed, half to herself. "Oh no, definitely not! He's a very respectable lawyer now, with a high-flying job in the City."

"Oh." Caitlyn was dying to ask more but wasn't sure how to word her questions. "Um... so does he come to visit sometimes?"

"No." Bertha's smile faded. "Evie can go and visit him any time she wants, of course, but Ewan and I decided when we parted that it would be best if we didn't see each other again."

"Oh... I'm... I'm sorry," said Caitlyn lamely.

Bertha gave her a wistful smile. "Don't be. It's for the best. And I shall always remember it as one of the happiest times of my life. My only regret is that life in the commune was so all-consuming, and I was so engrossed in my own affairs at that time—I didn't even return home to visit for several years, you know—that I didn't realise what was happening back home. It was a shock when I heard that Tara had run away."

Caitlyn jerked upright, all thoughts of Evie's father forgotten. "Tara?" she said. "You mean, your younger sister... my mother?"

Bertha nodded sadly. "I have to admit that we were never really close—oh, we loved each other as sisters, of course, but we weren't 'best friends', the way you and Pomona are. The ten-year difference between us was just too much of a gap, and I think Tara always saw me as more of the annoying older sister than as a friend. Plus, we were such different personalities, so it was difficult for us to relate to each other."

"So you don't know what happened—why she left?" asked Caitlyn breathlessly.

She'd tried so many times to find out more about what had happened to her mother, but she'd always come up against a brick wall. The Widow Mags flatly refused to discuss her estranged youngest daughter, and it had also been difficult to pin Bertha down in the past. Perhaps it was the atmosphere of the commune and the nostalgia of her past life, or perhaps it was being away from Tillyhenge and the shadow of her imperious mother, but this was the first time that Bertha had seemed open and willing to talk.

Her aunt grimaced, as if in memory, and said: "Well, at first I thought it was just another one of their fights—they were always at each other's throats, you see. If Tara and I were complete opposites, then she and Mother were too *much* alike, and that was even more of a problem! They were both proud and stubborn, and neither would give an inch. It got worse after I left home—I suppose because I was a buffer between them when I was there."

She sighed. "And Tara was so wild too. She was throwing tantrums and doing things to defy Mother at the age of three that I wouldn't even have dared to at thirteen! It didn't help that she'd always been an extremely powerful witch. Even as a toddler, she could perform advanced spells just by instinct, without any training. It was amazing to watch—but it did mean that she grew rather smug," said Bertha ruefully. "By the time she was seventeen, Tara was terribly cocky and reckless. She thought that she knew everything there was to know about magic and witchcraft, and argued with Mother constantly. So at first, I thought it was simply another one of their rows and that Tara would come home when she calmed down, but... she never did."

"And the Widow Mags—Grandma—never gave you

any idea what happened, like what they had fought about?" asked Caitlyn.

"I know that something dreadful happened, but Mother would never tell me the details. You know what she can be like," said Bertha with a wry look. She paused, then added, "I think there was a man involved. Someone Tara had met."

My father? thought Caitlyn wildly. Her mind was reeling from all the information that she had suddenly learned, and she didn't know what to think, how to react. Her mother sounded nothing like the saintly, maternal figure that she had built up in her mind—although she reminded herself that the Tara she was hearing about *had* only been seventeen. Recalling all the angst, rebellion, and emotional turmoil that she'd gone through at the same age herself—and she didn't even have her mother's bold, headstrong personality!—Caitlyn reflected that it was probably unfair to judge Tara too harshly.

She wanted to ask more, but Bertha was already walking towards the mansion, and she could see several women coming out to meet them. She would have to save further questions for later. Besides, if she was honest, she felt like she needed a bit of a break to digest all that she had learnt. What she really wanted was to crawl away somewhere quiet to be by herself with her thoughts, but this was neither the time nor the place. Caitlyn sighed, then took a deep breath, pushed the thoughts temporarily out of her mind, and went to join Bertha.

CHAPTER THIRTY-TWO

Several residents from the commune came out to welcome them, and everyone seemed incredibly friendly. As Bertha and her friend Stella became engrossed in a discussion about the best use of over-ripe rowan berries, Caitlyn accepted an invitation from a smiling young woman to take a tour of the rest of the house. The ground floor—like the grounds— was communal, and in addition to the kitchen, dining room, and laundry, there were several offices and work spaces, a meeting room, a music room, and even a dance studio.

As they went upstairs, Caitlyn realised that the upper floors contained private rooms and units, and she stopped with a smile as a little cat suddenly popped its head around one of the open doors. It was a "tuxedo cat", with a sleek black coat and white chest and paws, and bright yellow eyes that reminded her of Nibs.

"Hello!" she said, crouching down to stroke the little feline.

"That's Sparky," said her companion. "He belongs to the whole commune, although he does have his favourites among the residents. He spends a lot of time in Petra's room." She indicated the open door. At the same moment, they heard a soft voice with a slight accent calling:

"Sparky? Sparky, where have you gone?"

A moment later, an elderly woman came out of the room. She smiled as she saw Caitlyn and immediately invited her in.

"Oh no, I don't want to disturb you—" protested Caitlyn.

"Nonsense, I was just reading. Do come in!" said Petra, waving her into the room.

The woman was so insistent and seemed so eager for company that Caitlyn felt obliged to say yes. Leaving her companion, who drifted down the hallway to her own room, Caitlyn followed Petra into a large airy space with a bed in one corner, a small sofa in the other, and a wall of shelves filled with books, pretty knick-knacks, and framed photos on every level.

"Do sit down. Would you like some tea? You're visiting, aren't you? I haven't seen you before. Are you thinking of joining the commune? You'd love it here! It's wonderful having people around you all the time—you never feel lonely. Are you married or with a partner?"

Caitlyn parried the flood of questions and explained her connection with Bertha. It was obvious that Petra loved company, and the chance of a "fresh" conversation partner was a delightful prospect. As Caitlyn chatted, she saw that the other woman wasn't as old as she'd first thought; in fact, she realised with a start that Petra was probably no older—or possibly even younger—than Vivien Kwok. But in complete contrast to the beautiful Asian socialite, Petra looked much older than her years, with her skin prematurely lined and hollows around her eyes. Caitlyn wondered if she had suffered a terrible loss or illness, but didn't feel that she could ask.

"...and you say that you live in Tillyhenge?" asked Petra, stroking Sparky absently as the cat jumped up into her lap. "That name sounds familiar for some reason..."

"You've probably seen it mentioned in the news, in connection with the recent murder at Huntingdon Manor," said Caitlyn.

"Oh! Yes, of course—the murder at the masquerade ball." Petra gave a slight shiver. "It sounds terribly creepy. I was reading all about it in the tabloids just this morning. But that wasn't where I first heard the name—I remember now: it was from my daughter, Milena. She's a cellist, you know, and she tours with a chamber orchestra. She was playing at the Manor on the night of the ball."

Caitlyn belatedly remembered the cellist mentioning that her mother lived in a "community". She hadn't realised that the girl had meant a commune.

"Oh, what a coincidence—you're Milena's mother?" she said in surprise. "I've met your daughter. She was really nice and stayed overnight at the Manor to help with one of the guests. I had a chat with her the next morning, and I gave her a lift into Tillyhenge, where she was going to catch a bus to come and see you."

Petra smiled. "Milena is such a good girl. She always makes time to come and visit every week, if she's able to—although sometimes she's too far away, of course. The chamber orchestra plays all over the country. It's one reason why I moved into the commune, so I wouldn't have to be on my own when she was away. I don't have any other family, you see. But I'm lucky to have such a wonderful daughter. I'm so proud of Milena and all she's achieved."

"She plays the cello beautifully," said Caitlyn politely.

Petra beamed. "She's always been so talented. I brought her up on my own, you know, and I was really worried that she might fall behind the other children, but she's been amazing. She can do anything! Look..."

She got up and went over to collect a few framed

photos from the bookshelves. Sparky, who had just settled down on her lap, gave a peeved *meow* at being dislodged. He shook himself, then strolled over to Caitlyn and looked pointedly at *her* lap.

Caitlyn chuckled. "You cats are unbelievable."

Sparky said nothing, just looked at her with unblinking yellow eyes.

"Oh, all right," said Caitlyn with an exasperated laugh. "Up you get!"

A minute later, the black-and-white cat was happily curled up on her lap, purring and kneading the folds of her sweater. Caitlyn turned her attention to the photos that Petra had brought over to show her. They were all of a pretty, long-limbed, red-haired girl who Caitlyn was quick to recognise as a younger Milena.

"...this is when she came first in the school swimmers' championship... and here she is with the school choir..." Petra handed Caitlyn another photo. "And this is Milena with her athletics team... here she is doing her favourite: the javelin toss—she was so good, you know, that her coach wanted her to train for the Olympics."

"Wow," said Caitlyn with genuine admiration as she looked down at the picture of a teenage Milena rearing back to throw a javelin. "She's really multi-talented."

Petra nodded, her eyes shining with pride. "Yes, even as a small child, Milena could do so many different things! I thought perhaps she might become a professional athlete. But then we left Serbia and came to England, and Milena seemed to lose interest in sports. She turned to music instead." She rose and went back to the bookshelves to retrieve another photo. "But she seems very happy in the orchestra now, and she has made good friends. I am glad for her."

She handed Caitlyn a framed photo showing a group of men and women holding their instruments and posing formally in black ties and evening gowns. Milena was sitting in the front row, and as Caitlyn looked down at the picture, she realised that she actually *had* seen the cellist on the night of the ball— she just hadn't paid much attention at the time. It had probably been when Daniel Tremaine whisked her past the orchestra on the dance floor, or maybe even when she was dancing with James. She recalled glancing briefly at the assembled musicians and admiring the way Milena had sat so gracefully in her long black gown while she balanced her cello between her legs.

Then Caitlyn's eyes sharpened as she looked at Milena's gown in the photo again. It wasn't black, she realised, but a very dark, emerald green. Something prickled at the back of her mind.

"Um… does Milena have to buy a lot of different evening gowns to wear for her performances with the orchestra?" she asked.

"Well, she would like to have another, but at the moment, she only has that one," said Petra, looking down at the photograph. "Ballgowns and evening dresses are very expensive, you know, and since she has no opportunity to wear them at any other time, Milena feels that it would be better to save her money than spend it on buying another dress. She's a very sensible girl," added Petra proudly.

So she would have been wearing this dress on the night of the ball, thought Caitlyn.

The thought set off another disturbing vibration in her mind, and she found it hard to concentrate on the rest of the conversation as Petra took her through several more family photographs. All she kept thinking was: *could Milena be the murderer?*

CHAPTER THIRTY-THREE

Caitlyn was relieved when she could finally lift a sleepy Sparky off her lap, thank Petra for the visit, and bid them both goodbye. As she went back downstairs to search for Bertha, her thoughts were churning. *Can it just be coincidence that Milena was wearing a green dress on the night of the ball?* Caitlyn wondered if the cellist had a solid alibi. Inspector Walsh hadn't mentioned Milena specifically, but that didn't mean that she was in the clear. She could have been included with the other members of the orchestra and not been checked very thoroughly. Caitlyn felt her pulse quicken as she remembered that photo of a young Milena throwing a javelin. *A javelin is a metal-tipped spear...*

Petra's proud voice echoed in her mind: "*...She was so good, you know, that her coach wanted her to* *train for the Olympics..."*

At the same time, Caitlyn heard another echo—that of Inspector Walsh's voice telling her about the mystery surrounding the murder weapon: *"...the angle of the wound and the damage in the surrounding tissues suggest that the stang was driven into Tremaine's body with a force that could only have come from flying at great speed through the air... it would have required a superhuman effort to throw the stang at such speed and with such accuracy as to impale Tremaine in that way..."*

Superhuman effort? Or simply an effort that you wouldn't expect a "normal" person to have? Caitlyn mused. It might have seemed impossible under the usual circumstances, but for a girl who had once been such a good spear-thrower that she could have competed at the Olympics...

No, it was crazy to think that Milena could have been the murderer. After all, why would the pretty, young cellist have wanted to kill Daniel Tremaine? What motive could she possibly have? There was no connection between them.

Caitlyn was so deep in her thoughts that she wandered aimlessly about the grounds for twenty minutes before she found her aunt, at last, in one of the vegetable plots. Bertha was helping Stella dig up and divide rhubarb clumps, and she looked slightly comical brandishing a spade while clad in her customary purple kaftan. She seemed very happy, though, with her face flushed from the exercise and her eyes bright as she chatted with Stella. She was obviously in no hurry to leave, and Caitlyn soon found herself roped into helping in the vegetable patch. By the time they finally finished the job, cold, tired, and dirty, they were grateful to accept the big thermos filled with chunky vegetable soup that Stella had brought from the house.

"I've got some of my home-made quiche too," she added. "You must have some before you leave. Gosh, look at the time! We should have had lunch hours ago!"

It was past mid-afternoon by the time they finally loaded Bertha's car, waved their goodbyes, and drove away from the commune.

"Oh dear, we've been there for hours—far longer than I intended. Evie will be wondering what's happened to us!" said Bertha, glancing at the time on the car's dashboard. She gave a self-deprecating laugh. "I should have known, because this always happens when I visit the commune—I have such a lovely time there that I don't want to leave. It has such a warm, friendly atmosphere, don't you think? And I saw that one of the girls took you on a tour of the place? You seemed to be in the house for ages."

"I met one of the residents—a lovely lady named Petra—who was really keen to chat," Caitlyn explained. "She was showing me lots of photos."

"Oh yes, I know Petra. I've met her several times. You're right—she does love a good natter. Once she gets going, she never stops," said Bertha with a laugh. "Were the photos of her daughter? Petra is very proud of her. She's a musician, I think. The daughter, I mean."

"Yes, her daughter Milena is a cellist. She was actually playing in the chamber orchestra on the night of the ball."

"Was she really? What a coincidence!"

Caitlyn almost said: "Too much of a coincidence." But she bit back the words. Instead, she asked: "Do you know Petra well?"

"Only what she's told me." Bertha's kindly face sobered. "She's had a very tough life, poor woman. She ran away from a terrible situation back in Serbia, about twenty years ago, when her daughter was only seven or eight, I think, and they found refuge here in Britain. It must have been very hard being an immigrant who didn't speak much English and raising a child as a single mother. And of course, Petra had her own mental health issues to deal with as well."

"Mental health?" said Caitlyn in surprise. Although thin and haggard, Petra had seemed fine emotionally.

Bertha nodded. "She's much better now, so you wouldn't really know it, but she was a nervous wreck when she first came to live at the commune several years ago. She'd been involved in the resistance movement against the government back in Serbia, you see, and I think she might have been working with foreign spies—possibly even our own British agents. Then something awful happened."

"What?" asked Caitlyn, unconsciously holding her breath.

Bertha took her eyes off the road to look at Caitlyn gravely. "Well, Petra hasn't gone into the details, but from what she's told me, I think she was captured and subsequently tortured for information."

Caitlyn stared at her aunt, her thoughts whirling. "She was *tortured?*"

"Yes, it's horrible to think about, isn't it? The whole experience left her emotionally very fragile. She suffered panic attacks and other psychological issues for years. She has a morbid fear of being alone, for example, and used to break down into fits of hysterical terror sometimes. It was very hard for her daughter to support her through all that." Bertha brightened. "But as I said, things have improved a lot since Petra moved into the commune. She's become like a different person..."

Caitlyn hardly heard the rest of what her aunt said. Her mind was racing as she thought of her previous doubts about Milena being the murderer—mainly because the girl seemed to have no motive for wanting to kill Daniel Tremaine.

But what if the motive had been revenge? Caitlyn suddenly recalled Daniel Tremaine looking at the items in the Portrait Gallery and picking out the "Vlach magic talisman from Serbia"—an obscure occult item that surely most people wouldn't know about, unless they'd visited or lived in Serbia? Was it a coincidence that Tremaine, a British agent with a penchant for torture, could have spent time in Serbia, and that Petra Marković, a Serbian informant, was subjected to torture during her time working for the resistance? Surely there had to be a connection between them?

And what if Milena had somehow discovered that the handsome man at the ball was the same man who had tortured her mother all those years ago? As a loving child who'd had to watch her mother suffer the consequences of that ordeal, wouldn't she have wanted vengeance for what he'd done? And with her natural talent and abilities for javelin-throwing, she could have easily thrown the stang to impale Tremaine from across the room...

I have to get back to the Manor and tell James, Caitlyn thought urgently. *The police need to question Milena again. She could be the murderer! Which also means that Pomona would be released from suspicion,* she realised with delight.

She chafed at the delay for the rest of the trip, wishing that Bertha could drive faster, and, when they arrived back in Tillyhenge, she barely waited for the car to come to a stop before jumping out and bidding a hasty goodbye to her startled aunt. She was running across the village green, heading for her own car to drive back to Huntingdon Manor, when she spotted a familiar grey stallion tied to a tree at the side of the green. It was Arion, James's Percheron stallion.

Caitlyn faltered to a stop. *That must mean that James is here in the village.* She knew that he often rode Arion across the estate and into Tillyhenge, as it was actually a quicker route than having to drive via the roads, which circled around the valley. Tillyhenge was one of the last villages in England to still be owned by an estate, and James took his responsibilities as the local landlord very seriously. His down-to-earth manner and willingness to roll up his sleeves and "muck in" when helping his tenants had earned him great love and respect from the local residents. Now, Caitlyn paused and scanned the area, wondering which business or farm James might be at.

Then she noticed for the first time that there were several groups of people clustered around the green, with the largest group just outside the village pub. Everyone was talking animatedly, and there seemed to be a general buzz of excitement in the air. Caitlyn approached one of the groups and tapped one of the women on the shoulder.

"Excuse me... has something happened?" she asked.

"Oh, haven't you heard?" said the young woman excitedly. "They've got someone for the murder up at Huntingdon Manor!"

Caitlyn gasped. "Who is it? Has there been an arrest?"

The woman shrugged. "That's all I know." She nodded at the pub. "Lord Fitzroy's in there now with the police. They're questioning some of the pub regulars."

Caitlyn turned and rushed into the pub. She found her way barred by a young police constable as soon as she stepped inside.

"Sorry, miss—the pub's closed."

"I need to speak to James—I mean, Lord Fitzroy!" she exclaimed.

"His lordship is busy at the moment, helping the police with their enquiries—"

"This is about the murder investigation," she blurted. "Please, I have important information about the murderer!"

The constable hesitated, then turned and looked across the pub. In the far corner was a group of men, and Caitlyn spotted James's tall figure amongst them immediately. He glanced in her direction, and Caitlyn was heartened to see that in spite of their recent argument and hostile parting, his grey eyes warmed as soon as he saw her.

"Caitlyn!" He came hurrying across to greet her. "What are you doing here?"

"I heard that the police have arrested someone for the murder?" said Caitlyn.

"They haven't made an arrest yet," said James, looking slightly uncomfortable.

Before he could continue, Caitlyn launched into her revelations. "Don't you see?" she concluded after she had explained everything. "Milena could be the murderer! She's got the perfect motive. And she has the means—the ability, I mean. She could have thrown the stang with enough force to kill Daniel Tremaine because she used to be a champion javelin-thrower. Well, okay, maybe not champion, but you know what I mean." She leaned to the side to look beyond James. "Where's Inspector Walsh? Is he here? We must tell him about Milena as soon as possible. They have to bring her in for questioning again and recheck her alibi ..."

She trailed off as she noticed the expression on James's face. "What? What is it?"

James cleared his throat, looking even more uncomfortable. "Inspector Walsh has gone back to the station to organise a search."

"A search for whom?"

"For Pomona. There's a warrant out for her arrest."

CHAPTER THIRTY-FOUR

"*What?*" Caitlyn stared at James in disbelief. "Arrest Pomona? Why?"

"The police believe that she's responsible for Daniel Tremaine's murder."

"But why would they suddenly—"

"Because I told Inspector Walsh about the rubber snake you found," said James after a moment's hesitation. "He's confiscated it as evidence in a murder investigation. And together with Mr Bates's testimony, it puts Pomona at the crime scene just around the time the murder occurred. It also throws into question the credibility of her statement."

Caitlyn shook her head, her eyes wide with hurt and betrayal. "How *could* you, James? You went behind my back! You said you'd give me until the end of the day to decide—"

"And what would you have decided? Would you have confessed everything to the police? Or would you have kept on covering up for Pomona?" asked James scathingly. "You *knew* the right thing to do already—and yet you refused to do it."

"That's not true!" cried Caitlyn. "I just needed time to think and... and to prove that Pomona wasn't involved—"

"Why are you so sure that she's *not* involved?" demanded James. "Why are you so certain that Pomona isn't the murderer?"

"Because I know her!" Caitlyn snapped. "Yes, I know she's changed, and... and she might have done some things that are a bit... er... questionable... but Pomona isn't a killer! I know that in my heart. And besides," she rushed on, seeing that James looked unmoved. "If you just look at the 'facts', as you say, it makes much more sense for Milena to be the murderer. She had the necessary 'skill' to use the murder weapon. She could throw the javelin, for heaven's sake! Whereas Pomona can't even throw rubbish in the bin without missing it. Trust me, I know—I've had to share a bedroom with her."

"I thought you told me that Pomona was starting to gain some magical ability. So she wouldn't have needed Olympic skill with a javelin—she could have simply bewitched the stang to fly through the air. Just as she did with the knife aimed at Eddie Paver." James gave her a hard look. "You knew this, Caitlyn. You knew that Pomona could have used that weapon, and yet you still didn't speak up."

"What about motive then?" asked Caitlyn wildly. "That's just as important! Milena had a very good reason for wanting Daniel Tremaine dead, whereas Pomona had no connection with him. She barely knew him!"

"Perhaps she wasn't doing it for herself," said James.

"What do you mean?"

"Oh, come on, Caitlyn," said James impatiently. "It must have occurred to you that Pomona is under Blackmort's influence? Therefore, it's not impossible that he could have asked her to kill Tremaine for him. After all, he's helped her escape."

Caitlyn took a step back. "Escape? What do you mean?"

"Pomona has disappeared. No one has seen her since this morning. Mosley looked after her at breakfast and she told him that she was going for a walk in the grounds—but no one has seen her since then."

"Are you sure she's not still out walking?"

James shook his head. "The staff checked her room: one of her smaller travelling cases is missing. Her car is still there, though, so the only way she could have left is if someone picked her up." He nodded towards the group of men on the other side of the pub. "Neil Whitford, one of the regulars here, was out walking in the woods behind Tillyhenge this morning, and he claims that he saw a black helicopter overhead. It looked like it was about to make a landing."

Caitlyn drew a sharp breath as she recalled the sleek black aircraft that had transported Blackmort to and from the ball. "So you think Blackmort came to get her?"

"It's the logical assumption. But we have no idea where he might have taken her. We suspected London at first, but there's no one at his penthouse. That's why Inspector Walsh has gone back to the station—he's trying to mobilise his contacts to see if he can track down Blackmort's movements. From what he's ascertained so far, Blackmort appears to have left the country and gone on one of his mysterious overseas trips again, but there's no evidence that Pomona has left with him." James looked at her hopefully. "Do you know where she might have gone?"

"No. I have no idea."

"I thought Pomona might have mentioned something to you—somewhere she's stayed in the past with Blackmort, perhaps? She always seems to tell you everything."

Caitlyn sighed. "She used to. But not anymore."

"Well, if she does get in touch with you, you need to convince her to come back and give herself up," urged James. "The longer she runs from the law, the worse it will be for her. If she's really not involved in the murder, she'll be cleared of all the charges. I'll personally make sure that she has the best legal representation. But she needs to come back before it's too late."

In more ways than you realise, thought Caitlyn as she suddenly recalled Evie's words about the Mabon deadline. She felt a surge of worry and panic. She had to find her cousin. "I have to go," she mumbled to James, and, without waiting for his reply, she turned and rushed out of the pub.

It was late afternoon now, and with the shorter autumn days, the light was fading fast. Caitlyn hurried through the cobbled streets of the village until she arrived at *Herbal Enchantments*. She'd expected to find Bertha there, sorting through her new horde of goodies, but to her surprise, there was only Evie behind the shop counter.

"Mum's gone over to see Grandma," Evie explained. "She heard some of the gossip going around the village—you know, some of the nasty things that Vera and her friends have been saying— so she was a bit worried about Grandma being alone in the chocolate shop. Oh, but I'm so happy you came, Caitlyn, 'cos I wanted to tell you that I've found it!" She beamed. "I've found the spell we can use! It was in one of Mum's oldest spell books. And you know what else? I've thought of a great way to do the banishing ritual if you can't persuade Pomona to take part—we can just use a poppet!"

"Evie—"

The younger girl rushed on, reaching under the counter to grab a small doll-like figure and showing it to Caitlyn excitedly. "See, like this one... I thought of it when I saw the ones Mum put in the window display. We just need to create a connection to Pomona so that this poppet can represent her. Usually, you use a lock of hair or fingernail clipping or something, which you sew into the stuffing, but I'm worried that might not be strong enough this time. I think to make sure it works, you need to get the black diamond necklace from Pomona and put it on this doll. Then it will represent the 'new' Pomona and we can work the spell on..." Evie trailed off as she finally noticed the expression on Caitlyn's face. "What's wrong?"

Quickly, Caitlyn told her what had happened. "Pomona will have taken the black diamond with her—she wears it all the time—so unless we can find her, we won't be able to do the ritual, even using a poppet. But I have no idea where she is. Blackmort could have taken her anywhere! She might not even be in Britain anymore." She looked at Evie despairingly. "How are we going to do the banishing spell before sunrise tomorrow?"

Before Evie could answer, there was a loud *THUD!* and something struck the front shop window with a muffled impact. Caitlyn flinched and hunched her shoulders instinctively as she whirled around. Her bad experiences from the night before meant that she half expected to see a large stone come through the cracked glass. But there was nothing: the glass pane was intact, the view of the street outside showed no one out there.

"What on earth...?" she muttered.

"It was probably a bird flying into the glass," said Evie. "It's happened before. Mum says they get blinded by the sun or streetlights or something and then they fly wrong and go straight into the glass. Last time, we found a pigeon on the ground outside. Poor thing! It was okay, but really stunned. Mum said we should just let it rest in a box, in a quiet, dark place, and it should be fine—and it was! We released it the next morning." She came out from behind the counter. "We'd better go and check, in case there's another bird..."

When the two girls stepped outside, however, it was not a bird they found lying stunned on the ground beneath the shop window, but a large, fuzzy, brown fruit bat.

"Viktor?" said Caitlyn.

The fruit bat gave an irritable squeak, then it began to change, its body enlarging and elongating, its leathery wings morphing into arms clad in black sleeves, its furry, pointed face transforming into the wrinkled face of a very old man with a balding head, rheumy eyes, and two yellowed fangs protruding from a sunken mouth.

Hastily, Caitlyn glanced up and down the street, relieved to see that no one else was nearby to witness the shape-shifting. Then she grabbed Viktor's arm and hauled him into the shop.

"Viktor, you can't do that in broad daylight," she

admonished him. "People will be terrified if they see you shifting, and things are tense enough in the village at the moment."

"Who says it's 'daylight'?" grumbled the old vampire, rubbing his forehead where a sizable bump was beginning to develop. "If it was still light, I wouldn't have crashed into that blasted window. Really, the indignities I have had to suffer today! First squashed into a travelling case, and then knocked about by whoever was carrying the case... I shall probably have bruises for weeks!" He rubbed his arm peevishly. "And then when I finally manage to get out, I find that a bottle of body lotion has been spilled all over me, and now I reek of French vanilla and coconut... *ugh!*" He leaned forwards and wagged a bony finger in Caitlyn's face. "You should tell that cousin of yours to screw the caps back on her lotions properly—"

"Pomona?" said Caitlyn with a gasp. "Viktor, are you telling me you've been with her?"

"Eh?" The old vampire looked bewildered by her vehemence. "Well, I've been in her travelling case. Crawled in last night when I was looking for a good place for a snooze. Didn't fancy hanging upside-down in the Manor Library, and that nap I had in the cello case reminded me of the cosiness of hard moulding. Of course, I had to shift into my bat form to be small enough to fit in the case, but I decided it didn't matter since I could burrow under some of the clothes that were still in there." His voice rose with indignation. "How was I to know that the young lady would march in this morning and start throwing things into the case? I was just coming awake properly when she slammed it shut, and then I couldn't get out until she opened it again."

"Where?" demanded Caitlyn. "Where did you get out of the case? Was it far from here?"

Viktor considered. "Hmm... not far, I suppose, as the bat flies."

"Can you show me on a map?" asked Caitlyn eagerly. "Can I get there easily?"

"Why on earth would you want to go there?" asked Viktor. "Dreadful mess of a place. Construction equipment and bricks and scaffolding everywhere."

"Pomona's at a building site?" Evie said in disbelief.

"Well, part of it is built already. One wing. Not that it's easy to see, concealed behind all that scaffolding. The inside is decorated quite well, though," said Viktor with grudging approval. "All black, with ebony curtains, sable rugs, onyx bathrooms—even the mirrors are made of black obsidian. Reminds me of a castle I lived in once in Transylvania..."

Blackmort, thought Caitlyn. What Viktor described sounded exactly like the kind of place the "Black Tycoon" would inhabit. Did he have a house concealed in the countryside nearby? But surely there would have been gossip about that, and she hadn't heard anything. Although, if it was still only half built, as Viktor had suggested, then perhaps people had mistaken it for a construction site and hadn't realised that parts of it were already inhabitable. *A clever way to hide in plain sight...*

"Listen, Viktor, you need to tell me where this place is," she said, grabbing the old vampire's arm. "It's urgent. I need to find Pomona as soon as possible."

"Well, I can't *tell* you because I don't know myself. I can't point it out on a map," said Viktor huffily. "However, I *can* show you the way. If I can fly back in my bat form, I can retrace the route. Most of it will be through the forest, though."

"You mean I have to follow you cross-country?" said Caitlyn, dismayed. That meant that driving her car was out of the question, but there was no way she could follow Viktor on foot either. She would be much too slow... Then suddenly, she had an idea.

"Okay, you just lead the way and I'll follow," she told Viktor. "We have to start from Huntingdon Manor, though. Come on, we'll take the shortcut into the estate from the back of the village." She turned back to Evie. "Can you get everything for the banishing ritual ready, Evie? I'll try and make sure that I'm back here with the black diamond before sunrise."

"Not here," said Evie quickly. "We need a bonfire, so it has to be outdoors; somewhere secluded, where nobody will disturb us, and—"

"What about the stone circle?" asked Caitlyn. "There will be no one there after dark."

"Oh! Yes, of course!" cried Evie in delight. "Why didn't I think of that? It's perfect! It's a site of ancient magic, where the powers of nature meet, and it will help to magnify the strength of our spell."

"Good. Get everything ready and meet me there."

"Okay, but Caitlyn..." Evie reached out for her hand. "Please be careful."

"Don't worry, I will." Caitlyn glanced at Viktor, who was busy adjusting his fangs in a nearby mirror and gave a grin. "What can go wrong with my vampire uncle protecting me?"

CHAPTER THIRTY-FIVE

Caitlyn crept silently around the side of Huntingdon Manor, trying to stay within the shadows as she made her way swiftly through the landscaped grounds. Everything seemed quiet; the big house was silent, the lights dimmed, and she hoped that most of the staff had left for the day, although she knew that the ever-diligent Mosley would probably still be around, checking, monitoring, planning...

At least James wasn't back yet—she was thankful for that. She knew that it was silly, and maybe she should have gone straight to him for help, but she still felt so hurt and angry and betrayed by his recent actions that she didn't want to involve him. She felt as if she couldn't trust him anymore. What if he insisted on contacting the police and dragging them along? They could spook Pomona into going on the run again, and this time there would be no way of knowing where she had gone. No, she had to do this on her own.

Well, not completely on my own, Caitlyn reminded herself, glancing backwards to where Viktor was following her. Then she frowned. The old vampire was nowhere to be seen. She retraced her steps a few yards until she found Viktor standing by one of the windows at the back of the Manor. It was a tall sash window that had been opened slightly at the bottom, and the old vampire was bent over, his pointed nose pressed against the glass as he sniffed earnestly.

"Viktor! What are you doing?" Caitlyn hissed.

Viktor didn't seem to hear her—he was too busy sliding a long, bony arm through the gap and stretching to reach for something inside. Caitlyn scurried up to him, taking cover behind a large holly bush next to the window. She peered in through the glass pane and saw what looked like the inside of a large walk-in pantry, with a long counter running around the edges of the room, and cupboards and shelves filled with tins, jars, sacks, and boxes lining the walls. Sitting on the counter, on the other side of the window, was a bowl of ugly yellow fruit that looked like lumpy, misshapen pears, and next to the bowl were several open glass jars filled with a beautiful, rich, amber-red jelly.

It was one of these jars that Viktor was reaching for, his wrinkled face a mask of concentration as he tried to manoeuvre through the narrow window opening. Finding it simply too small, he grabbed the bottom rail of the lower sash and gave it an upward heave to open the window more. The wood was stiff and gave an ear-piercing shriek as it shifted at last.

"*Viktor!*" cried Caitlyn in a furious whisper.

She started forwards to grab him, but before she could move, there was a scream from inside the room, followed by a commotion of shouting, banging, and running footsteps. The next minute, Mrs Pruett, the Manor's cook, appeared on the other side of the window brandishing a copper pan.

"Thief! Vagrant! Get your dirty hands off my jelly!" she screeched, trying to smack Viktor on the head.

"Ow! *Ouch!*" cried Viktor, hunching his shoulders and ducking his head under the blows.

Caitlyn reached out an arm, grabbed the back of Viktor's ancient black jacket, and yanked him away from the window. She pushed him flat against the wall next to her, concealed behind the holly bush, and gestured frantically for him to stay quiet, just as she heard Mosley's familiar voice coming through the open window.

"Mrs Pruett! What on earth—"

"There was a thief! A horrible dirty old tramp—"

Viktor bristled next to Caitlyn. "I'm not a 'dirty old tramp'!"

"Shhh!" admonished Caitlyn, clamping a hand over his mouth. She held her breath as Mosley stuck his head out of the window and leaned out, looking around.

"I don't see anyone about, Mrs Pruett. Are you sure you didn't imagine things?"

"I certainly did not!" came Mrs Pruett's indignant voice. "I'm telling you, I saw him! He was trying to climb in through the window to steal my quince jelly!"

"Well, perhaps you shouldn't leave windows open like that," said Mosley testily.

Mrs Pruett sounded even more indignant. "I've always left windows open a crack. It's important to have good ventilation in kitchens and pantries..."

Their voices faded as they moved away from the window, and Caitlyn took the chance to escape as well, hustling Viktor in front of her and not stopping until they were well away from the main manor house.

"Viktor, what on earth were you thinking?" she said in exasperated tones when they stopped to catch their breath.

"I could smell quince jelly," said the old vampire sulkily. "There's nothing like English quinces at this time of the year... light, fragrant, marvellous! The quintessential autumn experience—"

"Yes, well, you nearly got the quintessential English prison experience," grumbled Caitlyn.

She sighed. She should have remembered Viktor's weakness. As a vampire of the Megachiroptera Order, whose members all transformed into fruit bats, Viktor was an avid fruitarian, and he could forget everything the minute he sighted a juicy plum or a bush filled with ripe gooseberries.

"We can't get caught by anyone, otherwise they'll stop us searching for Pomona," she reminded him. "We really need to find her, Viktor—it's urgent!"

"All right, all right," he grumbled. "No need to get your bloomers in a twist."

A few minutes later, they stole into the stable courtyard. It was an eerie change from Caitlyn's last visit, when it had been filled with hustle and bustle: the musical *clip-clop* of horses' hooves as they were led across the yard mingling with the cheerful whistling and conversation of the grooms and stable hands. Now, it was dark and empty, with only the occasional equine snort from the individual stalls breaking the silence.

Caitlyn hurried down the row of stalls, reading the names on the brass plates affixed above each door, until she came to the one she was looking for. She peeked inside: a stocky chestnut mare with a flaxen mane and tail stood, relaxed, with her head down. She lifted it and whickered a greeting as Caitlyn let herself quietly into the stall.

"Hello, Melys," Caitlyn said softly, reaching out and feeling the velvety muzzle in her open palm. "Sorry, sweetie, I haven't brought you any sugar lumps again, but I hope you'll still help me..."

Several minutes later, Caitlyn stood next to the mounting block in the courtyard, with the mare saddled and ready. *At least, I hope she's ready*, thought Caitlyn, running a doubtful eye over the horse's tack. She'd had to rely on her hazy memory of her few riding lessons—as well as Viktor's rambling instructions—to tack up, and she hoped that she'd done it correctly. For good measure, she checked the girth, adjusted the stirrups, and fiddled with the buckles on the bridle once more, then she climbed onto the mounting block.

At the top, she paused, her heart pounding. She'd never ridden a horse on her own. There had always been someone supervising before, like this morning, when James had been there guiding and encouraging her... And now she was planning to ride out alone, into the dark of night, with no idea of where she was going—was she mad?

Then the mare turned her head to look at Caitlyn with her big, dark eyes and whickered softly, as if to say: *"Come on! What are you waiting for?"*

Caitlyn chuckled, in spite of herself. Feeling braver, she took a deep breath, grasped the pommel with one hand, and heaved herself up into the saddle. Melys fidgeted slightly, then calmed as Caitlyn tried to remember everything James had taught her that morning. She tried to sit back and relax, settling her weight firmly into the saddle and making sure that she wasn't clenching the mare's sides with her knees. Then she picked up the reins and gave the horse a gentle nudge with her heels.

Instantly, Melys responded, turning automatically towards the wide arch that led from the stable courtyard out into the rest of the estate. Caitlyn felt a surge of confidence and she smiled to herself.

Looking up, she scanned the skies for Viktor and spotted the little fruit bat a minute later—a darker shape against the night sky, his black, leathery wings stretched out from his fuzzy, brown body, and his little foxy face turning left and right as he surveyed the landscape.

He swooped down next to her, gave a bossy squeak, then turned and flew off, making for a stand of trees in the distance. Caitlyn urged Melys into a trot and they followed, soon entering the forest that covered large parts of the estate. It was unnerving to ride in the dark. Although the autumn tree canopy was sparse, it was still dense enough to block out what little light there was from the moon and stars. Caitlyn felt as if she were riding blind—that whether she shut her eyes or opened them, she was faced with the same yawning darkness in front of her—and she had to fight a rising sense of panic in her chest.

But Melys trotted on, steady and sure-footed, and the mare's calm demeanour soothed Caitlyn's nerves. After a while, she found that she had stopped straining her eyes uselessly in the darkness and, instead, focused on her other senses: the soft whisper of Viktor's wing beats up in the sky ahead of them and the occasional squeak he gave to urge them forwards... the rustle of the leaves and branches from the canopy overhead... the muffled thud of Melys's hooves on the soft ground... and the earthy smell of mud and fallen leaves, mingled with the woodsy aroma of the trees around her... all overlaid with the warm, comforting "horsey" scent emanating from the mare's body.

Slowly, as she relaxed, Caitlyn found that she could see after all. Her eyes adapted, and shapes and textures emerged from the darkness. By the time they left the cover of the trees to step out onto open land, she was surprised by how much she could see of the night landscape. Now, as she reined Melys in atop a small knoll, she saw that there was a large property under construction on the small plateau of land beyond.

We must be on the estate bordering the Fitzroy lands, she thought. She had never been to this side of the valley before—it was on the opposite side of Huntingdon Manor to the village of Tillyhenge—but she did remember some gossip about it on the local grapevine. In particular, she recalled hearing that the land had been sold for development the year before, and there were rumours of a luxury country resort and spa being built there.

Now she could make a good guess as to who the owner of the new luxury development was: Thane Blackmort. Judging from what Viktor had said, it sounded like the mysterious billionaire was cleverly using the cover of a property development project and unfinished construction site to hide a secret country retreat.

Caitlyn took a deep breath, then urged Melys into motion again, heading down the slope towards the dark shapes of the half-finished buildings.

CHAPTER THIRTY-SIX

Caitlyn rode as close as she dared, then she dismounted and tethered Melys loosely behind a copse of trees before continuing the rest of the way on foot. She moved tentatively, keeping to the shadows and making as little noise as possible, and she was glad of her caution when she crept around a bulldozer a few minutes later and spotted a figure loitering by the side of the main building. It was a man, big and bulky, who reminded her of the "bouncer-like" bodyguards that Blackmort had brought with him to the ball. He was lighting a cigarette, bending his head down and cupping his hand around the naked flame to protect it against the wind, so luckily he hadn't seen her.

Caitlyn ducked down behind the bulldozer and considered her options. She could see a doorway just beyond the man, and she guessed that it led into the interior of the building, which was probably also where Pomona was staying. She had to get inside somehow. She peeked at the man again, hoping that he might set off on a patrol of the grounds or something, thus giving her the chance to sneak into the building, but he remained standing resolutely outside the doorway. Caitlyn sighed. It looked like he was going to be stationed there all night...

A cold hand suddenly gripped her shoulder and she whirled around with a muffled scream. Then she sagged with relief as she saw the stooped old man standing in front of her.

"Viktor!" she gasped, clutching her chest. "You've got to stop sneaking up on me like that!" She threw a glance over her shoulder and was relieved to see that the guard seemed unperturbed. The strong winds whistling around the corner of the building must have drowned out her cry.

"What on earth are you skulking around there for?" asked Viktor. "Your cousin's room is on the other side. Follow me, I will show you."

He led her to the other side of the construction site, approaching the main building from a different direction, and showed her a section of scaffolding which had been erected against the half-finished wall. The scaffolding was covered with sheeting, which screened the exterior of the building from view, and when Viktor lifted a loose flap and pulled her through to the other side, Caitlyn realised with surprise that the section of building behind the scaffolding wasn't actually incomplete at all. It looked like a fully intact wing of an elegant country manor, with lavishly furnished interiors visible through the glass windows.

Viktor beckoned her over to one of the windows. Caitlyn peeked in and her heart skipped a beat when she saw Pomona sleeping in an enormous four-poster bed, in the centre of a luxurious suite. As Viktor had said, it was furnished all in black, with black damask wallpaper, black velvet drapes and upholstery, and even an enormous black crystal chandelier hanging from the high arched ceiling. Yet somehow, it managed to look opulent and sexy, rather than dingy and morbid. And even in the dim room, Caitlyn could make out the black diamond, nestling against Pomona's throat, its usual vicious sparkle dimmed to a malevolent glow.

"I need to get in and remove that necklace from Pomona's neck," she told Viktor urgently. "Without that, I can't do the banishing spell that's going to release her from Blackmort's influence. Does the window open?"

"No, they are all sealed."

"Then how did you escape?" asked Caitlyn in surprise. "Surely you didn't go out through the corridors of the house?"

"Certainly not!" said Viktor. "Go through the house and run the gauntlet of guards both inside and out? What do you take me for?"

"Well, then how did you escape?"

"I used the chimney." Viktor peered through the glass and pointed to the wall beyond the four-poster bed, which featured an ebony mantelpiece around a large empty fireplace and a long chimney flue extending up the wall to disappear into the ceiling.

Caitlyn felt her heart sink. "The chimney? Does that mean I have to climb up on the roof to access it?"

"Great garlic, you would never fit," said Viktor, giving her a disparaging look.

"Thanks," said Caitlyn, wryly, trying not to feel hurt. "I know I've got big hips but—"

"No, no, it is not your hips," said Viktor impatiently. "The flue is barely wide enough for a child. I had to shift into my bat form to be small enough to fly out."

"Great," said Caitlyn, crestfallen. She looked back at the sleeping Pomona. "How am I going to get that necklace then?"

"*I* shall get it," said Viktor grandly. "I shall shift into my bat form and retrace my route back into the room, remove the necklace from your cousin's neck, and bring it back to you."

"But Viktor—"

It was too late. The old vampire had turned and, with a twirl of his black coat-tails, was gone through the flap in the scaffolding sheeting. A moment later, Caitlyn heard a soft squeak and the rhythmic flapping of leathery wings rising in the air and fading away. She sighed, then turned back to the window. *It'll be okay. It'll be fine,* she reassured herself. *Just as long as there's no bowl of juicy plums or something in the room...*

The minutes ticked past, and Caitlyn felt sweat begin to bead on her forehead, despite the chill of the autumn night. She stared through the glass pane, her eyes riveted on the yawning black opening above the hearth on the other side of the room. Surely Viktor should have made it down the chimney by now? What was taking him so long?

Just as she was wondering whether she should leave the shelter of the scaffolding herself to go in search of Viktor, she saw a cloud of ash come raining down and billow out of the chimney opening. The next moment, a fuzzy brown fruit bat plopped down onto the hearth. He shook himself and sneezed, then he climbed over the grate and began half hopping, half crawling across the room.

Caitlyn watched tensely as the little bat grasped the bedcovers in his tiny claws and slowly hauled himself up the side of the four-poster bed. Pomona sighed suddenly and turned over in her sleep, moving restlessly against the blankets, and Viktor ducked quickly behind a fold of the canopy hanging from the top of the bed. A second later, he peeked out and, seeing that Pomona had settled again, began to crawl carefully across the bedclothes towards her.

Caitlyn held her breath, her heart pounding, as she watched the little bat's slow progress. "Careful...

careful..." she whispered, even though she knew Viktor couldn't hear her.

He had reached Pomona's chest now and was hovering next to her neck, eyeing the black diamond choker with consternation. Caitlyn realised with dismay that the way Pomona was sleeping meant that the clasp for the choker was tucked beneath her and out of reach. *What's Viktor going to do now?* she wondered frantically. As she watched, the little fruit bat cocked his head, as if pondering the problem, then—to Caitlyn's horror—he reached up and rubbed the tip of one leathery wing against Pomona's cheek.

What is he doing? she thought in a panic. If Pomona were to wake suddenly and find a bat crawling across her bed—even as cute a bat as Viktor was—she'd probably scream the place down and bring the guards running... and that would be the end of everything!

But to her relief, instead of waking, Pomona simply stirred restlessly, then turned over on her side. Caitlyn swallowed a gasp as Viktor dived out of the way just in time to avoid being squashed, then she relaxed again as the little fruit bat deftly crept up to Pomona's shoulders and reached for the nape of her neck, where the clasp of the necklace was now exposed. A moment later, the necklace was undone and carefully pulled off Pomona's neck. Caitlyn stiffened, wondering if her cousin would feel the movement and miss the gemstone's cold weight against her throat. But Pomona didn't stir and, after a second, Caitlyn exhaled again.

Still, it wasn't over: Viktor had to get out. She watched as the little fruit bat grasped the necklace firmly in his mouth, then turned and climbed down the side of the bed, and began his odd hopping walk back to the fireplace. It was an agonising process to watch as—weighed down by the heavy diamond choker—he was even more slow and clumsy. But at last, he reached the hearth and climbed laboriously over the grate.

There he paused for a long time, and Caitlyn felt a new misgiving as she recalled that bats normally launched themselves into flight by dropping from a height and then beating their powerful wings to provide the uplift they needed. She had rarely seen Viktor take off from standing. It would be hard enough in such a cramped space, never mind carrying a heavy platinum-and-diamond necklace as well. Could he do it?

She held her breath and watched as the little fruit bat seemed to gather himself, then he launched himself upwards, flapping his wings manically. Caitlyn darted a look at Pomona, worried that all the movement and noise might wake her cousin, then jerked her eyes back to Viktor, who was still struggling to get airborne. He had managed to rise up to where the firebox narrowed into the opening of the flue and was desperately trying to manoeuvre into the narrow gap.

Caitlyn winced as she saw one of his flapping wings smack against the edge of the lintel and, for a moment, she thought he was going to fall back down. But the little bat was determined and with a combination of clawing, flapping, and scrambling, he somehow managed to get himself into the throat of the chimney. The next moment, he disappeared from sight. Caitlyn held her breath, her eyes still frozen to the spot where Viktor had been just a moment before, watching half in hope, half in dread. She knew that the chimney flue was long and there was still a chance that Viktor could get stuck halfway or simply fall back down from sheer exhaustion…

Then she heard the rustle of the scaffolding screen behind her, and she whirled to see Viktor stepping through the flap once more. His face was streaked black with soot, and the tops of his shoulders and balding head were liberally covered with ash, but he was back and safe—and holding the black diamond necklace triumphantly in his hands.

"Oh, Viktor!" cried Caitlyn, rushing to throw her arms around him in relief.

"Yes… *ahem*… very well, very well…" The old vampire patted her shoulder awkwardly. He cleared his throat, looking embarrassed. "No time for that. We had better leave at once."

"Yes, you're right," said Caitlyn, recovering herself.

She threw an agonised look back through the window, where she could see Pomona still sleeping in the depths of that huge, black four-poster bed. She hated leaving her cousin there, in that opulent, sinister space, but she had no choice. Taking a deep breath, Caitlyn turned away from the window and followed Viktor back out of the scaffolding cover.

As they hurried around the building site, making for the side where they'd arrived and where she had left Melys tied behind the copse of trees, Caitlyn felt a giddy mixture of relief and jubilation.

"We did it, Viktor! We did it!" she panted, laughing. She raised the hand clutching the necklace and looked at it, glittering in the moonlight. "I can't believe you actually managed to steal this! I nearly died watching you trying to get up that chimney—"

She broke off with a gasp of shock as they rounded the side of a stationary excavator and crashed straight into two burly men dressed in black. More of Blackmort's guards. They had obviously been patrolling the grounds and their eyes narrowed as they confronted the intruders.

Caitlyn's heart lurched with sickening horror as she stumbled back, and she found herself staring into the muzzle of a gun.

CHAPTER THIRTY-SEVEN

"Back up! Against the machine!" barked one of the men.

Slowly, Caitlyn backed away until the solid metal body of the excavator pressed against her back. She felt sick with chagrin. They had almost made it! A few more minutes and they would have escaped the building site and got away! Whereas now... what was going to happen to them?

"You! What's that in your hand?" snapped one of the men, waving his gun at her.

Caitlyn gulped, then reluctantly unfurled her fingers to show the black diamond choker clutched in one hand. The guards exclaimed in outrage. It was obvious they recognised Pomona's favourite accessory.

"How did you get that?" demanded the first guard.

He reached for the necklace and, instinctively, Caitlyn drew back. "Give it to me!" he snarled, lunging at her.

"Hold hard, my man!" cried Viktor, stepping in front of Caitlyn and puffing his bony chest out. "You will not touch a hair on her head, or you will have me to answer to!"

The two guards stopped and looked at each other, then burst out laughing.

"Look, Grandpa," said the second guard. "I'm not in the business of beating up old men, so just get out of the way, okay?"

Viktor bristled. "*Old man*? Who are you calling 'old'? I will have you know, I am only six hundred and thirty-four years old, which is barely middle-aged for a vampire."

"A what?" The guard grinned, then turned to his friend and made a twirling motion with one hand next to his head. "Thinks he's a vampire, this one... hehehe..."

"I do not *think* I am a vampire—I *know* I am one," said Viktor loftily. "And I shall prove it by putting you into a state of vampire hypnosis!" He raised both arms and leaned towards the two men. "Look into my eyes... LOOK into my eyes..."

The guards stopped and stared at the old vampire in bewilderment, and Caitlyn felt a rush of hope. Could it work? Was Viktor going to save the day?

There was a tense silence, then the air was filled by a loud snore.

From Viktor.

Great, thought Caitlyn with a sigh as she saw that the old vampire was still standing, leaning forwards, but now with his chin dipped to his chest and his arms hanging limply at his sides. *He's put himself to sleep!*

"Hey!" the second guard guffawed. "Check it out! The old geezer's fallen asleep!"

"Vampire hypnosis, my arse!" said the first guard. "Must be some barmy old sod who's escaped from a nursing home." He turned his attention back to Caitlyn, his expression hardening. "Now, where were we?"

He took a step towards her, but, at the same moment, Viktor came awake with a loud snort.

"Eh? *Hugghhh... gguuhh...* Hold hard, my man! You will not touch a hair on her head, or—" Viktor paused. "Wait, have I not said that already?"

The first guard growled, "Ah, I've had enough of this bullsh—"

"*Fie!* You do not use such language in front of a lady, sir!" cried Viktor. "Apologise at once or I shall wash your mouth out with carbolic acid!"

"Huh?"

The guard's dumbfounded expression was so comical that, in any other situation, Caitlyn would have laughed. Then she blinked in surprise as both guards began to cough and thrash their arms about, waving their hands in front of their faces. A thick mist had appeared out of nowhere and wrapped around them, obscuring their vision. Their voices, frantic and confused, came out of the mist:

"Hey! What's going on?"

"I can't see!"

"Harry, where are you, mate?"

"Aaggh!"

Viktor dusted his hands with satisfaction and turned to Caitlyn. "Vampire mist. That should keep them busy for a few minutes."

"You did that?" said Caitlyn, impressed. She had never thought much of Viktor's vampiric powers, despite the stories he often told of great battles he had fought in. So far, most of his attempts at things like "vampire hypnosis" had ended in a farce. But now she felt a new respect for him.

"Now, away with you," said Viktor, making a shooing motion at her. "I shall stay and hold them off."

"What? No, Viktor, I can't leave you! There are two of them and more might come. You're an ol—" Caitlyn caught herself before she said "old man". Hastily, she amended it to: "You're outnumbered."

"Outnumbered?" Viktor scoffed. "I will have you know that I once faced three basilisks alone and emerged victorious!"

"Yes, but that was probably a long time ago when you were a lot youn—er, I mean, when the situation was different," protested Caitlyn.

Viktor glowered at her. "I am an Ancient Guardian Protector, trained to do battle and shield others. Do not insult me by doubting my abilities. Now, go! Do what you need to save your cousin. There are only a few hours left before the sun rises on Mabon morn."

Caitlyn hesitated. She still couldn't quite shake off the image of Viktor as a rather frail and doddery old man, but she reminded herself that he *was* a vampire, after all, who had survived over six hundred years of wars, plagues, and catastrophes before she was even born. Besides, he was right: if she didn't get back to Evie with the necklace to do the banishing spell soon, then everything they'd risked that night would be for nothing.

"Okay, but... please be careful, Viktor," she begged, resisting the urge to hug him once more.

The old vampire turned back to the two guards, who were starting to emerge from the dispersing mist. Caitlyn gave him one last troubled look, then ran as fast as she could for the copse of trees where Melys was tethered. A couple of minutes later, she was mounted and heading back the way they had come, with the black diamond necklace tucked safely into a pocket.

Melys strained against the reins, as if she could sense the urgency of the situation, and Caitlyn knew that the mare wanted to break into a canter. She gripped the reins tightly and swallowed. Did she dare? She had never tried riding faster than a trot before—what if she fell off? But they didn't have a minute to lose, and it seemed silly restraining the horse when they could be going at double the speed...

Caitlyn took a deep breath, then leaned forwards and loosened the reins, giving Melys her head. At the same time, she nudged her heels hard against the horse's side.

"Go, Melys!" she breathed.

The mare's ears pricked forwards, then she surged forwards into a powerful canter. Caitlyn gasped, her heart flying into her mouth, as she felt herself rocked wildly back and forth. She clutched at the mane and tried not to think about falling off as the night landscape turned into a blur around her. The wind screamed past her face, bringing tears to her eyes and a numbing cold to her ears.

The dark shape of the forest loomed in front of them. Melys was heading unerringly for the gap between the trees—the start of the track which they had come on earlier—and Caitlyn barely had time to register this before they were in the woods and the trees had closed around them. The sound of the mare's hooves drumming on the forest floor joined the roar of the wind as they pounded down the track snaking through the trees.

Caitlyn ducked low over the horse's neck, but not fast enough to avoid getting slapped in the face by some of the branches. She winced from the sting and wondered if her face would be covered in scratches tomorrow. It didn't matter. All that mattered was that she was still clinging on. More than clinging on, in fact, she realised. She was actually starting to adapt to the horse's gait, her body instinctively swaying in the saddle to match the mare's movements.

Her fear faded slowly away, to be replaced by a sense of jubilation. She'd never thought she'd be able to ride this fast, much less in the dark, through a dense forest! She almost wanted to whoop with glee and delight. Then she recalled why she was riding through the dark of night in the first place and came back down to earth with a thump. She flung a look over her shoulder. It was hard to see, what with the moving horse and the dark confusion of the flowing landscape, but she didn't think that she was being followed. Still, that didn't mean that she could relax.

Turning back, Caitlyn hunched low over the mare's neck. "Faster, Melys—faster!"

CHAPTER THIRTY-EIGHT

They emerged at last on the other side of the forest and Caitlyn saw the familiar shape of Huntingdon Manor and its collection of outbuildings in the distance. But she turned the mare's head away from the manor house and instead directed Melys across the open field running alongside the landscaped grounds. This gradually rose up into a small hill, and at the very top, silhouetted against the night sky, was a circle of standing stones—the ancient sarsen boulders which made up the stone circle of Tillyhenge.

Caitlyn urged the mare up the hill and Melys obliged, snorting and puffing, her breath billowing out in great clouds of steam as she began climbing. When they neared the top, Caitlyn saw the glow of flames, and she broke into a smile of relief as she saw

Evie crouched next to a small bonfire in the centre of the stone circle.

"Caitlyn!" Evie sprang up and waved. "Oh my Goddess, I thought you were never going to come!"

Caitlyn brought Melys to a stop and dismounted, grimacing at the aching muscles in her buttocks and thighs. She felt like she would never be able to walk normally again! Gingerly, she made her way over to join Evie by the bonfire.

"Did you get it?" asked Evie eagerly.

Caitlyn nodded and dug into her pocket, then drew out the sparkling black diamond choker. Evie's eyes grew round, and she reached out reverent hands to take the necklace.

"Wow..." she said in a hushed tone. "I've never seen it up close before. It's... it's beautiful, isn't it?"

"It's horrible," said Caitlyn, eyeing the necklace with distaste. "Like a poisonous serpent or centipede or something..."

"Still, imagine all the power it could give you," Evie murmured, running a caressing finger over the glowing black jewel.

"Evie!" Caitlyn cried, snapping her fingers under her younger cousin's nose.

Evie started, then looked up with a shamefaced smile. "Uh... sorry."

"I think you'd better give me that," said Caitlyn hastily, taking the necklace back. She glanced at the items gathered around the bonfire. "Have you prepared the poppet?"

Evie nodded and bent to pick up a doll-like object. "Here. Look."

She had taken one of the simple figures in Bertha's shop window and added embellishments, including bright yellow yarn hair, pretty glittery fabric for a dress, and big blue button eyes. Caitlyn felt a stab of disappointment. She didn't know what she had expected, but it hadn't been this. The poppet was crude, like a home-made child's toy, and looked nothing like Pomona.

"It's not complete yet," Evie explained, seeing her expression. "We need the taglock—the thing from the person it's representing—that will create the link between them. And then it will awaken."

Caitlyn reached out and carefully draped the black diamond necklace over the head of the poppet, twisting the chain around twice, so that the length was shortened, and the black gemstone came to rest against the throat of the "poppet-Pomona". As she did so, Evie chanted softly:

"Poppet, awaken... no more encumber,
Pomona, you be... now rise from your slumber!"

Caitlyn waited, half expecting the poppet to move or something, but nothing happened. And yet somehow, as she continued staring at the doll, she began to feel that it did have the "essence" of Pomona, after all, despite nothing visibly changing.

"What happens now?" she asked Evie.

"Now, we do the banishing spell. I found a whole chapter in Mum's oldest spell book on banishing rituals, and I've brought all the things we need."

Evie indicated the pile of items, which included a black candle, a salt and pepper shaker, a little carving knife, and a vial of anointing oil, as well as an open book lying on the ground next to the bonfire. Caitlyn glanced at the spidery handwriting covering the open pages and realised they contained spell verses. She turned and looked worriedly at the other side of the hill, which rolled steeply down to the edge of the village. The Widow Mags's cottage was tucked right against the base of the hill, the gate of her back garden opening almost directly onto its slope. Caitlyn knew that the stone circle was easily visible from the cottage—she herself had often looked at the distant shapes from her attic bedroom window—but that was in the daytime. Hopefully, the dark of night would hide them from view now. Then she remembered the bonfire. Would the sight of an unusual orange glow on the hill attract attention?

As if reading her mind, Evie added reassuringly: "Don't worry, no one's there. I used the back lanes when I was coming through the village, to keep out of sight, and I came past the back of *Bewitched by Chocolate* 'cos that's the fastest way up the hill. I peeked in the kitchen window, and I saw Mum and Grandma talking to Inspector Walsh. They were just leaving with him to go down to the police station." She turned back to look at the bonfire. "If we're quick about setting up the spell ritual, we can put out the fire before anybody notices."

"Okay, so what do we have to do?" asked Caitlyn.

Evie indicated an area around them. "We have to make a circle around us with the salt, to create a protective barrier, and then we have to call Pomona to mind while chanting the spell. And then we need to carve a banishing sigil onto the candle, sprinkle it with the pepper and anointing oil, then light it and let it burn itself down."

"What? But... that could take hours!" Caitlyn protested. She glanced at the horizon. "It might not burn out before sunrise. Isn't there another way?"

"Yeah, there *are* other ways," Evie admitted, looking doubtful. "Like you could use a cleansing bath, with magical herbs, salts, and milk, but you really need Pomona to be willing to take part in that. Or... or there's burning."

"Burning?"

Evie nodded. "It's the fastest method. You chant the banishing spell and focus on the evil that has taken root, willing it to be consumed by the flames that burn the poppet. And then you throw the poppet into the bonfire. It's one of the oldest and most powerful magical rituals: purification and cleansing, by way of destruction, but..." She hesitated. "It's the one that will cause Pomona the most pain."

Caitlyn sighed. "Okay. I guess we don't have much choice. Tell me what I need to do."

Evie grabbed the salt shaker and thrust it into

Caitlyn's hands. "Sprinkle this on the ground in an anticlockwise direction and make a large circle around us—"

She broke off as the sky above them suddenly erupted in a tumult of noise and roaring wind, which whipped their hair back from their faces and flattened the grass around them. Caitlyn realised belatedly that she had been conscious of a faint rumble in the background, which had been growing steadily louder, but she and Evie had been so engrossed in discussing the banishing spells that neither of them had paid much heed. Now, they watched open-mouthed as a sleek black helicopter descended slowly from the sky, until it hovered just metres above the side of the hill.

A figure appeared at the open passenger door and perched on one of the landing skids for a moment before leaping from the hovering aircraft to land in the soft grass. Instantly, the helicopter rose again and disappeared into the darkness of the sky. As the throbbing of its rotor blades faded away, Caitlyn saw the figure rise slowly, then advance towards them. Her eyes widened as she saw who it was.

"Pomona?" she gasped.

CHAPTER THIRTY-NINE

Caitlyn watched, transfixed, as the figure walked across the top of the hill towards them. It looked like Pomona... except that this girl, with her cold, dark eyes and the cruel twist to her mouth, seemed nothing like her warm, bubbly cousin. A sinister aura seemed to emanate from her, which reminded Caitlyn of the eerie glow from the black diamond, and she felt an involuntary shiver run down her back.

Pomona stopped by the bonfire and held out her hand. "Give it to me!"

Caitlyn had jerked the poppet behind her back, and now she faced her cousin, trying to keep her face calm and expressionless. "Give you what?"

"The frickin' necklace!" snapped Pomona. "I know you have it! As soon as I woke up and discovered it gone, I knew it had to be you. You're jealous of me and my new powers, and you want to steal the black diamond for yourself—"

"No!" cried Caitlyn, goaded out of her feigned composure. "I didn't take it for myself—I took it to save *you*, Pomie!"

"Save me?" Pomona gave a sneering laugh. "You're kidding, right? What do I need saving for? Oh... oh... wait, you're gonna tell me that I need saving from the forces of Dark Magic or some other pathetic crap like that." She rolled her eyes. "Gimme a break! Spare me that self-righteous garbage—"

"It's not garbage!" said Caitlyn hotly. "Do you have any idea what you've become, Pomona? Do you realise how much you've changed? Have you looked at yourself—really looked at yourself—in the mirror?"

"Oh yeah, I've looked." Pomona smirked. "And I like what I see." She took a step forwards, her smile fading. "Now, give me the black diamond."

Caitlyn stiffened. "No."

Pomona narrowed her eyes. "I don't wanna do it, Caitlyn, but I *will* hurt you—really hurt you—if you don't give it to me."

Caitlyn stared at her. She couldn't believe that this was the same girl who had been her best friend since childhood, who had shared teenage angst and embarrassing secrets, who had laughed and cheered and fumed and cried, and always been there for her.

"Pomie, please... this isn't you," she whispered, searching Pomona's eyes for a glimmer of the girl she had once been.

"This is the new me!" snarled Pomona. "And I'm warning you, Caitlyn, you don't know what I'm capable of—"

"Did you kill Daniel Tremaine?" Caitlyn burst out. Suddenly, she had to know. "I defended you, Pomona! I told everyone that you could never commit murder... Was I wrong? Did you do it?"

"No, of course I didn't kill him," said Pomona scornfully. "I told you, I was, like, having a nap in the Library. Did you think I was lying? Hah! I'm not like you and the Widow Mags, always skulking in the shadows—I'm not ashamed of my powers!" Her voice dropped to a menacing tone. "And I'm warning you: I was just messing around in the chocolate shop last night. I won't be messing around now." She held her hand out again. "I'm only gonna say it one more time: Give. Me. The. Necklace."

Caitlyn raised her chin and looked her cousin straight in the eye. "Do your worst, Pomona. I'm not scared of you."

"Oh yeah?" Pomona gave a cold smile, then she turned her gaze on Evie, who was cowering a few feet away. "What about Evie? You not scared either, huh?"

"I... I..." Evie stammered, her face white.

"Leave Evie out of this!" cried Caitlyn, trying to jump between Pomona and the younger girl. As she did so, she brushed against the bonfire and the flames singed the poppet she was clutching in her hands.

"*Aaah!*" cried Pomona, jerking back.

Caitlyn froze. She lifted the poppet and stared at the blackened edges of the doll's arm, then she looked up to see Pomona rubbing her shoulder.

Her cousin's face turned ugly as she saw the black diamond necklace wrapped around the poppet. "Sympathetic magic! You've hexed me!" she cried, her eyes accusing.

"No, Pomie, we were trying to heal you!" said Caitlyn. "Please, let us help—"

She broke off as Pomona turned towards Evie and raised her hands in a threatening gesture, her eyes burning with malevolent fury. Caitlyn threw an agonised look at the items on the ground—the candle, the salt shaker, the anointing oil... There was no time to do the banishing spell that they'd originally planned. There was only one other option. Taking a shuddering breath, she raised her hand and flung the poppet into the bonfire.

Instantly, Pomona screamed and crumpled to the ground. She rolled and writhed in agony, and the air filled with her shrieks of pain and pleading. "Nooo! Stop! *Stop!*"

Caitlyn turned away, unable to watch. She felt sick with guilt and remorse, and her hands were shaking as she pressed them to her ears, trying to block out Pomona's cries.

"*Caitlyn... help me! Please...!*"

Oh God, I can't do this! thought Caitlyn, sinking to her knees, still trying to press her hands to her ears.

She caught her breath in a sob and looked wildly around. Her eyes caught sight of a wooden stick which had rolled away from the main pile in the bonfire. It was lying by her foot, slightly charred but still whole. She could easily pick it up and use it to fish the poppet back out of the flames. She hesitated, her hand hovering over the stick. Just a small action and she could stop Pomona's suffering...

"No!" cried Evie, appearing next to her and catching hold of her hand. "No, we have to let the fire do its work! It's the only way to save her."

Caitlyn took another shuddering breath and nodded, grateful for Evie's support. Trying to block out the sound of Pomona's cries, she fixed her eyes on the poppet in the flames. Then, as Evie began chanting the verses from the spell book, she echoed the words:

"Evil, you must make your way,
Ne'r more seen from this day—
Your grotesque form I thee banish,
And from this place you must now vanish!
So free thy captive from your chains,
And let her be herself again!"

Caitlyn gritted her teeth and watched as the poppet slowly turned into a charred black figure and then finally into a pile of ashes. Even the black diamond disappeared, which surprised her, as she didn't think diamonds could burn in a normal fire.

But it was definitely gone, and the flames burned bright and pure. Next to the bonfire, Pomona slumped to the ground at last and lay still.

"Pomie?" Caitlyn gasped.

She rushed across and crouched down next to her cousin, then gently rolled her over. Pomona was unconscious, her face pale and her breathing shallow. Caitlyn swallowed and reached out to feel the other girl's brow: it was clammy and feverish. But even as her fingers lingered, the skin began to cool and the perspiration evaporate, whilst colour began to slowly return to Pomona's face.

"Is she... is she okay?" asked Evie in a fearful whisper as she crouched down next to Caitlyn.

As if in answer, Pomona suddenly opened her eyes. They were a beautiful, clear, cornflower blue, and Caitlyn felt her heart leap with hope. She and Evie waited tensely as Pomona blinked, then slowly sat up and looked around in a daze. Finally, she turned back to the two girls and grinned at them.

"Holy guacamole, guys! You won't believe the dream I had!"

CHAPTER FORTY

Caitlyn hesitated outside the entrance to the Ballroom. For a moment, she was struck by a vivid sense of déjà vu: the bright light from the sparkling chandeliers, the Mabon decorations everywhere, the noisy hum of talk and laughter from the crowds of people dressed to impress, and the lively music filling the air...

This time, however, she was not wearing an exotic rented gown, but her own pretty sea-green chiffon dress, with her runestone necklace proudly displayed around her neck. And as she stepped into the Ballroom and looked around, Caitlyn saw that the music came not from a chamber orchestra but from a small village band made up of residents from Tillyhenge; the crowd, too, was not composed of sophisticated strangers clad in glamorous, masked costumes, but members of the Huntingdon Manor staff and the local community, all dressed in their Sunday best. And rather than swirling around the room in dramatic waltzes, couples were joking and giggling as they bopped and danced to the light-hearted tunes coming from the village band.

The one thing that *was* familiar, though, was the magnificent fountain with its five tiers of rich, buttery, salted caramel sauce, which still took pride of place at one end of the Ballroom. Caitlyn smiled as she watched the guests gathered around the fountain, eagerly dipping their pieces of marshmallow, fudge brownie, apple, or chocolate into the free-flowing salted caramel sauce. It was good to see so many residents from the village happily tasting the Widow Mags's treats and heartening to think that not everyone in Tillyhenge agreed with the mob who had vandalised the chocolate shop.

It was a fantastic idea of James's to have a private Mabon celebration just for the Manor staff and local residents, Caitlyn thought. After the tension and stress of the last few days, it was a wonderful chance to bring the local community together again, and she felt gladness fill her heart as she walked through the room, past so many happy faces. There was dairy farmer Jeremy Bottom, being cheered on by several other farmers as he took on the traditional challenge of drinking a yard of ale; there was Amy Matthews, the pretty young wife of the Manor's late gamekeeper, sipping red wine and chatting with Bertha; there was the usual group of busybodies from the village, heads together, happily gossiping as they stood around the caramel fountain; and across the room, there was Mrs Pruett, the Manor's cook, and a couple of the maids, all pink-cheeked with laughter as they watched Mosley fastidiously attempt to eat a toffee apple.

And unlike the Mabon Ball, this time, the animals had been invited too. Caitlyn chuckled to herself as she saw Nibs scamper across the Ballroom and up to Old Palmer, the Manor's head gardener. As the only member of the estate who hadn't instantly fallen in love with the little black kitten when he first arrived, Old Palmer had spent a lot of the early days yelling "You bloody cat!" and chasing Nibs out of his prize rose beds. But now he scooped the kitten up into his arms and proudly showed him off to some of the other guests. And across the room from them was the Manor's other furry resident, sitting at James's feet, while his master talked to the owner of the village pub. Bran's baggy face was pulled back in his habitual doggie grin as he panted placidly and leaned against James, who had to spread his legs to brace himself against the mastiff's weight.

There was no sign of Vera, though, nor of Eddie Paver, Angela Skinner, nor any of the other locals who were Vera's witch-hating allies. It looked like they had all snubbed the celebration. Caitlyn sighed. *Well, Rome wasn't built in a day*, she reminded herself. *And besides...*

She broke into a smile again as she glanced across the Ballroom and caught the surprising sight of the Widow Mags surrounded by several village children. They were watching wide-eyed as the old witch tempered melted chocolate on a marble slab, then deftly produced swirls and lattices, chocolate curls, and other fancy garnishes and decorations. It might not have been "real magic", but there was no doubting the awe and wonder in the children's eyes, and Caitlyn felt hope stir in her chest as she saw that some of the adult villagers were also joining the audience. To see people admiring and respecting her grandmother's skill, instead of just fearing and hating her, was the most heart-warming experience.

"Oh, I say—have you seen Evangeline anywhere?" came a voice behind her.

"You mean Evie? She's over there..." Caitlyn said absently, starting to point to where Evie was standing on the other side of the room. Then her voice trailed off as she turned and realised who was asking the question. It was Archibald Cummings, Viscount Astley.

"Oh!" She stared at him in dismay, then glanced back across the room to where Evie was now standing, her eyes bulging with horror.

"Ah! Much obliged," said Archie, giving her a comical bow.

Caitlyn made a rueful face and mouthed a silent "Sorry" behind Archie's back as he strode across the room towards Evie. But to her surprise, when he reached her younger cousin, he walked straight past her and kept on going, his eyes still searching the crowd. Evie stared at him in surprise as he blanked her completely, then a wide smile spread across her face. Caitlyn realised suddenly what she hadn't noticed earlier—that Evie was looking just like her old self again. Her hair was a frizzy, carroty-red mane hanging down her back, her cheeks were tinged with acne, and her bony chest and thin body did little to fill out her dress. And yet she had never looked so relieved and happy.

Then, as Caitlyn watched in delight, a lanky youth with blond surfer good looks suddenly came up to Evie and held his hand out to her, a friendly grin on his face. Evie stared at him, open-mouthed, for a full minute before she shyly put her hand in his. Then she followed him onto the dance floor, still looking starstruck that Chris Bottom had chosen to dance with *her* over all the other village girls vying for his attention. Her face was radiant and, suddenly, she looked absolutely beautiful.

Caitlyn felt a wave of happiness fill her heart as she watched Evie. Then she heard a familiar peal of laughter and her smile widened even more as she turned to look across the Ballroom and saw a vivacious blonde beauty flirting with several young men from the village. Pomona, as usual, was dressed more flamboyantly than anyone else in the room, in a gold lamé minidress that clung to every curve, matched with a pair of white cowboy boots. It should have looked ridiculous, but somehow, she managed to pull it off with flair and style—and the best thing of all, Caitlyn noted, was that her cousin's neck was bare, with no malevolent black jewel glittering at her throat.

Caitlyn drifted over to the little group and Pomona's eyes lit up as she spotted her. Leaving her admirers for a moment, she sidled up to Caitlyn and said in a stage whisper:

"Omigod, Caitlyn, have you met the new apprentice stonemason from the village? He's *so hot*! He's got, like, the most gorgeous brown eyes, and these big hands with long sensitive fingers..." Pomona sighed lustfully and fanned herself. "He was telling me all about his training, and I swear, I've never heard chisels and mallets sound so sexy." She gave a wicked grin. "He said his dream was to carve his very own gargoyle, and I'm like, 'Honey, you can come and work on my spout any time you like'."

"Pomona!" said Caitlyn with a shocked laugh. *Yup, the old Pomona was definitely back.*

Her cousin giggled. "Aww, come on, Caitlyn, stop being such a prude. There's no better way to celebrate a harvest festival than with a bit of *ripening* action, right? Speaking of which, have you and James kissed yet?"

"Pomie!" Caitlyn looked quickly around to see if anyone was listening.

"C'mon, I wanna know what I missed while I was off in Creepy La-la Land... did you guys kiss?"

"We... sort of," mumbled Caitlyn, looking down.

"What d'you mean 'sort of'? You either kissed or you didn't... Oh, wait, you mean James gave you a peck on the cheek or something? That doesn't count!" said Pomona scornfully. "I'm talking a proper kiss, with tongue—"

"*Pomona!*" Desperately, Caitlyn tried to change the subject. "Um... I'm... I'm glad you're able to joke about the whole thing. It was a lot more than just 'Creepy La-la Land', you know."

Pomona shrugged. "Yeah, well, I don't remember much about it. Which kinda sucks, you know, when you tell me I was able to do all these cool spells and bewitchments and stuff. Man, I could actually do *magic*—honest-to-goodness, real freakin' magic!" She pouted. "I can't believe I had all these awesome powers, and I can't remember a thing!"

"It's just as well," said Caitlyn darkly. "You were horrible, Pomona. You wouldn't have liked who you were." She hesitated, then added: "Um... you're... you're not going to see Thane Blackmort anymore, are you?"

Pomona tilted her head to one side. "Well, I don't know—there's something really hot about a powerful, sexy, evil billionaire... Just kidding!" She laughed, seeing Caitlyn's expression. She glanced back at the group of young village men, eyeing them with relish. "Don't worry, I'm gonna stick to local 'bad boys' from now on. The baker's son is pretty cute too, *and* did I tell you he's got a motorbike...?"

CHAPTER FORTY-ONE

Caitlyn stood by the buffet, feeling another wave of déjà vu as she considered the display of dishes in front of her. It was more modest than the one at the Mabon Ball, since James had been adamant that Mrs Pruett should have a complete break, and the only way she'd agreed to that was if the hired caterers provided a simpler menu. So the buffet consisted of mostly cold meats, hors d'oeuvres, and gourmet tarts, coupled with a smaller array of sweet cakes and treats from *Bewitched by Chocolate*.

Still, it reminded Caitlyn enough of the night of the ball when she had stood there, plate in hand, trying to decide what to taste. *And I never got to taste anything*, she reminded herself as she recalled the interruption by Vivien Kwok, followed by Pomona and Blackmort's arrival. This time, she decided, she was going to make sure that she enjoyed a mouthful of everything on display. *Starting with the salted caramel fountain,* she thought with a smile.

She joined the throng gathered around the showpiece and carefully speared a large slice of Granny Smith apple from the tray next to the fountain, then she dipped this into the rich, buttery caramel sauce flowing over the edge of one tier and down into the next. She rotated the apple piece until it was evenly covered, then lifted it to her lips and took her first bite.

Mmmm... definitely worth waiting for! The salted caramel was rich and buttery, with the wonderful toffee taste of caramelised sugar mingling with smooth cream and enhanced by a subtle layering of salt—all deliciously offset by the tart, crisp flavour of the apple. Caitlyn felt as if she could stay there by the caramel fountain, happily stuffing her face all day!

Then she spied some wooden crates artistically stacked next to the fountain, with some turned on their sides to display a range of autumn fruits and root vegetables nestled amongst piles of hay and burlap sacks. It was a beautiful display which really highlighted the "bounty of the autumn harvest", and it was crowned by a tray of glossy, sticky toffee apples placed on the topmost crate.

Suddenly, Caitlyn heard Viktor's voice echo in her head: *"...that old witch Mags knows what she's doing with caramel sauce, I'll give her that. Best toffee apples I've tasted in a century!"* She sighed as she felt a familiar pang of worry. She hadn't seen the old vampire since leaving him to hold off the guards at Blackmort's secret estate two nights earlier. Was he all right? Had he escaped? She told herself that Viktor had lived a long time and could look after himself, but still, she couldn't help the nagging feeling of concern.

She had relayed the story of Pomona's "abduction" to a sceptical Inspector Walsh, and he had been good enough to trace the location of the property and send a team there to investigate. But his officers had been met by an innocuous-looking building site and a team of bewildered engineers, surveyors, and architects, all denying that anyone could have been staying in the half-finished development. There had been no sign of the sinister guards that Caitlyn had met, nor of Blackmort himself—in fact, the "Black Tycoon" was rumoured to still be overseas. Meanwhile, although the police did find one section of the building with the interiors already complete— in particular a sumptuous bedroom suite fitted out with luxurious black décor, furniture, and upholstery—there was no sign that anyone had ever stayed there.

"It's just a demo room for investors and partners to see, so they can visualise what the final resort would look like"—had been the innocent explanation, and with no evidence to the contrary, the police had had to abandon their investigation. It was frustrating, but Caitlyn was less bothered by the remaining mystery and more by Viktor's continued absence. Had Blackmort's guards captured him and taken him away? What if they'd really hurt him? She felt a stab of guilt and berated herself once more for leaving the old vampire alone there that night...

Then her morose thoughts were interrupted by a shriek of disgust, and she looked up to see one of the village busybodies standing by the tray of toffee apples, holding one up at arm's length.

"L-look!" she quavered. "There's... there's teeth stuck in the toffee!"

"What?" cried Mrs Pruett indignantly, hurrying over to inspect the offending fruit.

Caitlyn arrived at the woman's side at the same time, and they both stared down at the caramel-covered apple. A large bite had been taken out of its curved surface, and embedded in the sticky toffee, at the edge of the missing chunk, were a pair of yellowed fangs. Caitlyn felt her lips twitch as a sneaking suspicion began to dawn.

"Ugh!" cried Mrs Pruett in outrage. "I personally inspected every one of the toffee apples before putting them out earlier. How did this get here?"

"Looks like someone's taken a bite and left their false teeth behind by mistake," guffawed one of the villagers standing nearby. "That toffee's really sticky. Practically yanks your tonsils out."

"Well, they should know better than to just take one bite and put the apple back, never mind leaving their teeth stuck in it!" said Mrs Pruett huffily. "When I find who did this, I'm going to give them a piece of my mind!"

Caitlyn swallowed a laugh as she stepped back from the crowd gathered around Mrs Pruett. Then her grin grew wider as her gaze fell on the stack of wooden crates and she looked properly at one of the open crates for the first time. Tucked amongst the butternut squash and scrubbed parsnips, the glossy red apples and russet-coloured pears, was a fuzzy brown bundle. Surreptitiously, Caitlyn leaned closer and saw that the small mound was in fact the rounded belly of a little fruit bat. He was curled up with his leathery wings tucked close to his sides, and his foxy little face a picture of sleeping contentment. She could even hear the soft wheezing of his snores.

So this is where Viktor has been! Here I was, worried sick about him, and he's been busy indulging himself into a toffee apple coma! she thought with a mixture of exasperation and affection. Casting a quick look around to make sure no one was watching, Caitlyn reached down and carefully pulled a flap of burlap sacking over the little bat, so that he was better hidden from view. Then she straightened and was about to return to the buffet when she heard her name being called. Turning, she saw Mosley approaching. The butler gave an apologetic cough and said:

"Miss Le Fey? His lordship was wondering if you would mind going to his study."

"His study?" said Caitlyn in surprise.

She glanced around the Ballroom and noticed that James was no longer where he had previously been standing. In fact, he seemed to have left the party altogether. She knew that there were still a lot of things unresolved between them—they hadn't had a private moment together since their "fight", just before she'd left to search for Pomona—but still, it was odd that James should choose now, in the middle of the party, to want to talk to her. Nevertheless, she put her plate regretfully back down and followed Mosley out of the Ballroom.

She was startled when she was shown into the study to find that it was not James, but Inspector Walsh who was waiting for her. Wasn't the murder investigation all wrapped up? Why did the police want to speak to her again? But as Inspector Walsh began talking, it became quickly apparent that the case was far from closed.

"What do you mean Milena's story holds?" Caitlyn asked, staring at the detective inspector in disbelief.

"I mean that her alibi checks out," said Inspector Walsh. "Several of her fellow orchestra members vouch for the fact that she was with them at various times throughout the evening, which means that she was never alone at any point and therefore could not have gone up to the Portrait Gallery."

"But... no, that can't be right. Someone in the orchestra must be covering up for her. Milena has to be the murderer! She had the perfect motive," insisted Caitlyn. "She had a strong reason for wanting Tremaine dead. He tortured her mother and—"

"No, in actual fact, he did not," said Inspector Walsh. "Petra Marković *was* tortured, yes, but not by Daniel Tremaine or any member of the British government. She was detained and questioned by the Serbian secret police and suffered torture at their hands. We have spoken to her at length and shown her photos of Tremaine and she denies ever having met him."

"But... but it all seemed to fit," stammered Caitlyn. "And Milena was a trained javelin-thrower, so she was one of the few people who could have thrown the stang with enough force... Are you telling me that it was all just a coincidence?"

Inspector Walsh gave Caitlyn a reproving look. "It's what we call circumstantial evidence, Miss Le Fey. It's the first lesson we learn in detective school: not to build a case simply on a convenient convergence of events and happy coincidences. I hope that's something you learn from this experience too."

Caitlyn flushed, then she asked: "But does that mean we're back to square one in the hunt for the murderer?"

CHAPTER FORTY-TWO

Inspector Walsh seemed less disturbed than Caitlyn expected by what seemed to be a massive setback. "Not exactly," he said. "If you remember, there were several other leads and options for suspects—"

"Oh God, you're not going to jump on Pomona again, are you?" groaned Caitlyn.

"Well, that's one of the reasons I wanted to speak to you," said the detective. "The key piece of evidence that placed your cousin at the crime scene has turned out to be a hoax."

Caitlyn blinked in surprise. "A hoax? What do you mean?"

Inspector Walsh reached into his inner jacket pocket and pulled out a plastic evidence bag. He handed it to Caitlyn, who stared uncomprehendingly at what was contained in the bag: a long lock of dark red hair.

"This is the bag that Lord Fitzroy gave me, purported to contain a rubber snake which came from the Medusa wig that Miss Sinclair wore on the night of the ball, and which was found next to the victim's body." Inspector Walsh gave her a hard look. "However, when I took it out at the station to give it to my forensics team, this is what it contained." He indicated the scarlet tresses. "Now, the only thing I can think of is that you somehow cleverly switched the item in the bag—"

"No!" gasped Caitlyn. "How could you think I would do that? I swear, I gave James the exact rubber snake I found in the Portrait Gallery. I have no idea how you've ended up with a piece of hair in the bag instead! Are you sure that it isn't something on your end? I mean, could someone have got things mixed up at the police station?"

Inspector Walsh shook his head decisively. "We have very strict protocols to ensure a robust chain of custody, which is crucial for evidence in a criminal investigation. There is no way that anything could have been switched after this was taken to the station. Which means—if *you* didn't do it—then how did a rubber snake in a sealed evidence bag suddenly turn into a lock of red hair?"

By magic, thought Caitlyn suddenly. In her mind's eye, she saw herself standing in the guest bedroom with Pomona and Evie, and the younger girl telling them about glamour spells:

"Glamoury is an advanced form of witchcraft where you use magic to make the world see you the way you want to be seen... you hide your reality... an illusion that's so real it fools everybody."

She looked back down at the lock of hair in the plastic bag and felt a wave of certainty. *Yes, it all makes sense!* That was why "Pomona" had been seen heading to the Portrait Gallery, even though she had really been asleep in the Library. Someone had used a glamour spell to project an illusion—an image of themselves wearing Pomona's Medusa costume, also transforming their hair to look like the distinctive snake-headed wig. And the glamour had been strong enough that even when Caitlyn had picked up the fallen lock of hair, it had still retained the illusion. She recalled Evie talking about how a glamour would wear off after a certain amount of time—and that was exactly what had happened. By the time Inspector Walsh had taken the "rubber snake" back to the police station, the power of the glamour magic had faded, so that the true form was revealed.

But that meant that the person who had gone into the Portrait Gallery that night, the person who had murdered Daniel Tremaine, had been someone capable of magic, Caitlyn realised. Someone who knew how to use glamour to disguise her true self, so that she could move unhindered through the Manor. It fit the method of murder too. The mystery of the stang flying through the air was solved now. It was not achieved by an Olympic javelin-thrower or anything so mundane—it had been done, just as Bertha had said, by magic: *"A powerful spell could animate an object and cause it to fly across the room, to stab or strike an enemy."* But who was this person who could wield such powerful forces of magic?

"Miss Le Fey?"

Caitlyn blinked and came out of her thoughts to see Inspector Walsh looking at her impatiently. He had obviously asked her something and was still waiting for her reply. "Sorry—I missed that. What did you say?"

"I said, given that you too have red hair, and you are the only other person who handled this piece of evidence, I assume you will have no objection to donating a sample for us to compare?" asked Inspector Walsh.

"No, of course not. But I can tell you that it's not mine. For one thing, you can check: there's no section of hair cut off anywhere from my head." Caitlyn held up some of her own tresses to demonstrate. "But for another, it's just not the same shade of red."

"Yes, well... we have to follow any lead we can," said Inspector Walsh, looking harassed. "I've had to deal with a few unsolved cases in my time, and they're never easy to accept, I can tell you. But this... I have never had an investigation go nowhere like this one, where every new lead simply throws up more questions than answers!"

Caitlyn hesitated, sorely tempted to tell him the real explanation for all the mysteries surrounding the case. But somehow, given the detective's well-known scepticism of magic and the paranormal, she doubted that he would be impressed by her rambling about "glamours" and powerful spells that could bewitch objects and turn them into flying weapons.

She was saved from having to make a decision when the door of the study opened and the young constable she had met on the night of the ball came in. He was carrying a tablet tucked under one arm and had his other hand under the Widow Mags's elbow as he escorted her into the room.

"Ah…" Inspector Walsh stood up and indicated the chair next to Caitlyn. "Please come in and sit down, madam."

"This'd better be important," grumbled the old witch. "I've just started tempering a new batch of chocolate on the slab, and if I don't get back soon, that's two and a half pounds of premium couverture chocolate wasted!"

"This will only take a moment, madam," Inspector Walsh assured her. He turned to the constable. "Have you got the footage, Stewart?"

"Yes, sir."

The young officer stepped forwards and handed Inspector Walsh the tablet. Caitlyn saw that the screen was taken up by a video player which had been paused so that the blurry picture was frozen mid-frame. She looked questioningly at the detective, who cleared his throat and said:

"As you may recall, I mentioned that we'd managed to collect some CCTV footage from the camera in the corridor outside the Portrait Gallery. Although it does not include the doorway to the Gallery itself, it does encompass the console table opposite and the large bronze vase on top of that table. Now, one of my more enterprising officers spotted a reflection on the side of the vase, which shows a figure entering the Gallery a short time after Daniel Tremaine."

Inspector Walsh paused significantly. "Which meant that if we could identify this figure, we could have the identity of our murderer. Unfortunately, it's a very blurred, distorted image, and of course, the dim lighting in the corridor makes recognition even harder. However, I have had our digital video specialists working on it ever since the night of the ball, and it seems that they had a breakthrough this morning." He leaned forwards, his eyes gleaming with satisfaction. "We now have an enhanced version of the footage, with a clearer view of the figure entering the Portrait Gallery. It is clearly a woman, wearing a long green gown, and..." His gaze strayed to Caitlyn's shoulder-length mane. "She appears to have red hair."

"Red hair?" Caitlyn bristled. "Surely you're not suggesting that I might have—"

"No, no, we know it is not you, Miss Le Fey," said Inspector Walsh, holding up a hand. "We have checked the matching time stamps and you are clearly visible in footage from the Ballroom at the same time that evening."

"Well, then... who is it?" asked Caitlyn, bewildered.

"I'm hoping you or your grandmother might be able to tell me," said Inspector Walsh, placing the tablet in front of them. "Can you tell me if you recognise this woman?"

He tapped the centre of the screen, and the video sprang back into life. Despite the enhancements, the picture was still hazy, the colours dim, and the edges of the video oddly bent and distorted. Caitlyn realised that it was because they were actually seeing a close-up of the curved side of the vase, and this footage was the reflection on the polished bronze surface. Even as she had the thought, she recognised the thick metal-studded door of the Portrait Gallery on the left-hand side of the frame.

Then a figure appeared on the right-hand side. It was a woman, slim and ethereal, with red hair tumbling in thick waves over her shoulders, and an athletic grace to her movements as she walked up to the Gallery door. Her back was to the vase, and so the reflection did not show her face—at first. But as she reached the heavy wooden door, she paused and flung a look over her shoulder, as if checking to make sure that she wasn't being followed. It was a quick movement, barely a couple of seconds long, but her face was clearly shown for a few fleeting seconds.

The Widow Mags, who had been silent up to now, made a choked sound in her throat as her gnarled hands reached involuntarily towards the screen. Then she swallowed and croaked:

"Tara?"

CHAPTER FORTY-THREE

The stables were warm and cosy, filled with the earthy scents of hay and leather and horses. Caitlyn breathed deeply as she stepped into the box stall, relishing the calm, homely ambience. The air was filled with the soothing sounds of the horses' breathing, the contented chewing of feed, and the occasional snort of equine conversation. She shut the door of the stall and leaned against it, closing her eyes and savouring the atmosphere for a moment. After the emotional upheaval of the recent revelations, she wanted—needed—some simple normality.

In the corner of the stall, a beautiful Welsh cob mare lifted her head and turned towards Caitlyn, flicking her ears and whickering softly in greeting.

"Hello, Melys," said Caitlyn, going forwards to cup

her hands around the velvety nose of the mare. Then she slid her arms around the horse's neck and hugged her close, drawing reassurance from the warm, solid body. The mare nosed the back of her shirt and blew gustily, making Caitlyn giggle and pull away.

"Look, I remembered this time," she said, putting a hand in her pocket and pulling out two sugar lumps. She held these out on the flat of her palm and smiled as the mare gently took the treats from her hand. "And you've certainly earned these, Melys! If it weren't for you, I would have never made it back in time that night."

She gave the mare another hug, then sighed and leaned against the side of the stall to watch absently as Melys moved over to her hay net and pulled out a mouthful of dried grass. The stall filled with the sound of the mare's placid munching, but this time, the cosy mood couldn't distract Caitlyn's thoughts from returning to the recent scene in James's study.

She shook her head, not quite sure what to think. Could the woman in the video—the woman who had gone into the Portrait Gallery on the night of the ball—have been Tara... her mother? It would certainly explain a lot of things. Her mother had been a very powerful witch, with natural abilities way beyond those of her years and training. So Tara would have had no problems using a glamour to disguise her appearance, and she could have easily bewitched the stang to fly through the air and impale

Daniel Tremaine. But then that would mean... Caitlyn shrank away from the thought. *Does that mean my mother is a murderer?*

A noise behind her made her turn around, and she felt her heart skip a beat as she saw the tall figure of James Fitzroy enter the stall. They stared at each other for a long moment, then James cleared his throat and said:

"Hi. I thought you might be here."

"Hi..." Caitlyn replied. Suddenly, infuriatingly, she felt the old shyness grip her again, and she turned back to Melys, pretending to fuss with the mare's mane. "I... um... I came to bring Melys some sugar lumps. I hope you don't mind."

"No, of course, I don't mind." James came over to stand next to her and reached out to pat the mare as well.

They were silent for a moment, then Caitlyn asked: "Has Inspector Walsh left?"

"Yes. A few minutes ago." He glanced sideways at her. "He told me about the enhanced video footage and the Widow Mags making an ID. She thinks the woman caught on camera is her daughter—your mother—Tara?"

Caitlyn nodded, not knowing what to say.

"Are you okay?" asked James gently.

Caitlyn nodded again, touched by his concern. "Yes, I'm fine. More sort of numb than anything else. I mean..." She raised agonised eyes to his. "My mother could have killed someone. I... I just don't know what to think. I don't know if I *want* to think."

"I can relate," said James gently. "I felt like that the night Gerald Hopkins told me my father had been a witch hunter, that my whole bloody family were involved in that foul pursuit. It's why, as soon as I heard about this, I came to find you."

Caitlyn felt her heart fill with love and gratitude. "That was sweet of you, James, to come especially—"

"Well, actually..." James hesitated, shuffling his feet. "I also came to apologise."

Caitlyn looked up at him in surprise.

He took a deep breath, then turned around to face her. "I shouldn't have gone behind your back with the rubber snake. It *was* your decision whether to tell the police about it or not, and I had no right to take that from you."

"You didn't trust me," said Caitlyn accusingly.

"No," James admitted, looking down. "And I'm sorry. Even if you'd chosen to protect Pomona, I suppose I should have respected that decision. I was just—" He broke off and then gave a bitter, self-deprecating laugh. "You know, I despised my ancestors for their allegiance to this secret society of witch hunters. I couldn't believe that my own father could be part of an organisation like that, a group that hunted down innocent women and tortured them, killed them, simply to pander to bigotry and superstitions. I was so shocked and disillusioned." He sighed. "We might not have been close, but I had always looked up to Father as a decent, compassionate man. But he'd put aside his own values, his own instincts of right and wrong, simply out of duty to his country. I thought it was despicable of him." James raised his head, his grey eyes meeting hers. "And yet, when it came to you and Pomona, I found myself doing the same. I was consumed by my duty to see justice done, even if it meant hurting and betraying those I most cared about."

Caitlyn reached out impulsively and touched his hand. "Don't, James... I think you're being too harsh on yourself. I mean, I admit it—I *was* angry and hurt by what you did, but you know, you weren't wrong. I *should* have handed that evidence over to the police on the night of the murder. So I suppose I was just as much at fault as you were." She paused, then added, "And I think I owe you an apology too."

"I beg your pardon?"

"You know, I was so frustrated with you—I couldn't understand why you were being so stubborn, why you kept resisting finding out more about this secret society. I couldn't appreciate why you wouldn't want to know more about your father's involvement and your own family history. But now..." She gave him a rueful smile. "Well, ever since finding out that my mother is not only alive but might even be—" She swallowed. "—a murderer... I think I can understand how you feel."

She dropped her gaze. "All I want to do now is to stick my head in the sand, not talk about it, not think about it..." She shook her head. "And it's crazy! Ever since learning I was adopted, I've wanted nothing more than to find my real mother—find out who she is, what happened to her, why she abandoned me. But now, I... I don't know." Her voice trembled. "I feel so confused and alone and scared."

James's hand closed around hers. "Don't be. Remember, you're not alone... not anymore."

He gave her hand a tug, pulling her suddenly towards him, so that they were close, chests touching. Caitlyn had to tip her head up to meet his eyes and she stared into them, her heart pounding. They had been here before, standing like this, lips inches apart... his eyes dark with intent... and his fingers, light and delicate, caressing the side of her face... skimming across her skin... making her shiver with awareness.

Last time they had been interrupted, but this time...

This time, James bent his head and kissed her, his lips soft and tender as his arms slid possessively around her. Caitlyn melted into his embrace, feeling as if her whole world had condensed into this dizzying, breathless moment. There was nothing except the touch of his mouth on hers, the feel of his strong body, and the fierce tide of joy and wonder that swept through her and filled her heart to bursting.

At last, James drew back and loosened his arms slightly. They were both breathing fast, and Caitlyn could see her tumultuous feelings reflected in his eyes.

"Do you know how long I've been wanting to do that?" asked James, reaching up to gently brush a tendril of hair back from her forehead. He chuckled. "You know, I think I've always known that you're a bit of a witch."

She laughed. "Yeah, right."

"No, I'm serious," said James, smiling tenderly. He leaned close again, his lips inches from hers. "Caitlyn Le Fey, you've bewitched me from the day I met you— and every moment since."

Then he drew her close for another kiss, and neither of them spoke again for a very long time.

THE END

ABOUT THE AUTHOR

USA Today bestselling author H.Y. Hanna writes fun cozy mysteries filled with quirky characters, lots of laughs, clever twists—and cats with big personalities! She is known for bringing wonderful settings to life, whether it's the historic city of Oxford, the beautiful English Cotswolds or the sunny beaches of coastal Florida.

After graduating from Oxford University, Hsin-Yi tried her hand at a variety of jobs, including advertising, modelling, teaching English and dog training... before returning to her first love: writing. She worked as a freelance writer for several years and has won awards for her poetry, short stories and journalism.

Hsin-Yi was born in Taiwan and has been a globe-trotter all her life—living in a variety of cultures, from Dubai to Auckland, London to New Jersey—but is now happily settled in Perth, Western Australia, with her husband and a rescue kitty named Muesli. You can learn more about her and her books at: www.hyhanna.com.

Join her Readers' Club Newsletter to get updates on new releases, exclusive giveaways and other book news!

https://www.hyhanna.com/newsletter

ACKNOWLEDGEMENTS

This book was quite a challenge to write and so I am very grateful to my team of beta readers who supported me through the (very rough!) first draft and then all the subsequent (endless!) revisions, and provided me with such helpful feedback: Kathleen Costa, Connie Leap, Charles Winthrop and Basma Alwesh.

My thanks also go to my editor, proofreader and the rest of my publishing team, for always going to great lengths to match my schedule. Thank you also to my readers for their wavering enthusiasm for this series, and for their patience as I juggled my commitments to different series, to find the time to devote to writing the next book in this world.

Lastly, as always, my love and thanks to my wonderful husband for his incredible support and encouragement. I really couldn't do it without him.